RHEA SILVIA

BOOK ONE
· THE FIRST VESTALS OF ROME ·
TRILOGY

RHEA SILVIA

DEBRA MAY MACLEOD
AND SCOTT MACLEOD

Copyright © 2022 by Debra May Macleod

All rights reserved. This book or any portion thereof may not be reproduced or used in any manner whatsoever without the express written permission of the author.

Any historical and/or legendary figures and/or events referenced in this book are depicted in a fictitious manner. All other characters and events are products of the author's imagination.

Cover design by ebooklaunch.com
Stylized V symbol designed by Jeanine Henning
Book design by Maureen Cutajar, gopublished.com

Paperback edition: ISBN 978-1-9994300-8-5
Hardcover edition: ISBN 978-1-9994300-9-2
Ebook edition: ISBN 978-1-990640-00-1

DebraMayMacleod.com

PROLOGUE

The City of Troy
April 1184 BCE

Ascanius wound his way through the city streets, trying to keep his bearings in the dark. He had never been so far from home this late at night before, and everything looked different. It was not just the strange shade of night, either. It was the streets themselves. Normally as clean as holy Hygeia, they were tonight littered with broken wine jugs and scraps of half-eaten meat still on the bone. Ascanius had to sidestep puddles of vomit from the revelers, most of whom were now sleeping it off in their beds, although those who lacked the endurance to stumble home had contented themselves by passing out in front of their neighbors' homes. One of them raised a wobbly head as Ascanius passed by.

"Boy, get home!" he slurred.

Ascanius quickened his pace and looked ahead. There, just inside the gates of Troy, and towering above the homes and even the temples, was the colossal wooden horse. He inhaled excitedly. It was just as the priest Laocoön had described it: perhaps thirty *podes* high, on a huge wheeled platform. A giant votive offering to the gods of Troy, the departing Greeks had left it at the gates of the city as an overture of peace after ten bloody years of war.

As he neared the structure, Ascanius slowed his step and crept toward it as quietly as he could. It would be awful if he got this close only to be shooed away. However, there was little chance of that. Even the guards posted to keep watch over the gift horse had passed out from too much celebration, too much wine. And why not? The long war was finally at an end.

Ascanius wrested a torch from the ground and held the flame in front of him as he moved beneath the giant horse's head. He looked up. By the flickering light, he could discern the painted crimson eyes of the horse, the marine-blue meander pattern that ran along the length of its barrel-shaped belly and the thick mane of wool—*it must have been pulled from a hundred sheep!*—that extended from its forelock to its withers. It was a wondrous thing indeed.

Captivated, he shuffled along, staring up at the silhouette of the horse's magnificent body high above him. The contour of its massive form blocked out a horse-shaped section of the starry sky, and he was gazing up, lost in awe, when something brought him back to his senses. A slight movement. A shifting. A stream of water landed on his forehead, running down over his ears and wetting his hair. He thought for a moment that it might be raining, but no rain fell on the ground around him. He sniffed. It was not rain.

It was…*urine*, coming from the horse.

He wiped the urine off his face just as a plank from the horse's midsection was kicked free from within. It fell, narrowly missing Ascanius's head, and landed with a solid thump on the ground beside him. A heavy rope fell down next, followed by the outline of feet and legs descending. Ascanius knew he should run—he was no fool—but the sight transfixed him. Another solid thump sounded behind him. He spun, blinking in disbelief to find a Greek soldier, dressed in full armor, standing an arm's length away. The soldier seemed as surprised to see the boy as the boy was to see him, but unlike the child, the man did not hesitate. He advanced, dagger drawn, and lunged at Ascanius.

Ascanius ducked, tripped, and landed hard on his knees. Ignoring the pain, he scrambled to his feet and ran. Behind him, he could hear the Greek soldier utter a hushed shout to his companions—"*Tha ton piáso!*"—before taking chase.

Ascanius wanted to shout himself, to wake the sleeping guards and the sleeping city, but he could not spare the breath in his flight. He had barely made any distance before the silence behind him broke into panic-stricken shouts, the sound of swords clashing, and even more horrifying, the unmistakable mechanical groan of the massive gates of Troy. *Opening*.

He ran faster and harder than he ever had before. He did not stop until he arrived home, gasping for breath. Rushing past his father's slaves who were busily sweeping the street outside their fine home, he pulled open the door and rushed inside where a group of men were sitting around the table, his father at the head. Like his father—who was kin to the Trojan king Priam and married to one of the king's daughters—these men had protested the Greeks' colossal gift and were convening to discuss how they might petition King Priam to drag it back out of the city.

One of the men, a priest named Gyas, pointed to Ascanius, amused. "Aeneas, your boy's been up to no good."

Aeneas sat back in his chair and put his palms flat on the table the way he always did when he was angry. As far as he had known, his son was asleep in his bedchamber. He could guess to where he had snuck off.

"Ascanius, I told you, it is not safe—"

Ascanius ran to his father and gripped his tunica. "Father, there were men in the horse! One of them pissed on me before they came out of its belly!"

The men around the table jumped to their feet, instantly shouting profanities and cursing their king's foolishness.

"Are the gates still closed?" Aeneas asked his son.

"No, Father. I heard them open."

The men cursed louder, their words now tinged with panic.

Drawn by the commotion, Ascanius's mother Creusa emerged from behind a heavy curtain, her eyes sleepy as she absently tucked her long black hair into the head wrap she always wore to bed. She was about to ask about the fuss when they all heard it—the blare of horns, the city's alarms, sounding in the distance. She locked eyes with her husband as he sprinted to the door, opening it a crack and peering outside.

The sounds of loud voices, heavy footfalls, and the *whoosh* of fire filtered into the house. Creusa could see Aeneas's shoulders rise with tension. He closed the door and looked back at her. "There are Greek soldiers already in the streets," he said. "They are setting the houses on fire. They will take the city; there is no doubt this time. I must go get my father."

Creusa hastily hung a long, tear-shaped amulet around her neck. She took Ascanius's hand and said to them all, "Meet us at the temple of the hearthfire. There is a way out there."

They nodded. As the senior priestess of Troy and a daughter of Priam, Aeneas's wife knew more about the temples than almost anyone in the city. Creusa said a whispered prayer, clutched Ascanius's hand tightly, and followed her husband and his men out the door and into the loud, fiery chaos of the streets.

They ran together down a long street and then turned down another. As they did, Ascanius screamed. The old man who lived there, along with his two pretty daughters and their husbands and children, all lay slaughtered on the ground. One child, a boy Ascanius always played with, had an arrow protruding from his throat. Blood dribbled out the corner of his mouth. He stared up at Ascanius with open, lifeless eyes and gripped his mother's hand in death. Ascanius gripped his own mother's hand even tighter.

He looked up at his father. Aeneas took his wife's face in his hands and kissed her. She said something to him that Ascanius could not hear in the turmoil, and then she pulled him away from his father to start down an adjacent street. Ascanius wondered whether his grandfather Anchises was still alive, or whether he was already lying dead on the ground like his friend's grandfather.

But then those terrible thoughts were interrupted by an even more terrifying image: fire. It was everywhere. It roared like Vulcan bursting forth out of every window, every doorway, licking and consuming all of the homes on his street, on the next street as well, and the next. It rose and crackled from every rooftop, reaching into the black sky and illuminating the city as if it were already morning. Ascanius wondered whether the real morning would ever come.

He wiped the sweat from his face—fear, combined with the suffocating heat of running through the inferno—and ducked behind his mother as she navigated their way through the blazes and brutality around them.

It seemed like two Greek soldiers were standing outside every door. They waited for the inhabitants—half-drunken husbands and half-dressed wives carrying babies—to flee their burning homes, and then stabbed them or slit their throats as they crossed the threshold. A dog that tried to defend its master was rewarded for its loyalty with a dagger to the skull. It dropped where it stood.

Eyes wide with fear, Ascanius looked up at the back of his mother's head. Her normally tidy hair had fallen out of her head wrap and the amulet around her neck swayed this way and that as she frantically looked for a safe path to the temple. As they ran, they heard the impassioned shouts of Greek soldiers proclaim the news with voices already confident of victory—"Odysseus has scaled the palace walls!"

The despair of hearing those words—her father and brothers would be in mortal danger—combined with the startling closeness of the voices rendered Creusa immobile. She stood falteringly in the street, leaving her and her son dangerously exposed. Another moment and the soldiers would spot them.

Ascanius's eyes fell upon a large, overturned grain basket in the narrow space between two homes. He tugged at his mother's arm and pointed to it. Regaining her wits, she pulled Ascanius toward it. Working together, they righted the basket and crouched behind it, both of them panting in fright.

Ascanius peered around the makeshift cover. On the other side of the basket, four or five Greek soldiers had stopped. They were pointing this way and that, arguing about whether to head to the temples or to Priam's palace.

They were soon joined by another soldier whose presence instantly silenced them. By the light of the blazing fires, Ascanius could discern the intricate imagery on the new soldier's shield: the sun, the moon and constellations in its center, encircled by scenes of people, fields, vineyards and cattle. He had heard Trojan soldiers talk about this very shield. It belonged to the mighty Greek soldier Achilles. The harrowing realization made him gasp, and his mother slapped her hand over his mouth to silence him. Full of dread, the boy moved his eyes upward and saw the face of Achilles, bearded, sharp, and hungry for the violence of war.

But even more dreadful was the man next to Achilles. His face was less hateful, but he held—no, it was impossible!—the Palladium, the guardian statue of Pallas Athena that was kept on the Trojan citadel. If the Greeks had broken through that fortification, if they had removed the statue from its temple, the city was indeed doomed.

Ascanius closed his eyes to stop himself from whimpering. After a barked order from Achilles, the men all ran off in the direction of the king's palace. Creusa exhaled. She shoved the grain basket aside and the two slipped back onto the street, running with their heads down, snaking between buildings, dodging crashing timbers, choking on smoke and covering their ears at the piercing shrieks of pain and terror from women, children and men alike.

At last, they reached the Temple of Vesta. Mercifully, it was less a priority for the Greeks than the citadel and the king's palace, and was quiet. It was unguarded, too, its regular soldiers presumably having left their post to fight the invaders, and the priestesses having taken flight to save themselves. Mother and son entered unseen.

The inside of the temple was dim, lit only by a few oil lamps and the glow that emanated from a large tripod terracotta bowl atop a weighty wooden altar. Inside the bowl were the persevering embers of the *Iliaci foci*, the hearthfire of Troy that burned with Vesta's eternal flame. Creusa picked up a glowing oak coal with her bare fingers, slipped it into the hollow of the amulet around her neck and packed it with wood ash.

"*Dea, nos defendi,*" she whispered. Goddess, protect us.

She knelt in prayer. Ascanius knelt beside her.

And then they waited.

Finally, the doors of the temple opened and Aeneas burst inside. His hair was matted with blood from a head wound, and a deep gash on his thigh had painted his leg red. With him were the same men from the house, a few of their benumbed wives, and Aeneas's graying father, Anchises. All of the men bore the scarlet wounds of battle. Ascanius ran to embrace his father, but Aeneas only thrust something solid against his son's chest—the wooden statue of Pallas Athena, dripping with the blood it had cost to win it back from the enemy.

"You saved the Palladium, Father!"

"May it save us," he replied. "Take it, son."

Ascanius clutched it to his chest with desperate reverence. The ancient statue had been hurled down from the heavens—it came in a thunderbolt, some of the priests said, or as a shooting star, said others—as a sign to Troy's founder, Ilus, ordaining him to build the great city in that spot. Thank the gods his father had reclaimed it—as a descendant of Ilus himself, it was his duty to do so. Perhaps all was not lost.

"Come," Creusa ordered, jumping to her feet. "There is a way out. Under the altar."

The men rushed to the altar and pushed mightily, sliding the hefty base of the sacred hearthfire forward to reveal a hidden tunnel below. A robust man with a torch took the lead, descending first, while Aeneas stayed behind. He gestured for his wife, son and the others to enter. When only he and Gyas remained above ground, they slipped into the tunnel together and reached up to grasp the handles on the underside of the altar. Although their muscles strained from the effort, they managed to heave it back into place.

The group moved through the narrow dirt tunnel slowly, ducking their heads to avoid the low ceiling of earth and squeezing through tight spots where the walls had partially caved in, their way lit only by the single torch in the lead. The sounds of crumbling loose soil and their own heavy breathing extended before and behind them. Ascanius brushed his shoulder against the side of the tunnel and felt something moist and fibrous cling to his arm. He did not bother to wipe it off, but hugged the statue of the goddess tighter.

As they moved along unspeaking, none of them dared to think about what was happening above—about how their family and friends were being mercilessly massacred by the enemy—yet none of them could think of anything else.

Aeneas called ahead to his wife. "Creusa, where will we emerge?"

"Five or six *stadia* from the walls," she answered. "In the woods, not far from the sea."

Finally, they neared the end of the tunnel where a single narrow ladder extended upward. They all stopped as Aeneas squeezed past his companions to climb up first. Clutching the top rung of the ladder, and blinking the falling dirt out of his eyes, he upheaved the rotten planks of wood that covered the tunnel's secret exit. Clumps of soil, rocks and roots tumbled down on top of and around him. He stuck his head out of the hole to look around.

As his wife had said, the tunnel's exit was some distance from the walls of Troy—but it was not in the woods. The trees were gone. He clenched his jaw. *The Greeks cut them down to build that bloody horse. We will be completely exposed.*

Aeneas turned his head to look behind him and in the distance saw his beloved city ablaze. The night sky over the walls glowed orange from the flames, and plumes of black smoke rose up. The shouts of the enemy, their cackles of laughter, traveled on the wind to him. He could hear the faraway, anguished cries of his Trojan countrymen float through the air to haunt him like bodiless ghosts.

He turned his head again, this time looking ahead. The blackness of the sea stretched out before him, and he could hear gentle waves lapping against the shoreline. He looked to his right—the woods were there, but at least another *stadion* away.

Aeneas lifted himself out of the tunnel. He spun around on his knees and reached down to help his companions rise from the earth one by one, whispering to each of them to stay low and silent. They emerged in turn, some looking toward the burning city, others forcing themselves not to. When they were all out of the tunnel, Aeneas spoke.

"We need to run to the woods," he said. "Go quickly!"

They sprinted as one, as a herd of exiles fleeing the implausible horror of their exalted city's ruin, toward the cover of the thick trees. Aeneas grasped his wife's wrist in one hand and his son's in the other. The sanctuary of the woods grew closer and closer with every desperate, hopeful step.

But then Creusa stumbled. She clutched her stomach in pain and dropped to her knees. Aeneas looked back at her, at the arrow that had impaled her and the dark pool of blood spreading across her belly. She stared up at him and they met eyes in the flickering torchlight.

Aeneas grabbed Ascanius by the back of his neck as they stopped. "Stay behind me."

He scanned the shoreline and spotted two Greek sentries, their eyes also searching and their bows drawn. One sentry saw him and fired, but his arrow struck a tree stump as Aeneas knelt beside Creusa.

She gasped, unable to speak. With bloodied and shaking hands, she reached for the amulet around her neck. Understanding, Aeneas quickly removed it and lowered his head to place it around his own neck. When he looked back up at Creusa, she fell silently onto her side.

Knowing the swiftness of her death was her last gift to him—a final chance to save their son—Aeneas turned back to the horrified boy. "Your mother sees us from the hereafter," he said, "and she wants you to run."

So Ascanius, fighting his tears and the disorienting terror of his mother's absence, gripped the goddess even tighter in his arms and raced alongside his father, grandfather and the others. They were nearly at the woods when Aeneas saw the elderly Anchises falling behind. Filled with a sudden rage—*I will not lose another!*—he lifted his father onto his shoulders and kept running.

They kept running even as they sensed the shelter of trees around them. They kept running all night long, ignoring the branches that stabbed at their legs, the sounds of unseen creatures around them, the strangeness of the deep woods and their own unfathomable fatigue.

When morning finally broke, and when Ascanius could not take another step, Aeneas directed them all into a cave. It was a rough, unhappy shelter, but it was better than the tomb.

Shivering, Ascanius helped his grandfather sit on the hard cave floor and took the old man's trembling hands in his own. "It is all right, Grandfather," he said. "We are together." He tried not to think of his mother's body still lying in the open, abandoned, breakfast for the crows.

Aeneas slumped to the rocky ground beside his son and father. All around him, he could hear the voices of his men—traumatized, exhausted, grief stricken—in prayer. Aeneas prayed, too. He prayed to his divine mother, the goddess of love, for the soul of his beloved Creusa. He prayed to the god of war for the safety of Ascanius and for vengeance against those who would abuse his royal bloodline.

As Ascanius rummaged around the cave foraging for kindling, Aeneas's hands moved to the amulet around his neck. It was still warm from the smoldering oak coal within, so he passed it to his son. Ascanius removed the coal and placed dry grass and thin strips of wood on and around it, gently blowing on the little pile to wake the sleeping flame within.

Aeneas thought of his fallen wife and his fallen city.

As the despair rose up, he swallowed it down, again and again, until something harder took its place. Conviction. He moved to kneel beside his son. The fire, ignited with the embers of Troy's sacred hearthfire, crackled to life and spread out to consume the kindling.

"Someday, my son," said Aeneas, staring into the fire, "some way, you and I will use these Trojan flames to forge a city that will last forever."

CHAPTER I

*Alba Longa
772 BCE
(Four hundred and twelve years later)*

Princess Rhea Silvia held up a conch shell, put it to her lips, and blew. The sound startled both her father, King Numitor, and her brother, the prince Egestus, who reclined on adjoining couches. They laughed as she inspected the shell, her lips pursed in disapproval.

"Is this really to be my engagement present?"

"In Tusculum, that is considered a gemstone," replied her brother, grinning. "Mamilian will expect to see it hanging from your neck the next time he sees you."

The king raised an eyebrow at his son. "You should not mock him, Egestus. When you are king, your sister's husband will be the strongest ally you have in Latium."

"Alba Longa does not pander for allies, Father. You taught me that. Cities like Tusculum are fortunate we ally with them, not the other way around."

"That is so," said Numitor, "but diplomacy is a strength too, and a less costly one than war."

Rhea extended an arm and held the seashell at eye level. "I think my husband-to-be needs a lesson in diplomacy himself," she said lightly, peering into the shell, "unless there is gold in here somewhere…"

They laughed again, and the gray-haired king smiled at his children. As twins, Rhea and Egestus had always shared a special bond. It was a blessing to him as a father. More than that, their devotion to each other meant that the alliance between Alba Longa and nearby Tusculum, the latter being the second strongest city in Latium, was assured. He rose, bade them goodnight, and left.

The siblings slumped back onto their cushioned dining couches and looked at each other, the humor in their eyes having left with their father.

"A shell?" said Rhea. "Really, a shell? Am I so cheaply bought?"

"It is not an insult to you," Egestus replied. "It is a message to me." He reached over to take the shell from his sister's hands, putting it to his ear. "Ah, yes, here is the voice of Mamilian now. He says, 'Egestus, you fool, once your sister bears my son, Tusculum will rule all of Latium, including Alba Longa.'" He held the shell back out to his sister. She crossed her arms and refused to take it, so he let it drop to the carpeted floor. They both stared at it. "This marriage is not to Alba Longa's benefit, no matter what our father says."

"He is too trusting," said Rhea.

Egestus turned onto his back and stared at the ceiling, absently rubbing his short black beard the way he always did when he was worried about something. Which these days, was all the time. "He is weary of war and the constant threat from the Etrusci. He wants to believe your marriage to Mamilian will inspire stability throughout Latium, once and for all. We cannot fault him for that. He has always had a peaceful heart. The fault lies with Mamilian's nature, not with our father's."

"You are correct, of course," Rhea agreed. "But then you always are, Egestus. I mean no disrespect to our father, but you will make a better king than he." Her voice grew heavy. "I do not want to go to Tusculum. I do not want to bear Mamilian's son, only to see him and his father challenge my own city."

Egestus rubbed his beard harder, frustrated.

"You will be smooth faced by morning if you do not stop," said Rhea.

Egestus offered a half-hearted smile. There was no doubt in his mind that Mamilian planned to do exactly what his sister had said. He would be a fool not to. Egestus and Rhea had an enviable lineage: they were direct descendants of the great Trojan Ascanius, founder of Alba Longa, and son of the mighty Aeneas—Aeneas, who was said to be the mortal son of the goddess Venus.

Mamilian, who himself claimed to be descended from the Greek hero Odysseus, and who Egestus suspected was just as war-minded and wily, was no doubt eager to add Rhea's noble bloodline to his own legacy. Their son—half Aeneas, half Odysseus—would boast a lineage that could conquer and rule the world, never mind Latium.

A dark thought came to Egestus. If some injury or illness befell Rhea while she was pregnant, one that prevented her from carrying a child to term...but no, that would only be a temporary measure. Mamilian would breed her more regularly than his best mare. He would not stop until she gave him a strong, living son, one that could prove to be an even greater threat to Egestus than Mamilian himself.

Sighing, Rhea stretched and stood up. As she made to leave, Egestus reached up from his couch to grasp her hand, stopping her.

"If you bore a boy..." he looked away, his black eyes expressionless in thought, "...could you bring yourself to kill it?"

Rhea thought about this. "No."

"Would your loyalty still lie with me?"

Again, she thought. "No, brother. I would favor my child. The gods have made it so with women."

Egestus kissed his sister's hand. She ruffled his hair affectionately and left the room, left him on his couch with only his thoughts, and those growing darker by the moment.

❖ ❖ ❖

It was a crisp spring morning and the sanctuary of Jupiter Latiaris stood high and mighty atop the lush green Mount Albanus. Rhea gazed up at it from her position on the edge of the lake far below. The mountaintop shrine to Jupiter was a divine sight. It reached higher into the sky than any of the temples around it, seeming to pierce the clouds, though her current reverence was soured somewhat by the smell of fish that she suspected the fishermen could never quite scrub clean from their little boats, several of which sat overturned along the shore.

She skipped a smooth, round stone along the surface of the green water. As the trail of ripples spread out into concentric rings, a trout jumped, its iridescent body catching the sunlight for a brief, shining moment before again disappearing below the surface of the water. It was a perfect day.

Another stone skipped along the water's surface and Rhea spun to face her cousin, Nemeois, who was standing behind her eating cheese from a cloth. He held out a piece to her and she took it, biting it in half.

"The priests and politicians are already arriving for the festival," he said, "and thankfully not empty handed." He inspected a piece of cheese. "They must have excellent goats in Satricum. I suppose it makes up for the women."

Rhea threw her half-eaten cheese at him. "And yet not one of them is so hopeless that she will marry you," she said, grinning.

"That is a sobering thought, cousin. Have you heard the news?"

"I hear a lot of news."

"My father has proposed that Egestus marry Lady Cloelia."

"That is old news, Nemeois." Rhea took the last piece of cheese from the cloth in his hand and pushed it between her lips. She chewed thoughtfully and added, "My father will formally announce the engagement at the banquet, after the sacrifice."

"Then it seems you and your brother will both be married by summer."

"It seems so."

"Do you not approve of the match?"

"Of course I do. Father has always respected the Cloelii, and Lady Cloelia is a fine choice."

Rhea kept chewing. There was no doubt that Cloelia would be a faithful wife to Egestus. She would give him children he could be proud of. Two years his senior, she had already born a son for her first husband, although the infant had died almost a year ago of the same sickness that had taken his father, a soldier named Geganus. Cloelia was proven fertile, proven resilient. And her next son, Egestus's son, would be the crown prince of Alba Longa, and someday its king. Perhaps it could be some reward for her suffering.

But does she really deserve such a reward? thought Rhea. *I should be queen and my son made king. Instead, I am being sent away, bought only by a conch shell...*

Nemeois absently kicked a stone into the water. "Tusculum is not far away," he said, guessing her thoughts. "It may take some time, but it will feel like home."

"Says the man who gets to stay home," replied Rhea. She waved a hand in the air. "I am sorry, Nemeois. You are right, of course."

He put his arm around her shoulders. "Ugly men are always right," he said. "It is how we remain useful."

"You speak the truth," said Rhea. "I have found that handsome men are often useless."

"Do you find Mamilian handsome?"

"Ha, an unanswerable question," Rhea laughed, twisting a rope of her long black hair in her fingers and leaning lazily against her cousin. "I must either state he is ugly or useless. It is too bad you are not in line to be king, Nemeois. Strategy runs through your veins faster than blood."

"I would not wish the crown of oak on my worst enemy," he replied flatly. "When was the last time you saw Egestus enjoy any sport? Or any woman? He picks through his food as though each bit was a problem he is trying to solve...that olive is Tusculum, that piece of cheese is Etruria, that slice of meat is the Julii. No, I prefer to spend my time skipping stones in the water with pretty girls." At that, he turned around to wink at the younger of Rhea's two handmaids. The girl, named Lela, winked back. Nemeois was known for his flirtations, and Lela had learned that it was easiest to just play along.

Rhea jabbed a finger into her cousin's shoulder. "Go away, Nemeois," she said. "Leave my poor lady alone."

"Your *poor lady* cannot resist me," he said, and then before Lela could protest, smiled in greeting as Cloelia approached, her own lady in tow. "Ah, I must be on my best behavior now," he bowed, "the next queen of Alba Longa arrives. She may have me beheaded for it."

Cloelia smiled warmly. Rhea pursed her lips. She doubted Cloelia had the stomach to order the beheading of a chicken, never mind a man.

Nemeois departed and the two noble women, trailed by their handmaids, walked leisurely away from the shore until they reached the road that ran alongside the lake. The road branched up toward the old city and the high-walled palace grounds in one direction, and off toward the citadel in the other direction. They both headed to the palace.

"What brings you outdoors so early, Lady Cloelia?" Rhea asked.

"I am fond of early mornings, Princess," replied Cloelia. "I inherited the trait from my father. He often goes out fishing before dawn. He likes it when I wave to him from shore."

"He fishes himself? Instead of sending slaves?"

"Yes." She smiled. "Many years ago, when my father was a young man fighting the Etrusci alongside your father, one of his slaves tried to poison him. To this day, he only eats what he himself has fished, hunted or plucked from a tree."

"I did not know that."

"You watch," said Cloelia, still smiling, "at the banquet, just watch him. You will notice that he barely takes a bite. It amuses me, since there is no logic in it. He has no such reservations about wine. He would drink it out of a slave's hand if he had to."

"That I did know," said Rhea. For a moment, she worried that she had overstepped, but then Cloelia nodded her head in agreement at her father's well-known vice. Rhea continued. "Are you visiting my brother this morning?"

"Yes, Princess."

"Good, we shall walk together." After several minutes of easy conversation about the upcoming festival, Rhea spoke cautiously. "Lady Cloelia, you should know that Egestus…"

"Egestus what, Princess?"

Rhea shook her head. *Do not do this, Rhea,* she said to herself. "Nothing."

"Princess, I am his betrothed. Like you, I care only for his well-being."

"I do not mean to worry you," Rhea said reluctantly, "and it is a private matter, but you should know that my brother shares the same vice as your father."

Cloelia looked at the ground. "I see."

"I only mention it because I do not want you to be surprised by his behavior. It has at times startled me. How a kind man can turn cruel so quickly is beyond me."

"My Greek tutor is fond of saying that Dionysus has a dual nature," said Cloelia. Distracted by the revelation, she said nothing else until they reached the tall, fortified gates of the palace. Two guards opened them wide to reveal the lush green gardens and white stone exterior of the palace. As they passed through, Cloelia touched Rhea on the shoulder. "Thank you for telling me, Princess. You are already such a kind sister to me."

"It is best you do not tell him that I told you," said Rhea.

"I agree," Cloelia replied.

As the great gates closed behind the women and their handmaids, Rhea smiled at Cloelia in parting and then continued toward her private quarters at the far end of the palace.

Cloelia stood unmoving for a moment as her handmaid—a

dark-skinned, middle-aged woman named Melete—stood at her shoulder. Cloelia looked at the older woman. "I love my father," she said, "but life as a child was not easy under his roof. After Geganus died, I had no desire to return to it, but what choice did I have?"

"I know," said Melete, "and I know life is still not easy under his roof." The handmaid's eyes followed Rhea as the princess passed through the doors of her quarters and disappeared into the palace. "I do not mean to speak against the princess, but…"

"Speak freely, Melete."

"I have watched the prince since he was a boy. He can be ruthless, but I have never seen him lose his judgment from wine or any other force. Perhaps the princess isn't as supportive as you think."

"The princess has been nothing but supportive," said Cloelia. "She wants this marriage to succeed as much as I do."

Melete said nothing further as the two women began walking toward the palace stables. It was where Egestus could be found most mornings. This morning was no exception. Cloelia studied him as they approached: his black hair and short black beard, his thin lips that were always pressed together as if in worry, his eyes that were always narrowed in thought. Even now, as he groomed his horse in the light of the morning sun, he seemed to be cast in darkness.

"Good morning, Your Highness," she greeted him.

He looked at her pleasantly enough, though unsmilingly, and Cloelia felt a sudden pang of sadness. *How I miss Geganus*, she thought. *How I miss our son, our life.*

She forced herself to smile at Egestus and quietly congratulated herself for doing a better job of faking it than he was.

CHAPTER II

According to the Alban priests and scholars, as well as Rhea's many tutors, Aeneas had fled the besieged city of Troy with his son Ascanius, his father Anchises, and a group of loyal followers. They carried with them the Palladium and embers from the *Iliaci foci,* sacred embers that housed the powerful spirit of Vesta, goddess of the home and the Trojan hearthfire.

As the band of desperate refugees moved through the woods day after day, it fell upon the young Ascanius to keep the embers alive. Having nothing more than the clothes on his back, he asked the spirit of the woods, Silvanus, for guidance. Silvanus inspired him to use his surroundings—the trees, the moss and lichen, the grass—to preserve the embers and keep them aglow during their harrowing journey. That is how he was able to bring the *Iliaci ignes Vestae,* the Trojan fires of Vesta, to the city of Lavinium in Latium.

When Ascanius became a man, he taught his wife how to keep the embers alight, and together they traveled to found Alba Longa, bringing the goddess's eternal fire with them and keeping the old Trojan flames alive in their new city. And when Ascanius became a father, he named his firstborn son Silvius in honor of the spirit and the woods that had nourished that fire. Thus, the Silvian dynasty was born.

Rhea's dynasty.

She knelt before the Shrine of Vesta on the citadel. Beside her knelt her cousin Amulia and eight other young Alban women who were betrothed to marry. Behind them stood the priests, royalty, and nobles from the finest cities in Latium, including Lavinium, Bovillae, Lanuvium, Tusculum, Satricum, Cora, and more. They had all gathered in Alba Longa for the *Feriae Latinae*, the annual spring festival that celebrated the confederation of their thirty member cities. And every year, the rites began here on the citadel, with Alban maidens gathering embers from the sacred fire.

It was a fire that, according to tradition, every betrothed maiden had to maintain in Vesta's temple for a minimum of six months before she could wed. A religious duty and a rite of passage for highborn Alban girls, it was a way to honor the goddess and symbolically prepare for marriage and family life: by learning to perform basic rites and care for the communal hearth, they were preparing to care for their future household hearth.

After her betrothal to Mamilian, Rhea had completed her own tenure as a *sacerdos Vestalis*, a maiden priestess of Vesta. For six months, she had lived in the *sacerdotes*' convent on Mount Albanus, close to Vesta's temple. Under the guidance of the senior priestesses, she had daily, and often nightly, tended to the sacred fire. She wished she was still there, surrounded by her sister sacerdotes, instead of here with Mamilian, their wedding now so close and so inevitable.

Rhea looked into the flames that burned high and hot upon the shrine. Spotting the perfect red-glowing oak coal, she plucked it out of the ash with iron tongs and placed it on the bed of moss and lichen she had gathered from the base of the sacred oak tree in the Silvian grove. She placed more fresh green vegetation on top and wrapped it all in a sheet of peeled tree bark to hold the *Iliaca flamma dormiens*, the sleeping flame of Troy, as if it were a slumbering infant wrapped in a blanket.

When she was certain the other women had properly made and secured their *sarcinae sanctae*, their sacred bundles, she stood and turned to face the gathering of people. She bowed in respect first to her father, King Numitor, and then to each of the city kings, priests and dignitaries in turn, before walking toward an exceptionally tall horse. She forced her lips into a smile as she looked up at its rider. Mamilian.

Just as his horse outsized those around it, Mamilian did, too. He was taller than average, with wide shoulders, light brown hair, and a perennial smug smile on his full lips. He sat straight and confident as he grinned down at Rhea. She had the immediate sense that he enjoyed seeing her below him. A slave placed a mounting stool at her feet and, with assistance, she climbed onto the back of the horse, wrapping one arm around Mamilian's body and clutching her *sarcina* with the other.

He turned his head to speak to her. "Are you comfortable, Princess?"

"Yes, thank you, Mamilian," said Rhea, privately thankful that her cloak had fallen where it was meant to, thereby hiding the bunched dress underneath.

Mamilian's horse shifted on its feet as the procession arranged itself in front and behind them. The parade of horses stretched from Vesta's shrine on one side of the citadel to the Altar of Diana on the other, as everyone waited to begin the journey to the religious center of Alba Longa and, indeed, all of Latium—the top of Mount Albanus where the city's temples, including the grand sanctuary of Jupiter, were located. Mamilian's horse shifted again, and Rhea tensed her legs to hold her balance. The beast was so large that her leg muscles were already strained from the effort. She distracted herself by thinking how good the banquet would be, and found herself licking her lips at the memory of the cheese from Satricum.

Rhea watched her father's horse move to the head of the procession with Egestus's horse alongside him. Egestus twisted his body around to offer his sister a rare smile, and she leaned to the side to return it. His smiled faded, though, as he met eyes with Mamilian, who was clearly unimpressed by his position: staring at the ass end of Egestus's horse was a reminder to him, and everyone else, that Alba Longa was still the undisputed head of the Latin Confederation.

Mamilian sat upright on his horse and Rhea tensed. It was bad enough she had to wrap her arm around him and sit splay legged on the back of his horse. She did not relish the feeling of his solid back pressed into her breasts. It was entirely too intimate.

"Can you kindly sit forward, Mamilian," she said.

"Of course, Princess," he replied, although he waited several moments before doing so.

At long last, the procession was ready. A horn sounded and the pipes began, their music accompanied by the chants of the priests and the clip-clop of horse hooves. Mamilian prompted his horse to move and it began to walk forward, not breaking into a trot until there was ample space between it and Egestus's horse in front.

As the lively procession moved along the road, traveling easily enough over the tight-fitting polygonal basaltic stones that paved their way from the citadel to the mountaintop, the people of Alba Longa and tourists from neighboring cities ran alongside, cheering and throwing flowers at the feet of the horses. Children perched in treetops or stood on rooftops for the best view of the parade and the colorful city flags held high upon staffs. Rhea could not help but envy their capacity for simple joys. When had she lost that capacity herself?

She tried to ignore the unsettling warmth of Mamilian's body so close to hers and instead focused on the warmth of the *flamma dormiens* in its bed of moss and blanket of bark. Little wisps of smoke were escaping from cracks in the bark, proof that the coal inside was still alive and well. Rhea hoped they would reach the sanctuary before it combusted into a flame: the journey along the sacred road was meant to pay homage to Ascanius's precarious passage with the divine embers, and it would be humiliating if her sarcina, in particular, were defective.

As the incline of the mountain grew more severe and the horses in the procession quickened their pace to compensate, Rhea slid forward and gripped Mamilian tighter, not wanting to slide off the back of the horse.

"We are there," he said over his shoulder. "Look, there is the beast."

Rhea peeked around Mamilian's body. The sacrificial white bull was indeed already in place, standing near the great rectangular sanctuary of Jupiter, at the feet of a larger-than-life statue of the god: powerful and bearded, Jupiter held his thunderbolt like a spear, his thick hair tousled from the winds of heaven, his face severe yet somehow fatherly.

Unlike other temples, this one had no roof or covering whatsoever—all the better to honor the god of the sky, the king of the gods, who watched from above. That open-air design, and the height of the sanctuary, allowed the people of Latium to get as close to the heavens as possible. And just in case the celestial significance was lost on anyone, a sprawling astronomical observatory—constructed only recently, after an Alban priest had visited a similar structure in Greece—was located among the other temples that stood on the mountaintop, giving god-seekers the best place in Latium to marvel at the cosmic wonders overhead.

The sacred bull snorted as one of its stewards hand-fed it some kind of sweet grain. Another handler fussed over the long, colorful ribbons that were tied arounds its horns, arranging them in a way that Rhea supposed he thought was most becoming to a bull. The beast seemed entirely unconcerned by the presence of two axe and knife-wielding men who stood only a few steps away, studying its head and neck with singular purpose.

A horn sounded and the procession stopped. King Numitor and Egestus dismounted first, followed in succession by everyone else—royalty, priests, and nobles. Armed guards kept order amongst the throngs of people who had made the journey on foot and now stood or knelt with palms up, muttering prayers or petitions to the gods.

Two soldiers approached Mamilian's horse and helped Rhea dismount as gracefully as she could while still holding the now very warm, almost hot, sarcina in her hands. Mamilian waited until she was safely on the ground, and until her handmaids had finished removing her cloak and straightening her white dress, before he dismounted as well. He stood before her, letting his eyes move quickly over her body.

"You look ripe enough to pick, Princess," he said.

Rhea swallowed her offense. "Thank you, Mamilian," she replied.

"Soon it will be thank you *husband*."

Rhea said nothing, but felt his eyes on her as she walked toward the sanctuary, followed by the other maidens who carried sarcinae, each of whom had similarly arrived on the horse of her betrothed.

The priests raised their arms to the sky—to Jupiter—and called out the prayers, asking the god's protection first of Alba Longa and then all the city-states of Latium. This reinforced the solidarity and shared purpose of the Confederation: to honor the gods, to keep the peace, and to ensure that each city in the alliance would defend the next from the more aggressive peoples who lived nearby, the foremost of these being the Etrusci, who called themselves the Rasenna. They lived to the north, on the other side of the great Tiber River.

Rhea led the other sacerdotes to a large bronze bowl that sat on the wide stone altar before the sanctuary. Inside the bowl lay thin strips of dry kindling. She set her sarcina inside the bowl and used a piece of kindling to carefully pry it open. As she did, smoke from the smoldering ember escaped, and she leaned over to blow, gently stirring the ember back to life. A flame burst forth, licking outward to consume the kindling. Relieved, she stepped back to allow each maiden in turn to add her sarcina to the fire. Within moments, strong orange flames roared in the bronze bowl, crackling and popping as they devoured the wood.

The chief priest of Jupiter, his head hooded in deference to the gods, called out. "*Dei, nos respicite*," he began. "*O Jupiter Pater, O Vesta Mater*, see us wake the sleeping fire of Troy in Latium, as decreed by our ancestors, as we have done for generations and will always do! See it burn on this great mountaintop, high in the sky over Alba Longa and all the cities of Latium! *O Jovis divine*, look down on us, as we look upward to you." A senior priestess of Vesta stepped forward with a bowl of salt and sprinkled the grains between the bull's ribbon-wrapped horns, thus purifying the animal for the god. "See this fine sacrifice we offer to you," continued the priest, "father of all!"

A loud bellow and it was over. The axe and knife-wielding men had done their work. The white bull collapsed to the ground, immediately surrounded by priests who began the task of skillfully cutting out its choicest innards, carrying the slippery contents to the bronze bowl, and setting them in the sacred flames. The smoke and the smell rose up to Jupiter, even as Rhea tried not to gag at the stomach-churning stench of the altar sacrifice.

I will never understand what pleases the gods, she thought.

❈ ❈ ❈

"Prince Egestus, let's share a drink together." Mamilian, standing behind Egestus's chair in the palace's banquet hall, placed his hand on the seated man's shoulder and squeezed. "We are to be brothers soon. We should learn to get drunk together."

Without turning around to face Mamilian, Egestus met eyes with Nemeois who was sitting on the chair beside him, obviously in mid-conversation and chewing a mouthful of the sacred bull's best flesh. Egestus jutted his jaw forward, signaling Nemeois to leave, which he promptly did. Mamilian replaced him in the chair, settling into the amber-colored upholstery with the confidence of a king taking his throne. He called for wine and cocked his head at Egestus, his smile somewhere between amused and arrogant.

Egestus did not react, but rather looked at Mamilian in the same cautious, analytical way that he looked at everyone he distrusted. As Mamilian leaned forward to clasp his wine cup, Egestus leaned back. To someone who did not know him, the crown prince might have looked intimidated by the larger man.

"I have heard good things about Alban wine," said Mamilian. He downed the cup of wine in his hand and raised his eyebrows, impressed. His eyes moved deliberately to Rhea, who stood on the other side of the crowded, music-filled hall, laughing at whatever anecdote her uncle Amulius was relating to her. "I hope your women are as good as your wine."

Egestus emptied his own cup.

Mamilian turned his attention to Cloelia who was happily dancing with Numitor, spinning and singing as the king clapped. "Congratulations on your engagement," he said to Egestus. "There isn't a man in Latium who hasn't admired Lady Cloelia's—how should I say it?—*well-formed* nature. I guess the heir apparent gets his pick, eh?"

"My uncle suggested the match."

"But you didn't put up a fight, did you?"

"Why would I?"

Mamilian clucked his tongue. "Well, it's just that your history with her late husband…it must make things a little awkward, no? I mean, the two of you were good friends. And now him in ashes, and you bedding his rosy wife…"

Still, Egestus said nothing. He had a habit of only speaking when he was certain the words would be to his benefit. It was a type of self-discipline that never failed to frustrate his detractors. Unfortunately, Mamilian was not the type of man to be dissuaded by an uncomfortable silence. The prince's strategy was as clear to him as still water.

"I'll leave you to your thoughts, sir." Mamilian stood and looked down at the top of Egestus's head, waiting for him to say goodbye. When he did not, Mamilian gave an imperceptible nod and left, crossing the floor of the banquet hall in large strides until he reached Rhea's side.

Nemeois returned to his seat beside Egestus. Chewing the side of his mouth, he followed Egestus's gaze. Mamilian had his hand on Rhea's back and although the princess was smiling, her kinsmen knew her well enough to know that she would be secretly seething at her betrothed's presumptuousness. Egestus put his elbows on the table and rubbed his beard.

"Will Numitor not reconsider the match?" Nemeois asked him.

"We couldn't get him to reconsider it before it was made public. There's no way he'll do it now, not with all of Latium knowing about it." He rubbed his beard harder. "It would look like we're threatened by Mamilian...like I am threatened by him. My father has put me in an impossible position. How can he not see that? How can he not see what impending disaster I will inherit as king?"

Nemeois curled his upper lip as he stared at Mamilian. "Once you are king, you can dissolve the marriage."

"The peace treaty with Tusculum would dissolve with it."

Nemeois thought. "Rhea is a daughter of Alba Longa. She has no love for Tusculum or Mamilian. When he impregnates her, perhaps she would be willing to somehow…"

"I have already explored that path with her. It leads nowhere. You know Rhea. She plays at being hard, but she has a pliable heart. If Mamilian ever wises up enough to be pleasant to her, she will grow to love him. It is inevitable. Once she leaves this house and gets into his bed, she will be his, not ours, and he knows it."

Nemeois knew it, too. He rolled through the options in his mind, but each seemed more futile than the last. Frustrated by his failure to offer the prince a solution, and distracted by his own uncharacteristic lack of strategy, he had not noticed Cloelia approach.

"I wonder if I may sit with the prince for a while," she said.

"Oh, forgive me, Lady Cloelia," Nemeois replied, standing. "We will speak tomorrow, cousin," he said to Egestus. "Try to enjoy the banquet. Even royalty doesn't usually eat this well."

As Cloelia sat beside him, Egestus sat up straight and set his palms on the table. She placed her hands on top of his. "I have been watching you," she said. "You have not moved from this spot in hours. The guests all eat and dance, but I have not seen you take a bite of food or sing to a string of music."

"You know I am not the jovial sort, Cloelia. You mistake me for your first husband."

Cloelia pulled her hands off his, unsure whether he intended the statement to be as hurtful as it sounded. She folded her hands in her lap and pulled her lips into a tolerant smile.

Egestus looked at her. Unlike most of the women at the banquet, she wore no elaborate hairstyle, preferring to pull her dark hair back into a simple braided bun. And why not? Her face was flawless. There was no need to accentuate her features or try to distract from them.

He had always been taken with her beauty. Whenever he had visited Geganus's home, he had watched his friend's wife out of the corner of his eye. The way she moved and spoke, the way she smiled at him with her full lips and deep brown eyes. He would think about her all the way home and then, in his bed, he would fantasize about her. He would have coupled with her without pause, without regret, if Geganus were still alive, despite their long friendship. Yet with Geganus dead…for some reason Egestus did not understand, the betrayal seemed somehow worse. Or perhaps, as Nemeois was fond of saying, passion burns hottest when it is forbidden. Now that Cloelia was his to take at will, he did not care for her quite as much.

Nonetheless, thoughts of his former fantasies had stirred his physical desire, and Egestus glanced around the hall. The city-states of Latium had sent their finest women. Perhaps he would take Nemeois's advice and try to take some enjoyment from the banquet. If nothing else, it might take his mind off his troubles for the night.

Cloelia could see it in his eyes—the way they suddenly looked past her, as if she wasn't even there, to move almost predatorily over the many beautiful women who danced and socialized, all of them, married and maiden alike, doing their best to catch the crown prince's attention. It was too late for them to become his wife, but a mistress was the next best thing. Cloelia put a hand back on top of his, pressing down so he could feel her warmth. His eyes moved back to hers.

The prince stood, his hand first slipping out from under Cloelia's, but then taking hold of it. Except for a number of disappointed would-be mistresses, the revelers around him took little notice as he left the banquet hall with his soon-to-be wife, passing through the huge double-doors and into a wide corridor lined with painted terracotta statues of the gods. Egestus led her silently down one wing of the palace and then another, until they reached the prince's private quarters.

A slave stood before his bedchamber door. When he saw the prince had Cloelia with him, he bowed, but avoided making eye contact with her. "Your Highness, is there anything you require?" he asked his master.

Egestus shook his head as he led Cloelia into his bedchamber: it was even larger than she had expected, with carved mahogany furniture, plum-colored drapery and linen as red as garnets. He proceeded to his bed and sat on the edge. His eyes narrowed as he studied her, and Cloelia lowered her head. She felt the years of history between them, the awkwardness, and underneath it all, she felt his simmering attraction to her. She knew he expected her to inflame it. All of Alba Longa expected her to inflame it.

I can still refuse, she thought. *He will not be so surprised…perhaps he will even be relieved. I can return to my father's home… No, I cannot do that.*

A feeling of resolve came over her. She had agreed to this engagement and Egestus was a decent man. Why take a risk with a man she did not know as well, whose vices might be far worse? If she could please him tonight, it would change things. They would grow closer.

"I do not know how you prefer things," she said softly. She waited for him to say something, prayed he would give her some kind of direction, but nothing. Holding on to her resolve, she moved her hands to her shoulders and slipped off her dress. The fabric fell to the floor, leaving her standing naked in front of him. Next, she raised her arms and unpinned her hair so that it fell in thick locks over her bare breasts.

Egestus raised his chin, still studying her. Finally, just when Cloelia thought she could not stand there exposed for another moment, he stood and began to undress. Seeing his arousal, she silently thanked Venus and waited unmoving as he neared her. His expression still unreadable, he brushed her hair off her breasts and gently slid a palm over them. Cloelia stepped even closer toward him, bringing her mouth closer to his, inviting him to kiss her.

But then a change came over him. His fingers tightened over her breast and Cloelia gasped in surprise and pain, stepping back. Egestus clutched her head between his hands and all but yanked her forward, placing a hard kiss on her lips, probing her mouth with his tongue and cutting off her breath. She let out a murmur of protest, but it was met, unbelievably, with a slap across the face. Shocked, she nonetheless let him pull her to his bed where, a moment later, she found herself on her hands and knees as he entered her from behind in a single stroke.

He released quickly with a low grunt, took a deep breath, and then withdrew from her, wiping his genitals off in the sheets and then lying down with his back to her. Stunned by his callosity, Cloelia gathered the sheets around her nakedness. Her head was spinning and her cheek stung. A rising sense of humiliation competed with confusion and she sat back on her heels to get her bearings, trying not to cry as she considered her options. Should she speak to him? Should she leave? Should she lie down beside him?

Deciding the last option was best—there was nothing to do now but see it to the end—she lay down on the opposite side of the bed and steadied her breathing. She did not bother trying to sleep.

❈ ❈ ❈

With most of the distinguished guests having turned in to their guest quarters, the banquet hall was left to the younger and mostly unattached crowd—the cousins of royalty, the adult children of dignitaries, high-ranking soldiers, popular mistresses and favored slaves. Without their important parents or patrons around, they were free to relax.

And Rhea was free to leave. She said a last round of goodnights and left the hall, exhaling tiredly as she turned into the torchlit corridor. Her older handmaid Thalia walked alongside her. A regal-looking woman herself, with long silver hair and bright black eyes, she snapped her fingers at Lela who stood leaning against a statue of Mars, giggling as Nemeois kissed her on the neck. The younger handmaid pushed Nemeois away and ran to catch up to her mistress.

"I am sorry, Princess, I was just—"

"We know what you were doing," said Thalia.

"My father has given Nemeois permission to take her," chided Rhea. "It is not your place to refuse the king. You should know that better than anyone."

The older handmaid raised her eyebrows at her mistress. It was not like Rhea to chastise her: Thalia had raised the royal twins after their mother died, and was the closest thing to a mother either of them could remember having. For a while, she had even taken their mother's place in the king's bed, despite being married at the time—thus the personal gibe.

"Of course, Princess," said Thalia.

As the three women walked along, Rhea tried to lose the sensation of Mamilian's hand on her back. "It is not my place to refuse the king, either," she said to herself as much as to her handmaids.

That realization—that she was as powerless as her servants—made the anger that she had been suppressing all night break free, and she turned around, retracing her steps along the corridor until she arrived at the king's private wing. The guards bowed and opened the doors for her. Lela and Thalia waited outside as Rhea strode over the soft-carpeted floor into the king's sitting room. As she had expected, he was awake, reclining in a cushioned chair by the fire and staring absently into the thick orange flames.

"Can you not sleep, Father?" asked Rhea, as she sat on the chair beside him.

He patted his stomach. "I ate too much." He reached over to pat her knee. "You fulfilled your duties perfectly at the sacrifice this morning. Everyone was very impressed."

"That includes the gods, I hope."

"I have no doubt, daughter."

"I spoke to my cousin Amulia tonight. She is very happy with her engagement to Arus of Lavinium."

"It is a good match."

"I know you and my uncle consulted with her about it before you made your decision."

"My dear Ilia…" he said, employing the endearment he often called her, the one that hearkened back to her Trojan lineage.

"And yet you could not consult with me before offering me to Mamilian? Does it not matter to you that I hate him or that, worse, he hates me? You show more kindness toward your niece than toward your own daughter!"

"Rhea, please, listen—"

"I wish Egestus were already king. He would never trade me for a conch shell and a vain hope of peace."

"Don't be naïve, Rhea. Egestus will always put Alba Longa first, just as I have. That is the burden every king is born with. You may someday be surprised by what your brother is willing to do in the name of Alba Longa."

Rhea stood and stormed out of the sitting room, ignoring her father's pleas for her to return, to listen. She marched through the carpeted corridor to return to where Thalia and Lela were waiting, and then kept marching, face flushed and fists clenched, until she reached her own quarters. She collapsed onto a high-backed couch that stood in front of an unlit fireplace and covered her face.

Thalia knelt on the floor in front of her. "My sweet girl," she said. "Lela and I will come with you to Tusculum. You will see, life will be no different there. The trees are just as green and the sky just as blue. We will eat, walk in the gardens, bathe, laugh, and honor the gods, just as we do here. It is so close to Alba. We can visit often."

"Why? My father will not miss me."

"Your father will weep every morning for months," said Thalia, "but he must be a king first and a father second. Mamilian has been critical of Alba's expansion, and his family has had a personal feud with the Julii here in Alba for generations. I know you think your father is a fool, but he is not. He knows the only way to prevent a war in Latium is for Mamilian to love you as much as he and the prince do. He is placing the peace of Latium's two closest allies in your hands. He knows you are the only one who can achieve it."

"By whoring myself out to Mamilian."

Lela knelt beside Thalia and looked up at her mistress. "Princess," she said, "forgive me, but if I had a choice of whom to whore myself out to, I would choose Mamilian over Nemeois."

A cough of laughter broke through Rhea's tears. "Perhaps."

Thalia shrugged. "Mamilian is a handsome man," she said. "There is no denying that. Once you couple with him, you will feel differently. You will love him. The closeness of the marriage bed, the feel of his arms around you in those quiet hours, they will create a bond between the two of you."

"I cannot see it happening," said Rhea. "Mamilian does not have a kind bone in his body."

Lela smirked. "But he has one bone that you should know—"

"Lela, stop it," Thalia scolded the younger handmaid, although she herself struggled not to smile.

The ribald comment had its desired effect on the princess.

Rhea laughed and gave a heavy sigh that seemed to relax her whole body. "Pour me a bath," she said.

The two women stood. Thalia moved off to prepare a warm bath while Lela entered the princess's nearby bedchamber, lighting an oil lamp and arranging her bedclothes and linen for sleep.

Rhea sat up. Her hair was messy from her outburst, and she pulled out her hairpins. It felt good. The pins had been pinching her scalp all night. As she stood and her hair released onto her shoulders, a ribbon fell from it and landed on the floor. She looked down at it, trying not to think how much it reminded her of the ribbons that had been tied around the horns of the sacrificial animal.

CHAPTER III

In the weeks leading up to his wedding day, Egestus had tried and failed to shrug off the melancholic attitude he had toward the event. And so, almost immediately after the marriage vows had been exchanged, he had quietly slipped away to visit the one place that best matched his mood. His mother's tomb.

He kissed the hut-shaped urn that contained her ashes. He had no memory of her, but imagined she looked much like she did on the frescos painted on the walls of her tomb—a soft-faced woman, with hair and eyes as black as his own. He set her urn back in its stone niche and stared into the painted black eyes.

"Blessed Juno, Egestus! What are you doing here? Half of Alba is out looking for you."

The voice jolted him from his reverie, and he turned to see Rhea descending the few steps into the room-sized tomb, pulling her light woolen cloak tighter with one hand and holding up her torch with the other. In the dim light, she looked around the barrel-vaulted space. The abundance of fine pottery, pretty statuettes and votive offerings made it obvious that Egestus came here often.

"There are more votive sculptures in here than at the Heroön of Aeneas," she said. "Tell me, brother, what would people say if they knew you'd left your own wedding party to sulk at the necropolis?"

"I am not sulking. I am thinking. And clearly I must ask the gravediggers to go deeper if I wish to find some peace. I'll land in Hades before I'm left alone."

"Poor Cloelia. What new wife wants her husband to spend their first night together in his mother's tomb, instead of in their bed?"

"Since when do you care about Cloelia?" Egestus sat heavily in a low-backed chair: its carved chestnut legs and sapphire-blue cushions exactly matched the chair his painted mother rested on in one of the frescos. No doubt, it had been one of her favorite pieces. "And just so you know, sister, our first night together was over two months ago. On the night of the spring festival. She came readily to my bedchamber and undressed for me like a whore."

Rhea's torch sputtered and died, leaving the siblings in their mother's tomb with only the light of a few oil lamps to see by. The princess squinted and stared at her brother: his drawn expression and the shadows cast on his face made him look older. Sad. She knelt at his feet. "Egestus, what is the matter?"

"Why did you tell Cloelia that I become cruel with drink?"

Rhea felt a rise of anger. So much for Cloelia's discretion. "I told her no such thing. She should not spread such falsehoods about me."

"She never said that you were the one who told her. She said that she overheard it at the festival. But I know it was you, Rhea."

"Is that what's bothering you?"

"No. But why did you say it?"

Rhea shook her head. "It has always been just the two of us…"

"We will always be close, Rhea. Tusculum is not—"

"Yes, I know. Tusculum is not far away. If I hear that one more time, I will throw myself off the top of Mount Albanus. Now come, brother. You are already a grave sort, and this place does not help. Let us go back to the party. The guests were already wondering where you were when I left. They will be full of conspiracies by now."

Egestus put his hands on his knees and sighed. "How will I explain my absence?"

Rhea glanced around the lamplit tomb and pointed to an ivory table upon which sat several rich pieces of their mother's jewelry. "Bring Cloelia a gift. Tell her it was the queen's, and that you personally retrieved it from the tomb for her."

The prince chuckled. "You're sharp as a snake's tooth, sister."

"I played with Nemeois too much as a child," she said wryly.

Egestus lifted himself out of the chair and took the few steps across the tomb to inspect the jewelry: gemstone bracelets and necklaces, gold rings and dangling earrings.

And the dead queen's diadem, the one their mother had worn as a princess. Rhea saw it in the same moment her brother did. It was all she could do to not cry out *No, not that!* as Egestus picked it up. He ran his fingers over the vibrant gold, formed into the shape of oak leaves, and turned to face Rhea.

"I suppose this is only proper, right?"

Rhea nodded, suddenly feeling as somber as her surroundings. "Of course, brother. Cloelia is the crown princess of Alba Longa now."

※ ※ ※

By the time the royal siblings returned to the wedding celebration at the palace, the guests had gathered in the well-treed garden. King Numitor and Lady Cloelia—now Princess Cloelia—each carried a basket full of palm-sized *oscilla*, ornaments that bore the faces of the gods. Laughing, they held out the baskets as each guest selected an ornament and then moved off to hang it on the branch of a tree. Soon, the lower branches of the garden's many trees were full of ornaments—the faces of the gods spinning in the wind to bless everything they saw—and children were climbing upward to hang even more from the higher branches.

Rhea leaned against the trunk of her favorite tree, a large oak that was said to be centuries old, and watched Egestus approach his wife. She greeted him with an uncertain smile, but the smile widened as he held out the diadem to her. She hesitated, clearly waiting for him to put it on her head or perhaps make some kind of announcement, but he did neither, so she handed the basket to one of her handmaids, took the diadem from him, and placed it on her own head as her other handmaid helped to ensure it looked as regal as possible.

Not wanting to see any more, Rhea pushed herself off the tree trunk and walked toward an oval fountain accented with statues of long-necked swans. She sat on the teal-padded cushion of a long stone bench and stretched her legs out in front of her, smoothing the fabric of her dress and letting the sunlight warm away the last chills from the underground tomb.

A figure appeared before her and blocked the light.

"May I sit, Princess?"

Rhea looked up to find Mamilian grinning down at her. She managed a thin smile. "By all means."

He sat beside her—closer than was necessary, so that their bodies touched—and leaned back casually on his arms.

"Did you enjoy the wedding ceremony?" Rhea asked him.

"I'm not one for ceremony," he replied.

"The feast, then?"

"Yes. Although the cooks in my home prepare things differently. You will prefer it."

Rhea turned her head away from him. "I'm sure."

She spotted Egestus walking out of the trees and toward a circle of chairs arranged under an orange canopy where Nemeois was sitting with his father, Amulius. Seeming to sense her gaze, Egestus turned and looked curiously at her for a long moment before joining his kinsmen.

"Let's join them," said Mamilian.

He rose and offered his arm to Rhea. Doing her best to contain an irritated sigh, she accepted. They walked awkwardly arm in arm to the canopied seating area.

Amulius raised a wine cup as Mamilian and Rhea sat. "May the gods bless your upcoming marriage as they have blessed the prince's."

"They have no reason not to," Mamilian replied.

Nemeois cleared his throat. "I hear Tusculum is home to a fine new theater. I will look forward to watching a performance."

"We have the best Greek actors anywhere in Latium," said Mamilian, "and now we have the best theater, too. Our engineers are unmatched."

"Tusculum is a learned city," Nemeois replied, hoping the compliment would cool Mamilian's boasting.

"Our scholars are also unmatched," Mamilian continued. He rearranged himself in his seat and wagged a finger at Egestus. "As a matter of fact, our scholars have long believed that Tusculum was founded by Telegonas, son of Odysseus. My own ancestor."

Amulius scoffed. "Tusculum was founded by the Silvii," he said. "The history is certain."

"History is never certain, sir. How can it be? All who witnessed it are dead."

Egestus refilled his cup with wine and drained it in two swallows. In a rare show of agitation, he threw the empty cup onto the ground. "The Silvii founded all the major cities of Latium," he said. "It is why Alba Longa is the head of the Confederation. That will never change, Mamilian, regardless of what your boy-fucking Greek scholars say."

Rhea put her hand on Egestus's knee. "Brother," she said. "It has been a long day. Perhaps it is time to rest indoors."

Mamilian waved his hand dismissively in the air. "The fault is mine," he said. "I should know better than to talk politics on a social occasion. Yet I always say, what can it hurt to have a minor difference of opinion? I have noticed many differences between our cities."

"And many similarities," mediated Nemeois. "We honor the same gods."

"We do," Mamilian agreed, but before any sense of ease could return added, "and yet even there, I have noticed differences." He leaned far forward in his chair, speaking directly to Egestus. "Here in Alba Longa, the priests cover the top of their heads during the sacred rites. That is not always so in Tusculum. Do you know why?" When no one responded, he continued. "The reason, again, can be found in history. When Aeneas, your ancestor, first landed in Latium after fleeing Troy, he stopped to pray at a temple. While giving thanks to the gods, he saw his enemy Odysseus, my ancestor, enter the same temple. Terrified of being recognized by the greater warrior, he covered his head to disguise himself."

Egestus clenched his jaw. Amulius made to stand up, but Nemeois discreetly shook his head first at him, then at Rhea. *Let the prince handle it.*

"Later, when Aeneas left the temple," Mamilian continued, still leaning forward and speaking only to Egestus, "his men asked him why he covered his head. To avoid appearing a coward, he told them he did so to honor the gods." Mamilian opened his arms. "Thus the Alban tradition was—"

In the blink of an eye, Egestus sprang from his chair, grabbed the handle of the terracotta wine jug on the table beside him and swung it hard at Mamilian's head, sending the larger man tumbling off his chair, onto the ground. Still consumed by his fury, Egestus straddled Mamilian's body, clutching the wine jug's handle and striking him from above with the now broken vessel. Blood sprayed up to dot his face, but he did not stop until Amulius wrested the jug from his hand and Nemeois pulled him off the fallen man.

"Egestus!" shouted Amulius, struggling to restrain the younger man. "Calm yourself! It is your wedding day, for the love of the gods!"

Looking as shocked as he was injured, Mamilian clambered to his feet. A flood of blood ran from his nose and he coughed and spat, wiping his face with the back of his arm and staring incredulously at Egestus.

"It's the heat," Nemeois attempted. He put his arm around Mamilian's shoulder, patting his chest conciliatorily. "What's a wedding without a fight, eh? Come, friend, let us find a spot with more shade."

Mamilian did not move, but only stared in silent fury as the prince turned and marched toward the palace, disappearing inside.

Rhea looked at Mamilian. *It serves you right*, she thought. "I will speak to my brother," she said, stepping away from her fuming betrothed and the crowd that had gathered.

She entered the relative coolness of the palace walls, gathering the bottom of her dress so that she could run to catch up to Egestus who was already halfway down the wide corridor toward his quarters. She was about to call out to him when he stopped in his tracks, slumped against the wall and slid to the floor. He put his head in his hands. Rhea approached and stood over him, saying nothing.

Egestus tiredly rested the back of his head against the wall. He was not sure what omens he had invoked by creating such a scene on his wedding day, but he was certain they were not good ones. He looked up at his sister. Her dark hair was illuminated by a slant of sunlight streaming in from an open window, giving it a golden glow, like she was a demi-goddess looking down at him, curiously amused by his human frailty.

He rubbed his eyes as he thought back to the sight that had first disturbed him: Rhea and Mamilian sitting intimately on the bench in the garden. Until then, Egestus had mostly felt sorry for Rhea. However, in that moment, seeing her sitting so closely to Mamilian, seeing them having a private conversation, he had felt something else. Fear.

He felt fearful of her. Fearful of what she could become if she fell in love with Mamilian. If she bore Mamilian's son, and if her ambition someday matched her husband's, the two of them might decide that their son was not only the rightful king of Tusculum, but of Alba Longa and all of Latium.

Egestus lifted his eyes to meet hers, but she only looked at him quizzically. He looked past her, at the statues of the gods that lined the corridor, until his eyes fixed on the two largest statues—Jupiter and Juno. The king and queen of heaven. Husband and wife.

But also brother and sister.

❋ ❋ ❋

It was one of the rare occasions that Egestus could remember waking up with a wine-induced headache. It throbbed incessantly before he even sat up, and when he did, a wave of nausea had him searching for his chamberpot, finding it just in time to vomit into it. Ignoring Cloelia's expressions of concern, he pulled a tunica over his head and shuffled out of his bedchamber and out of his quarters. He needed some air.

He stepped into the courtyard just in time to see Nemeois tuck a messy lock of hair behind the ear of Rhea's handmaid, Lela. He gave her a kiss on the lips and then slapped her backside as she grinned, offered a bashful bow to the prince, and slipped back inside the palace.

"I don't have to ask how your evening went," said Egestus.

"Better than yours, I presume," Nemeois replied, "and I'm afraid your day won't be any better."

"Oh?"

"I got one of Mamilian's advisers drunk last night—the slave Haemon, the one with the two missing fingers—and he let it slip that Mamilian has proposed a marriage between his future son with Rhea and the newborn daughter of the Etruscan king in Veii."

"The Etrusci will never agree to it."

"The Etrusci believe they are descended from Odysseus. Apparently, their king and Mamilian have found a common ancestor. That will go a long way toward an alliance between them. You can bet Mamilian will have Rhea with child by the fall."

"He'll be screwing her in the wedding carriage on the way home from the altar," said Egestus. He rubbed his beard. Mamilian forging an alliance with Latium's strongest and most hostile neighboring tribe felt like a waking nightmare. "Gods," he muttered. "If Mamilian made this proposal without consulting my father, does that not break the peace treaty?"

"It's a gray area," said Nemeois. "Either way, it's unlikely that it's enough to make the other cities in Latium declare war on Tusculum, especially since Mamilian will spin it as a step toward peace with the Etrusci."

The crown prince wandered further into the courtyard, consumed by his thoughts and feeling his face flush with anxiety. He reached a fountain and dipped his hands into the cool water, splashing it on his face and rubbing the back of his neck. *I feel the balance of power shifting,* he thought to himself. *I can feel Mamilian gaining ground, breathing down the back of my neck.*

"Should I call a meeting with your father?" Nemeois asked.

"That would be pointless," replied Egestus. "My father is blinded by false promises of peace. I will have to find a solution myself." The prince stared into the fountain's water. It was clean and sparkled with the light of the morning sun, its surface calm except for the tiny ripples of distress formed by a small iridescent green beetle floating on top. Egestus scooped it out of the water and tossed it into a flower bush. "We will speak later," he said to Nemeois.

Egestus crossed the courtyard to return to the palace, heading directly to Rhea's quarters. He entered to find Thalia and a tidier but still sheepish-looking Lela selecting the princess's clothes for the day. Ignoring their greetings, he saw Rhea standing outside on the terrace, still in her nightdress, brushing her hair and staring off into the green hills. He joined her.

"What got into you yesterday?" she asked, still gazing off into the hills. "It is not like you to bite Mamilian's bait."

Egestus put his hands on the balustrade and squinted in the sunlight. A black-winged scarlet bird, the one Albans called the *flamma aestatis*, the flame of summer, landed on the far end of the terrace. It cocked its head this way and that, chirped at the siblings and flew off toward a nearby tree.

"There cannot be any more beautiful place in the world than Alba Longa," he said. "It is no wonder that Ascanius was destined to create his legacy here. That legacy lives on in you and me, Rhea. No one else." He rested his elbows on the balustrade, linked his fingers together, and stared at his hands as he spoke. "What would you do to become the queen of Alba Longa?"

"That is a cruel question, Egestus, especially when I'm about to be exiled to Tusculum."

"Answer the question."

"I would do anything."

His fingers tightened so that the skin of his knuckles turned white. "Do you know how the pharaohs of Egypt hold on to their power? How they maintain the pure bloodline of their royal ancestors?"

Rhea stopped brushing her hair. An aberrant silence followed. After several long moments, Egestus found the courage to look at her. Her eyes were narrowed in thought, locked on to the little scarlet bird that was now perched in a tree, chirping and hopping, made joyous by the warmth of the sun and the dew on the leaves.

"It is forbidden," she said finally, her voice near a whisper.

"By whom? The king? I will be king soon enough."

"The gods, then."

"The gods do it themselves. And much worse."

Rhea examined the hairbrush in her hand as she spoke, her voice still low and uncertain. "We would *marry*?"

"Yes."

"What about Cloelia?"

"I will divorce her or find some reason to banish her. I'll have her executed if you want. I cannot trust her." He thought back to his first night with Cloelia. How she had undressed for him and initiated their coupling. Did she have so little regard for her late husband? If he too were to die, would she so quickly drop her dress for another man? "She has no capacity for loyalty. You're the only one I can trust."

"But would we actually have to…"

Egestus stood up straight. "Yes, but only to create issue. Pure issue. The uncorrupted bloodline of Aeneas and Ascanius. You will be Queen Rhea Silvia of Alba Longa and I will be King Egestus Silvius. Our son—" he stumbled at the strange sound of that, but recovered "—our son will be the future king. The true blood king of Alba Longa. That is a better destiny for your son than the one Mamilian has planned. He will marry the boy to an Etruscan princess. What pride will you take in creating such a bastardized bloodline?"

Rhea took her bottom lip in her mouth. "How would we…" she fidgeted with the hairbrush, pulling some loose strands of hair from the bristles. "How would it happen?"

"The same way it always happens. I would make sure that I was ready, so it would be over as soon as possible. We could do it in the dark, without even looking at each other. It would just be a physical act."

"Like eating or bathing," Rhea said sardonically. "Yes, I can see the similarity."

"Wine will help." He forced himself to face her again. This time she met his eyes, so he pressed on. "It would be no different with Mamilian, except…"

"Except what?"

"Except he will not be gentle with you. After what happened yesterday, he will hurt you to hurt me."

Rhea began to brush her hair again, hoping it would hide the fact that her hands had started to tremble.

"If you want to be queen of our city and mother to the next king, this is what it will take, Rhea. This is the price of it. It's the curse of royalty, of those who want their pure bloodline to continue. We would not be the first." He paused. "When will you be ready to conceive?"

She shook her head. "Don't ask me that."

"When did your blood last come?"

"That is none of your business."

Egestus blinked at the scarlet bird, now puffed up and sleeping contentedly on a branch. The thought of Rhea's menstrual blood made him see the bright red feathers differently, and he felt another mild wave of nausea. He reached out to touch her arm, to comfort her, to reassure her they were still brother and sister, but she pulled away.

"I need to get dressed, Egestus."

"We will speak more of it later."

Rhea nodded in a way that made Egestus certain they would not. He released a heavy sigh and departed, leaving her alone on the terrace with her thoughts.

CHAPTER IV

Her handmaid Thalia was right. The trees were just as green in Tusculum. Rhea sat back in the horse-drawn carriage as it reached Mamilian's palace, an island of soaring masonry and painted statues positioned regally among a manicured forest of cypress and stone pines. She had been here before, as a child: her father had visited Tusculum on business and she had accompanied him, though she did not remember the palace being quite so grand. Mamilian had clearly expanded the grounds after his father's death.

"I remember when you visited," he said. "When we were children."

She put her hands in her lap and looked at him, sitting with his arms crossed across his chest on the other side of the carriage. "I'm surprised you'd remember such a thing," she said.

"I remember it well." He unfolded his arms and pointed outside the carriage, to the fortification wall that surrounded the expansive grounds. "You and I walked all along the top of that wall. We stayed out until well after dark. They had to come looking for us."

"I forgot about that. My father was so worried."

"My father was irate," said Mamilian. "He beat me for it."

"I am sorry to hear that."

"It is no matter." Mamilian lifted his chin, still looking at the encompassing wall of the grounds as the carriage traveled along the stone path closer to the palace. "It was worth it."

Rhea leaned forward to get a better look out the carriage. The movement shifted her wedding veil and she reached up to remove it from her hair, feeling the absence of one curled lock. It was tradition for brides to place a lock of hair on the Altar of Juno, and she had done so during the morning exchange of their vows. She could still see the black lock lying on the scarlet altar. She and Mamilian had stood before it as he poured wine and then milk over the top, an offering to Juno, the queen of heaven and the goddess of marriage.

The wedding reception had also taken place in Alba Longa, at the palace, and had been pleasant enough. That is, there had been no secret trips to the necropolis to sulk, and no one had struck anyone else with a wine jug.

Yet she and Mamilian had barely spoken during the reception. The throng of important guests from the confederate cities of Latium, and the endless stream of speeches, well wishes and gift giving had occupied their every moment. Rhea had been grateful for the commotion of it all. It had kept her distracted from thinking too hard about what was really happening.

When the time had come to depart Alba Longa, she had surprised herself by climbing willingly, more or less, into the wedding carriage as she and Mamilian set off for Tusculum. She had peeked outside the carriage to see her father and brother bid farewell to Mamilian. Her father had spoken private words to him, during which he had nodded in understanding, indulging the parting words of a doting father.

After that, Mamilian had extended his arm to Egestus, and the prince had clasped it. Only Rhea knew Egestus well enough to know that the expression on his face was not one of civil accord, but rather one of restrained hatred. As for Mamilian, she did not yet know him well enough to read his true feelings, though she suspected they were no different from her brother's.

Mamilian's carriage slowed as it reached the main entrance to the palace—a high, wide staircase that led up to a pair of ornate wood doors reinforced with iron—and stopped at the base of the stairs. Mamilian stepped out of the carriage and held the curtain back with one hand, helping Rhea step down with the other. She smiled graciously at the many palace officials and household staff that had gathered to welcome her: they bowed respectfully and offered her warm greetings as she passed by them to ascend the staircase.

She entered the palace to the sound of lively pipes and stepped directly onto a carpet of colorful flower petals strewn across the floor. More slaves greeted her, offering chilled water, wine, meats and sweets. It seemed to Rhea that they were genuinely happy to see her and were doing their best to honor her as their new mistress. With the death of Mamilian's mother years earlier, it had been a long time since a woman had overseen the household. *They are probably hoping I will be more pleasant than Mamilian*, she thought.

Mamilian entered the palace closely behind her. "Welcome to your new home," he said. The words seemed sincere enough, but there was an unmistakable tone of victory in the way he spoke them, as if he was congratulating himself at the same time that he was welcoming her. "Your ladies are here," he said, just as Rhea noticed Thalia and Lela standing expectantly several paces away. They had arrived in Tusculum ahead of Rhea, having traveled with her wardrobe, jewelry, and other personal belongings.

Lela was smiling widely—the whole thing was an adventure to the young woman—while Thalia seemed more reserved, searching Rhea's expression, looking for a sign of how the wedding had gone. Rhea smiled at her. *I am fine. Everything is all right. Do not worry.*

Mamilian put his hand on her back. "You must be tired," he said. "Shall I show you to our bedchamber? You can rest before I show you the rest of the palace. I've had several new rooms added and expanded the courtyard in anticipation of your arrival. I have been told you prefer to hold social events outdoors."

Rhea didn't respond. She hadn't heard anything after the words *our bedchamber*, and after several awkward moments of silence, the reason seemed to dawn on Mamilian.

"No, I did not mean it like that," he said. "I only meant that you could lie down for a while or freshen up. Your ladies could stay with you, if you are more comfortable. All is at your command, Rhea."

"Of course, thank you," Rhea said, suddenly embarrassed by how inexperienced and child-like she must have seemed to Mamilian, a man whose womanizing was as well-known as Nemeois's. "I would like to see more of the palace."

"Very well," said Mamilian.

They walked along, Mamilian twice offering her his arm, but she pretended not to notice, instead distracted by the colorful frescos of birds and vineyards that covered the walls, and the fine furnishings and fabrics that filled the many rooms and halls they passed. Mamilian's home equaled the royal palace in Alba Longa in every way.

As they turned into the open air of the courtyard, Rhea found she was shivering. Night had started to fall, and the chilly air, combined with the emotional and mental exhaustion of the day, suddenly seemed to settle on her. She looked up and saw the moon was already out. A thud of reality hit her—this was her new life, her new home—and she had to turn her head away from Mamilian to hide what she feared would be a tear of homesickness.

"Let's go inside and sit by the fire," said Mamilian. He took her hand without asking and gently pulled her back into the palace. "We can see the courtyard tomorrow in the sun."

Mamilian held her hand as they made their way to their bedchamber. He opened the door and dismissed the slaves who were arranging linens and stoking the fire, himself crouching in front of the fireplace to rearrange the wood until the flames crackled and snapped with renewed vigor. The heat radiated out to Rhea, and she lowered her shoulders. Mamilian stood up and faced her. To Rhea, he suddenly seemed as unsure of how to proceed as she was. He stepped closer to her and again took her hand. This time, he raised it to his lips and kissed it.

"You will have no reason to believe me," he said, "but I intend to be a good husband to you."

She looked up at him: it was the first time that she really let herself study him. Although they were close to the same age, fine lines had already started to appear around his dark brown eyes, no doubt from spending more time outdoors than she, riding and hunting in the woods.

Mamilian noticed her scrutiny and misinterpreted it. "I will do everything," he said. "Take off your dress."

She stepped back from him. "You said I didn't have to."

"I thought you wanted—"

"Do you care for me so little?" she asked. "You lay flower petals on the floor for me, but then disrespect me? It is not easy for me, not like it is for you. Do you know that we have only taken a meal together a few times, and never privately? And yet you want me to undress for you like…" she thought about the way Egestus had described Cloelia's willingness to couple with him "…like a whore?"

To her surprise, Mamilian laughed. "You are no whore, Rhea." He smirked, although more indulgently than smugly. "All right."

"Good. You can sleep in a guest room."

He laughed again. "I will not. We will both sleep here, but we will not couple."

Deciding that was the best she could hope for, Rhea called for Thalia and Lela. They helped her bathe and prepare for bed, Rhea moving as slowly as she could through it all. By the time she returned to the bedchamber, and as she had hoped, Mamilian was lying on his side with his back to her. Praying he was already asleep, she stood by the bedside for a few moments before pulling back the linen and slipping underneath as quietly as she could.

The bedchamber was dim, lit only by a single oil lamp, leaving Rhea to blink into the near darkness. The bed was comfortable and the room was warm, but the strangeness of it all made her certain that sleep would never come. She turned to lie on her back and stared up at the black ceiling above.

"Things will be better in the morning," whispered Mamilian. "You will see."

His unexpected kindness threatened to make her cry, but she swallowed the feeling and forced herself to speak normally, even as she made sure her body was as far from his as possible.

"Thank you, Mamilian."

"Good night, wife."

※ ※ ※

"So you didn't even couple with him?" Lela slumped her shoulders and stared incredulously at Rhea. "He didn't force you to? Honestly, I thought the man would be a beast. I thought you'd be sore as—"

"Oh, be quiet, Lela," said Thalia. She set a plate of peaches and warm bread on the table for Rhea and then sat opposite her mistress, raising a hand to her brow to shield her eyes from the piercing light of the morning sun that streamed into the palace's central courtyard.

Lela huffed. "I wish my biggest problem was how to reject a man like that."

Thalia picked a peach slice off Rhea's plate and bit into it. "You cannot reject him again tonight."

"Why not? He will not die if he has to wait." She smirked as she dipped a piece of bread into a bowl of olive oil. "Lela can wear my nightdress and sneak in when the lamps are out."

"Gladly," said the younger handmaid.

"Mamilian will be proud of himself for being patient with you," said Thalia. "The patience won't last another night."

Rhea chewed thoughtfully, speaking through her food. "I know. But Egestus said that Mamilian would hurt me to hurt him."

"That is nonsense," said Thalia. "You are his wife now. He will be more respectful."

"Last night he told me that he intended to be a good husband."

"See?" brightened Thalia. "Then be a good wife. If you are worried about it being painful, take a little extra wine before bed."

"You can use some olive oil on yourself to help it go in," said Lela. "I used to do that all the time when Nemeois started taking me. Then I got used to him." She shrugged. "I kind of miss the fool, to be honest."

"Gods, things *have* changed," said Rhea.

"For the better I hope," said Mamilian, entering the courtyard. He approached the table, gesturing for the handmaids to remain seated as they both made to stand up. "No, enjoy the sun," he said. "I have some matters I must deal with right now. Rhea, we will sit together this afternoon, yes?"

"Yes."

Mamilian eyed the two handmaids—his expression somewhere between civility and suspicion—and moved off to join his slave and adviser, Haemon, who was waiting for him on the other side of the courtyard. They walked toward the far wing of the palace where Mamilian conducted business and met with his staff, advisers and visitors.

Once inside, Haemon raised his eyebrows in curiosity. "Well?"

"No. Tonight."

"What was wrong with last night?"

"New bride," replied Mamilian. "I couldn't exactly ravish her on her first night here, not if she is to favor me over that prick brother of hers. It took the patience of Perseus, though. I was a rock all night long and couldn't even slip out of bed to find a slave to relieve me. She woke up every time I moved."

Haemon snorted a laugh. "There is a messenger here from King Velsos of Veii. He has sent you a wedding gift. You will want to see it."

Mamilian turned the corner to see a larger-than-life statue of Odysseus, cast in bronze, standing in a niche in the wall. Its presence took him by such surprise that he could not remember what statue stood in the spot the day before. Made to look like the Greek hero was standing on a rocky shore looking out to sea, the sculpture boasted a craftsmanship that Mamilian had never seen before.

The Etruscan messenger knelt before Mamilian. "My master, the great King Velsos of Veii, supreme ruler of the Rasenna, gifts you this fine sculpture on the occasion of your wedding. The fearsome King Velsos sends word that his newborn daughter is well, and expresses his desire to hear that your wife is with child. The benevolent King Velsos sacrifices to the gods that the accord between Veii and Tusculum remains constant."

Mamilian ran his hand over the exquisite bronze statue. "Tell your king that I am honored by his magnificent wedding gift, and that my wife is healthy, and soon to be with child. Tell him that the bond between Tusculum and Veii could not be broken, not even by the unyielding Odysseus who forged it." Mamilian gestured to two slaves who stood a few steps away from the statue, cloths still in hand from having polished it, as he spoke to the king's messenger. "My men will see that you are fed and rested before you leave. You are welcome to fresh gear and horses. In fact, choose the finest horse in the stable and present it to your master for me, with thanks."

"As you wish, sir," bowed the messenger.

After another admiring study of the bronze, Mamilian led Haemon out of earshot. The adviser spoke first. "The *great*, the *fearsome*, the *benevolent*, King Velsos," he mocked. "Mighty Jupiter best be warned about the Rasenna. But you heard the man. He is eager to formalize the betrothal of your offspring."

"I hear you, Haemon," said Mamilian. "I will couple with her tonight." He cast his eyes back to the bronze. "And every night after until she's with child."

❉ ❉ ❉

It had been a long day for Mamilian, and an unusual one. Most of his days followed the same routine: business, breakfast, more business, lunch, then riding his fine horses and hunting for deer, rabbit or pheasant in the hills, before taking dinner, getting drunk, mounting whatever slave was close by, and going to bed.

Today, he had spent all afternoon with Rhea, strolling leisurely through the courtyard and gardens, showing her the vineyards and stable, and asking if she wished to change any of the design or furnishings in the palace. Yet he was surprised to find that the experience was not altogether unpleasant. Having been born into royalty, she was certainly more demanding than most of the women he had known, but she was also more interesting and far more useful. He could already see the kind of future they could have together.

As night fell, they retired to their bedchamber where Mamilian again knelt before the fireplace to stoke the red embers and add kindling. Once the fire was crackling its warmth into the room, he rose and turned to Rhea. She was standing in the middle of the room, her expression pensive and her eyes staring coldly at the conch shell on the fireplace mantel. His betrothal gift to her. The one she had never acknowledged. He still felt bitter at the snub.

"I am sorry you did not like your gift. My adviser Haemon told me you would prefer gold or gowns, but I thought—"

"That I should not cost so much?"

Mamilian frowned. "I thought that, as a princess, you had enough gold and gowns, and that you would prefer something more meaningful from your future husband."

"How could a seashell be meaningful?"

Mamilian hung the stoker on the fireplace and brushed soot off his hands. "It is the emblem of Venus. I rode to the coastline myself to get it for you. I picked it from among hundreds on the shore of the great sea."

Rhea searched his face with her eyes, searched for some sign of deception, but could find none. Mamilian seemed as confused as she was.

"I sent a messenger with it," he said. "He was to explain its meaning. Did you not receive him?"

"No," replied Rhea. "It was not a messenger who presented it to me."

"Who, then?"

"Egestus. But he didn't give me any message." Rhea felt her chest tighten with anger. "He said you sent it to insult him."

"I need no seashell to insult Egestus."

As the weight of her brother's deception descended on her, Rhea moved to sit on the edge of the bed. She had always relied on Egestus, always thought of him as her second self. To now know that he had kept this truth from her so that she would hate Mamilian as much as he did…it all made sense now. *He's lucky I'm not home*, she thought, *or I would strike him!*

Mamilian sat on the bed beside her. "It is the past, Rhea," he said. "We will start again."

She let him draw closer and didn't resist as he put his hands on her face, bringing his mouth closer to hers, kissing her lightly and then more deeply, letting her body relax and respond. To Rhea, his strength and even his former aggression suddenly seemed somehow appealing, and she allowed him to push her onto her back on the bed. She felt her nightdress rise up as his hand moved underneath, exploring and caressing her body.

She looked away as Mamilian hastily undressed and held her breath as he lowered his body onto hers. He urged her to open her legs and she did, her face flushing with anticipation, but she gasped in pain as he entered her. Her arms came up to push him away, but he held them down and kissed her neck, thrusting slowly and gently until the pain became a rhythmic pleasure for both of them, peaking in a strong, shared climax.

For a while, Mamilian did not move. He stayed on top of her, inside of her, as his breathing returned to normal and the sense of frantic want faded away. Finally, he withdrew and lay beside her, brushing her hair off her face in a way that, despite their short time together, seemed genuinely affectionate.

Rhea squirmed to pull her nightdress back down. She sat up slowly as the strange blend of discomfort and gratification that she felt began to ebb.

"I need to wash myself," she said.

He touched her back, smiling at her as she rose and disappeared behind the dressing curtain to a washbasin. Spent and already fighting sleep, he rolled onto his back.

She was only gone a few moments.

Which made it even stranger that, upon her return, Mamilian was nowhere to be found.

CHAPTER V

Thalia woke to the feel of a hand clamped over her mouth. She opened her eyes to find Mamilian's slave, Haemon, glaring down at her.

"Not a sound," he said. When she nodded in consent, eyes wide and chest pounding, he removed his hand. "Why was there no blood?" he demanded.

"What do you mean?" she asked breathlessly.

Mamilian stepped out of the shadows and toward the bed, his frame towering menacingly above her, lit only by the flame of the oil lamp on her bedside table. "There was no blood on the sheets after I penetrated your mistress. Why not?"

The handmaid sat up, holding the bedcovers to her chest. "I don't know," she said. "The princess is a virgin, I can assure you."

Mamilian leaned over and put his arms on either side of Thalia, bringing his face close to hers. "Then why was there no blood?"

"Master Mamilian, I promise you, she is—she *was*—a virgin when you took her. I have known the princess since she was a young girl. I would know if she had been with a man."

Frustrated, Mamilian pushed his arms off the bed and stood up. "Take her downstairs," he said to Haemon. He glared at Thalia. "Keep quiet."

Haemon grabbed Thalia's arm and yanked her out of the bed. She stumbled and fell, but he clutched her arm harder and dragged her across the bedchamber, out the door and down the long, dark hallway, not slowing as they descended a long flight of stairs. It was even darker at the bottom of the stairwell, though Thalia could hear the creak of yet another door opening. She forced herself to remain silent, not to ask where he was taking her or why, nor to cry out at how badly he was hurting her arm, even though her hand was numb from his vise-like grip and her fingers throbbed from the pressure.

The slave pushed her through the door into total blackness. The chilly air contracted the skin on her bare arms, and she instinctively recoiled at the feel of loose dirt under her bare feet. The air was dank and smelled of old wine. Haemon entered the cellar after her, holding up an oil lamp and staring accusatorily at her by the light of its flame.

Thalia looked around. Amphorae of wine and oil were stacked neatly against the walls, some—most likely the choicest varieties—were half-buried in the dirt floor, the cool insulation working to preserve their quality and taste. She nervously clasped her hands in front of her as she heard more footsteps coming down the stairs.

"Your master is mistaken," she whispered to Haemon. "You must make him understand."

"We'll see about that," he said.

Mamilian entered the cellar with a sleepy-eyed woman following closely behind. He put his hands on his hips, breathing loudly through his nose, his face drawn in anger and confusion. "There was no blood on the sheets," he said to the woman with him. "Why not? Should there not be blood?"

Gaia, the long-time female slave who had for years served as the palace midwife, rubbed her eyes. It was the middle of the night and with the last birth in the palace having been decades earlier, she was no longer accustomed to—or tolerant of—being so abruptly woken from sleep. It only took her a moment to understand the reason for her master's distress.

"There is not always blood," she said to him. "The hymen can be broken in all sorts of ways. Inserting the menstrual wool can do it, as can horseback riding, especially if the animal has a wide back. You can't always assume the worst."

Haemon looked to Mamilian. "King Numitor assured us that she was intact," he said, seeming to agree with the midwife's optimism. "He would not mislead about such a thing."

"How did she react to penetration?" Gaia asked Mamilian.

"It seemed to be painful for her," he replied. "She was inexperienced, that is for certain." He paced half the length of the cellar, and then paced back. "But there was no blood."

"After you were done…what did she do then?"

"She left to wash."

"Then she probably washed the blood away," said Gaia. When the answer didn't seem to appease Mamilian, she added, "I can examine her, if you wish."

"What will that show?"

The midwife shrugged. "Won't know 'til I get in there."

Mamilian sat heavily on a low stool and leaned his back against the wall. "No, I can't do that to her. If I'm wrong, she'll never forgive me." He chewed his bottom lip, his anxious stare settling on Thalia. "Tell me the truth. You will not be harmed if you are honest."

"I have been nothing but honest."

"Bloody Jove," he said. He spoke to Haemon. "Get it out of her. Whatever it takes."

Haemon used the flame of the oil lamp to light a second lamp affixed to the stone wall, making it only slightly easier to see in the musty cellar. He reached out to clutch the back of Thalia's head, his fingers tightening into a fistful of her hair. Thalia raised her arms to try to pry off his fingers, but it was no use.

"Please," she cried out, "I swear to the gods, I am telling you the truth!"

Haemon forced her to take several steps forward, toward a round tub of wash-up water near the center of the cellar. Even in the low light, the film of oil on the water's surface was visible, as was the crusted wine that colored the inside of the tub's rim. He kicked Thalia's legs out from underneath her. She fell hard onto her knees. Still clutching her hair, he thrust her head into the stagnant water, nearly gagging himself at the stench that billowed out of it.

Thalia's hands let go of his and flailed frantically around, splashing helplessly in the water and batting at the sides of the tub. Finally, she pressed her palms against the bottom of the tub and pushed up as hard as she could. The back of her head nearly broke the water's surface, but Haemon leaned over and pushed it in deeper.

A grotesque-sounding gurgle and a burst of bubbles from below the water signaled it was time: Haemon snapped Thalia's head upward. She gasped for air, clutched her heaving chest, and began to sob. "Please, stop! I swear, I am telling you the—" Haemon forced her head back underneath the water.

After three more episodes of torture, each bringing Thalia closer to drowning than the one before, Haemon pulled the exhausted woman's head out of the wash-up tub and tossed her limp body onto the dirt floor. For a moment, he feared he had gone too far, but then her body convulsed and she retched, vomited, and began to weep.

By the time the handmaid recovered enough to push herself to her knees on the dirt floor, now muddy from the repulsive combination of fetid water and her vomit, she heard a new but familiar voice in the cellar. Lela. She wiped the oily water from her eyes and looked up helplessly at the younger handmaid.

A girthy but stooped male servant had a good grip on the back of Lela's neck as she twisted and swore at him to release her. She broke free, running to her friend.

"Gods, Thalia!"

Mamilian grabbed Lela around the waist before she could reach her. She tried to fight him off, but relented as he squeezed the breath out of her.

"I have a question for you," he said into her ear, "but first, there's something I want you to see." He nodded to Haemon.

As Lela watched, Haemon wrapped his left arm around Thalia's throat, locking her in a stranglehold that quickly turned her face blue. He raised a knife and—without a beat of hesitation—sawed off her nose. He dropped the fleshy stub to the dirt floor as if it were the skin of an apple he had just peeled.

Haemon released Thalia. The handmaid's hands flew to her face and she sucked in a bubbly, bloody breath of air, blowing it out in the form of a long, piercing scream.

Haemon cuffed her hard on the side of the head and she fell over, silent.

Mamilian felt Lela's body sliding downward. He loosened his grip and the handmaid fell to her knees, her stare fixed on Thalia's mutilated face. Her body swayed and she shook her head, fighting to not faint.

"My mistress," she said, her words weak but hateful. "She will have you—"

"Was she a virgin when I married her?"

Lela looked up at him and blinked. "What?"

"Was Rhea a virgin when I married her?"

"Yes, of course she was."

Mamilian reached out to take the bloody knife from Haemon's hand. In one motion, he stepped toward Thalia's unconscious body and thrust the blade deep into her throat. Her body twitched weakly and then went still. A blackish pool of thick blood spread out around her head, soaking her silver hair. Lela clasped her hands over her mouth and leaned forward, screaming into the dirt floor.

"Is there any chance," Mamilian continued, now pointing the blood-wet tip of the knife at Lela, "any chance whatsoever that she was with a man before me? Did you ever hear her mention a man before me?"

Lela sat back up and wiped the tears from her face. Suddenly struck with the spine-tingling realization that her own life now hung in the balance, she stuttered out an indecipherable sound.

Mamilian took a step closer to her. Lela forced herself to think through the paralyzing fear. And then she remembered. Her mouth dropped open and she looked up quickly, too quickly, at Mamilian.

Mamilian narrowed his eyes and squatted in front of her. He placed the tip of the blade against her throat. "Who was he?"

"I don't know if they coupled," Lela stammered, "I don't think they did. I just overheard them…talking about it."

"Who was he?" Mamilian repeated. His tone made it clear that he would not ask again.

Lela closed her eyes. "Prince Egestus," she said.

※ ※ ※

Mamilian would not see her, would not speak to her. And Thalia and Lela—Rhea had not seen either of them since the night before. No one would tell her where they were. The only person who would speak to her at all was the slave named Gaia, the scowly middle-aged woman who had brought her a tray of food for breakfast, but she had only repeated the same words: *Master Mamilian has asked that you prepare for a journey*.

Rhea looked out the window of the bedchamber. Below, at the base of the tall staircase that led up to Mamilian's grand home, several slaves were loading a horse-drawn cart with large trunks. Her belongings were being packed up. She was being sent home. As she watched, Mamilian emerged from the house to speak with one of the slaves. He looked up at the bedchamber window and saw her watching him, but turned away without acknowledging her.

He knew. It was the only explanation.

Coupling with Mamilian had not been painless, but there had been no blood. It was not like when Egestus had...her stomach turned at the memory. That had been far more painful and the blood had surprised her. But then, what exactly had she been expecting?

Egestus had come to her half-drunk, smelling like his favorite mistress. He had stumbled into her bedroom with a slurred, *Rhea, turn over.* She did as he said, not giving herself time to rethink it—they had already agreed on it, after all—and he straddled her body, pushing her face into the pillow and thrusting into her. The pain had felt like she was being split in half. When it was over, he had sat on the edge of her bed for a long time while she tried, unsuccessfully, not to cry.

There was no other way, sister, he had whispered, before leaving her alone.

The next morning, Rhea had lied to her handmaids, claiming that her cycle had come unexpectedly in the night. Lela believed it unquestioningly and went on to change the sheets without a second thought, but Rhea could see in Thalia's eyes that the older handmaid suspected there was more to it. Thalia never missed a thing.

Did Thalia betray me? Rhea wondered. *Did she tell Mamilian of her suspicions?*

That was unlikely. As the senior handmaid of the princess of Alba Longa, it was Thalia's sworn duty to ensure that Rhea remained a virgin and therefore marriable to whatever powerful ally the king wanted to strengthen ties with. If she failed in that duty, she would be condemned. Executed. A terrible thought occurred to Rhea. *Did Mamilian kill her?* She watched him scold a slave. *Of course he did.* Her mouth went dry with the certainty of it.

Gaia appeared in the doorway. "Mistress Rhea, it is time to leave. Come with me."

Rhea thought about refusing until she was allowed to see her handmaids—at least Lela—but the brusque slave did not seem like the type to indulge a tantrum, not even from a royal princess, so she wrapped her cloak around her shoulders and followed Gaia through the palace. Here and there, the few flower petals that had escaped the slaves' brooms lay forgotten along the wall, wilted remnants of her welcome only two days earlier.

She followed Gaia out of the palace and down the front staircase to where her carriage was waiting for her. The early morning air was light and filled with bird song, and the carefree aura seemed a strange, even mocking, backdrop to the severity of the circumstances. As she stepped into her carriage, she caught sight of Mamilian mounting his horse.

Rhea was getting what she wanted. She was going home. And yet the look of betrayal on Mamilian's face, and the way he moved, as if full of rage one moment and sadness the next, made her stomach sink. Even if she had not taken the marriage seriously, he had. She had not expected that from him. And then there was their night together and his surprising tenderness.

She sat back on the cushions inside her carriage as the horses jerked forward and began to clip-clop lazily along the stone path away from the palace. As the long, fortifying wall of the grounds came into view—the wall she and Mamilian had walked upon as children—Rhea looked away. Soon, the clip-clopping grew faster and harder as the horses reached the main road to Alba Longa and picked up speed for their journey, snorting with excitement at the relative freedom of the open road and the ease of traveling over the smooth, flat stones.

Peering through the curtains, Rhea stared vacantly outside the carriage at it passed by rich villas, sprawling vineyards, and roadside shrines to Apollo and Mercury. She took off an earring and tossed it out of the carriage to land by a shrine to Mercury, a gold offering to the wing-footed god of travelers, praying that he would make the journey pass swiftly.

She knew that Egestus's bold plan to protect the purity of their Silvian lineage and royal bloodline, and to advance their shared birthright to rule Alba Longa, would send shockwaves throughout Latium—starting with their father. He wouldn't care that the

Egyptians did it. He wouldn't care that the gods did it. He would resist. She took off her other earring and tossed it toward the base of a shrine to Apollo: *Apollo, god of healing, help Father forgive us...help him understand.*

As her carriage rolled onward, Rhea resisted the urge to stick her head out to look for Mamilian. She was not sure if he was riding ahead or behind. She still did not know where Lela was, either. There was no evidence that she or Thalia were dead. Yet by the time Rhea heard the quacking of mallard ducks flying overhead—a sign they were near the lake and therefore the Alban palace—her heart was pounding with that worry and with a string of new worries, a fresh one forming in her mind with each turn of the carriage's wheels.

The reality of it all, and the storm she would have to pass through before calm could be restored, was starting to descend upon her.

At last, the horses pulled her carriage up the road that led to the Silvian palace. Ahead, Rhea could hear voices—Mamilian was speaking to the guards. She heard the familiar squeak of the hinges as the great gates to the palace grounds opened and the horses moved slowly through them. By the time the carriage stopped in front of the main entrance to the palace, Egestus and the king were standing outside waiting, having been alerted to their arrival by a messenger who had ridden ahead of the convoy. Rhea stepped out of her carriage. Her father's face was wrinkled in concern, full of questions, but Egestus wore the same composed, analytical expression as always. Unlike the king, the prince was not surprised by his sister's hasty return to Alba Longa. If anything, he had expected it a day earlier.

Mamilian bowed to the king. "Your Highness," he said. "May we speak inside?" He did not acknowledge Egestus.

"By all means," replied Numitor. He turned and re-entered the palace with Mamilian behind him.

Egestus waited for his sister and spoke under his breath. "I'm assuming he knows."

"He could tell," she replied.

"Did you tell him…" he paused, "that it was me?"

"No. But I haven't seen Thalia or Lela since last night. I am worried about them."

Egestus didn't seem to share her concern. He had bigger things on his mind than the welfare of his sister's handmaids. He placed a hand on Rhea's back and led her into the palace, down the statue-lined corridor, and through the open doors of the royal stateroom to join Numitor and Mamilian.

A giant fireplace framed with sculpted floral designs took up nearly a quarter of one wall, crackling heat into the royal meeting chamber as the king ascended the raised platform at the front of the opulent room and sat upon his high-backed throne. Once he was settled, Mamilian, Egestus, and Rhea took their seats on the carved mahogany chairs below. Numitor leaned forward, about to speak, but was interrupted by Nemeois and his father Amulius hurriedly shuffling into the room: both wore the looks of men who had suddenly been pulled away from other matters. Amulius's face was stern, but Nemeois shot Rhea a perplexed stare: *What in the name of the gods is going on?*

The king spoke first. "Mamilian, I am not displeased to see you and my daughter. You are always welcome in Alba Longa. I am only surprised to see you here so soon after your wedding. I trust all is well?"

"I'm afraid not, sir," said Mamilian. He gripped the armrests of his chair. "I must nullify the marriage between your daughter and myself."

Numitor sat up straighter, as if the words themselves had physically struck him. "Why?"

"Your daughter was not a virgin when I married her."

The king stood. "How dare you say so, sir!"

"It gives me no pleasure to say so."

Mamilian twisted in his chair and motioned to two of his slaves who stood just inside the stateroom. They disappeared for a moment and then reappeared, each carrying an end of one of Rhea's larger wardrobe trunks. They set it before the king. One of the slaves untied the rope knot that held it closed and lifted the lid—to reveal Lela inside, her body curled into a ball, her face blanched, and her hair pasted to her face, wet with sweat and heat. The slave gripped her arm and yanked her to her feet, as if instructed to make the moment as dramatic as possible.

Rhea slapped her hand over her mouth and slumped back into her chair, while both Numitor and Amulius drew in sharp breaths. Nemeois was not as reserved. He sprang to his feet, his face burning red with indignation and his voice booming.

"Have you lost your mind, sir?"

Mamilian looked to Lela. "Tell your king what you told me."

Trembling, the handmaid faced Numitor. She hung her head. "I—I..."

"Say it, girl!" barked Numitor.

"I overheard them," she confessed. "Prince Egestus and Princess Rhea...they were talking about the two of them coupling. So their bloodline would be pure. So that my mistress could be queen of Alba Longa." She raised her head to look up at Numitor. "But Your Highness, I don't know if they—"

Mamilian turned to face Egestus. "Did you fuck your sister, Prince?"

If the bluntness of the obscene question was meant to rattle Egestus, it failed. Instead, the prince simply sat back in his chair, seemingly unperturbed by it all.

"Take care," the king warned Mamilian. "You tread on seditious ground."

"Look at your son," replied Mamilian. "Look at his face. Tell me I'm wrong."

Numitor's eyes shifted to Egestus for a silent moment. "Speak, son."

"We should discuss this in private, Father. It is a family matter."

"Mamilian is still her husband. You will speak now."

Egestus raised his chin, an edge of defiance in his voice. "This marriage was a mistake," he said. "I pleaded with you to reconsider it. Rhea did, too, but you would not hear us."

Numitor's face contorted in shock, in outrage, and he stood, taking two unsteady steps forward as if about to strike Egestus. Amulius rushed to his side, catching his shaken brother just before he fell over and easing him to the floor.

The usually politic Nemeois exhaled so loudly that the sound echoed off the walls of the stateroom. The adviser raked his fingers through his hair, his baffled stares moving between Mamilian, Egestus and Rhea, and then the king, who now sat child-like on the floor with Amulius passing him a cup of water. Nemeois could see the peace treaty between Alba Longa and Tusculum dissolving before his eyes. He grasped for a solution. Finally, he faced all parties, his palms held out, petitioning for calm.

"Nothing has to change," he said. He turned to Mamilian. "What does it matter if she is not a virgin? Half the brides in Latium are not. Her stature and the accord between our cities are what matters. She can still give you a—"

"No, she cannot," said Egestus.

It took several moments, but then the smug certainty with which the prince spoke made his meaning clear.

Mamilian nodded his head. "Of course. How foolish of me. You would not have sent her to my bed unless she was already with your child."

"No," agreed Egestus. "I would not have." He leaned forward in his chair, his glare shooting across the room like an arrow to strike Mamilian. "There is nothing you can take from me, Mamilian. Not my city. Not Latium." He glanced at Rhea. "And certainly not my blood."

CHAPTER VI

Like most of the information she received about her husband, Cloelia had learned of Egestus's maneuverings from gossiping slaves: the prince had undermined the marriage between Mamilian of Tusculum and Princess Rhea, and impregnated his sister with the pure blood child of his lineage.

King Numitor had raged and then taken to his sickbed to recover from the nefarious duplicity of his children. Meanwhile, Egestus and Nemeois had gathered Alba Longa's advisers and great men together, and they had spent a long, sleepless night strategizing about how best to frame the news to the other cities in Latium.

The royal drama had stupefied everyone. Everyone except Cloelia. She could have predicted it. She could also predict what would happen next. One of Egestus's top advisers—most likely Nemeois himself—would be dispatched to inform her that Egestus was divorcing her so that he could marry his sister. Her handmaid Melete had been right all along about the princess.

Therefore, when Nemeois approached her in the palace courtyard just after sunrise, looking as grim as Charon, she was not surprised. She folded her hands in her lap as he sat next to her.

"I have already heard," she said.

"I am sorry, Lady Cloelia," he replied. "The prince has divorced you. I am to escort you back to your father's home."

Cloelia felt the tears well in her eyes. She tried not to blink, but she could not stop, and the movement sent a heavy tear streaming down her cheek. "Is there any other way?" she asked. "Perhaps I could be permitted to stay in one of the guest residences? I only require my one handmaid, Melete, and no other slaves."

"I'm afraid that won't be possible," he said, his attention suddenly distracted by Lela.

The young handmaid was carrying an armful of laundry across the courtyard, from one wing of the palace to another, and smiled warmly when she saw him.

Following the dramatic revelation that Lela had known—or at least should have known—of the royal incest, Numitor had ordered her immediate execution. It was only Nemeois's fervent petitioning that had saved her. He had pleaded with the king, saying the girl was guilty only of naiveté, not deception, and that she was too simple minded to be involved in such a complex scheme. In the end, Numitor had relented.

Cloelia wiped the tears from her eyes. "You cannot marry her, you know," she said.

"Excuse me?"

"Lela. She is an acceptable mistress, but she could never be your wife."

"I know that, Lady Cloelia." He was about to ask why she would say such a thing to him, but in the selfsame moment, he understood. He was only surprised that he had not anticipated it. Then again, he was distracted by greater matters.

His mind worked it over. His marrying Cloelia would please his father, who had always favored the Cloelii, and who had first proposed the marriage between her and the prince. More importantly, it would appease the other cities in Latium. They would assume the crown prince had arranged it out of care and respect for his former wife. If those reasons were not enough, and they were, Cloelia was beautiful. It would be no labor to share a bed with her. And Lela? Cloelia's predicament meant that she would have to uncomplainingly tolerate Lela as Nemeois's mistress.

"I must go to Marino today," he said. "When I return, if you will have me, we will marry."

Cloelia reached out to take his hands in hers. "Do you need to leave right now? Or can we spend a little more time together?"

Nemeois felt the heat from her smooth hands warm his own. Cloelia's expression—a mix of desperation and seduction—stirred his groin. He glanced around to make sure that Lela was nowhere to be seen and then rose, pulling his bride-to-be to her feet and leading her into the palace.

※ ※ ※

"Why did you not give me his message about the seashell?"

"Because I know you, Rhea. You would've fallen for it. Do you really think Mamilian rode for days to the shore and picked a shell for you, like some lovesick boy? It was a trinket one of his slaves found at the market."

Rhea put her hands on her hips. "Maybe," she muttered, inspecting her guest quarters: a huge bedchamber with a washing and dressing room, and a sitting room with an unusually large fireplace.

The quarters were in a villa in Marino, a town by the Ferentine Spring, where leaders of the cities in the Confederation traditionally met to resolve conflicts on neutral ground. After Mamilian's unceremonious dissolution of their marriage, and the revelation that Egestus and she planned to rule as future king and queen, Nemeois had promptly called a meeting to reassure the other leaders of Latium that Alba Longa was still stable, still unassailable as the leadership city of the Confederation.

Egestus bit into the apple in his hand and spoke as he chewed. "Don't be mad at me. I just didn't want him playing you like that."

"He seemed sincere."

Seeing the doubt on his sister's face, Egestus scoffed. "Gods, he got to you, didn't he?" He stood and walked to the window. "It doesn't matter. You can't plant two seeds in the same spot. Nothing can stop our child from coming now."

"How did Cloelia take the news of your divorce?"

"I don't know. I had Nemeois tell her."

"What if she's pregnant?"

Egestus leaned against the window's ledge. "She isn't. Her handmaid said her blood came this month."

"What if she were, though? What would you do?"

The prince smiled at his sister. She was testing him, making sure that his commitment to their cause was as steadfast as her own. "If she were with child, I would order it killed before it took its first breath. In fact, I would kill it myself, just in case some misguided fool didn't have the stomach to carry out the order. Our son will have no half-blood challenger, sister."

The answer seemed to please Rhea, and she moved to his side, both of them leaning on the window's ledge.

"It is not so different between us now, is it?" she asked him. "Because of what we did?"

"It is no different, Rhea. When we are king and queen of Alba Longa, when the child comes—our little prince—you will see. We will love him more than our own lives, and all of this will be worth it."

"What if the child is a girl?"

"Then we will have a princess to fall in love with, and we will try again." He threw his half-eaten apple out of the open window. "But it will be a boy, I know it. I have sacrificed to Mars for a son, one that will grow strong enough to rule Alba Longa and all of Latium."

"Why stop there?" Rhea taunted playfully. "Why not all the world?"

Egestus scraped the sole of his sandal against the floor, chuckling. "I thought that might sound too grandiose to you."

Rhea placed her head against her brother's shoulder. It felt good to be close to him again in a way that wasn't strange…that didn't remind her of that night. "Do you think Father will forgive us?"

"Eventually, yes. Politically, it may not matter, though. I met with Albus Julius this morning, and he said that all the great families of Alba Longa are behind me. He was not exactly supportive of our actions, but as you know, the Julii, the Curiatii, and the Geganii have been critical of our father's policies for a long time. That includes your marriage to Mamilian. Everyone but Father could see Mamilian's true intent. They are eager for me to take the throne."

"Will Father abdicate?"

"I don't know. It won't make a difference either way. The cities of Latium will see what we've done as an act of desperation, as a way to maintain stability despite Father's growing ineptitude. They will acknowledge my authority, even if he still wears the crown."

"They've already been looking to you for years," said Rhea.

"May the gods keep it so," Egestus replied. He put his hand on Rhea's belly and for the briefest of moments, his perpetual frown softened. It returned in an instant. "We should go. Everyone should be assembled by now."

"Will Mamilian be there?"

"Yes."

Rhea's eyes fell and Egestus brushed a lock of hair off her cheek. Instead of comforting her, the gesture brought back a memory—Mamilian lying beside her in bed, after their lovemaking, gently brushing the hair off her face.

"Are you all right, sister?"

It was a trinket one of his slaves found at the market, she told herself. "I am fine," she said. "Let's go."

❄ ❄ ❄

The Temple of Concord, built to honor Concordia, goddess of agreement and accord, stood near the Ferentine Spring in the town of Marino, close to a sacred grove of oak trees that honored the Silvii. A sprawling complex of civic, recreational and religious buildings had been erected around it, most recently a large bathhouse that the townspeople of Marino—proud of their role as neutral host to the Confederation's assemblies—had built to pamper the leaders of Latium's most influential cities while they were visiting.

On the far side of the temple's cella, past the life-sized painted terracotta statue of the conciliatory goddess, a set of double-doors led into the open-air meeting space of the Latium Confederation: thirty semicircular rows of stone seats, built into the natural slope of a hill, and bordered by columns and a green wall of cypress trees.

Egestus and Rhea entered the theater-like meeting space to find it was already full—the only person yet to arrive was King Numitor—so they took their seats in the front row, beside Nemeois and Amulius.

Egestus leaned back in his cushioned seat, his lips pressed together and his brow furrowed as he assessed the gathering. The oldest and most influential families in Alba Longa were present, including the Julii, the Servilii, and the Curiatti. Also present were the leaders of other cities in Latium, the foremost being the cities of Lavinium, Laurentum, Satricum, and Cora. And, of course, Tusculum. Mamilian sat forward in his seat as he noticed Egestus, though his gaze soon settled on Rhea who sat regally next to her brother.

Rhea felt his stare and fought the urge to acknowledge him. How would she even do so? Would she smile? Would she mouth a silent *I am sorry*? Would he be able to read her expression and understand that, if she had injured him, she regretted it? Her father had forced the marriage upon her, despite her protests. It was not her intent to harm anyone, but only to assert herself with the only option available to her.

The thought of that option—marriage to her own brother—and what it really entailed, forced her to suppress a wave of self-consciousness. She had known most of the men present since she was a child, and they had always doted on her as a princess. What would they think of her now? Yet as she discreetly looked around, they appeared no different from usual: chattering and telling stories, bragging about their children, horses and mistresses, and debating which vineyards produced the best wines or whose flocks had the finest sheep, cattle or goats.

The chattering fell silent as King Numitor arrived, followed immediately by the priests, one of whom carried a heavy terracotta bowl full of cow innards—the result of the sacrifice to Concordia they had performed earlier. The king ascended the low dais that faced the rows of seats and sat upon his throne, looking weary and refusing to meet the gaze of his children. The priests gathered before the altar to Concordia that stood before the dais.

On top of the altar, within a wide bowl, burned a crackling fire—the *Iliacus ignis*. The fire of Troy. According to rites, an Alban sacerdos had taken embers from the sacred fire in the Temple of Vesta on Mount Albanus and transported them to Marino, fanning them into the fire that would now purify the offering to Concordia and bless the conference.

One of the priests called out the rites, scooped out a handful of the cow's bloody insides, and set them into the sacred flames. The smoke ascended to the goddess in thick, black plumes. No sooner had the pungent odor reached Rhea's nostrils than another priest tossed incense into the fire and the rank smell was muted by the sweet, pine-like fragrance of cypress.

Having performed their religious duties, the priests took their seats and Nemeois stood, first bowing to the king and then speaking to the men around him.

"Revered fathers of Latium," he said, "under the authority of King Numitor, and with the blessings of the gods and our ancestors, we, *populi Albanses et quibus nomen Latinum est*, hold council on the consecrated ground of Holy Concordia."

He had no sooner stopped speaking when Mamilian stood.

"Fathers of Latium," he said, "we all know why we are here. By usurping the marriage between Princess Rhea and myself, Prince Egestus of Alba Longa has breached the treaty that binds us in peace and prosperity. If that were not enough of a transgression, he has impregnated his own sister with plans to marry her. The laws and the gods of Latium prohibit incest, even royal incest. It is *nefas*, a crime against the gods."

Albus Julius, the respected patriarch of the powerful Julii—a family second only to the Silvii themselves—rose to his feet.

"If the crown prince has committed a crime against the gods, then he can atone for it," he said. "We are not here to decide a religious matter. And how Alba Longa governs itself is no concern of yours, Mamilian. We are only here to compensate you and Tusculum for the breach of the marriage contract."

"There has been a larger breach than that," countered Mamilian, "and a much greater loss. Every city here has suffered from Prince Egestus's disregard for our treaty, not just Tusculum." He spoke to the gathering. "I have for months been privately petitioning for peace with King Velsos of Veii. It was recently agreed between us that my future son by Princess Rhea would be betrothed to Velsos's newborn daughter. Revered fathers, never in our time have we seen such potential for lasting peace between the peoples of Latium and Etruria. And never before have we seen such potential lost. Prince Egestus has put his own vanity, his own ambition, before this confederation's interests. War with the Etrusci is now as imminent as ever."

"War with the Etrusci has been imminent for generations," said Albus. "It is nothing new." He held out his arms and addressed the men around him with sudden showmanship. "As for the prince's vanity and ambition, Mamilian, they are second only to your own. Do not pretend that you bartered some alleged betrothal for the sake of peace. You have used your inflated claim of descent from Odysseus to ingratiate yourself to the Etrusci. If I were not such a decent man, I would accuse you of conspiring with them to conquer Latium!"

A lively uproar, mostly of assent, was quieted by King Numitor.

"I call for order!" he shouted. "What good is our alliance if we treat each other so? We do the Etrusci's work for them!"

Albus bowed to the king. "My apologies, Your Highness. You are correct, of course." Again, he addressed the gathering. "Revered fathers, I do not disagree that Mamilian, our friend and honored compatriot in this confederation, has suffered a loss. I therefore propose that three stadia of agricultural fields, including all beasts upon them, be annexed to Tusculum as compensation for his dissolved marriage to Princess Rhea and—"

"Make it six stadia," said Mamilian.

"Make it one," Egestus replied. He put his hands on the armrests of his chair, silently challenging anyone to disagree. No one did.

Albus shrugged. "One stadion it is, then."

Mamilian's expression—already one of profound insult—contorted into a sneer. "You call yourselves revered fathers? You are a pack of foolish old men, rushing to the defense of an incestuous prince who has coupled with his own sister, who has planted a rotten seed in her belly, whose crime against the gods will be yours to answer for! You act as if you indulge his indecency for the good of Latium and the stability of your cities. That is a lie. Self-interest and profit is your only motivation. You seek to reap the favors of a depraved prince, and you abandon your own morality to receive them! How can such a confederation endure?"

"Sit down, Mamilian," ordered King Numitor. His shoulders stooped. "Six stadia," he ceded, "and an additional two hundred head of cattle from the prince's holdings."

A collective mumble of surprise sounded from the gathering.

Though his nostrils were still flared in indignation, Mamilian slowly composed himself and sat down. The king's public concession had allowed him to maintain some dignity.

Numitor signaled to the priests, prompting them to rise and begin the rites that would draw the conference to a close. The meeting had gone as well as could be expected. And in Numitor's long experience as king, it was the wine and food that followed such heated assemblies that actually mended wounds and strengthened Latium's alliance.

Yet before the priests had even fully risen from their seats, Nemeois rose from his.

"With your permission, Your Highness, there is one more matter."

"Go on."

"Lady Cloelia is here. She wishes to speak to the council."

Egestus glanced at Rhea. She shook her head, as puzzled as he was.

"This is no platform for a jilted wife," said Numitor, his patience wearing thin.

At that, the king's brother, Amulius, stood. "Your Highness, as the former wife of Prince Egestus, the lady's request is not unreasonable. She claims to have information that is vital to this council's proceedings."

An immediate, inexplicable sense of dread settled over Rhea. *Why would Cloelia be here? Why would she presume to speak before the council?* A low murmur ran through the rows of seats as the men debated whether to allow it.

"If there is information that is vital to this council's proceedings," said Egestus, "I am certain it is not a woman who would bring it to our attention."

Shouts of agreement went up, and the priests again stood, assuming that was the end of it.

"Lady Cloelia claims her information concerns the safety of King Numitor," said Amulius.

The priests sat back down. A heavy silence fell over the council. Everyone could feel the change, the dark turn. Rhea took Egestus's hand.

"What is happening, brother?" she whispered to him.

"Nemeois has betrayed us," he whispered back, rubbing his beard. "Let me think."

Amulius gestured to Cloelia. She walked apprehensively across the stage-like floor to first bow to the king and then to the entire council.

"Revered fathers of Latium," she said, her voice meek but loud enough to be heard by all. "It is my most grievous duty as a daughter of Alba Longa and the Cloelii to speak to you today. Yet I must tell you what I have learned." She drew in a weighty breath and exhaled slowly. "There is a plot against the king's life." Amid a rise of agitated murmurs, she faced the royal siblings. "It is the intention of Prince Egestus and Princess Rhea to murder their father, so that they may rule as king and queen in his place."

Albus jumped to his feet. "That is an absurdity!" he shouted, and pointed at Nemeois. "Nemeois, you seditious wretch of a—"

But before he could finish the insult, Nemeois spun around and—to the sound of a collective gasp of horror—swiped a blade across Egestus's throat, just as the prince was himself rising from his seat to speak.

The flesh of the prince's throat separated in such a thick, deep gash that even the man sitting on the farthest seat away from him could see it. A gush of blood pulsed out of the wound, followed by another. Egestus's face instantly drained of color and both of his hands instinctively flew to his open throat in a desperate effort to stop the blood. It was impossible. It spurted and flowed past his fingers, like the waters of a raging river flowing over fallen trees.

Egestus tried to take a step, but his legs gave out and he collapsed onto his knees. Rhea screamed and knelt at his side, her hands diving on top of his, trying to tamp the blood but instantly becoming as blood-soaked as his.

"Help him!" she cried out.

Men leapt from their seats to help—but stopped at the sight of Nemeois and Amulius standing war-like before the dais, daggers drawn, as another fifty or more armed men filed in from the temple's double-doors. They were soldiers from Amulius and Nemeois's personal guard, and their eyes gleamed with the same power-hungry ferocity as their masters'.

"This is sacrilege!" Albus shouted in disbelief. "Violence and soldiers in the temple? I call for order!"

Nemeois rounded on him. "You shall have it, Albus."

Except for the sound of Rhea's sobbing, all grew strangely, suddenly silent. The princess buried her face in her brother's hair, his body already feeling different as the last of the life ebbed from it. She did not look up as she heard her uncle speak to the king.

"King Numitor," proclaimed Amulius, "my brother. Under your rule, the royal prince and princess have committed sacrilegious incest. They have conspired to commit patricide and regicide, and thus threatened the kingdom of Alba Longa and the stability of Latium. It is my duty, as a son of the Silvii and a prince of Alba Longa, to replace you on the throne."

Nemeois approached the benumbed Numitor. He wiped the blood from the blade of his dagger on the king's tunica and pointed the tip at him. "You are no longer fit to be king, Uncle," he said. "You will step down from that throne, or I will drag you off of it."

Rhea heard her father's voice, low and mumbling, behind her. He sounded more like a confused old man than a king. She lifted her head and turned to look at him. His face was as fallen and colorless as Egestus's.

"They are lying to you, Father!" she cried. "We love you. We would *never* betray you!"

She struggled to stand, her legs threatening to buckle under her, as Egestus lay unmoving at her feet. Her hands were wet and scarlet with his blood. Drops of blood ran down her fingers to drip onto the stone ground.

Slowly, shakily, Numitor stood. He stepped away from the throne and off the dais. Amulius shouldered by him, hitting him hard enough to make him tumble to the floor, as he himself ascended the throne. Once he was sitting, his eyes conveyed a silent order to Nemeois.

Nemeois raised his dagger—and advanced on Rhea.

A hundred voices called out "Stop!" but one was louder than the rest. Mamilian. He sprinted from his seat and in an instant was before Nemeois, standing between him and Rhea.

"It is sufficient," he said. "What you have done…" his eyes moved to Egestus's body, and then back to Nemeois "…it is enough."

A chorus of stunned voices agreed with him. "Spare the princess!" someone called out. "You have the throne," someone else shouted. "Will you now butcher a woman in the temple?"

As Nemeois lowered his dagger, Albus Julius and two men from Lavinium—Rhea knew them, but suddenly could not remember their names—rushed to her side. "Come, Princess," one of them gently urged her. "We will take you to Lavinium. You will be safe there."

"The princess will return with us to Alba Longa," declared Amulius. His gaze lowered to Numitor, who now knelt on the floor with his eyes fixed on the dead body of his son. "I am the king of Alba Longa now. I will decide my family's fate."

CHAPTER VII

"Where is the princess, Nemeois?" demanded Lela. "Answer me at once!"

Cloelia took three steps toward the young handmaid and slapped her across the face. "Do not speak to the crown prince that way!"

Lela put her hand to her burning cheek and glared at Nemeois. The *crown prince*? She held her breath. "Where is Prince Egestus?"

"Most likely in ashes by now," Nemeois replied. He faced her squarely, as if daring her to challenge him again, but she only let her arms drop to her sides in shock.

"Where is the king?" she asked. This time her voice was subdued. She feared the answer. "Is he also…"

"Alba Longa has a new king. King Amulius. Numitor has been exiled."

Lela let the information wash over her. She steadied herself. "And Princess Rhea?"

"She lives," said Nemeois.

"Tell me where she—"

Again, Cloelia slapped Lela's face, though harder this time. It felt good to do it. "You do not make demands of the prince."

Lela resisted the urge to touch her cheek again. She didn't want to show Cloelia how much it hurt. Instead, she pointed at the gold diadem on Cloelia's head. "Prince Egestus divorced this wench," she said to Nemeois. "Why do you still permit her to wear the diadem of a princess?"

"Lela, calm down," he pacified.

"I am still the crown princess," Cloelia said, trying but failing to keep the goading from her voice. "Prince Nemeois and I have married." She stared at Lela, relishing the look of bewilderment and then betrayal that passed over the handmaid's face as the meaning of her words sunk in. "Husband," she said, taking Nemeois's hand. "Send her away."

Lela took a step back from Nemeois. "Yes, send me away. To the princess."

"I can't do that, Lela."

"Then never call on me again."

Lela spun around and marched out of the room. Cloelia tried to hold on to Nemeois's hand, but he pulled it away and ran after his mistress. "Come back here!"

After a few more angry strides, Lela slowed, burst into tears, and put her hands to her face. "What have you done, Nemeois? What have you done to your kinsmen? To Rhea? She and the prince loved you as their brother. The king trusted you with his life."

Nemeois gripped her shoulders and pushed her against the wall, bringing his face close to hers. "Listen to me," he commanded. "Egestus and Rhea were planning to kill Numitor—"

"You know that is not true!" said Lela. "At least be honest with yourself, Nemeois. You saw an opportunity to be crown prince and you took it."

"So you condone what they did? Coupling? Creating an inbred heir and offending the gods?"

Lela spat out a spiteful cackle. "Do you really believe the gods are troubled by such things?"

"Numitor's incompetence was spreading like a plague," said Nemeois. "He'd lost the trust of every great family in Alba Longa, and just about every city in Latium."

"That is why they looked to Prince Egestus."

"Egestus was too busy having a pissing contest with Mamilian to rule properly. It was just a matter of time until he bullied Tusculum out of the Confederation. And then what? Latium would be split apart. Weakened. Never mind war with the Etrusci, we'd be at war with each other."

"You have always had the tongue of a sorcerer, Nemeois," said Lela. "You could talk Vesta out of the flames, but you will never talk me into believing that you did this for Alba Longa. You did this for *you*."

Lela pushed hard against his chest, causing him to stumble back. It was all the space she needed to slip by him and hurry down the corridor, her sobs echoing off the walls. Nemeois watched her go, her words—*You could talk Vesta out of the flames*—resonating in his mind…and solving a problem that he'd been grappling with since leaving Marino.

Cloelia appeared at his shoulder. "Husband, it is not proper for you to put your mistress before me."

"An argument in a corridor is hardly preferential treatment," growled Nemeois. "I have a meeting with the king. I will see you at supper." He turned and walked off in the same direction as Lela, stopping before the carved double-doors that led to the king's throne room and leaning against the wall to think.

The royal coup had gone mostly as expected. Most of Nemeois's plans did. The only thing that didn't fit into Nemeois's original plan was the continued existence of Rhea. He had expected the revered fathers would protest her killing, but not Mamilian. As the person most directly injured by her, he had anticipated Mamilian's support. When that hadn't come, when Mamilian had instead stood against it, Nemeois had been given little choice but to relent.

Perhaps that was for the best. Nemeois didn't regret killing

Egestus—it had to be done—but the sight of his cousin grasping at his bloody, gaping throat was not an image he cared to carry in his mind any longer than necessary. It would have been worse with Rhea. Nemeois had always felt greater affection for her than for her brother.

And then there was Lela. She already hated him for the coup: Amulius was on the throne, but Lela knew, as did most, that Nemeois had masterminded the overthrow. Had he taken a dagger to Rhea as well, Lela would probably kill him in his sleep…that was providing he ever managed to get her back into his bed.

Still, things were good. Although he found Cloelia more grating by the moment, she was surprisingly eager to please in bed and was resettling into her role as crown princess. Egestus and Numitor were gone, and very soon, Rhea would be gone as well.

Nemeois entered the king's throne room just as a group of Amulius's advisers were exiting. He compelled himself to smile at the men, though he felt his irritation rise. As far as he was concerned, there was no reason for his father to continue to meet with other advisers, not after his own son's strategizing had proved so successful.

He inspected his father on the throne, reposing on the seat of royal power with an air of overconfidence. A statue of Jupiter stood on one side of him and a torch with a thick flame stood on the other. He wore a scarlet tunica with wide wrist cuffs. The oak crown—crafted in gold—lay on a table beside him, as did a cup of wine and a platter of meat.

"Father," he bowed. "I have been thinking about Rhea. I have come up with a—"

"Yes, my advisers were just offering their thoughts."

Nemeois tensed. "Did any of them present a solution?"

"Execution."

"Our task now is to calm the waters," said Nemeois, "not create a new storm. The revered fathers have already spoken against her execution, as have the Julii and the other families of Alba

Longa. It would be unwise to further antagonize them so early in your rule."

Amulius frowned. "Exile was also suggested."

"Also unwise," said Nemeois. "Rhea has too many sympathizers. It wouldn't be long before some self-styled hero tried to make a name for himself by rescuing her." He cocked his head. "Any other suggestions?"

"Temple life."

"I thought of that. She's a Silvii, so confining her to the Temple of Vesta would be an option, but she'd have to live in the sacerdotes' convent. It's too busy there, and too busy in the temples generally, for that matter. As a priestess, she would still be involved in religious and civic functions, and would have every opportunity to garner sympathy, likely even organize a revolt, knowing Rhea. She needs to be out of sight. Out of mind."

"What do you suggest then?" Amulius asked, his nerves grated.

"As you know, there is a shrine to Vesta in the necropolis, at the tombs of the Silvii. She could serve there. She could live there."

"In the necropolis?"

"Why not? Her tomb is more comfortable than many homes in Latium. There is only one way in and out of the necropolis, and it is already well-guarded. She could serve as the shrine's sole priestess."

"A priestess who is with child?"

"There is no one in the necropolis to see her belly swell. It is the wisest option, Father. You will appear merciful by letting her live despite her crimes. And by giving her a purpose, one that suits the dignity of her lineage, the people's conscience will be sated. They will forget her."

Amulius picked a piece of meat off the platter at his side and chewed it, washing it down with the rest of the wine in his cup. "Do it," he said. "Let the foolish girl live out the rest of her days with Pluto."

✽ ✽ ✽

No one would tell Rhea where they were taking her. No one would tell her where her father was. His royal guard—her own guards—were nowhere to be seen. Instead, Amulius's guards ushered her into her carriage, closed the curtains, and gave the order to move.

They traveled along the paved road for some time, until a certain series of winding turns struck Rhea as familiar. She opened a curtain—what would they do, stop the carriage and beat her?—and inhaled a quick breath as she realized where they were taking her. To the necropolis. To kill her.

Standing up as best she could in the moving carriage, she reached for the door, but found it secured from the outside. She kicked it as hard as she could until she heard a snap. The door swung open. She jumped out, landing hard on a paving stone, but quickly picked herself up and scrambled for the trees.

"She's running!" a guard shouted.

For a hopeful moment, Rhea thought she might make it, that she might reach the trees and run in such a haphazard fashion that the guards would lose track of her. In that hopeful moment, she envisioned the whole scenario in her mind: she would run all day and night, until she found a farm or a villa, then she would sneak in and steal a horse, riding it all the way to Lavinium where she knew she would be granted sanctuary.

But the moment passed and the hope faded. She hadn't made it more than a few steps before Nemeois dismounted from his horse and caught her. He wrapped his arms tightly around her chest and spoke into her ear. "You will not be harmed, Rhea," he said. "Calm yourself."

"You take me to the necropolis, but say I will not be harmed?"

"You have my word," he said.

"Your word?" Rhea tore herself out of his grip and faced him, pointing to the tombs of the dead that could be seen through the iron gates of the necropolis. "*Their* words are worth more than yours!"

Nemeois grabbed her arm and pulled her toward the gates as two guards opened them. "You should not speak to me like that, Rhea. If my father had his way, I'd be bringing you here in an urn."

Once they were inside the necropolis and the gates had closed behind them, Nemeois let go of her arm and continued to walk along the main cobblestone path. Seeing no other option, Rhea walked alongside him, down the endless neat rows of mausoleums and ornamented tombs, some styled as small temples and others dome-shaped, some freestanding and others subterranean or built into grassy mounds of earth.

For a city of the dead, the necropolis seemed remarkably alive. Towering green trees housed colorful chirping birds that fluttered here and there. The fine statuary—swans, deer and rabbits—and pretty gurgling fountains added more color and sound, and baskets of fresh flowers, fruit and herbs lent sweet fragrance. It was a man-made Elysium, one that sought to bring as many familiar comforts and pleasures to the beloved dead, and to their visitors, as possible.

Nemeois and Rhea entered the massive royal section of the necropolis that was dedicated to the Silvii, the entrance marked by two larger-than-life statues of Aeneas and Ascanius. As they passed by her mother's tomb, Rhea's eyes looked ahead to her own waiting tomb. Egestus's tomb stood next to it.

Nemeois followed her eyes. "Egestus was cremated in Marino. His ashes were brought here yesterday," he said.

"And so you are the new crown prince." Rhea wiped away the tears, but did not look at him. "You have no choice now, Nemeois. Now you will have to do the very thing you accused Egestus and me of doing. You will have to kill the king. Your father will live a thousand years before he will let you take the throne."

"That is no concern of yours."

"Uncle always hated the fact that my father and brother preferred your counsel over his."

"My father sees my worth."

"Perhaps," she narrowed her eyes quizzically, "but he has a favorite bastard son by one of his mistresses, does he not? Yes, I remember he brought the boy to a festival a few years back. It was Egestus who forbade him from formally acknowledging the boy...he did it to protect you. The boy must be a man by now. You had better take care, Nemeois. You might find a blade across your own throat soon enough."

"It has been a hard day for you, Rhea. So I will not take offense at your words."

"You can take offense if you like," she replied.

They walked on. Just before they reached the side-by-side tombs of the royal siblings, Nemeois stopped at a tall shrine to Vesta. At its apex, a statue of the seated goddess looked down at him and Rhea, her face serene and all seeing, a bronze firebowl at her feet. Inside the bowl sat strips of kindling and, on top of those, a fresh sarcina that contained a smoldering oak coal.

As if it had been waiting for her arrival, the bark of the sarcina ignited from within, and the ember it housed flared out to consume the insulating vegetation. Infant flames crept outward in search of more, and Rhea instinctively reached out to place thicker strips of kindling in their path. The fire crackled to life.

"The ember was taken from Vesta's temple this morning," said Nemeois. "The Ilian fire of our ancestors. You will watch over it here."

"I suppose it is safer for you to keep me here than at the temple," she said.

"It is safer for the sacred fire as well," Nemeois replied. "Our enemies will attack the temple before the necropolis. You are therefore performing a great service to Alba Longa."

"How clever, Nemeois."

Nemeois gestured to the siblings' tombs and they moved on.

Rhea had been to the necropolis many times in her life to visit her mother's tomb and to pay her respects at the sepulchers of her great Silvian ancestors. On the occasion of her and Egestus's eighteenth birthday, the two of them had been obligated to visit in order to approve their own final resting places. It had seemed to them a trivial formality—after all, they were young and the end was many years away—but the awareness that Egestus's ashes were now actually inside his tomb…as Rhea neared it, she felt a grim, almost mocking, sense of fate.

She arrived at the entrance of the temple-shaped structure to find the bronze-inlaid wooden door ajar. Without waiting for Nemeois, she pulled it open and stepped over the threshold. The air felt cooler and thinner inside the stone walls of the multi-room tomb, but the colorful frescos painted upon them depicted scenes of rich abundance from Egestus's life. In one scene, he was feasting at a banquet. In another, he was hunting in the woods. In yet another, he was speaking to the revered fathers at the Temple of Concord. Fine furnishings filled the interior of the tomb, and Rhea's eyes were drawn to a gold crown of oak leaves—the crown of an Alban king—resting upon the red cushion of a throne-like chair. It was a crown that their father had crafted for his son in happier times.

In the middle of the chamber sat Egestus's sarcophagus. Inside the sculpted stone coffer, unseen and protected, was the urn of his ashes. It was all that was left of him, all that remained of his face, his voice, his ambition. Rhea placed a palm upon the sarcophagus and turned her head to look into the eyes of the life-sized statue of Mars that guarded it. The god of war's piercing gaze, bearded face and severe expression reminded her of Egestus more than any tomb painting could. She left the sepulcher to rejoin Nemeois in the sunshine, though it gave her no warmth.

"Your tomb has all the comforts you will need," said Nemeois, pointing to the similarly temple-shaped tomb that stood next to Egestus's. "As I told my father, you will live better here than many in Latium…once you get used to the stillness, of course. You will have no slaves, but down that path"—he jutted his chin to direct her—"you will find facilities and supplies, and stockpiles of wood, everything you need to live and perform your duty to the goddess."

"Will I have visitors?"

"Your supplies will be replenished, but no, you will not be allowed visitors. The necropolis will be sealed off until…" his voice trailed off.

"Until when?" she asked. He did not answer. "Until I die?"

Nemeois turned to leave. Rhea clenched her fists—*do not call out to him*—she told herself, but dignity gave way to desperation and the sudden absolute despair of her reality, and she grabbed his arm.

"Cousin," she pleaded, "please, do not leave me here! I will do as you wish. I will kneel to you and uncle. Please do not go!"

The pleading continued all the way to the main gates of the necropolis where Nemeois enlisted the help of two expressionless guards—neither of whom seemed proud of the task—to restrain her as he passed through. Once he had, the guards closed and locked the gates behind him, imprisoning the princess of Alba Longa within the high walls of the city of the dead.

Rhea clutched the metal bars of a gate and shouted through them, even as Nemeois mounted his horse. "Cousin, think back on our childhood, our lives! Have I not always loved you as a brother? Do not leave me here! Be merciful to your sister!"

But as she watched him disappear down the road, back toward the city of the living, she realized that she was now as dead to him as everyone else in the necropolis.

CHAPTER VIII

Cloelia gathered the sheets around her naked body and sat up in King Amulius's bed. She examined his sleeping face. Even in slumber, he looked as though he could bark out an order or complaint at any moment. He reminded her so much of her father. He could drain a jug of wine in one swallow, flew into fits of rage without provocation, and exploited his position of power to lay with every woman unlucky enough to cross his path. For the newly crowned king of Alba Longa, that included his son's wife.

Yet there was a fundamental difference between Amulius and her father. While Cloelia's father was often loving toward his child, Amulius was consistently critical of Nemeois. He had no reason to be. As far as Cloelia could tell, the son surpassed the father in all things. Then again, perhaps that was the reason for the ill treatment. As she watched him, he grumbled in his sleep and turned over. Good. He was in a deep sleep, the kind that meant he wouldn't mount her again tonight. He disgusted her. He coupled like an animal, full of grunts and snorts, and dismounted with all the grace of a drunk falling off his horse.

She reached for her tunica on the floor, dressed hastily, and slipped out of the king's bedchamber, scurrying back to her own. Nemeois was there, lying in bed, although as usual he was awake and staring at the ceiling in thought. She stood in the doorway for a moment before crossing the room to her washbasin, cleaning herself, and then joining her husband in bed as the first hue of sunrise colored the sky outside the window.

"Did he tell you anything last night?" Nemeois asked without looking at her.

"He mostly talked about his bastard son, Ammon. He plans to bring him to Alba Longa and have him live here, in the palace."

"Gods," Nemeois muttered. "Will he acknowledge Ammon as his son?"

"He didn't say outright, but I think so." Cloelia hesitated. This was the exact situation that Nemeois had feared might happen, and it was still about to get worse for him. "Also…he plans to marry Ammon to Lela."

Nemeois sat upright. "What?"

"He had the idea of marrying Ammon to Lela. He said it was a suitable match and—"

"*He* had the idea? Or was it your idea, Cloelia?"

"It was his idea," she lied. "You know that he does all he can to spite you."

Nemeois threw himself back onto the bed, scratching his scalp in frustration. Cloelia was right about that much. His father's ego and audacity swelled with each day he sat on the throne. But this was too far. It was unthinkable for a king to acknowledge a bastard son. The act did not just betray Nemeois and the memory of his mother, but also the royal customs of Alba Longa. And then there was the proposed marriage.

That bastard will never put his arms around Lela, he thought.

He kicked the sheets off his legs and got out of bed, walking naked to the window and staring out. A slave heard him rouse and took a step into the bedchamber, but Nemeois waved him away. He pulled the previous day's tunica over his head, fastened it around his waist with a belt and left his bedchamber. He strode barefoot toward the courtyard.

As expected, Lela was already there carrying an overflowing basket of laundry from one wing of the palace to another. She saw him and quickened her step, making a show of ignoring him.

"Lela," he said. "Wait. I have to talk to you."

"Am I permitted to see the princess?"

"No."

"Then I have nothing to say to you."

Nemeois took a few jogging strides to catch up to her. He grabbed the edge of the laundry basket in her arms, compelling her to stop. "Well, I have something to say to you."

"I have work to do. Your wife will beat me if I don't have my chores done before she wakes."

"She will never lay another hand on you, and you know it. I have some information. We need to speak privately."

"We can speak when I'm done my chores," she said, and jerked the laundry basket out of his hands. "And when you let me see the princess." She trudged into the palace as he watched her go.

Nemeois heard laughter behind him and turned to find his just-woken father, red-faced and bloated after a night of indulgence, also staring after the handmaid. "That one's a little wasp," he said. "Maybe I'll—"

"You'll do nothing," flared Nemeois.

Amulius raised his eyebrows, as if sizing up his son. "Relax, Nemeois. You take things too seriously these days." He patted his stomach and kept walking in the direction of the baths. Nemeois was glad Lela wasn't anywhere near the baths this morning. He knew his father would expect to be serviced by whatever unlucky female servant was stationed there.

Yet it was just a matter of time. The new king seemed to have made it a personal challenge to couple with every female in the palace, no matter how young or old, no matter whether she was married or not. Nemeois had already seen his eyes wander to Lela more than once, no doubt curious to discover what his son found so appealing about the young woman…or perhaps simply to soil the one woman he knew Nemeois truly cared about. Marrying her to his bastard brother Ammon would certainly accomplish that.

He leaned against the edge of a wide stone fountain, remembering Rhea's words to him in the necropolis: *You'd better take care, Nemeois. You might find a blade across your own throat soon enough.*

A flame-breasted bird landed beside him and dipped its thin black beak into the fountain's water, twitching its head nervously at him.

"My cousin is neither a princess nor a priestess," Nemeois said to the bird. "She is a prophetess."

✽ ✽ ✽

Rhea had come to realize something very quickly in the necropolis—she was not a woman who was accustomed to being alone. She could not remember a single moment in her life as a princess when she was not with someone else. Even if she did occasionally find herself alone in a room, someone was always just on the other side of the door, ready to appear and serve her, whether it was one of her handmaids, a slave, or a guard.

She had passed her first solitary night in the city of the dead outside, lying wide awake on one of the stone benches by the shrine to Vesta. The warmth, sound and moving presence of the living flame had kept her company—and sane—as the sky changed from blue to black and then blue again.

She had passed her second night in much the same way, although she had managed to drift off to sleep for short periods, thanks to the lullabies of the necropolis's resident nightingales. She couldn't yet bring herself to enter her tomb, despite Nemeois's assurances it would have all the comforts she would need. She spent her third night on the stone bench.

On the morning of the fourth day, she woke to find her surroundings now quite familiar. It made her feel bolder, so she lit an oil lamp with flame from the sacred fire and pulled open the carved wooden door of her multi-room tomb, venturing inside with the goddess to inspect the lively frescos and furnishings within. The tomb had been improved and stocked with more household items since she had last seen it, including a couch from her quarters in the palace and a soft bed. Setting down the oil lamp, she labored to drag two large clay pots of pink roses inside, positioning them so they could catch the morning sun through the open door. The cheery addition brought a colorful, living presence to the space. As the sun set on the fourth day of her captivity, she climbed into the small but downy bed in her tomb and slept well.

On the dawn of this day—her fifth—she woke dry-eyed, surprised to reflect that she had not wept at all overnight. She left her tomb and, as she had done every morning since the start of her imprisonment, walked to the spring creek that flowed through a section of the necropolis. There, she washed herself in the clear water, careful not to step on a snake coiled just under the surface, an unmoving toad clamped in its jaws.

After that, she journeyed to the main gates of the necropolis where the guards had already left her food and other supplies, having squeezed it all through the thinly spaced bars. She never saw the guards, never heard them. No doubt, they had strict orders: don't look at her, don't speak to her, and don't let her see you. Tucking a round loaf of bread with olives baked into it under her arm, and chewing a fig as she walked, she made her way back to the tombs of the Silvii, passing the statues of Aeneas and Ascanius.

She stopped before the Shrine of Vesta and added some fresh wood to the fire. "Holy Vesta," she prayed. "Bless the soul of my brother Egestus. Bless Alba Longa. And if you can see past my faults, bless me, too." She tore a handful of bread off the loaf and tossed it into the flames as an offering to the fiery goddess, something the priests had told her was the oldest of Trojan household customs.

Reaching Egestus's tomb, she passed through the half-open door and sat cross-legged on top of his sarcophagus while she ate her bread, staring into the eyes of the statue of Mars that stood beside her. Looking at the god's face—it was so similar to Egestus's—kept the image of her brother's face alive in her mind. In fact, had he walked into the tomb at that moment to join her, she would have teased him for commissioning a statue of the war god that looked so much like himself. She could imagine him talking to the sculptor—*There's another sack of gold for you if Mars has my features.*

The imagined interaction made her smile, but the happiness was hollow and soon collapsed into sorrow, making her throat tighten as the tears came. She forced them to stop. *I have cried for four days straight*, she told herself. *I am as weary of my self-pity as the gods are.*

Finishing her bread, she slid off Egestus's sarcophagus and looked around. The wind had blown some dirt into the sepulcher through the open door—Rhea left it at least partially open at all times—so she departed her brother's tomb and set off to look for a groundskeeper's supply shed. There had to be a broom in there.

And anyway, it was good that she kept busy. She had learned very quickly not to let her mind wander. When it did, horrible thoughts and fears crept in. The fear that Nemeois would never relent. That the revered fathers would never intercede. That a rescue would never come. That she would die here, among the dead. The fear that, in a way, she was already dead.

Stop it, she told herself. *Stay busy.*

She walked faster along the rows of tombs and monuments, past the statues of the dead, past votive statues of the gods, all the while reminding herself that, despite the silence, she was still alive. The singing birds, chattering squirrels, rustling of leafy trees, and the crackling of the sacred fire all served as proof that there was still life, still movement, still sound in the world.

Finding a groundskeeper's shed behind a grove of trees, she searched through the various tools and equipment until she found a broom, some cloths and a boar-bristle brush. Yet instead of heading directly back to Egestus's tomb—what was the hurry?—she strolled along the rows of royal Silvian sepulchers and mausoleums, each as magnificent and beautiful as the next, pretending that she was simply a visitor to the city of the dead on this sunny day.

Taking her time, she made sure to stop before each of the life-sized statues that stood beside each tomb, gazing into the faces of the *reges Albani*. The Alban kings.

Silvius, son of Ascanius.
Aeneas Silvius.
Latinus Silvius.
Alba Silvius.
Capetus Silvius.

When she reached the tomb of Tiberinus Silvius, she noticed that the door had been left ajar—likely by a negligent groundskeeper—so she entered. A large sarcophagus sat in the center of the sepulcher, its surface painted with lush scenes of the Tiber River, the great river that bore the king's name. Rhea used the boar-bristle brush to remove some sticky cobwebs that clung to the sarcophagus before leaving, closing the door tightly behind her and brushing a few stubborn spider webs off her tunica.

The door to the next tomb—that of Romulus Silvius—was also open a crack, so again, Rhea slipped inside, wishing she could be rescued from the necropolis for no other reason than to chastise the groundskeeper for his laxity. Yet the outside elements had not entered this tomb and the inside was clean and tidy. The frescos that ornamented its walls looked as though they had been painted only yesterday, not some eighty years ago.

Noticing a small stone passageway on the other side of the sepulcher, Rhea curiously made her way to it and slipped through. She emerged in a deeper, low-ceilinged room. This one was damp and cooler, with little daylight able to reach it. It instantly reminded her of one of the deeper rooms within Egestus's tomb. As in his, the walls were lined with various weapons and armor: splendid daggers, swords, helmets and breastplates hung from floor to ceiling.

"You and our great-great-grandfather shared a similar temperament," she whispered to Egestus. The hushed sentiment echoed within the stone walls. As she turned to leave, she accidentally stepped on the gilded handle of a dagger that had fallen off the wall. She thought about hanging it back up, but decided instead to take it with her. She tucked it into the back of her belt, feeling somewhat warrior-like herself.

She meandered along the tombs of the Alban queens—those whose ashes had been interred in their own sepulchers rather than in the larger mausoleums of their kingly husbands—and stopped briefly at the tomb of Queen Cassandra. Her mother. The last time Rhea was here, she was retrieving Egestus on his wedding day. Had he been pondering his plan to couple with her on that day? Had he been communing with the spirit of their mother, seeking guidance? Rhea would never know when the idea first came to him.

Returning to Egestus's tomb, she swept both the dirt and the crumbs from her breakfast bread outside. That duty done, she headed back to the spring creek to wash her hands in the clear, running water. As she knelt on the ground, she searched the shallows for the snake with the toad in its mouth, but it was gone. Another would be in the same spot tomorrow.

Over the past several days, she had begun to follow the pattern of the little lives that, like her, lived in the city of the dead. The birds in the trees, the snakes in the grass or along the shallow edge of the creek, the lizards that scrambled up the sides of the stone tombs, the squirrels that visited her for bits of dry bread, and the occasional rabbit that hopped carefree by the tomb-homes of dead kings.

But there was another little life that she thought about, too. The one growing inside her. She put her hands on her belly and stood. *What if I am still imprisoned when the child comes?* she worried, as she walked along. *I will have to give birth alone. What if the child dies?*

By the time she arrived back at the Shrine of Vesta, the fire was down to embers. She added strips of dry kindling and gently blew. It crackled back to life.

"Spirits of the Silvii," she prayed. "I call upon you and ask you to protect the child within me. Ancestors, I am only here because of my devotion to you."

A thought came to her as she looked into the sacred flames, so she searched through the box of wood next to the shrine until she found a suitable piece: wide in the middle, with multiple projections. Pulling the dagger out of her belt and kneeling on the ground, she cut into the wood, carving it into the very rough form of an infant—head, legs and arms, with two eyes burrowed out with the tip of the dagger. She stood and placed her makeshift votive sculpture into the fire.

Rhea held her palms up in prayer, feeling the heat of the flames on the back of her hands and watching the fire consume the wood figure. "*O Vesta Mater*, I make this offering so that you may watch over the child within me as I now watch over your sacred flame. Great goddess of fire, I offer my life to you, from this breath to my last, to serve as your constant sacerdos Vestalis, your lifelong priestess, so that you may deliver him into the world alive and healthy…no matter my own fate."

CHAPTER IX

Lela peeked around the corner. By the light of the torches, she saw King Amulius sitting chest deep in a large, sunken oval bath as two female slaves massaged his shoulders and three more added fresh buckets of hot water to the bath. The king reached out of the water for his cup of wine, knocking over a tall pitcher that shattered loudly on the tile floor. Another slave rushed past Lela into the bath chamber to clean up the shards and mop up the wine before it dripped into the water. That would send the king into a rage.

Nemeois appeared silently at Lela's side, also peering around the corner to frown at his father. "The man requires six women just to take a bath," he whispered. Yet another slave hurried past, this one carrying a new pitcher of wine. "Make it seven," he added.

"He was looking for me tonight," Lela said quietly. "He wanted me to massage him. I had to hide behind a dead pig in the kitchen."

Nemeois folded his arms across his chest. "Albus Julius came to see me today. He was irate. He said the king propositioned his sister."

"There is also a rumor that he groped the wife of Titus Quinctius."

"I'm sure I'll hear about that in the morning," said Nemeois. "Titus has a jealous nature to begin with." He reached out to touch Lela's hair. When she didn't protest or pull away, he leaned in cautiously and placed a soft kiss on her lips. "I cannot stand the thought of him touching you," he said. "Be careful."

"Go to bed, Nemeois," she replied. "Your wife will be wondering where you are."

He gave her a wounded look and touched her hair again, but this time she turned away, so he gave up and walked off. Lela stole another glance into the bath chamber. Now, the king spotted her.

"Come here, girl," he said.

Lela's breath caught in her throat. She walked with her head down into the bath chamber and stood above the king with her hands clasped in front of her. "Yes, Your Highness?"

"My neck hurts. Come massage me." He dismissed the two female slaves at his back with a grunt, and they scrambled out of the water, shuffling naked out of the baths, exploiting the opportunity to disappear from the king's view.

Lela froze. "Your Highness, I am not skilled—"

"Get in the water," he said.

Lela swallowed, her mouth suddenly dry. Reluctantly, she gathered the bottom of her tunica at her knees and walked down the five steps into the warm water. Despite her efforts to hold the fabric down, it floated up and billowed around her, exposing her bare legs. The show of modesty inflamed the king's arousal, and he reached out to grab her arm, pulling her through the water until she stood in front of him.

"Take off your tunica, girl," he ordered, his words slurring from the wine.

"Your Highness, it is not my place to refuse, but I should tell you that I am a favorite of the crown prince—"

"The *king* tells you to take off your tunica."

Even though the water was very warm, Lela began to shiver. Again, her unwillingness only seemed to encourage Amulius. "Do it now," he ordered.

Her eyes darted to the three slaves who had returned with more hot water. It was humiliating enough that the king would see her exposed: she didn't relish the thought of subordinate slaves also seeing her naked body…and whatever Amulius planned to do to it.

Seeing her self-consciousness, the king splashed water into the face of the closet slave. "Leave us," he said. The slave quickly put her empty bucket against a wall and all but ran out of the bath chamber, followed by the other two women. "We're alone now," said Amulius. "No need to be shy." He leaned back against the side of the oval bath, lifting his arms out of the water to rest them on the cool tile floor while he gazed lustfully at her.

Lela's heart pounded. Nemeois was the only man who had ever seen her naked. She looked at the king's face, trying to see Nemeois's features in them, searching for something that she could cling to, something that could help her pretend she was undressing for the son and not the father. Finding nothing, but at least grateful it was dim in the torchlit bath chamber, she pulled her wet tunica off over her head. Instinctively, both of her arms moved to cover her bare breasts and she held her legs closely together, hoping the low light and the water would obscure the king's view of her body.

Amulius let out a low groan of arousal. "Come now, little wasp. Put on a show for your king."

"I don't know what you mean, Your Highness."

"Touch yourself. Run your hands over your body."

Lela's shivering grew more visible. The feeling of degradation, compounded by the dread of what the king could do to her, brought her to the edge of tears.

Amulius grabbed the wine pitcher by the edge of the bath and filled a cup. He drained the cup in two swallows, then refilled it and held it out to Lela. "Drink."

Lela reached for the cup, the movement exposing more of her breasts. As she drank, a bit of wine spilled over the brim and ran over a breast, stopping at a nipple. As she wiped it away, she saw one of the king's hands move under the water to stroke himself.

"May I have another, Your Highness?"

"Pour me another first."

She stepped to the edge of the bath and reached for the wine pitcher, filling the cup to the brim and passing it to the king. When he did not take it, she held it to his lips and tipped it until he had drunk it to the bottom. Then she poured him another, again putting it to his lips. As he drank, she felt his hands under the water, moving between her legs. She stepped back.

"Pour the wine over your breasts," he said.

Lela tipped the rest of the wine in the cup over her chest. The red wine ran down over her breasts. She set the cup on the edge of the pool and slid her hands over her breasts, between them, spreading the wine over her body.

"Come closer," Amulius instructed.

Lela stepped toward him. He reached out to take her hands, directing them under the water, urging her to stroke him. As she did, he brought his face to her breasts and began to lick the wine off her. She felt his tongue glide over her bare flesh and shuddered.

Taking her by surprise, the king gripped her arms tightly and lifted her onto the edge of the pool. Kneeling before her, and swaying slightly from the wine, he spread her legs. She tried to close them, but he gripped her inner thighs and held them apart, putting his head between her open legs, his tongue probing her.

"You're enjoying this, aren't you?" he asked as his fingers squeezed her thighs and moved up her body to caress her breasts.

"I am ashamed to say it," she forced herself to say, "but you please me more than your son."

With a smile of self-satisfaction on his lips and his eyes glazed over from the wine, the king's body again swayed in the water, this time nearly tipping over. He shook his head in an effort to avoid passing out and reached for the edge of the bath for balance, as if suddenly alarmed by the extent of his impairment. His hand never made it there. Instead, he felt Lela's legs wrap tightly around his neck.

Leveraging all of her weight and the benefit of her position, not to mention the king's disabling intoxication, Lela squeezed her legs around Amulius's neck as hard as she could and forced his head under the surface. The surprise of it made him suck in a large breath of water. He tried to come up—and almost did—but she leaned over more, pushing the top of his head under the water with all her strength. She held it there long after his feeble underwater thrashings had ceased.

An unnerving silence filled the watery chamber, the only sound being the rise and fall of Lela's panting breaths as she perched on the edge of the bath. Finally satisfied that the king was dead, she kicked his motionless form away from her. She slipped back into the water, frantically searching for her soaked tunica and trying to avoid the king's body: it hung in the dark water close to her, face down, his arms dangling under him. Only the curve of his spine broke the surface.

Her searching fingers found her tunica floating by the water's edge and she grabbed it, wringing it out as she climbed the five steps out of the bath. When she pulled it over her head, it clung to her trembling body like a wet, wrinkled second skin. She breathed in and out, composing herself, willing her heartbeat to slow and silently rehearsing what she would say to the other slaves. She took a last look behind her at the king's floating form and spotted the wine jug on the edge of the bath. Quickly, she kicked it over so that the red wine spilled out to darken the water even more.

As she exited the bath chamber, Lela saw the three young women who had been filling the bath with hot water now sitting on a bench some distance away, eating olives and chatting. One of them gave her a sympathetic look as she approached.

Lela tugged at her soaked tunica. "The king wants to see"—she pretended to forget the name—"that short-haired girl from the mills."

"Iona," said one of the slaves. "She's probably in bed. I will go fetch her."

"Should we go back in?" another of the slaves asked her.

Lela shrugged indifferently. "It's up to you. Personally, I'd wait for Iona and let her take the worst of it. He's drunk."

As she walked off toward the palace, her legs shaking more from the dramatic ordeal than the chill, Lela risked a glance over her shoulder. To her relief, the two remaining slaves had taken her advice. By the time Iona arrived, everyone would assume the king had drowned alone from his drunkenness.

Everyone but Nemeois, that was.

✽ ✽ ✽

Rhea awoke, jarred from her dream by a sound. No, not a sound. A *voice*. She lifted herself onto an elbow and shifted her body until her feet hung over the side of the bed and she was able to stand. It was a task that her ever-growing belly made more difficult each morning.

She stood unmoving in her tomb-home, holding her breath and listening intently—had she imagined the voice? Had it been part of her dream? It had been months since she had heard another human voice anywhere but in her dreams, so perhaps her mind was just playing cruel tricks on her. But then she heard it again.

"Princess Rhea!"

Rhea gasped—it was Lela!—and rushed to the door of her tomb, pushing it open and running outside, her gait cumbersome with pregnancy, toward the statues of Aeneas and Ascanius.

"Lela, I am here!"

As if the heroic father and son had delivered the handmaid to her themselves, she saw Lela on the path between them, running toward her. The two women embraced, faces wet with tears, both of them falling into sobs.

"You are alive!" exclaimed Lela.

Rhea clasped Lela's face in her hands, hope shining in her eyes. "Am I to be freed?"

"Princess," said Lela, putting her hands on top of Rhea's. "I am sorry, but no. I have only been permitted to visit you."

Rhea nodded, the tears still streaming down her cheeks. The exhilaration of Lela's appearance fractured and re-formed into a sinking despair. She had spent six months alone in the necropolis. One hundred and eighty times she had woken in her tomb and performed the same routine—washing her body in the spring creek, collecting her food at the gates, and tending to the sacred fire and the tombs of her ancestors—without any human company. One hundred and eighty times she had told herself the same thing: *It will not be forever. Nemeois will have mercy on me. If not, one of my father's allies will rescue me, and my child.*

Lela noticed the anxiety on the princess's face: the way her breathing quickened and her complexion paled, as though she might faint from the excitement of her handmaid's startling arrival, followed too soon by the crushing news that her captivity was not at an end. She took Rhea's hands, squeezed them, and gently directed her to a stone bench.

"Sit down, Princess. Breathe."

Rhea took a few unsteady steps to sit down. "Am I never to be freed?" she asked.

"We must never lose hope," Lela replied, sitting beside her.

Despite her months in captivity, the princess seemed largely unchanged to her handmaid. Her hair was longer and her belly was large and round with pregnancy, but she looked healthy enough. Even her tunica was clean and kempt, in the hopes, no doubt, that each new day would bring a rescue.

"What of my child?" asked Rhea. What is to become of him?"

"That is why I am here. Nemeois wanted me to see how the pregnancy is proceeding. He says I can come back when you are close to delivering, to help you."

"And afterward? Can I keep the infant here?" Her eyes searched Lela's, but found no comfort in them.

"No, I am to take it with me after it is born," she said. Seeing Rhea's panic rise, she again took the princess's hands in her own.

"Your cousin Amulia has petitioned Nemeois for the child's life. She says that she and her husband will raise it in Lavinium."

"Nemeois will deny her. He will never let him live."

"It might be a girl," Lela replied encouragingly. "He will not be threatened by a girl."

"It is a boy. Egestus sacrificed to Mars for it."

"Nemeois wants to appear merciful," said Lela. "Benevolent. If Amulia cannot persuade him, perhaps I can—"

"He will be immovable."

"I talked him into letting me come here, didn't I?" She kissed Rhea's cheek and braved a smile. "Venus has given me power over the man."

Rhea looked at her seriously, her thoughts clearing as her emotions began to settle. "How did you persuade him?"

Lela wavered—*how honest should I be?*—and then risked it. "I killed the king for him."

"You lie."

"I do not. Amulius is dead."

"How?"

"I enticed him to call me into the bath. He was drunk, and I drowned him."

Rhea shifted on the bench as the child inside her kicked. "Lela…was it…terrible?"

"More terrible for Amulius."

"So Nemeois is king," mused Rhea. She shook her head disbelievingly. Even she had not expected him to reach quite so quickly for the throne.

"Yes," said Lela. "His first royal order was to have his half-brother executed on the Via Latina. He had his soldiers tie ropes to the man's arms and rip them from their sockets. He bled to death on the road."

"What has he done with my father?"

"Numitor has been exiled," said Lela. "Nemeois swears he has not killed him."

"He wouldn't dare. Now that he's king himself, he won't want to set any precedents," she quipped. "Nemeois is not that short sighted." She shifted, not from discomfort, but from hesitancy. There was still one question she wanted to ask, but could not quite bring herself to. She wasn't sure what was stopping her. Pride? Regret?

But her handmaid knew her too well. "Mamilian has married a noblewoman from Satricum," she said. "I saw her. She has the face of the Gorgon. If he looks at her while they are coupling, their children are sure to come out as stone blocks."

The warmth of laughter spread through Rhea's body and she smiled, embracing her handmaid and friend as closely as she could with her pregnant belly. They stood and walked hand in hand through the city of the dead, along the statues, mausoleums and tombs, their conversation turning away from politics, toward something more pressing. The survival of Rhea's child.

The survival of the true king of Alba Longa.

The first stars were already out by the time Lela departed the necropolis. It would be another month until she returned. Another month until Rhea heard another human voice.

But then to remind her that she was not alone, the unborn king kicked inside her. A message, perhaps, that he was already preparing for a fight.

CHAPTER X

The handmaid Melete adjusted the crown on Queen Cloelia's head. "You look more beautiful than ever," she said. She dabbed fragrant oil from a clay jar onto the queen's swan-like neck and pinched her smooth cheeks for color. "Pregnancy suits you."

"Do I look more beautiful than Lela?"

"You know the answer to that."

"I should have her poisoned," said Cloelia. "Or perhaps she can fall from her horse."

"Nothing can happen to her," replied Melete. "The king will know you were behind it."

Cloelia smiled and put a finger in the air. "I have it! I'll have her raped by one of the butchers from the kitchen. Nemeois won't touch her after that."

Melete crossed her arms and cast the queen a scolding look. "You are transformed," she said. "You are not the gentle woman I once served."

"I am transformed," agreed Cloelia. "It happened the first night that Egestus used me like a whore. I walked out of his bedchamber transformed into a lioness, just like Atalanta leaving the temple." She pretended to lift the back of her dress. "If you look just under here, you will see my long tail."

"Stop it," said Melete, "and stop plotting against Lela. So what if he beds her? The more often the better. He'll tire of her that much sooner. Anyway, every king thinks he is Jupiter entitled to couple with any mortal he wants. You should be grateful it is her, and not some blushing young noblewoman who could replace you." She patted the queen's belly. "Although that would be even more impossible now."

"Rhea will deliver her baby any day now," said Cloelia. "Nemeois is letting Lela play midwife. She is leaving this morning." The queen huffed. "Although my husband couldn't be bothered to tell me. I had to hear about it from the laundry slaves."

"Good," said Melete. "Why should the king trouble his queen with such sordidness? Anyway, Lela is her handmaid. It is proper that she would attend the birth."

"I don't trust her."

"Then trust your husband. King Nemeois is no fool. I'd wager the princess is better guarded than the Eleusinian rites. As for the baby, he'll make sure the inbred grub doesn't live long enough to taste its mother's milk. You can be sure of that."

"I hope you are right, Melete."

The handmaid straightened the gold necklace around the queen's neck. "When have I ever been wrong?"

❊ ❊ ❊

Rhea had been having nightmares about the birth for months.

Long ago, she had overheard a female slave talking about a woman whose labor had become obstructed. She had screamed in agony for two torturous days, with only soiled sheets and exhaustion to show for it. When a more experienced midwife had at last been brought in, she had crushed the baby's skull in an attempt to extract it, but to no avail. Finally, the woman's pelvis had been fractured to allow the baby—long dead by that point—to pass. The woman then promptly bled to death. According to the slave who had witnessed it all, the blood had flowed like a scarlet waterfall.

That image—a scarlet waterfall—now intruded into Rhea's dreams nightly. She woke countless times during the night and rose sleep deprived in the morning, often unable to shake off the vision until midday. She wished she had never heard the story. Going into labor in the city of the dead was enough of a nightmare. She didn't need the exaggerated account of some gossiping birth slave making it worse. At least she hoped it was an exaggeration.

She also hoped that her offering to Vesta would be enough to protect the infant's life, and her own, during the delivery. With the birth so imminent, the goddess had already granted a mercy: Nemeois now allowed Lela to enter the necropolis at dawn every morning and to stay until the stars were out in case Rhea went into labor. Her presence was some comfort. Lela was no midwife, but at least Rhea would not be alone. At least she would have a hand to hold. At least her baby would have a chance of survival.

She had been kneeling by the spring creek on this cool dawn, washing her face with the cold water, when the first labor pain struck. It had felt like a sharp menstrual cramp and had taken her by total surprise. By the fifth contraction, it felt like a thousand menstrual cramps at once—sharp, tight and relentless. Her water had broken shortly thereafter, startling her and bringing even stronger, more disabling contractions. During the brief moments of respite between them, she had found the strength to stagger her way to Egestus's tomb, entering clumsily and knocking over a chair.

Crippled by yet another contraction, she wrapped her arms around the statue of Mars and clung to it, crying out. As if ordered to hurry by the god himself, Lela burst through the door, her eyes wide, carrying a laundry basket of fresh linens and supplies.

"It is happening!" Rhea grunted. "He is coming!"

Lela entered the tomb, took a last glance outside to ensure no one was there, and closed the door tightly behind her. Normally, the guards had strict orders to not enter the necropolis, but in light of the impending birth, Nemeois had likely given them alternate orders. Lela was not about to take any chances. No one but herself and the princess could know what happened inside the stone walls of the dead prince's tomb.

Moving carefully in the dimness, she set down the basket and used the flame of an oil lamp to light the torches affixed to the walls, illuminating the space. She shrugged off her cloak and moved to Rhea, lifting the bottom of her mistress's tunica and knotting it under her breasts. As the princess stood with her legs apart, still clinging to the statue of Mars for support, Lela retrieved the linens from the basket and spread them over the floor. She knelt beside Rhea, reaching up to rub her back and encourage her through the contractions, each coming faster and more intensely than the one before.

"It hurts," Rhea sobbed.

"I know," said Lela, trying to remember everything the midwife had instructed her to do. She peered between Rhea's legs: another contraction, another push, and the top of the baby's head emerged. "It is coming very fast," said the handmaid. She thought back to what the midwife had said: *Too slow is bad, but too fast is also bad.*

"I have to push," groaned Rhea.

Lela reached for a clean cloth and held it under Rhea's body, ready to catch the newborn. She could see the infant's head emerge fully—a red, frowning face followed seconds later by the rest of its body, landing softly in the linen in Lela's hands. She wiped the fluid off its face and set it gently on the floor, clamping and cutting the umbilical cord just as the midwife had demonstrated.

Rhea looked down at the squirming newborn as it let out a high pitched and rhythmic cry, its black, blood-soaked hair pasted to its wrinkled forehead.

"You were right!" exclaimed Lela. "It is a boy! He is perfect."

The boy opened his eyes, moving them back and forth, as if already scrutinizing his surroundings.

Rhea gazed down at him, feeling a swell of pride. "His eyes are blue," she panted.

"Like sapphires," replied Lela.

"Like the sea," said Rhea, "from which Venus was born." Still clutching the statue, she exhaled and wiped a rivulet of sweat off her forehead. "My father said that Egestus's eyes were blue when he was born. They turned black after a few weeks." Her eyes moved to the fresco of Egestus on the wall. She stared into his face, the joy of her son's healthy birth competing with the refreshed sorrow of her brother's death. He was not here to see his son. He was not here to protect him.

Another contraction—unexpected, intense—made her shriek, and she felt the urge to bear down again, to push. Lela hastily swaddled the boy and again knelt beside Rhea, inspecting her.

"What is happening?" the princess cried.

Lela gasped. "Blessed Juno, there is another! Push!"

The second infant came out quickly, almost so quickly that Lela might have let its wet, moving body slip through her fingers. She caught it just in time. Embracing her role as midwife more confidently now, she wiped the fluid and blood from the newborn's face, cut the cord, and presented the infant to Rhea.

"Royal twins!" Lela nearly shouted. "Brothers!"

Drained and drenched in sweat, Rhea lowered her tunica. She eased herself to the floor and lay on her side as Lela swaddled the second infant and moved both babies closer to their mother. They squeaked and squirmed as Rhea pulled down the neckline of her tunica, putting the blue-eyed one to her left breast. Lela gently stroked the soft head of the other, the gray-eyed sibling, the younger brother by only moments.

"They are so tiny," whispered Rhea. Her eyes were moist with wonder and love. She could feel her milk and warmth spread into them. As the one nursed, she reached out to the other, touching his small pink lips.

"Tiny and impatient," said Lela. "The midwife told me you could be in labor for a long time. The gods were merciful." She pushed herself to her feet, the front of her tunica soggy with blood and fluid. "I need to get some fresh water from the creek. I will be right back."

She put on her cloak and left the tomb, closing the door behind her. Grabbing two buckets, she ran to the spring creek and dipped them into the clear water—and then she burst into tears. It was the look on the princess's face. The way she gazed at her infants, twin sons that she would only have a few moments to know before death closed in on them.

Composing herself, she headed back to the tomb, anxiously looking for any signs that Nemeois's guards had entered the necropolis. If they had heard the princess cry out, they would know she had delivered, and would not wait long before taking matters into their own hands. And then the twins' one chance at life would be lost. She had to move quickly.

Arriving back in Egestus's tomb, Lela wordlessly dipped a cloth in the spring water and washed each babe in turn, wiping the second infant down even as he nursed at Rhea's breast. When he too had swallowed a few mouthfuls—it would have to be enough to sustain them—she wrapped the brothers in fresh linen before turning to the princess and cleaning the blood off her body and legs.

That done, Lela steadied herself. What came next would be the worst part.

Quickly, she ducked into an adjacent room in the tomb and returned a moment later with the small bassinet she had brought into the necropolis with her a few days earlier. She brought it to Rhea's side. The two women met dread-filled eyes before forcing themselves to look inside the bassinet—at the dead newborn lying within. The sight of it—lips purple, skin peeling—made them both recoil.

"Where did you get it?" Rhea asked.

"From a mass grave just outside Aricia," Lela replied.

"No one saw you? You are sure?"

"I am sure, Princess. I dressed like a peasant and brought a votive offering. Anyone looking would have thought I was praying. Anyway, nobody looks twice in a place like that."

Taking a deep breath, Lela slipped her fingers underneath the baby's corpse, fighting to ignore the horrid feel of the wasting flesh against hers, and lifted the small body out. She placed it on one of the bloody linens.

Rhea watched her for a moment, then closed her eyes tightly and rested an open hand on the warm, living body of her firstborn son. "I will name him Romulus," she said.

"And his brother?" asked Lela.

"Remus."

"Princess," said Lela. "I am sorry, but we cannot delay. It is too dangerous. The guards may enter at any moment, if they haven't already."

Rhea opened her eyes and looked at her two sons. Both had drifted into a deep sleep, drunk with a few precious mouthfuls of their mother's milk and the exhaustion of birth. "I know," she wept.

Not even trying to fight the tears—that would be pointless—she knelt up and reached for the laundry basket that Lela had brought with her. Working with frantic haste, she arranged the bottom of the basket, spreading out a few essential items and thick blankets, just as she and the handmaid had planned. And then, Romulus first and Remus second, she placed her sleeping twin sons side by side inside the basket.

As she did, Lela moved hurriedly, barely keeping her panic at bay as she struggled to wrap the naked body of the dead newborn in the bloody birth linen in a way that covered the very worst signs of decay. When she was sure she could do no better, she placed the tiny corpse back inside the bassinet. That morbid task accomplished, she leaned over to look inside the laundry basket, and then reached out to squeeze her mistress's shoulders.

"Princess, they are sleeping deeply. I must go now. It is the perfect time."

Rhea hesitated and nodded. She stared intently at Lela. "When you see the king of the Etrusci," she said urgently, "be sure to kneel before him." She put her hand on the edge of the basket. "Put the basket at his feet and say these words: 'Mighty King Velsos, Princess Rhea Silvia of Alba Longa begs for your mercy and friendship. She presents to you the rightful king of Alba Longa, Romulus Silvius, born in captivity, but destined to unite our great people in strength and splendor.'"

"I will say it," assured Lela, "just as you have instructed. I promise."

"Remember, Lela, he is the one with the blue eyes. The firstborn."

"I will remember, Princess."

Even as she watched Lela loosely pile bloody linen on top of her sleeping infants, Rhea's mind raced with doubt. *Is it right to send them to the enemy? Yes, it is their best chance of survival. I cannot trust my allies in Latium. Nemeois is too feared. They will betray me.*

Lela lifted the basket's shoulder strap over her head and stood, positioning it at her side and making sure the most soiled linens sat on top to cover the sleeping twins. Finally, she bent down to grab the handles of the bassinet with the dead baby inside. She looked down at Rhea.

"May the gods protect us," she said.

Rhea tried to speak, to pray, but only a loud sob came out. "Go," she managed to sputter.

"I will not fail, Princess," said the handmaid. She gave her mistress a sad smile—how broken she looked, kneeling on the bloody floor of the torchlit tomb, sobbing uncontrollably—and stepped outside into the full light of day.

Immediately outside the tomb, there stood two armed soldiers.

"Let me see the child," ordered one of them.

"I am to bring it to King Nemeois," Lela replied.

"Actually, *I* am to bring it to the king." He ripped the bassinet out of Lela's hands. Holding the handles with one hand, he reached inside with the other, lifting a corner of the linen to inspect the child. He instantly recoiled at the sight.

"It was stillborn," explained Lela. "A girl."

"Why does it look like *that*?" he asked.

"Because it was stillborn," she repeated, trying to cover her fear with a tone of annoyance. She spoke condescendingly. "That means that it was dead inside her before it was born."

The guard gave her an insulted look. "I know what it means. I'm not an idiot."

The second guard unsheathed the dagger at his side and looked inside the bassinet, though without reaction. His eyes shifted to the laundry basket. "What's in there?"

"Soiled linen," said Lela.

The guard jabbed the tip of his dagger into the laundry basket, using the blade to lift the bloody linen—that same moment, he heard a shriek and turned, startled, to see Princess Rhea Silvia, her tunica bloody from birth, stumbling out of her brother's tomb.

"Give me my daughter!" she cried out, and lunged for the bassinet in the first guard's hand.

"Jove's ass!" exclaimed the guard with the bassinet, stepping backward as the distraught princess descended on him. "It's dead," he said to her. He nodded toward the tomb. "Get back inside."

The princess knelt at his feet and clutched one of his legs. "Leave her here with me!" she screeched frantically. "I must perform the rites!"

The guard shook her off. "I have my orders. King Nemeois wants to see it for himself."

The second guard stepped away from the laundry basket and moved closer to Rhea. "Princess," he said. "I am sure the king will allow the rites to be performed in Alba Longa." He glanced at his companion and at Lela, and turned toward the path that led toward the gates of the necropolis. "Let's go."

Lela adjusted the laundry basket at her side and followed the guards. She didn't risk looking back at Rhea, even as she heard her waning wails—"My daughter, bring back my daughter!"—behind her.

"Your mistress has lost her mind," said the guard with the bassinet.

"My mistress has lost everything," replied Lela.

The guard rolled his eyes. As they reached the gates of the necropolis, the soldiers on the other side opened them enough to allow the trio to exit. The guard with the bassinet noticed a couple of the soldiers eyeing it curiously.

"Kid's adorable," he said.

He lifted the linen, and the other soldiers peered in, instantly gagging and shaking their heads in disgust. The guard laughed and mounted his horse, still holding the bassinet. He kicked his horse's sides and it broke into a canter, heading in the direction of the Alban palace. His colleague, the one who had nearly discovered the twins in the laundry basket, mounted and followed behind him.

Lela watched them go. She was about to walk toward her own horse when one of the necropolis's guards, whose manners were slightly more refined than the two who had departed, walked the animal over to her.

"Here you go, my lady."

In a heart-stopping moment, he lifted the basket's strap off the handmaid's shoulder and held it while she climbed onto her horse. He glanced at the bloody linen on top, but looked away just as quickly. He had seen a hundred men die in various battles and drunken fights over the years, but a woman's blood—blood that came from *down there*—well, that was a different matter altogether.

Once mounted, Lela smiled down at him. "Thank you," she said.

He passed the basket up to her. She secured it over a shoulder and held it at her side with one hand, gripping the reins with the other, just as the guard gave her horse's rump a slap. The beast jerked forward into a quick trot and clip-clopped along the road.

After the first turn in the road, Lela reached into the basket to move the linen off the infants' faces. They were both still sleeping contentedly, faces pink and healthy.

Not letting herself feel any relief, she pulled the hood of her cloak over her head. It was a modest cloak—not one of her finer ones—and that, combined with the plain but reliable horse she had chosen, would make her an inconspicuous traveler on the road. She didn't stand out, and she didn't look as though she had anything worth stealing.

Clutching the reins tighter, she prompted her horse to break into a full gallop, hating the thought of the infants jostling in the basket at her side. They were swaddled tightly and well padded. It would have to be sufficient. It was a long way, but if she rode with few stops, she could make it to the Tiber, and to Etruria on the other side, before nightfall. With the gods' help, the royal twins would be suckling an Etruscan wet nurse before they ever felt a hunger pang.

But it wouldn't be easy. The guards in the necropolis had been lax. Once their superior officers learned that Lela had left the necropolis shortly after the guard with the stillborn—and yet was not behind him on the road back to the palace—they would know something was wrong. They would immediately send out a search party to look for her.

Shortly after that, Nemeois would realize that she had betrayed him. He would fly into a rage. He would dispatch every soldier he could spare, every assassin he could hire, to track her down. He would dispatch his fastest messengers, too, equipping them with enough gold to bribe every leader and every citizen in every town in Latium to find her—to travel the roads, to check in their stables and sheds in case she was hiding.

One thing was certain: if she didn't exploit the short head start she had and make it to Etruria today, she would never make it.

She rode hard when the road was open, past the towering

stone pines and thick laurel trees that lined its borders, then slowed and allowed her horse to recover as she wound through hills and navigated around heavier traffic—horse-drawn carts and carriages, travelers on horseback and on foot—returning to a gallop as the way cleared. She raced past stretches of stone-walled villas and rows upon rows of grapevines.

She stopped twice to let her horse graze on the tall grasses. She fed him handfuls of barley from a satchel to keep his energy up, and led him to drink from a stream. Both times she stopped, she checked on the infants. At first, they had slept contentedly, still sated by full bellies. Now, she could hear faint grunts and squawks of discontent, and when she peeked at them, they wrinkled their red faces and wriggled, eyes closed, as if impatient with her progress.

Draining the last of the fresh water from her waterskin, Lela twisted around to look over her shoulder. For the last while, she had noticed two men on horseback riding some way behind her, but now it seemed they were gradually closing the distance. She prompted her horse to pick up the pace.

Her destination was the town of Fidenae. Situated on the banks of the Tiber River—the wide, watery boundary between Latium and Etruria—the town had a strong Etruscan presence. Once there, she knew she could be persuasive enough to find someone who could arrange an audience with the Etruscan king in Veii.

Her chest tightened as she realized the riders behind her had also picked up the pace. Testing her theory, she broke into a gallop around a blind turn in the road and felt a hammer of panic as the sound of their horses' clip-clopping grew faster and harder.

Seeing a small break in the trees, she veered her horse off the pavement and into the woods, driving the animal forward, weaving through the trees and feeling her heart drum in her chest at the shouts of the men behind her, now in obvious and heavy pursuit.

I'll never make it to Fidenae! she thought. *But I can still make it to the river!*

It was hard going. The trees soon thinned but the ground grew muddier, sapping her horse's velocity and allowing the men's stronger horses to gain on her. Worse, the two voices had doubled to four, all calling out to each other. "She's this way!" "I see her!" "Don't let her reach the river!"

A black cloud of insects swarmed around her head and mouth. Lela coughed and swatted them away just as the banks of the Tiber opened up before her. She looked up and down the river, but seeing no boat, urged her horse forward. It plunged into the water.

At that same moment, she felt the hot, piercing pain of an arrow impale her ankle, penetrating through her anklebone to lodge firmly in her horse's flesh. The animal whinnied in pain and reared up, wrenching Lela's ankle free of its body and throwing her and the basket into the water.

Lela sank under the water. An image formed in her mind—Thalia, in Mamilian's dank cellar, her head in a tub of water, her body limp. *No! I will not drown!* Fighting the current and the oppressive weight of her water-logged cloak, she managed to right herself and break the surface, gasping for air. Her relief was short lived, though, as she spotted the infants' basket floating close by. Its smooth clay bottom had prevented it from immediately sinking, but it would not float for long.

Sloughing off her cloak, she began to swim toward the basket, the current tugging at the arrow that protruded from her ankle and sending bolts of blinding pain up her leg. She swam through it, until the approaching shouts of the men made her stop. If they saw what was inside the basket, they would put a sword through the infants on the spot. With no other choice, she turned back toward shore, just as a soft cry slipped through the sound of the water's current to reach her ears. It was the most heartbreaking sound she had ever heard.

She watched the basket spin gently on the water's surface before the current caught it and swept it faster and farther downriver. "Gods forgive me," she whispered, knowing the helpless infants were now at the mercy of the river, the mercy of fate—two forces that were rarely merciful.

Once the basket was out of sight, she clambered back onto the muddy shore, hearing the men's voices in the distance and then shockingly nearby. Taking in a great breath, and not giving herself time to think about it, she yanked the protruding arrow out of her ankle. An involuntary cry of agony flew out of her mouth.

"There's the little bitch!"

Lela tried to stand, but the pain in her ankle shot through her body anew. She collapsed and began to pull herself along the shore, dragging her injured foot behind her like a wounded animal. She sensed a shadow above her and cried out as a man, wheezing for breath, stepped directly on her bleeding ankle, pinning her to the ground. She pressed her face into the mud and screamed as more men ran past her.

"Find the basket!" yelled the wheezing man. He grabbed her by the arm and flipped her onto her back. Straddling her body, his weight crushing the air out of her, he knelt on both of her arms and brought his face close to hers. "What was in it?"

"Dirty linen," she whimpered.

"Why would you run with dirty linen?"

"I—I wasn't running. I thought you were bandits."

"How do you know we aren't bandits?" When she didn't answer, he pushed more of his weight down onto her arms. "What was in the basket?"

"I told you! Soiled linen, that is all!"

The man stood and pulled a hatchet out of his belt. Lela tried to raise her numb arms to fight, but before she could even extract them from the sticky mud, he swung the blunt end of the rusty blade downward. It struck her other food, her good foot, so hard that the bone snapped and her ankle jutted out at a grotesque angle. She howled in pain and rolled onto her side.

The wheezing man bent over. "Tell me what was in the basket," he said, "or I'll start on your wrists."

CHAPTER XI

As King Nemeois watched Cloelia chat idly in the courtyard with Melete, doing her best to suppress that look of self-satisfaction that she knew irritated him, he felt his disdain for his wife grow even more. Disdain, though she deserved gratitude.

It was Cloelia who had likely saved his kingship and possibly his life, too. The queen's chronic distrust of Lela had motivated her to surreptitiously order four of her personal guards to secretly follow the handmaid in and out of the necropolis in the days leading up to the birth of Rhea's child. That is how Nemeois had learned that Lela, the only woman he had ever truly loved, every truly trusted, had betrayed him.

Returning a thin smile from Cloelia, Nemeois left the courtyard and entered the palace, heading directly to Lela's bedchamber where her mortally wounded body—she had not responded to torture—lay on her bed.

Despite her betrayal and her obstinacy, he could not bring himself to let her die. He had instructed the priests of Apollo and Asclepius to make offerings to the gods on her behalf, and had summoned an old Greek healer—he seemed like a madman to Nemeois—to treat her. *Her humors are corrupted*, the Greek had said, while applying some kind of noxious-smelling herbal concoction to her wounds.

He entered the bedchamber to find that the priests and the Greek madman had left, but three slaves were still busily caring for her. One was wiping the sweat off her forehead with a damp cloth. The other two were changing the bandage on her right foot. The axe head had shattered her anklebone and the Greek had spent half the morning digging around in there, picking out white fragments of bone. By the time he was finished, her ankle was three times its normal size: the flesh was splitting in places from the swelling, and her skin was blue and black. Yellow pus oozed nonstop, no matter how many bandages were applied to it.

Nemeois sat on a chair at Lela's bedside. She turned her head slightly to look up at him, and he forced himself to not react at the sight of her white face, clenched jaw and mottled skin. The sheets were wet with sweat, but changing them caused her so much pain that the slaves left them as long as possible. The mattress under her had already been replaced twice.

He looked down at her right hand. It was bandaged from her knuckles to her mid-forearm to stabilize the fracture to her wrist. Her left hand was in the same condition. He gently stroked the skin on her fingers. It was cold to the touch.

Nemeois took the cloth out of the slave's hand and dabbed Lela's forehead. "Why didn't you just tell them where it was?" he asked.

She squeezed her eyes closed. He knew it was difficult for her to answer. Her muscles were in spasm and she struggled to open her mouth enough to speak. Saliva ran down the side of her cheek and he wiped it away, suppressing the urge to break into tears then and there, in front of her and the slaves. It seemed unreal to see his Lela reduced to this—she should be in the courtyard, carrying laundry and casting him a flirtatious or scolding look. She should be in his arms. But he knew that would be impossible now, even if she lived.

"I had three midwives examine the infant you gave the guard," he said. "They all said it had been dead for days. It was no stillborn." He lowered his head and kissed her on the forehead. "I love you," he whispered, "but I will have you tortured worse than this if you don't tell me what was in the basket." She turned her head away from him, and he sat up straight. "Was it a boy? Who were you taking it to?"

Lela closed her eyes and Nemeois raised his, acknowledging the gruff-looking man who had entered the room. Steeling himself, the king stepped away from the bed.

Ignoring soft protests from the female slaves who had been caring for Lela, the man replaced Nemeois on the chair beside the handmaid's bed. He gripped the top of her head in one of his unusually large hands, forcibly cranking it toward him. She opened her eyes and blinked up at him, letting out a pitiful whimper.

"Now honey," he said. "Either you open that pretty mouth and tell me what was in the basket, or I will gouge out both your eyes with this knife." He held the blade threateningly above her for a moment, and then pressed the sharp tip against the bottom of her left eye. A rivulet of blood ran down the side of her face. Lela whimpered louder—and then let out a muffled screech of horror as the tip of the blade pierced her eyeball. Clear fluid and blood spilled out. Lela made a pathetic attempt to lift an arm in self-protection, tortured mumbles escaping her lips.

"Stand back!" ordered Nemeois. "She is trying to speak." He rushed to her side, compelling himself to focus on her right eye. It seemed the only part of her body that wasn't injured. "What was in the basket?" he whispered into her ear, desperately wishing she would speak so he could end her pain. "A boy or a girl? You can say that much and then all of this will be over. You will live and be cared for, I promise."

Lela looked up at him, tears mixing with blood to coat her cheeks. Her face contorted in pain as she forced her mouth to open. "Dirty linen," she muttered.

The look of sympathy faded from Nemeois's face, and he frowned at the man with the knife. "Keep going," he said.

But then Lela made yet another disturbing sound, a gurgling sound, and he looked down to find her face had turned a shocking shade of blue. Thick red blood seeped through her lips.

"She's bitten off her tongue!" Nemeois exclaimed. "She's choking!"

The three female slaves rushed to surround Lela's head. The eldest shouldered the horrified king out of the way and frantically used some kind of metal instrument to try and pry open her mouth. Nemeois stepped back until he reached the door. He placed a hand on the wall to steady himself and looked away, but the sounds coming from the bed were unmistakable—Lela was drowning in her own blood, suffocating to death before him. Despite his crown, despite his faculty for strategy, despite his feelings for her and his faith in the gods, there was nothing he could do to stop it.

After too many agonizing moments, her whimpers and twitches finally ceased. The eldest slave looked up at him and shook her head. "I am sorry, Your Highness. She is gone."

Nemeois swallowed, suddenly finding it hard to breathe himself. Feeling lightheaded and grave at the same time, he nodded curtly to the slave and pulled open the door—to find Cloelia standing immediately on the other side. She stared into his bloodshot eyes, her thoughts as clear to him as if she had spoken them aloud: *Is she dead? Oh, please say yes.*

He said nothing. Instead, he brushed by her, leaving her to find out for herself. He strode purposefully down one wing of the palace and then another, until he reached the statue-lined corridor and the main entrance. The guards opened the doors and he stepped outside into a suitably gloomy, overcast day. Ignoring the raindrops that fell on his uncovered head, he kept walking until he reached the stables.

The two guards who had most closely trailed Lela, including one with an odd wheeze in his voice—he was the one who had broken her bones—were both there, repairing some equipment. They bowed in deference as he neared.

"Your Highness," they greeted in unison.

"Tell me," said Nemeois.

"Sir," began the wheezy man, "the queen ordered us to follow the handmaid when she left the necropolis. Her Highness feared that she was conspiring with the princess's sympathizers to overthrow you, perhaps mobilizing them in the country somewhere. We trailed her until around midday when she spotted us and made a run for it."

"And the laundry basket?"

"We didn't think about it at first," he replied, "but when she bolted and didn't drop it, we started to wonder why. That's why, after we caught her, we searched the area for it until well after dark. We combed the woods and followed the banks of the river. The next morning, we rose with the sun and searched again, expanding our search area even wider. There wasn't a stone or a branch we left unturned, Your Highness."

"Did you hear anything from the basket? Any crying?"

"No, sir. We never got that close to it. We had no reason to think an infant might be inside. We assumed it was stuffed with gold for bribes."

"I see," said Nemeois.

"Sir," said the man, his already hoarse voice made raspier by the stress of his precarious position. "We didn't know there'd been a swap until we met your search party on the road the next morning. As far as we knew, the princess's baby had already been taken to you." The man noticed the erratic way the king's eyes glanced over him, over his companion, and then back to him. *How did I get myself mixed up in this shitshow?* the guard wondered. *I should have stayed at the gates and never agreed to palace duty...*

"You're sure the search party was thorough?"

"Very thorough, sir. We showed them exactly where we last saw the basket. They retraced our steps and spread out even more." When the king looked away to stare off into the distance, his thoughts clearly churning, the guard cleared his throat. "Your Highness, if I may be so bold"—he waited for the king to nod permission, then continued—"the basket would've sunk within moments. Even if it did float to shore, no newborn could've survived a cold night of exposure. On top of that, the whole area is crawling with bloody wolves. We heard the beasts howling all night. They even had the horses spooked. If the infant didn't drown or freeze to death, it was dragged off and eaten."

The two guards stood in front of the king, heads lowered in respect, waiting for his response. It was no secret that Lela had been his favorite for a long time. Both of them hoped they had not exceeded their orders.

Nemeois took his lip in his mouth, considering their words. He would have liked nothing better than to gut both of them where they stood. He couldn't bear to think of Lela suffering in the cold, in agony, that night: one foot shot with an arrow and the other broken, both wrists shattered, unable to stand or even brush the hair off her own face. But ultimately, these men had been more loyal to him than she had been, and a king who punished loyal men out of spite only put himself in harm's way. Look what had happened to his father.

"Ready my horse," he ordered.

"Yes, Your Highness."

❋ ❋ ❋

Rhea leaned against the volcanic stone wall of her tomb, listening to the raindrops fall outside. On cool days like this, she brought Vesta's fire inside, housed in a wide bronze bowl, where it warmed her tomb-home and brought life to its stillness. The door was open and she watched the smoke slip gracefully out while the sounds of chirping birds excitedly pulling worms from the wet ground slipped in.

Although her belly was still distended from giving birth only days earlier, she felt surprisingly well. Physically well, at least.

Mentally and emotionally, she was tortured. Her thoughts tumbled over each other day and night. *Did Lela make it to Etruria? Did King Velsos take mercy on my children?* The unanswered questions, the constant uncertainty, had consolidated into a tight fist of worry in her chest.

But there was something else, too. Hope. It was more than possible that Lela had made it to Fidenae, or at least to the Tiber, where she could find her way across the river to Etruria. And the king of Veii in Etruria…he was an enemy, yes, but one who at least respected King Numitor's right to rule. He would have no respect for the king's usurpers.

A heartbeat away from declaring war in the best of times, it was likely that Velsos would relish the opportunity to free the Alban princess, kill the usurper and put her son on the throne, thus establishing a new alliance between Veii and Alba Longa. The dramatic action would make him look powerful and righteous in equal measure. It would also give him more influence in Latium's politics. *How could he not agree?* thought Rhea.

She heard footsteps outside. *Could they have come this soon?* She darted out of her tomb.

Nemeois stood in the rain, his hair dripping wet and a pained grimace on his face. Rhea put her hands to her mouth and sank to her knees.

"No," she breathed.

"I wanted to tell you myself," said Nemeois. "Lela failed. You killed her. She had a horrible death, Rhea. She suffered so much…" He wiped his eyes with the back of his arm. "Your suckling is dead, too. Eaten by wolves in the forest."

Rhea blinked up at him. *Your suckling. He thinks there was only one.*

He had not found them. Lela had not failed—not completely. Misinterpreting her confused silence as sorrow, Nemeois spat on the ground, turned around slowly and walked away in disgust.

Rhea waited until he was out of sight before she rose to her feet and entered Egestus's tomb. Lela was dead, but Romulus and

Remus…there was still a chance, however slight, that they were still alive. And if they were, there was only one way she could help them now. Dripping with rain, she closed the door behind her and removed her tunica, leaving it on the floor in a wet pile and feeling her bare skin prickle from the cold. She moved to Egestus's sarcophagus and clutched the gilded handle of the dagger lying on top, the dagger she had taken from the tomb of their ancestor, King Romulus Silvius.

She stood naked in front of the statue of Mars, gazing into the god's black eyes, eyes that seemed to come alive by the flickering light of the torches to gaze back at her in desire. She could feel the presence of the war god in the tomb with her, as real and animate as another body moving in the stone-walled space, circling her, inspecting her nakedness and becoming more aroused by the moment.

"Raging Mars," she whispered, "fierce god of war and vengeance, I offer my body so that you will protect my sons and avenge their father's death." She clutched her left breast and, gripping the dagger with her right hand, placed the sharp blade against the soft flesh. "Savage Mars, I offer my body so that you will take my sons as your own." And then she cut.

The pain was instantaneous, but Rhea did not stop. She kept cutting—screaming and staring into the eyes of the war god—until the mound of flesh that used to be her breast came off in her hand and fell to the floor. Blood flowed down her bare body in red rivers, traveling over her still swollen belly and down her legs to pool at her bare feet.

Gasping, desperately trying to breathe through the pain, Rhea lifted the blade to her right breast, her hand drenched in blood and trembling violently. Yet as she stared into the god's eyes, she felt her own begin to involuntarily close. She struggled to remain standing on the slippery blood-covered floor, but knowing she did not have the strength, slowly lowered herself to her knees, fighting hard to remain conscious.

But fighting the god of war was futile. Surrendering, Rhea looked up once more into his face—the face of a god, the face of her brother—and then lay naked and bleeding at his feet, closing her eyes and leaving the rest to him.

CHAPTER XII

*Near the Palatine Hill
753 BCE
(eighteen years later)*

The fast-moving waters near the earthen banks of the Tiber River were clear, although the eels hunting there for food didn't care. They relied on their sense of smell rather than their eyesight. It was what had drawn several of them into the wicker basket trap—it had been temptingly stuffed with fat frogs—that Caelus had lowered into the river. The young man tugged on the rope attached to the submerged trap.

"It's just about full," he said.

His brother, Cinus, leaned against a fig tree and eyed the branches above him. He hadn't yet eaten today, and he would have loved to snap a juicy fig from a branch, but it was too early in the spring for the tree to bear fruit.

"Good," he replied. "Some of the ewes in the west herd will be lambing this morning, I'll wager. Father will be up by now."

Caelus pulled on the rope and hauled the eel trap onto shore. Inside, several large eels squirmed against each other, their slick, slippery bodies twisting into and out of knots. "These things are huge," he said, pleased. Eels were a favorite of their father's, and the brothers liked to slip down to the river before he awoke to surprise him with a good catch for salting.

Cinus grabbed a cloth sack from the ground while Caelus lifted the trap, the brothers working together to open the trap door and dump the moving contents into the sack. While Caelus returned the eel trap to the water, Cinus secured the top of the sack.

"We'll have to take a few out before Father sees them," said Caelus. He wiped his hands dry in his tunic. "Otherwise he'll salt all of them."

Cinus slung the sack over his shoulder. "We'll hide a few for lunch."

The brothers turned from the river and headed back toward the Palatine Hill. It was at the base of the hill's east side where their father, Faustulus, had a house and a little land, drawing a decent enough income by tending to a large herd of sheep owned by the Alban king, Nemeois.

They moved through the tall grasses toward their farm, past the myrtle trees, trampling the purple and yellow flowers that colored the landscape, and walking to the sound of a woodpecker drumming loudly against the trunk of one of the many stone pine trees on the slopes of the Palatine. Finally arriving at the thatch-roofed, round hut they called home, they both suppressed the same rise of sadness. In days past, their mother, Larentia, would have seen them approaching and come out to greet them, fussing with their hair and making a show of admiration for their catch. *Such fishermen! Such hunters!* she would say, before taking the catch indoors and preparing something delicious. But not today. Today, she was in her sickbed, too weak to even feed herself, never mind cook for them.

Cinus headed directly to the hearthfire that burned in the center of the house and piled their catch on a wobbly wooden table, while Caelus pulled back a heavy curtain to check on their mother. She was sitting up in bed, staring out the window that Faustulus had fastidiously carved out of the wattle and daub wall, watching him cross the field to enter a large barn.

Caelus tried not to react at her pallid face and messy hair, hair that was noticeably thinner each day, but which nonetheless could not rob her of all her beauty. When she saw him, she straightened the neckline of her tunica, trying to tidy herself. She knew her deteriorating condition was hard for her sons to see, especially Caelus. Even as a young child he had been more contemplative, but also more sensitive, than his brother, although he did his best to hide the latter quality.

She held out a frail arm and smiled weakly. "Look," she said, pointing to the ledge under the window. "The orchids you brought me were wilting last night. This morning they are blooming. Do you see how fast divine Chloris works?"

Caelus smiled, hoping the mask appeared more sincere than it felt. *If only the goddess could do the same for you*, he thought.

"We had a good catch of eel this morning," he said. "I will bring you a plate for lunch."

"I had some grapes when I woke," she replied. "I will not be hungry. You eat them."

"You will change your mind when you smell them, Mother. It will whet your appetite, you will see."

"All right," she conceded. "I will eat some. Now go help your father. He's been in and out of the barn all morning, like a little robin flying back and forth to its nest."

"More like an old crow," Caelus grinned, his smile widening when she rewarded him with a soft chuckle.

He squeezed her hand and left, closing the curtain behind him to afford her some privacy. He passed through the small house and broke into a run once he was outdoors, clearing the sunlit field and ducking into the relative dimness of the barn. The familiar smell of animals, of feed and manure, filled his nostrils. His dog—a large, muscular working breed that his father had won while gambling with a wealthy but unlucky herdsman—stuffed a wet nose into her master's palm.

"Go lie down, Cerva."

The dog gave a wet sneeze and trotted out of the large barn as Caelus strode further into it. He found his brother and father in a far stall, helping a ewe deliver her second lamb. The first lay in the straw—looking stunned in the moments after birth and struggling to master its teetering head—but the second was locked in the birth canal, its elbows lodged in such a way as to prevent its passage.

Cinus squatted at the rear of the ewe, gently pushing the lamb back into the birth canal just far enough to release the legs and extend them forward. With the skill of someone who has performed a task a thousand times, he pulled on the lamb's forelegs until they emerged fully from the mother, the rest of its body following easily now to land softly in a pile of clean straw. Cinus cleaned its mouth and presented it to its mother. Within moments, the ewe was fussily licking both of her lambs clean.

Just noticing Caelus's arrival, Faustulus moved to stand beside his son. "This is the third to deliver since sunrise," he said. "It'll be a good season."

"Mother is awake," said Caelus. "She says she'll have lunch with us. That's a good sign."

Faustulus pursed his lips but kept his thoughts to himself. Tall and rugged, his black beard streaked with gray and his face weatherworn, he had a habit of retreating into himself the moment his wife's condition was mentioned. He walked to the next stall.

The lambing continued uneventfully all morning. Ewe after ewe delivered successfully and then rested, though their keepers never did. Faustulus only found respite from his worries through work and thus never stopped. His sons were his echoes and did the same. They tended tirelessly to their duties, and took turns working in the lambing barn and inspecting the larger herd that roamed the fields.

Relieving his brother in the field, Cinus strolled among the grazing herd of healthy sheep, Cerva at his side, the dog's thick head constantly looking this way and that for predators. As they walked along the bottom of a rolling hill, the dog's ears perked up and she growled, nose lifted high and nostrils reading the air.

Cinus gripped her collar just before she could dart off. A moment later, three figures emerged, arriving from the direction of the road, cutting a path toward Faustulus's house. The middle figure—well dressed and boasting the king's golden oak emblem on his cloak—spotted Cinus and raised his arm in a somewhat formal greeting.

Cinus felt his own hackles go up alongside Cerva's. It was Vibio, the king's *magister pecoris*, who oversaw King Nemeois's herds in the region. It was his duty to tabulate herd numbers, including live births and deaths attributed to disease or predators, and report those numbers, as well as the general quality of the herd's level of care, to the king. Cinus couldn't stand him. It seemed to him that, like many men who possessed trifling power, Vibio wielded it like a heavy sword.

"*Salve*, Cinus," said Vibio as he approached. He glanced uneasily at the growling dog in Cinus's grip. "That beast of yours thinks it's the hound of Diana. Better keep a grip on the thing. It tore through my fucking tunica the last time I was here."

"I'm sorry to hear that," Cinus said unconvincingly as he patted Cerva on the back. "You've come too early, Vibio. We'll be lambing for days yet."

Vibio turned to his roughly dressed subordinates—men Cinus suspected did the real work—and spoke curtly to them. "Wait for me here," he said, then addressed the frowning young man. "Come, Cinus. Let's visit your father. I'd like to see what the king can expect for numbers at the summer market. And let's make it quick, I have four more farms to visit today."

Still gripping Cerva's collar, Cinus led Vibio across the well-grazed field and toward the main barn. It was close to lunch, and with most of the ewes having either already delivered or not quite ready to deliver, it was a good time for a break. As such, Faustulus and Caelus were both washing the worst of the blood off their forearms in a large tub of water at the threshold of the barn.

Cinus neared, his face stern with the displeasure of Vibio's presence. His brother tensed and stepped back at the sight of the perpetually unwelcome official, but Faustulus smiled amicably.

"Vibio," he said. "I did not expect you so soon in the season."

"Well, in my experience, surprise inspections are the only useful kind," replied Vibio. He looked around, as if expecting someone else. "Is your wife still alive?"

Cinus took an aggravated step toward the official, but Faustulus put a hand on his son's shoulder. "She is," he said.

"Hmm." Vibio wandered deeper into the barn, craning his neck to look into the stalls as he passed, impressed by the number of lambs. "Very good." He put his hands on his hips and faced Faustulus. "How many head lost to predators since winter's count?"

"Nine," said Faustulus.

"Nine? That's sixteen less than the next best farm."

Faustulus gestured to Cerva. "The dog is very well-bred."

"That's good to hear," said Vibio, his tone more sardonic than sincere. "Unfortunately, I lost many head over the winter from my own private stock. You wouldn't object if I took fifteen or twenty of yours back to my farm, would you? Between the record number of lambs I'm seeing in here and that fine dog—she looks like she could take on a whole pack of wolves—you won't even miss them."

Again, Cinus took a step toward Vibio, this time his lips pulled back into an aggressive sneer. "You can't do this to us every bloody year, Vibio. You have—"

"What have I done?" asked Vibio, placing a hand on his chest and feigning bafflement. "Other than accept a friendly gratuity for reporting back to the king what an outstanding shepherd your father is."

"You receive payment enough from the king. What would he say if he knew that you were—"

This time, it was Faustulus who interrupted. "Enough," he said to his son before nodding to Vibio. "Take what you feel is fair."

Vibio bowed mockingly and then smiled widely to display a mouthful of yellow teeth. "Thank you," he said. "I have a cart on the road. I will have my men drive twenty head to it." His eyes moved over Faustulus and the two young men, over the blood, straw and grime on their rough tunicas, before he brushed a piece of straw off his expensive cloak. "*Valete*," he said, bidding them goodbye.

Once he was out of earshot, Cinus turned angrily to his father. "Why do you let him get away with that? Why do you not tell the king? You are a respected herdsman. He will hear the truth from you."

"It is not worth inviting trouble," Faustulus replied. "The king will not care about such petty injustices. Vibio turns a profit and reports higher numbers each year. That is the only truth the king cares to hear."

"A king should have more cares than just his own," said Cinus.

Faustulus regarded his son. "Yes," he said thoughtfully. "A king should."

✻ ✻ ✻

The sun was already down by the time Faustulus instructed his sons to go into the small village of Pallantium, near the Tiber. While he had framed it as a chore—go get mother's favorite wine, go see the barber—what he really wanted was for the young men to enjoy themselves for a few hours, to visit some friends or even one of the regular prostitutes that frequented the village's sole tavern.

But neither Cinus nor Caelus were in the mood for such things. The memory of Vibio's insult, his extortion, was too fresh in their minds. They chose a table at the back of the tavern, ignoring the pipes and singing, and sat stewing in their own anger. Caelus scratched at his cheek and wiped away a streak of blood. The tavern's barber had thrown in free shaves after cropping their shaggy black hair, but his wine-fuelled workmanship reflected the price.

"We should come earlier in the day to get shaved," he said to Cinus. "Before the barber gets drunk. He might not carve us like hogs."

An attractive young woman wearing a long yellow tunica, an orange headscarf covering part of her thick ebony hair, floated up to the table, catching the last of their conversation.

"Maybe if you didn't smell like sheep, he wouldn't be so inclined to shear you like one." She smiled flirtatiously at Cinus, accentuating the strong features of her angular face. "Why don't you come around back? I'll give you a bath."

"Not now, Magia," said Cinus.

"Oh, come on…"

"I can't afford you tonight."

"It's on the house."

Cinus pushed her hand off his shoulder. "Go on, Magia."

The girl sighed. "Your loss." She turned to leave, but paused. "How's your mother?"

Cinus shrugged. "She sleeps a lot."

Magia bent over and gave both of the young men a quick kiss on their cheeks. "I will pray for her," she said, before moving on to the next table. She had no sooner left than another woman spotted Cinus and began to make her way toward him, veering away at the sight of his discouraging scowl.

Although the twins shared many traits—black hair and dark eyes, strong backs and well-featured faces—Cinus displayed more of Faustulus's ruggedness and thus tended to attract more female attention than did his comparably subdued, boyish brother. Not that it mattered. Unless Caelus also had a shot of coupling with a passably pretty girl, Cinus wouldn't indulge.

A slave placed a wood board stacked with bread and olives on their table, as well as another pitcher of wine. As if attracted by the bounty, two of Cinus and Caelus's friends appeared from the shadowy corners of the tavern, dragging chairs from other tables to join them and helping themselves to the food and drink.

"Why so sour, boys?" asked the first to sit down.

Caelus tore a piece of bread out of his friend's hand and stuffed it into his own mouth, pushing two olives in after it. "Do you need to ask, Acrisius?" he said, chewing. "Vibio came by today."

The two friends groaned in unison. The second, a close friend of Cinus's by the name of Fabius, downed a cup of wine. "The bastard took five head from my father yesterday," he said. "How many did he take from you?"

"Twenty," murmured Cinus.

"Ouch."

The door to the small tavern opened. A gust of cool air from the early spring evening blew in, making the flames of the candles and oil lamps on the tables waver. Glancing toward the door, Cinus slammed his cup on the table and snarled an obscenity as Vibio himself sauntered to the first empty table and sat down, immediately calling for wine.

"We should've known he'd come here," said Acrisius.

As the group of friends watched, Vibio leaned his chair onto its back legs. He reached out, pinching Magia in her rear as she passed. The woman stopped and swung around in pain. She glowered at the king's official and began to walk on, but Vibio grabbed her arm and yanked her onto his lap.

"You shouldn't frown like that, honey," he said. "It makes you look ugly."

Cinus stood up quickly, knocking over a cup of wine. It spilled on his brother's tunica.

"Cinus," Caelus said warningly. "Leave it. Father wouldn't want you to—"

"Father isn't here. And maybe if he'd stood up to the thieving prick years ago, we wouldn't be stocking Vibio's barn with animals from our own."

Fabius gripped the sleeve of Cinus's tunica. "Caelus speaks sense," he said. "Your father doesn't need any more trouble. He has enough to deal with already."

Cinus twisted his tunica out of Fabius's grip and marched to Vibio's table. Magia shook her head at him. *Don't do it.*

But it was too late. Even as she mouthed the words, Cinus pulled her off the official's lap, then raised his fist and struck Vibio hard across the jaw, sending him tumbling to the floor. "The lady's spoken for tonight," he spat.

Vibio glared up at his attacker in disbelief. He rubbed his jaw with one hand, the other grasping the table for support as he clambered to his feet, blood trickling down his chin. He tongued the inside of his mouth, gagged, then reached inside with two dirty fingers and withdrew a broken yellow tooth. He threw it at Cinus.

"You've assaulted an official of the king," he said, his speech distorted by his rapidly swelling lips. "I'll make sure you lose more than a tooth, boy."

Spitting a mouthful of blood on the floor, Vibio snatched an amphora of wine off the table, stuffed a cork into it, and stormed indignantly out of the now silent tavern, the eyes of every patron following him as he went. He was barely out the door when Cinus pulled Magia toward the back exit, the one that led to the prostitute's private quarters. He didn't look back at his brother, didn't speak a word to his friends, all of them standing around the table, slack jawed with the shock of his outburst.

Caelus stared after his brother. As the other patrons in the tavern resumed their conversations—their lives—Caelus slumped back into his chair. Cinus's tantrum could cost them everything. "Jupiter, have mercy," he said under his breath.

Acrisius sat down beside him and patted him on the back. "Vibio was drunk. Maybe he'll forget about it come morning."

"He wasn't that drunk," countered Caelus, "and you know he won't forget. He holds a grudge worse than Juno." He scratched his cheek and drew blood. The razor cut had opened up again. Wrapping his cloak around his shoulders, he bid his friends a solemn farewell and headed outdoors.

His face flushed with dread, Caelus mounted his horse—Cinus's horse was still tethered to the post—and rode away from the tavern, racing for the comfort of home, but knowing he would not find any there. Between his mother's heart-wrenching illness and his brother's tragic mistake, those days seemed to be gone forever.

※ ※ ※

It was past midnight by the time Cinus left Magia at the tavern. He had been too angry, too distracted to receive any pleasure from her. Yet when his anger faded, he found it soon replaced by feelings even worse. Self-reproach. Regret. Fear.

How could he have been so impulsive? How could he have so stupidly invited a reprimand, or worse, from the Alban palace? His only hope was that Vibio would place the blame where it belonged—on him, not on his father. Fabius's words resonated in his mind: *Your father doesn't need any more trouble. He has enough to deal with already.* How he wished he had heeded those words.

"*Futuo*," Cinus whispered to himself, seeing his breath form a cloud in the cool night air. He mounted his horse and yanked on the reins too hard before easing up and prompting the animal to trot along the narrow, empty road. Torches lined its length at regular intervals, providing a little light for villagers riding or walking home from the tavern.

He traveled along the road, the sounds of his horse's breaths and clip-clopping hooves accompanied by the usual sounds of night: the hoot of owls, the distant howl of wolves and the rustling of unseen creatures in the trees along the road.

Cinus squinted in the darkness as the silhouette of a horse and man appeared on the road ahead of him. He thought about turning around. It could be anyone, but if it was Vibio, he couldn't risk another altercation. Then again, if it was Vibio, perhaps he could make amends before the king's official reported back to Alba Longa.

Taking a deep breath, he pressed on. The man before him was standing with his head back on his shoulders and the bottom of his tunica hiked up, urinating on the road. Another few steps and the flickering light of the torches illuminated his face.

"*Salve*, Vibio," attempted Cinus.

"Keep moving, boy."

Cinus dismounted and walked cautiously toward Vibio, his hands held up in a gesture of peaceful surrender. "I lost my temper earlier," he said.

Vibio lowered his tunica and faced Cinus. "Because you think I treat you unfairly?"

"No," Cinus lied. "I was trying to impress the girl, that's all. It was stupid. I am sorry."

Vibio looked at him, his chin raised in a smug posture of condescension.

"Prove it."

"What?"

Vibio bent over to retrieve his amphora of wine off the ground and took a long draw, dribbling red liquid down the front of his expensive tunica. "Prove you're sorry," he said, stepping forward. "Kneel."

Cinus backed away, but held Vibio's gloating gaze. "No."

"Kneel, boy, or I'll have your father's farm confiscated and all three of you arrested for subversion. Who will care for your poor dying mother then?" He belched before taking another sloppy suck of wine. "Then again, she always was a looker. I'd be happy to check in on her for you. She already spends most of her time in bed, so why not?"

Cinus clenched his fists as an onslaught of competing emotions—loathing and rage, fear and vulnerability—coursed through his veins, making his heart pound and his head throb. What could he do? He could not stand to see his proud father carted off to prison like a criminal, torn from his sick wife's bedside, leaving her in her last helpless days to the whims of men like Vibio.

His eyes downcast, Cinus bent a knee and lowered himself before Vibio. The yellow-toothed official snorted in derision as he tipped his head back and drained the wine from his amphora. He held the last mouthful in his cheeks for a moment, then spat it out on Cinus.

The affront was enough to tip the scales of Cinus's emotions. He sprang to his feet and wrapped his arms around Vibio's midsection, propelling himself forward and forcing the official to stumble backward. Vibio landed hard on his backside, a winded *oomph* escaping his lips. Clambering to the man's side, Cinus gripped his hair and viciously smashed the back of his head against the cobblestone until the thud of bone against stone gave way to the mush of tissue and blood, and he realized Vibio's skull had caved in.

His chest heaving, Cinus let himself fall onto his back. Splayed out on the soundless road, he blinked up into the black sky. Nearby, and indifferent to the human drama, his horse shook its head and let out an impatient neigh. The animal wanted to be home in its stall, chomping fine hay and resting.

In the far distance, a burst of raucous laughter—most likely more patrons leaving the tavern—floated through the still night air. The sound spurred Cinus to action. He pushed himself to his feet, grasped Vibio's arms, and hauled his limp body into the trees. Returning to the road, he slapped the rump of Vibio's horse. Startled, the animal jerked its head upward and trotted forward a few paces before meandering off the road in search of tasty grasses along the woodland edge.

Cinus mounted his horse. The surge of blinding rage was receding now, replaced by the harrowing clarity of what he had done. How much worse he had made things.

Riding breathless past the last of the torches that lined the road, Cinus broke into a frantic gallop home, noting that the farther he rode from the faint lights of the village, the more the black sky overhead seemed to swallow him whole, like a Titan devouring Dionysus.

Except it was not a god who would devour him and his family. It was the king.

CHAPTER XIII

Since the altercation with Vibio the previous night, Cinus and Caelus had come to realize an unpleasant truth: the anticipation, the apprehension of a horrible thing happening could be as bad as the horrible thing *actually* happening.

They moved through their day as if it were any other, lambing in the barn, cleaning out stalls, tending the herd as it grazed, and pulling porcupine quills out of Cerva's nose. They helped their mother wash and eat and tucked her back into bed before quickly heading back out to help their father with chores. They ran to the river's edge and pulled out their eel trap, returning with four meaty eels for lunch. They ate, forcing down the food while also forcing down their worst thoughts. Would there be any repercussions from the previous night's events?

When it came to those events, however, the brothers had far different recollections. Caelus thought the worst of it was Vibio's lost tooth and bruised ego. He had no idea that his brother had smashed in the skull of the king's official on the road. Cinus had no intention of telling him, either. What was the point? If soldiers from the palace came for him, his brother—his whole family—

would learn the truth. There was no point making them suffer through each waking moment the way he was.

After supper, Faustulus carried Larentia from her bed to a cushioned chair outdoors so that she could enjoy the sunset. Caelus lit a fire with the flame of an oil lamp, while Cinus scraped a plate of leftovers on the ground for Cerva. The dog eagerly slurped it up and nudged Cinus's leg for more.

"That's all there is, girl," he said.

But the dog's attention was already elsewhere. She perked her ears and growled, hackles raised, looking toward the distant road.

"She hears something," said Faustulus. He tied a rope to her collar just in time to stop her from darting off. Unconcerned, the shepherd sat next to his wife and held a cup of wine to her lips. She took a sip.

"It is sweet, no?" asked Faustulus. "Just as you like."

Larentia smiled. "Just as I like." She looked at her sons, both of whom were staring nervously toward the road, as if they alone could hear the frightening footfalls of a hungry wolf pack descending upon them. "What is wrong?"

Cerva barked and ran to the end of her short rope, straining against it. Several moments later, the unmistakable sound of horses—at least three or four galloping together—traveled through the still air of the early evening to reach their ears.

"Strange at this hour," said Faustulus.

Yet even stranger was the appearance of the riders once the family could finally see them. Four muscly soldiers, boasting the fine gear of King Nemeois's army. Cinus's stomach sank at the sight. Caelus chewed his lip.

Please keep riding, the brothers prayed. *Do not stop here.*

But as the riders slowed and turned onto their father's property, they could no longer deny it. It was happening.

Cinus spun around to face Larentia, dropping to his knees in front of her and kissing her hands. "Mother," he said. "Forgive me. Know that whatever happens, I love you."

Larentia's already pale face blanched even more. "Cinus, what are you talking about?"

He stood and embraced Faustulus. "It is my fault, Father. Do not intercede. Think of Mother and Caelus."

"Cinus, what have you done?" asked Faustulus.

But Cinus's answer was drowned out by the pounding of horse hooves as the Alban soldiers arrived at the home. Two soldiers dismounted and strode boldly, with the authority of men invested with the king's powers, to stand before the shepherd.

"Which of your sons is named Cinus?" demanded one of them.

Cinus shouldered past his father. "I am."

Caelus pressed his palms together and held his hands before him. "Sir," he placated, "it was only a drunken scuffle in a tavern."

The man cocked his head at Caelus. "The drunken scuffle I can live with," he said matter-of-factly, "but I must take issue with one of the king's chief herdsmen having his head bashed in on the road."

"What? That has nothing to do with us. Vibio was alive when we last saw him."

"Well," said the soldier, "when I last saw him, half his brain was picked out by vultures."

Faustulus stepped in front of Caelus to address the soldier. "Vibio was corrupt," he said. "There are fifty men between here and the Quirinal that would want him dead. If he was murdered, it was by the will of Orcus, not the hand of my son."

"I'm sorry, old man," said the soldier, "but he's coming with us."

"No!" Faustulus moved toward the soldier. The escalation sent Cerva into a barking fit and she pulled madly against the rope. The soldier glanced uneasily at her, clearly more intimidated by the shepherd's dog than by the shepherd himself. Cinus grabbed his father's arm.

"Father," he said. "Do not resist. It is pointless." He put his hands on either side of Faustulus's face. "The Fates have spoken."

He patted his father's shoulders affectionately and then looked at Caelus. "Take care of our parents, brother."

"Take care of yourself, brother," Caelus answered weakly.

Caelus put his arm around his father's shoulders. Together, they watched the soldiers climb back onto their horses, Cinus dutifully mounting to sit behind the more subordinate of the two, his face turned away from his family. Caelus felt Faustulus's shoulders begin to shake—he was sobbing—but couldn't bring himself to look at the anguish in his father's eyes.

They stood silent, shocked, as the king's soldiers rode away from the house, back to the road and then out of view, the sound of their horses' receding hooves leaving a lingering sense of doom in the air behind them. Their family had been torn apart.

Yet when they turned back to Larentia, Caelus and Faustulus realized the tear had gone even deeper. Larentia's lifeless body lay slumped in the cushioned chair, her eyes unseeing, and a final, painful expression of despair on her face.

※ ※ ※

It had been the worst night of Caelus's life. The house that he had grown up in, that had always been alive with the sounds and activity of family life, seemed unfamiliar and unsettling. The absence of his mother and brother was palpable and disorienting, and both he and Faustulus felt it. They hardly spoke to each other—the grief, the shock, of the two sudden losses made speaking too exhausting. It was difficult enough to just keep moving.

Yet certain things needed to be done. Caelus cleared the table by the hearthfire as Faustulus carried his wife's dead body inside. Together, they gently laid her on top, standing over her with palms raised to the gods. They passed a sleepless night at her side, praying for her soul.

After their prayers, but before the sun had risen, Caelus stood outside while Faustulus undressed his wife, cleaned her body and anointed it with oil. Wrapping her in the best linen they had, he took a last look at her face. It was a face he had watched change from girlhood to womanhood and through sickness, to this. To death. Knowing he would never look upon it again in this life, he kissed her on the lips and covered her head in fabric.

Faustulus tried not to weep. Caelus had been through enough and he didn't want his son to hear or see him fall apart. But it was no use. The memories of his life with Larentia would not stop tossing and turning in his mind, and at one point he found himself speaking aloud to her. They had not spent a day apart from each other in thirty years. He had no idea how to live without her.

In the dark stillness of night, the father and son labored wordlessly to build a funeral pyre. Neither of them wanted to cart her off to the village's *ustrinum*. They chopped wood and stacked it high as Cerva panted restlessly and stayed on their heels, unsure of what to make of the strange happenings. When the pyre was ready, Caelus set burning torches all around it—they would light Larentia's way to the afterlife.

Finally, Faustulus carried his wife's body outside and placed it on the funeral pyre, setting it ablaze with flames from their household hearth. The fire crackled and roared. Thick orange flames consumed Larentia's flesh and reached into the black sky, red embers snapping out of them and drifting upward to join the stars, disappearing with them as the dark night gave way to the glow of dawn.

As the sweet songs of the morning birds brought the day to life, Caelus and Faustulus scooped Larentia's ashes and remaining white bone fragments from the pyre and placed them in a hut-shaped urn. Sealing the urn, a red-eyed Faustulus smiled sadly to his son. "I will bury it in the garden," he said. "But first…" he faltered, and walked unsteadily to a chair by the house, sitting heavily upon it.

"First what, Father?" asked Caelus.

"First, we must turn our thoughts to your brother. You will go to Alba Longa. There, you will…" he closed his eyes and pushed the heels of his hands against his forehead. "Son," he said. "There is something you must see." Setting the urn on the ground, he rose tiredly from his chair and walked slowly, as if pulling a great weight behind him, to the lambing barn.

Caelus followed him into the barn. The familiar scent of the feed and animals, and the sound of the bleating lambs were reassuring: his world had collapsed inward, and yet those things remained unchanged, a reminder that life had not stopped altogether, even if it felt to him like it had. He glanced into the stalls, noting several new births and, as far as he could tell, only one death. A mother ewe was licking the face of one lively lamb while its sibling lay unmoving in the straw.

They reached the back of the barn where an assortment of old, broken tools had been arranged neatly on the ground, awaiting a repair that would most likely never come. Faustulus knelt down and pushed several to the side. He scooped handfuls of dirt aside until—to Caelus's surprise—he exposed a few planks of rotting wood, the makeshift cover of an underground cellar.

"I didn't know this was here," said Caelus.

"I covered it up years ago," replied Faustulus. He pulled up on a plank of wood, but could not get enough advantage to lift it. "You are stronger than me," he said to his son. "Remove it."

Caelus knelt on the dirt floor. One by one, he removed the rotting planks, sending showers of dirt into the blackness below. When the last plank was gone, he leaned over and squinted into the cellar, his eyes adjusting to the darkness.

There was nothing of interest inside. Whatever valuable Faustulus had gone through the trouble of hiding, someone had obviously found it. He sat back on his heels. "There's nothing down there," he said. "Just one amphora of wine—looks like it cracked a lifetime ago—and an old laundry basket."

"Take out the basket," said Faustulus.

Caelus lay flat on his stomach and reached down into the cellar, pulling out the laundry basket. He knelt beside his father and peered inside. Only a crumpled blanket lay on the bottom.

Faustulus gripped the edge of the basket. "Eighteen years ago," he said, "I was setting an eel trap in the river when I heard a wolf. It was not a distant howl, but a low growl, threatening and very close. The fool I was, I had brought no weapon, so I froze in fear, not sure where she was. I spotted her several paces ahead of me, standing over a laundry basket that was lodged along the shore"—his fingers tightened on the basket—"it had come to rest against the old fig tree by the bend. When the wolf saw me, her hackles went up. I expected her to attack, but she only lowered her head and ran off into the trees. Curious, I pulled the basket out of the river, and what I saw inside..." his voice broke.

"Father, what did you see?"

The old man stared into the basket, remembering. "I saw you and your brother," he said. "You were swaddled tightly inside, your faces still wrinkled from birth."

Caelus absorbed the impact of his father's words. He and Cinus...orphans? "No, it is not true," he said. "Why would you say such a thing? We are your sons."

"You are my sons," said Faustulus, "but only by the will of the gods, not by blood."

Caelus's shoulders fell as yet another wave of loss, another torrent of unwanted change, washed over him. "So we were abandoned," he said. "Nameless orphans, discarded with the dirty laundry."

"No," said Faustulus. "You and your brother are not nameless, and you were not discarded."

"Really?" Caelus asked, his voice rising to anger. "How do you know that?"

Faustulus touched Caelus's cheek. "My dear boy, look under the blanket."

Caelus studied the basket. Its wicker sides were frayed but intact, and the thin lining of clay along its lower half was cracked and brittle with age. He pulled out the dusty blanket inside—and felt his breath catch in his throat at the glittering sight that lay beneath.

It was a crown of oak leaves, forged in solid gold.

CHAPTER XIV

Caelus's stomach churned. His thoughts did, too. He patted his horse's neck as the animal drank lazily from the wooden trough beside the stable, his mind already mapping out the journey to Alba Longa. It wasn't far—only a half-day's ride on horseback—but it would still be the farthest he'd ever traveled from home.

And once he got there...then what? He still had no idea how he would find or free Cinus. All he knew was that he had to get there, fast, and figure out a way.

Sensing his son's nerves, Faustulus handed him a half-loaf of bread. Caelus tore off a piece and chewed it, forcing himself to swallow.

"Thanks," he said, staring absently into the water in the trough. His horse, Xanthos, drank so languidly that the water's surface remained as undisturbed as the animal. Caelus wished he felt half as calm. He swallowed another mouthful of bread.

"The closer you get to the city, the busier the road will be," said Faustulus. "When you're within fifteen or twenty stadia, you're more likely to be stopped by palace soldiers than by bandits. They'll both be equally dangerous to you." He held an empty waterskin out to Caelus.

The younger man eyed it for a thoughtful moment before accepting it. Faustulus had cleverly sewn the Alban crown inside, and Caelus could feel the sharp edges of the gold oak leaves pressing against the worn sheepskin. He slipped the waterskin's rope over his head so that the pouch hung, inelegantly and insignificantly, from his neck.

"Am I really a…a *prince*?" The word, the idea, was preposterous. Only the day earlier, he had been lambing in the barn, covered in blood and manure, chewing on salted eels. "How is it possible?"

"Shortly before you were born," began Faustulus, "there was a coup at the Ferentine Spring, where the leaders of Latium hold conference. King Numitor Silvius, your grandfather, was overthrown by his brother, Amulius. He imprisoned Numitor's daughter, who was with child. She gave birth in captivity."

"Gave birth," mulled Caelus. "To me and Cinus."

"Yes," said Faustulus. "But the usurper didn't last long on the throne. He drank himself into the grave, and his son Nemeois claimed the throne after him. There is no doubt that Nemeois planned to kill the princess's offspring, but she found a way to save both of you. That is how you came to be in the river—it was an act of desperation on her part, no doubt." He sighed sadly. "I found you the day after Larentia and I lost our own child. I brought you home and placed you in her arms, but I had no sooner done so when soldiers came knocking on the door. Nemeois's soldiers. They were interrogating everyone along the river, everyone in the village, asking the same questions. 'Did you find a basket? Have you heard of an orphaned infant being found near here?'" Faustulus shook his head as the memories returned. "It was terrible. They slaughtered any newborn baby they came across, just in case it was the princess's. You and your brother were only spared because"—he laughed humorlessly—"because Vibio happened to come by at the same time as the soldiers. He told them that Larentia had been expecting, he had seen it with his own eyes. That, and her still swollen belly, was enough to ease their suspicions and they left us alone."

"Did Vibio suspect who we were?"

"No," said Faustulus. "He had no reason to."

"When did you know who we really were?"

"Soon after the soldiers and Vibio left," said Faustulus. "Larentia took the linens out of the basket to wash them. That's when she found the crown hidden at the bottom. Your mother, your real mother, she must have placed it there to prove your lineage."

"Our mother," Caelus turned his head to look at the funeral pyre. Small wisps of smoke drifted up from the embers, all that was left of the scorching heat that had consumed Larentia's body. "What was her name?"

"Princess Rhea Silvia."

A long pause. "Is she still alive?"

"I don't know. Most likely not."

"And my father?"

"I don't know."

Caelus reached out to retrieve the bridle that hung from a nail on the outside of the stable. He slipped it over Xanthos's head, securing it in place. There was one more question he wanted to ask—yet he hesitated, afraid that it might come across as too selfish, too ambitious, especially considering Cinus's precarious state. Still, he couldn't stop himself.

"Cinus and I are both princes of Alba Longa," he said, "but only one of us is the crown prince." He met his father's eyes. "Do you know which of us is the elder?"

"No," said Faustulus. "I do not."

But you suspect, thought Caelus. *You suspect it is Cinus. Of course. He has always been stronger than me.*

Faustulus took a step closer to him. "Right now, the most important thing is that you find him. That you free him. It's only together, as brothers, that you can reclaim what is yours. When King Nemeois learns of your existence, he will stop at nothing to kill you. Both of you. You are sons of the Silvii, in the direct line of royal descent. You are more entitled to the throne than he."

Caelus walked Xanthos several steps from the stable before mounting him. He sat straight on the animal's back, feeling the weight of the crown around his neck, and gazed pensively in the direction of the main road. It ran alongside his father's farm for a stretch, and then snaked into the distance, winding and disappearing between the stone pines. He wished he could see farther…farther down the road, further into the future.

Another wisp of smoke from the dying funeral pyre drifted by. From atop Xanthos—who was now restless and snorting below him, eager to go—Caelus looked down at his father.

"I will find a way to save Cinus," he said. "I will bring him home."

"He's already home," Faustulus replied. "He just doesn't know it yet."

※ ※ ※

Proculus Julius had been attacked by animals before. He had been attacked by wolves, lynxes and wild boars, but only after trapping them. He had even been attacked once by a mad goose—the creature was as vicious as any wolverine, though no one believed him—after accidentally happening upon its goslings. But those animals had not *stalked* him.

The large brown bear, the one he could hear rustling in the woods along the road, was stalking him. He clutched the handle of his dagger tighter and glanced nervously into the trees, trying to catch a glimpse of the beast and yet hoping not to, and especially trying to shake off the anxiety that came with being so vulnerable, so alone. Without the speed and security of his horse under him, the road seemed different. Dangerous. Proculus wasn't accustomed to the feeling.

He cursed himself again for letting his horse graze on a grassy slope some way back. It was there, while sampling a particularly lush shrub, that the animal had stepped into a deep rabbit burrow and, panicking at the stumble, managed to break its leg badly enough for the bone to break through its flesh. Proculus had seen no other option but to kill the animal where it lay.

And now he was on foot, praying to Callisto and Diana that the predatory bear in the woods wouldn't do to him what he had done to his horse.

From behind the wall of trees that ran along the side of the road, there came a sniff and then a low growl. A branch snapped. Proculus held out his dagger, well aware of how pathetic a defense it was against the bear. He had only seen it briefly through a break in the trees, but that had been long enough to gauge its size. It was big. Unusually big: a predatory male, perhaps new to the area and so aggressively establishing its territory.

When he had first noticed it, Proculus had tried to scare the beast away by throwing rocks and shouting, but that had only agitated it, causing it to huff louder, angrier. His only hope now was that it would realize he was no threat, get bored, and wander off. He had been clinging to that hope for too long now.

He was still clinging to it when the bear launched out of the trees and charged at him. It moved fast, faster than he would have imagined possible for an animal of its size, and was upon him in an instant. He hollered out in pain as its thick, white teeth sank into the flesh of his right arm. A moment later, he found himself on the ground with the bear's massive, long-clawed paw on top of his chest, pinning him in place, its shocking weight pushing the air out of his lungs.

The animal's large black nose nuzzled into Proculus's neck as it sniffed curiously at its prey, deciding where best to pull off the first strip of flesh. Proculus felt the bear's breath against the delicate skin of his exposed throat, triggering every instinct to fight back, sensing that death was imminent.

Yet despite the surge of adrenaline, despite summoning all his strength and desperation, he was helpless, immobilized by the bear's unyielding mass. He felt his consciousness slipping away—

with the animal's weight still pressing down on his chest, he could not take in a breath. Any moment, he knew his ribcage would crack and his heart would be crushed.

Even as the light of day gave way to the blackness of unconsciousness, Proculus's mind raced. *He'll devour me when I pass out! He'll rip out my insides like a gutted fish!* He tried one last time to scream, but the only sound he heard was…shouting?

It was not him who was shouting. It was someone else, someone he could not see in his fading state, but someone who had nonetheless shouted loudly enough to draw the bear's attention away from him. The animal woofed in a way that sounded almost dog-like and swung around, lifting its massive paw off Proculus's chest.

Proculus gasped for breath and scrambled to his feet, still unable to see clearly. He blinked rapidly in the direction of the voice, willing his vision to return. As he staggered around, he felt his foot hit his dagger—he had not even remembered dropping it—and bent down to search for it on the ground. His extended fingers tightened around the handle in almost the same moment that his eyesight returned.

Without hesitation, he rushed forward where a man about his age was facing the bear, whipping at the animal's snout with what appeared to be the reins from his horse. He had no real hope of hurting the beast, but his antics were baffling enough to the bear that it shook its head in irritation—one of these strange creatures was bad enough, but two were more trouble than they were worth—and lumbered off into the woods.

Face dripping with sweat, eyes still wide with panic, and blood streaming down his right arm from where the bear had bitten him, Proculus stumbled toward the stranger.

"Thank you, friend," he said. Panting, he squeezed the man's shoulder. "You saved my life!"

"I have never seen a bear on the road before," the man replied, his eyes scouring the trees, just in case the animal decided to make a second attack.

"Neither have I." Proculus made a quick study of the man. He was dressed in a rough tunica, and his horse, which he had dismounted several paces down the road, was clearly past its prime. "I am Proculus of the Julii. What's your name?"

"Caelus."

"Who is your master?"

Caelus met the nobleman's eyes. "I have no master, sir. I am a free man."

"Ah, forgive me," Proculus said sincerely. "Where are you headed?"

"To Alba Longa."

"Ah, me too," said Proculus. "Do you live there?"

Caelus hesitated, wondering how much he should reveal. "No. My brother has been falsely accused of killing a king's official. I must speak on his behalf."

Proculus took a step back. "*Falsely* accused, you say? Are you certain?"

"Even if I were uncertain," said Caelus, "it would change nothing. I will speak for him." He turned around and began walking back to his horse, speaking over his shoulder. "*Vale.*"

"Wait," said Proculus. "I mean no offense, brother, but how do you intend to gain an audience with the king, or even get the past the city gates, dressed like…well, dressed as you are?"

Caelus stopped and looked down at his tunica. It was white enough, but a little too short and stitched in places, his mother having mended it the best she could after Cerva had ripped it in play. It stood in stark contrast to Proculus's attire—a snow white, though now bloodstained, tunica with a richly embroidered hem and gem-studded gold cuffs on both wrists.

"Do you have family in Alba Longa? Friends?" asked Proculus.

Again, Caelus hesitated. "No," he said.

"Then you will need a place to stay. Come with me. You can stay at my house. It's the least I can do. We'll find you a finer tunica. And my father is an adviser to King Nemeois. He will make sure you are given an audience."

Caelus put his hands on his hips and stared at the ground. It was against his nature to accept any kind of charity. Yet this man's help, his connections, could be invaluable. Caelus was in no position to let ego stand in the way.

Proculus seemed to understand. "You just saved my life," he said. "My mother will want to stuff you with food." He winced and clutched his bleeding arm, his face suddenly blanching. With the adrenaline and shock of the attack receding, the pain was setting in.

Marching up to him, Caelus bent over and tore a strip of fabric off the bottom of Proculus's tunica. "Let's put your sister's fancy tunica to use," he said, wrapping it around Proculus's bloody arm. "You're pretty enough without it." He tied the fabric tightly enough to stop the flow of blood. "Are you able to ride?"

"Yes," replied Proculus. He pointed at the weathered Xanthos. "But are you sure that poor beast can carry us both? Look at that swayback! Our sandals will be dragging on the ground."

Caelus laughed and mounted Xanthos. "Don't judge so quickly by appearances, friend," he said, and held out an arm to help Proculus mount behind him.

As they rode along—Proculus chatting incessantly in Caelus's ear the whole time, and Xanthos snorting with the discomfort of two riders—the trees along the road slowly began to give way to villas, vineyards and monuments, all signs that they were nearing the large city. Caelus leaned forward slightly, succumbing to a stomach cramp.

Although he knew it was not true, he imagined that every passerby could see straight through the waterskin around his neck to the gold crown sewn inside. He imagined that at any moment someone would pull him from his horse and drag him before the mighty Nemeois, where his own kinsman—it was impossible to think of the *king* as such—would cut off his head on the spot.

Finally, they reached the tall gates of the city where a cluster of armed soldiers were conducting a thorough inspection of people entering and leaving. Caelus had only seen an Alban soldier a few times in his life—the last time was the previous day, when Cinus had been arrested—and the sight of their gleaming armor and weapons, their aggressive manner, made his heart pound.

He patted Xanthos on the neck as he waited to be inspected, an act meant to reassure himself as much as the horse, and glanced up, taking in the distant spectacle of Mount Albanus. The temples were larger, grander and more colorful than anything he had seen before. Long ago, Cinus's friend Fabius had visited Alba Longa with his father and had returned with tales of its magnificence, though they had all assumed he was exaggerating for effect. Caelus could see now that, if anything, Fabius's awed account had failed to capture the city's splendor.

In that moment, the audacity of his presumption—to be a prince of this powerful city—and the absurdity of it all struck him anew, even stronger this time, as he saw the city's expanse and wealth with his own eyes. It was inconceivable that all this majesty could possibly be his: the soldiers at the gates, the temples on the mountaintop, the luxury homes, and the structures on the distant citadel...all his. He felt like an imposter, a foolish child pretending he was something greater than he was. He had a better chance of being Jupiter, king of heaven, than Caelus, prince of Alba Longa.

And yet, there was the gold crown that hung from his neck. It was proof of his lineage, proof that he was in fact a prince of all that surrounded him. As he ruminated on that, the same ambitious question came to mind: *Who is the elder, me or Cinus? Which of us has the right to wear this crown not merely around his neck, but on his head?*

Caelus's lofty thoughts fell hard, though, as the travelers ahead of him cleared, and the stern gate soldiers waved him forward with scrutinizing eyes. Prince or not, he was powerless. He was in enemy territory. The city's grandeur and forces were nothing to marvel at. They were to be feared. If the contents of his waterskin were discovered...well, he couldn't bear to think of what would happen then, and not just to him, but to Cinus and their father, too. He held his breath as a bellicose soldier marched toward him, but breathed a sigh of relief as the man recognized Proculus sitting behind him and adopted a friendlier gait.

"*Salve*, Master Proculus," said the soldier. He gave a concerned look at the makeshift bandage on Proculus's bloody arm. "Bandits?" he asked. "Where? I'll send out some men."

"Not bandits," grinned Proculus. "A bear, if you can believe it."

"*Di boni!*" said the soldier. "You'd best get that tended to." Without so much as another glance at Proculus's humbly dressed companion, he waved the men onward to pass through the gates of the city.

Caelus spoke over his shoulder to Proculus. "Where are the prisoners kept?" he asked.

"He'll most likely be in the fields or maybe in the stone quarries," replied Proculus. "Most prisoners are worked before they're killed. My father will be able to find him."

"Why would your father care to help me?" asked Caelus.

Proculus laughed. "Because I am his only son, and if it weren't for you, the vultures would be hissing over my open ribcage right now."

"How long has your family been in Alba Longa?"

"Since its founding," Proculus said proudly. "The Julii are descended from Ascanius, just like the Silvii, but the Silvii are the royal line. Next to them, we are the greatest family in Latium."

"Is your father loyal to the king?"

"Of course," said Proculus, surprised by the question. "Why would you ask such a thing?"

"No reason." Caelus smiled broadly to deflect the sudden suspicion he heard in the young man's voice. "It's just that, where I come from, two cocks can't live in the same henhouse."

The levity worked, and Proculus laughed aloud. "The politics of Latium are slightly more complex than your henhouse."

"Don't be so sure," said Caelus. "Things can get ugly in a henhouse."

As a flock of quacking mallards passed overhead on their way to the nearby lake, the two men atop the swayback horse proceeded along the busy road, moving aside as carts and carriages claimed the right of way. There was a greater variety of people here than Caelus had ever seen in the tavern or shops near his home—the wealthy looked even wealthier and the poor even poorer—with foreigners, their accents and attire standing out, giving the noisy city a sense of exoticness he had never experienced before.

But then a scuffle between two men arguing in a language Caelus did not recognize drew the attention of a cheerless-looking Alban soldier. He arbitrarily gripped one of the men by the scruff of his tunica and dragged him gracelessly toward a prison cart, throwing him inside and spitting on him for good measure. The sobering interaction once again sharpened Caelus's focus. He had to find Cinus before one or both of them were killed.

As Xanthos continued down the road, Caelus looked up to study the grounds of the expansive royal estate. It was built into the slope and along the upper ridge of a mountain, although the thick trees and fortified peperino stone wall that encompassed the palace prevented him from getting a good look.

He wondered whether the king was inside the palace right now. If so, what was he doing? Distributing land among the cities of Latium? Feasting on delicacies? Sleeping with a mistress? Ordering the execution of some irrelevant shepherd's son from a tiny village in the country? Caelus had no idea how a king spent his time.

Finally, they arrived at the estate of the Julii. Guards opened the locked gates to allow them in and they dismounted, Caelus walking Xanthos toward the grand doors of the home's portico where two slaves quickly approached. One of them took the reins from his hands.

"Master Proculus!" exclaimed the older slave. "What happened to your arm?"

"I had an accident on the road. Is Father home?"

"Yes, and your mother, too. She will be fussing over you before your sandals are off."

"I will try to slip past her," said Proculus.

"You will not succeed," replied the slave, as both servants led the old horse off in the direction of the stables. Caelus saw the younger slave give Xanthos a curious look. No doubt, visitors to this house usually arrived on less ragged backs.

Another pair of slaves opened the large wooden doors to the house, and Caelus followed Proculus inside, trying not to appear too dazzled by the richness around him. Before this, the finest home he had ever been in was the country villa of a successful trader who had once hired him to deliver eels, but that house was a near-hut compared to the Julii's.

As the elderly slave had predicted, a soft middle-aged woman instantly appeared and clasped her hands to her face when she saw Proculus's condition. She rushed to his side.

"What in the name of the gods happened to you?"

"Mother, calm yourself," he said. "It is—"

"Do not tell me to calm myself!" she chastised. "Look at you! I told you not to ride alone, but you never listen to me, do you?"

"It is not as bad as it looks. The bleeding stopped a long time ago."

Drawn by the commotion, a stately looking man emerged from an adjacent room. A blue riding cloak was draped over his shoulders, as if he had recently returned from the outdoors. "Proculus, I've been looking everywhere for"—his eyes fell upon the bloodstained fabric wrapped around Proculus's arm—"How did that happen?"

"You won't believe it, Father," said Proculus, "but I was attacked by a *bear* on the road."

"A bear?"

"Truly, yes." Proculus put his hand on Caelus's shoulder, presenting his guest to his parents. "I prayed to Callisto to save me, but it was this one who dropped from the sky to do it."

Proculus's father and mother gaped at Caelus for several long moments. They exchanged looks of bewilderment and then looked at him again. Proculus frowned, confused by his parents' reactions—at the mere sight of the slightly disheveled young man, their mouths had dropped open in a way that might have been comedic had they not seemed so dead serious. For some inexplicable reason, they were not looking at Caelus with the usual warmth they showed a guest.

Rather, they were looking at him as if they had seen a ghost.

Albus narrowed his eyes as he considered the young man his son had brought home. That face—the thin lips pressed together in thought, the black eyes, the furrowed brow that was already showing lines of worry.

"Who is your father?" he asked.

Proculus cleared his throat, taken aback by his father's abruptness. Caelus sensed it, too.

"My father's name is Faustulus," he replied. "He owns land along the Palatine Hill and tends a large herd for the king."

"Why have you come to Alba Longa?"

"My brother was brought here as a prisoner, but it was a misunderstanding. I must see the king to explain."

Albus only looked at his wife, the two of them communicating with their eyes.

"Father," said Proculus. "Caelus saved my life. I told him you would arrange for him to speak with the king."

Albus looked at his son, nodding pensively. "I will speak to the king on his behalf."

"Perhaps it is better than I speak with him myself," said Caelus.

Albus shook his head. "I will take care of it," he said, his eyes still scrutinizing Caelus's face and his voice heavy with suspicion. *Because if the king sees that face*, he thought to himself, *you and brother will find yourselves in a darker place than prison.*

CHAPTER XV

Sitting naked on the edge of his bed, King Nemeois felt his hips thrust forward involuntarily as the woman kneeling between his legs did her work. The surge in pleasure made his muscles tense and he squeezed the handle of the dagger in his right hand, holding the blade steady against her throat but careful not to press too hard. It would be a shame to accidentally kill someone as talented as her, especially before he was finished.

The woman moved her tongue with expert precision, making Nemeois groan and move his hips forward again. Yet instead of succumbing, he clutched her hair and pulled her off him. Directing her to leave the bedchamber, he turned his attention to the other woman in the room—this one was kneeling on the bed, bound by the wrists to one of the bedposts.

Nemeois couldn't remember the last time he had taken a woman who didn't have a blade to her throat or wasn't tied to something. He knew it was paranoia. Since that night nearly twenty years ago, when Lela had murdered his father Amulius in the bath by distracting him with pleasure, Nemeois had become increasingly convinced that he would perish in a similar way. He wouldn't put it past one of his enemies, or even his wife Cloelia, to bribe some particularly skilled whore to murder him when he was at his most vulnerable.

He knelt behind the bound woman and clutched her hips, pulling them back toward him and forcing her to grip the bedpost for support as he thrust into her. He stroked slowly, trying to lose himself in the feel of her, staring at her backside by the light of the morning sun that filtered through the window drapes.

Yet, as always, unwanted thoughts found their way into his mind. Thoughts about the treasury, the upcoming treaty talks, the unrest among his soldiers, the constant complaining of the Julii and other elites, the land disputes between Alba Longa and Tusculum…it never seemed to end. He squeezed his eyes shut and thrust faster, purposefully, all but forcing the orgasm to happen. Sated—or perhaps just tired enough to be satisfied—he untied the woman. She crawled off the bed and bowed to him before skittering naked out of the room.

Unfortunately, his solitude did not last long. The door opened and Cloelia entered with a scowl. "Must you couple with your daughter's handmaids?" she asked. "There are twenty slaves within reach."

"I know," said Nemeois, "but I prefer the ones you disapprove of. It amplifies the pleasure." He rolled onto his back, not bothering to cover himself with the sheet. He knew the sight of his nakedness and fading erection would irk her.

"I do not care that you have mistresses," she said, "but I am your wife. You should visit my bed—"

"Why? We have done what is necessary. We have two healthy children." He didn't mention the two she had miscarried. "There is no need for more." He rose from the bed and stood naked in the center of the room, arms out in a questioning deportment. "Did you come here just to scold me? Or do you have an actual purpose?"

"Mamilian's messenger just arrived. He is in your study."

"About time," said Nemeois. A male slave approached the king with a fresh tunica and Nemeois pulled it over his head, chewing his lip at Cloelia as the young man fastened a rope-belt around his waist. "Let's see what he has to say." Knowing his wife would have trouble keeping up with him, he left the bedchamber and took large strides down the corridor to his study where Mamilian's messenger awaited.

"Your Highness," the man bowed.

"What is your master's answer?" asked Nemeois, just as Cloelia scurried into the room behind him, nearly puffing.

The messenger opened his mouth to speak, paused to bow to the queen, and then delivered his message. "My master graciously accepts the proposed betrothal between his daughter, Penelope, and your son, Prince Amatus. My master sends his ten most exceptional stud stallions, in gratitude and friendship. Finally, my master assures Your Highness and the crown prince that he will deliver his daughter pure and intact on her wedding day."

Nemeois smiled. "Good," he said. "Tell your master I am greatly pleased by his answer."

"Yes, Your Highness." The messenger bent at the waist and backed out of the room.

"Albus Julius will not be happy," said Cloelia. "He hoped to marry his eldest niece to Amatus."

"He won't be happy," echoed Nemeois, "but he won't be surprised, either. I told him Mamilian's daughter was my first choice. This bickering with Tusculum has to stop. Anyway, it's hardly something for you to worry about." The king brushed past his wife. "I will see you at supper."

Nemeois exited the study and again walked down the corridor between the rows of statuary, this time toward the royal stateroom. Through one of the open windows, he caught sight of his seven-year-old daughter, Amata, standing in the middle of the courtyard outside, hands on her hips, head back, looking up at the clear blue sky as the morning sun warmed her face. Her name meant *beloved one*, and it reflected how everyone felt about her: although she had only inherited a portion of Cloelia's beauty, she had been blessed with all of Nemeois's wiliness—and then some—and was the darling of her tutors. Like her father, she was an early riser. Nemeois slunk stealthily outside and snuck up on her from behind. He clapped his hands, and she spun around, startled.

"Father, don't sneak up on me like that!"

"How dare you say that!" said Nemeois. "Who was it that crouched behind a statue of Diana for hours last night, just so she could spring up and see her own father jump out of his skin?"

The girl laughed. "Let's call a truce."

"A truce? What do you know of a truce?"

"Nikandros has been teaching me about the Latium treaties," she said. "So I suppose I know a lot."

"Nikandros better be careful. You'll be tutoring him soon."

"I will tell him you said so," she replied and ran off, presumably in search of her tutor.

Nemeois sighed. How he wished that he could muster half as much enthusiasm for treaties these days, especially since the conference at the Ferentine Spring was only a few days away. The thought of the revered fathers quarrelling amongst each other, always vying for a little more power or a little more wealth, and then blaming him when they did not get it, made his shoulders slump.

He turned to re-enter the palace, walking unhurriedly to the stateroom as his senior slave fell into step beside him, briefing him on the morning's appointments. He listened with one ear, waving away a female slave who approached with a tray of fruit and hot drink. Arriving at the hall, he passed by the two soldiers who flanked the doorway and found the day's first appointment—Albus Julius—already waiting inside, reclining on a mahogany chair, his elbow on the armrest and his chin resting in his palm as if he were about to drift off to sleep.

Albus rose as the king walked past him to sit on the high-backed throne at the far end of the courtly room. "Good morning, Your Highness," he said, bowing his head.

"Good morning, Albus. You look as unrested as I feel."

"I was up late preparing for the conference. There is never enough daylight."

"The lamps burn late here as well," said Nemeois. He thought about breaking the news to the nobleman then and there—Amatus would marry Mamilian's daughter, not Albus's niece—but decided to wait. He was not up for the argument. "I'm told you're here on a mercy mission...some prisoner from the country."

"Yes, Highness. The issue stems from the activities of your magister pecoris out by the Palatine Hill, a man by the name of Vibio. The one who was recently found dead"—Albus waited for confirmation that Nemeois was aware of the situation, and the king nodded—"well, apparently he'd been skewing herd numbers out there for years. He would take a dozen or more head from each shepherd for himself, then report them as stillbirths or as lost to predators. I had a couple of my men ride out and ask around. Vibio had his share of enemies."

"I'm assuming the man you're here to plead for was one of them."

"Yes," said Albus. "His name is Cinus. He's the son of a respected shepherd in the country. My son, Proculus, is a friend of his brother. The boy was accused of killing Vibio, but denies it. And considering the number of enemies the man had—"

A man appeared in the doorway. The badge on his cloak—the face of Bacchus, god of wine—identified him as a messenger from the conference town of Marino, and the king's attention shifted to him. "Your man is pardoned," Nemeois said to Albus, at the same time motioning for the messenger to enter, his mind already moving to other matters.

"Thank you, Your Highness," said Albus. He bade the king good morning and left the meeting chamber, continuing out of the palace to where his horse awaited. As he mounted, he spotted Prince Amatus returning from the direction of the stables, one side of his body caked in mud. The crown prince was not known for his horsemanship.

"*Salve*, Albus," said the prince. He flicked a large chunk of mud off his arm and smiled sheepishly. "An improvement on yesterday," he said. "Only half of me is filthy this morning."

Albus chuckled. As usual, the prince's self-deprecating humor, the quickness with which he admitted his own flaws, only seemed to amplify his competence and good nature. "You are a fast learner, Prince Amatus," he said. "You will ride like Bellerophon before summer."

"Is Proculus not with you?"

"No, I only had a quick matter with your father."

"Well, tell Proculus that one of our best mares is ready to foal. I'd like him to come by. I am hoping for a colt."

"I will do so. Good day, Your Highness."

The prince waved a friendly farewell to the older nobleman as Albus walked his horse away from the palace, past the guards at the gate and onto the road, breaking into a trot as he headed to the stone quarry where he suspected Caelus's brother was being held.

It was a short ride on a fast horse. Even before reaching the entrance to the expansive quarry, which was built into the Alban Hills, Albus could hear the skull-rattling thuds and clangs of hundreds of hammers hitting stone, the constant din of which was punctuated by the sound of cart wheels grinding over gravel and the shouts of soldiers and supervisors—"Get up, you lazy sack of shit! Keep working! Break that stone, or I'll break you!"

By the time he arrived at the gates of the quarry, the sound was near deafening. A leathery-skinned guard sauntered up to him, shoving a yellowish piece of bread into his mouth. He spoke through the bars, crumbs spilling out of his mouth.

"Can I help you, sir?"

"I'm looking for a prisoner," said Albus. "He would've arrived the day before yesterday. From the country."

"We get a lot of prisoners from the country."

"Open the bloody gate," said Albus. "And get me the quarryman."

The guard made to spit, but then noticed the medallion of

Venus on Albus's gold wrist cuff—the symbol of the powerful Julii family—and thought better of it.

"As you say, sir," he replied.

The gate opened and Albus dismounted, leading his horse into the quarry. The guard took the reins from him and pointed to a shack that sat beside a massive mound of rubble. "The boss is in there," he said.

Careful not to trip or twist his ankle on the thick carpet of rock chunks underfoot, Albus picked a path to the shack and pulled open the rickety door to find the head quarryman lowering the bottom of his tunica, a dejected-looking slave boy on his knees before him, wiping his mouth with the back of his hand.

"For the love of the gods," scowled Albus. "Is *this* what the city is paying you for?"

The quarryman hastily adjusted his belt. "I was on my break." He waved the boy away and offered Albus a slight bow. "How can I help you, sir?"

"I'm looking for the prisoner who was accused of killing one of the king's chief herdsmen. He goes by the name of Cinus and came in a couple days ago from some backwater village in the country…near a hill called the Palatine. The king has pardoned him and he's to come with me."

Taking the nobleman at his word, the quarryman punched the air unhappily and grumbled. "Bloody Hephaestus," he said. "I lose all the good ones."

He hobbled out of the shack, clearing mucus from his throat and spitting on the rocky ground, his sputum as coated in dust as the rest of him. Albus followed behind, studying the grime-and-sweat covered faces of the workers all around. They seemed to be the walking dead, beyond exhaustion, gripping the handles of hammers or axes with bleeding hands, their backs permanently bent from swinging tools, pushing carts and carrying buckets of stone.

The quarryman stuck his head into the jagged mouth of a tunnel and barked a phlegmy order to someone inside its dark depths.

Several moments later, a young man emerged limping from the darkness, blinking into the light of day. Even the layer of dirt on his face, even the dried blood that painted his forehead, even the bruised left eye that was swollen shut, could not mask it.

Twins. Of course.

The quarryman grabbed Cinus by the fabric of his already torn tunica, ripping it more in the process and shoving him toward Albus. "You're to go with this man." He whistled to a worker whose cleaner, untorn tunica suggested a more supervisory role. "Take these two back to the gates," he said. Then he left, climbing goat-like over a pile of boulders to where a group of prisoners were passing around a waterskin and taking what was undoubtedly an unscheduled break. "Get my whip!" he shouted, and the prisoners rushed back to their hammers and axes.

Cinus sized up Albus, trying to camouflage his weakened condition with an assertive stare. Why was this nobleman claiming him? *If he thinks he's going to bugger me*, he thought, *he has another thing coming*. The quarryman had already tried it, and Cinus had left him with a swollen testicle for his efforts. The beating he had taken for it was worth it.

Albus anticipated Cinus's thoughts. "Your brother Caelus," he said discreetly, as they both trailed the supervisor out of the quarry. "I'm here on his behalf."

The hard expression on the young man's face cracked, replaced by a countenance of acute, unexpected deliverance. Cinus knew his brother would try to free him, but deep down he had feared that Caelus was simply not resourceful enough to find a way.

"Thank you, sir," Cinus said, his voice just above a whisper. "Where is my brother now?"

They reached the gates, and the same guard who had taken Albus's horse returned the animal to him. The nobleman walked the horse several paces away so he could not be overheard.

"He's waiting for you at my home, with my son." Albus mounted and looked down at Cinus's bruised and swollen left ankle. He reached down, offering the young man his hand. Cinus accepted it and mounted behind him.

"Who are you?" asked Cinus.

"Keep your head down and keep quiet," said Albus. "We don't have far to go."

Cinus sat obediently, joyfully, behind the stranger. Whoever he was, it was all Cinus could do to not hug his torso in gratitude and relief as the thuds, clangs and shouts of the quarry gradually faded away, and the only sound he could hear was the liberating clip-clops of the horse's hooves on the road as his emancipator rode him away from the stone-faced version of Hades.

CHAPTER XVI

Even though the muscles in his back and legs were in spasm, and even though his empty stomach growled for sustenance, Caelus had not moved since dawn from his kneeling position before the family shrine of the Julii. He ignored the muscle cramps and hunger pangs, and uttered prayer after prayer to Vesta. When Proculus's mother had brought him bread—it was the best he had ever smelled—he only passed it over the flame of an oil lamp on the shrine and asked that the remainder of his share be put into the household hearth as an offering.

Although Albus Julius was confident that King Nemeois would pardon Cinus, there was no guarantee that the young man would still be alive, especially if he was in a prison quarry. Deadly rockslides and summary executions from exploitative guards and supervisors who acted with impunity were all too common there. The idea that his brother could be at the mercy of such a place...Caelus lowered his head before the shrine.

"Great goddess," he whispered yet again. "Protect my brother. Bring him home."

Home. It was not incorrect to say so. For although Cinus did not know it, this strange city was his true home.

Caelus heard a familiar, though raspy, voice behind him.

"Why do you pray to the Virgin? It is Venus who fancies me."

Caelus sprang to his feet and turned to embrace his brother. They held each other for a long moment before Caelus gripped Cinus by the shoulders and held him at arm's length to examine him. His face was bloody, his left eye was swollen shut, and his clothes were torn. One ankle was so distended and blue that it looked as though the flesh would burst. Yet he wore a smile on his face.

Cinus glanced around at the affluent surroundings. "Who are these people?" he asked. "How did you meet them?"

"I met their son, Proculus, on the road to Alba Longa. His father knows the king, and he agreed to help me find you."

Cinus chuckled, still giddy with the relief of his rescue. "Unbelievable," he said. "I thought I was done for." He wiped away a stream of fluid that ran down from his swollen eye. "We should leave for home at once. Mother and Father will be worried sick."

Caelus squeezed his brother's shoulders, suddenly realizing—Cinus did not know. The smell of their mother's funeral pyre wafted into his memory and he stared at his brother, his expression vacillating between grief and uncertainty. How to say it? What words to choose?

"Mother..." he began.

He was almost relieved when he did not have to say more. Cinus's face contorted and tears streamed down his cheeks, mixing with the dirt to create a sludge that slid slowly down his face. Cinus took a step toward his brother, nearly collapsing into him. He rested his head on Caelus's shoulder, his own shoulders wracked by sobs.

"We will go home," Caelus said, supporting his brother's fatigued body. "Father will be so happy to see you."

Another voice, this one deeper, spoke. It was Albus Julius. "It is not my business," he said, "but your brother should rest before he travels. He could barely sit upright on the back of my horse."

"Yes," added Proculus. The young man was standing beside his father, also watching the dramatic reunion unfold. "We will send a messenger to your father immediately."

Feeling suddenly overwhelmed by his own exhaustion and emotions, Caelus nodded. One of the Julii's horses could make it home much faster than Xanthos anyway, and the sooner Faustulus could receive the good news, the better. He opened his mouth to thank his host, his first friend in this new city, but his throat was dry and tight, and no sound came out.

"You're welcome," said Proculus.

※ ※ ※

As it happened, Cinus and Caelus stayed for an additional two nights at the home of the Julii. Cinus's ankle had taken a brief turn for the worse and required splinting. The young man had hobbled around as best he could on crutches to let the swelling go down, which by the morning of the third day, it had.

Not that Cinus minded the delay. He had never enjoyed such luxurious living: the high ceilings and posh furnishings, the baths and the fountains, and of course, the food, which Proculus's mother, Adrastia, served him nonstop. As soon as he had devoured one dish, she had the cooks prepare him another. Being around her—her soft, round body and her smiling, maternal face—was familiar and comforting. There were other comforts to be had, too. The female servants were prettier and more accommodating than their counterparts in the country, and Cinus had welcomed their particular style of hospitality as they slipped into his guest room at night.

Yet while Cinus was happy to indulge himself while he could—he'd be back in the barn in a day or two, cleaning stalls instead of feasting and coupling with city girls—Caelus did not seem to be enjoying himself at all. He walked around in silence, preoccupied by his own thoughts. When he did speak, it was to ask Adrastia for a tonic to soothe his stomach. Twice Cinus had heard his brother retching into his chamberpot. He knew Caelus wasn't ill. It was just his nerves. Between the death of their mother and the stress of finding a way to free him from the prison quarry, no doubt his brother's constitution had been stretched to the breaking point.

Of course, Cinus had no way of knowing the truth. Caelus's distraction, his nerves, had nothing to do with their mother's death or the drama of Cinus's imprisonment. Rather, his anxious state stemmed from the gold crown that was sewn inside the waterskin hidden underneath his guest bed.

Caelus had still not told his brother about it. He didn't know how to tell him. More importantly, he didn't know how Cinus would react. Would he dismiss Faustulus's account as lunacy or a fantastical delusion of grandeur? Would he say it was senility, perhaps catalyzed by the grief of his wife's traumatic death? Or—and if Caelus was honest with himself, this was the real reason for his hesitancy—would Cinus grasp onto the greatness of it and immediately claim the status of the firstborn for himself?

Regardless, Cinus deserved to know the truth and Caelus resolved to tell him today. They would lunch at the home of the Julii and then take to the road where Caelus could tell his brother the whole story in private. After that, they could devise a plan together.

A pretty slave girl entered the dining room with a large platter of mouthwatering pheasant meat, and everyone took their places: Albus, Adrastia and Proculus reclined on three adjoining couches, while Cinus and Caelus—wearing fine tunicas gifted to them by their hosts—sat opposite them. As usual, the conversation was as delightful as the food, with Proculus leaping up to yet again reenact the way he and Caelus had fought off the bear, his father applauding their courage and his mother covering her face in horror. Amused by his own antics, Proculus collapsed onto his couch with a sigh and casually looked at the brothers.

"Now that you're cleaned up, Cinus, I can hardly tell the two of you apart," he said.

Cinus flexed an arm and patted his biceps. "This is how you can tell us apart."

Everyone laughed, except for Albus. "Did you know that twins are common with the Silvii?" he asked. It was an abrupt question. Out of place.

Caelus stopped chewing. His eyes darted to Albus, who was staring intently at him.

Noting the change in tone, Cinus spoke through his food. "Who are the Silvii?"

Albus ignored his question, his eyes still leveled on Caelus. "It's true," he said. "It's in the royal blood. Prince Egestus and Princess Rhea, they were twins. Before them, King Numitor and the usurper Amulius, they were also twins."

At that, a slave entered the room carrying a polished silver tray. On top lay Caelus's ratty waterskin—with the stopper removed. No doubt, Albus knew exactly what was inside. Caelus nearly choked on his mouthful of pheasant. He swallowed hard and leapt to his feet, ferociously jabbing a finger at Albus.

"That is my property, sir! Do you always snoop through your guests' belongings?"

"I have never had occasion to before," replied Albus, "but you are no ordinary guest, are you?"

Cinus had no idea what was happening, but the sudden change in the room—the tenseness and the edge of accusation in their host's voice, and his brother's uncharacteristic outburst—made the food nearly fall out of his mouth.

"Caelus, mind yourself!" he chastised.

Albus rose from his couch to stand face to face with Caelus.

Caelus spoke to the slave. "Bring that to me."

Albus nodded his permission, and the slave approached Caelus with the tray. The young man seized the waterskin and stopper off it and pushed the stopper back into place. He clutched the pouch tightly in his hands.

"Caelus," Albus said flatly. "What is sewn inside that pouch?"

"My family's few valuables," Caelus replied. "My father's bracelet and my mother's jewelry. I thought it wise to hide them while I was on the road."

"Well, there is no need to hide your valuables here," said Albus. "You are among friends. Please, let us see them."

Caelus stood straighter. "Are you accusing me of stealing from you, sir?"

"No," said Albus. "You are not being truthful, but you are no thief."

Baffled and embarrassed by his brother's stubbornness, especially in the presence of such generous hosts, Cinus stood. "Gods above," he said. In one motion, he swiped the waterskin out of Caelus's hands and ripped it apart. Its frayed seams easily snapped open. Whatever was inside fell to the floor with a clang. They all looked down at it.

The crown.

Blinking in confusion, Cinus bent over and picked it up. His eyes moved between Caelus and Albus, wondering why neither of them seemed remotely surprised by the fact that a gold crown had just tumbled out of his brother's waterskin. His mind searched for a reason and found the only rational one. *Caelus must have stolen it...perhaps he thought he could use it to barter for my freedom from the prison quarry...*

And yet their host was not angered by the revelation.

Instead, the corners of Albus's mouth slowly lifted into a satisfied but unthreatening smile. "Do you know which of you was born first?" he asked Caelus.

Caelus pressed his lips together. "No."

"No, I suppose you wouldn't," said Albus. "But I know someone who might."

"Who?" asked Caelus.

"Your true mother," their host replied. "Princess Rhea Silvia of Alba Longa."

* * *

"How long have you known?" asked Cinus.

"Father told me the morning I left to find you," replied Caelus.

"He showed me the basket he found us in. It was hidden in a cellar, under the barn, and the crown was inside it."

Cinus sat on the edge of the large fountain in the courtyard of the Julii, staring up at a statue of Pegasus: the winged horse seemed to be jumping out of the water, as if about to fly upward to the gods' heavenly stables. He reached into the cool water and splashed some onto his face with one hand. His other hand held the gold crown. "Why didn't you tell me sooner?"

"I didn't know how you'd react. I was going to tell you later today, when we were on the road. When no one was around to hear or see us."

"Maybe," said Cinus. "Or maybe you just enjoyed having it over me."

"That is not true." Caelus sat beside his brother. "We need to figure out what to do. We have no money, no army…"

"But you have a name," said Albus. He entered the courtyard with Proculus at his side. The younger man's normally carefree, frivolous demeanor was gone, replaced by a seriousness that Caelus suspected was inherent in his esteemed lineage. As Proculus had once said, next to the Silvii, the Julii were the greatest family in Latium.

"A name doesn't pay soldiers," said Cinus.

"No, but it inspires them," Albus replied. "I'll handle the rest for now. The Julii are bound by history, by our ancestors, to be loyal to the Silvii. Like you, we are descended from Aeneas and the founder, Ascanius. It is our duty to restore the crown to the true Silvian king." The older man canted his head at the brothers: if Nemeois was unwilling to advance the Julii in Alba Longa, then perhaps these new princes would. "Of course, our loyalty has always been generously rewarded by the crown."

"Help us take what is ours, and it will be," said Cinus.

Caelus looked at the ground. Cinus had only just learned of their lineage, and already he was assuming an air of authority. In fact, he hadn't let go of the crown since he had picked it off the floor at lunch.

"Where is our mother?" Caelus asked Albus.

"She is in the necropolis"—he raised a reassuring hand as the brothers thought the worst—"but not dead. Nemeois has kept her imprisoned there since he took the throne. She is tasked with keeping Vesta's sacred flame alight within its walls."

"What about our grandfather, Numitor, or our uncle? Are they alive?" inquired Caelus.

"Prince Egestus was murdered by Nemeois before you were born," Albus replied simply, "and Numitor died years ago in exile."

Before either of the brothers could ask who or where their father was, the sound of approaching footfalls—marching, militaristic—and the loud shout of a commanding officer drifted into the courtyard. Caelus jumped to his feet, imagining a small army of King Nemeois's soldiers storming the Julii's estate to arrest them.

"Are they here for us?" he asked breathlessly.

Proculus patted him on the back and smiled. "Yes, my friend. From this day forward."

CHAPTER XVII

It was still too early in the spring for the fig trees to bear fruit, but some of the strawberries couldn't wait. They hung like red jewels among the green leaves. Rhea squatted down to pick them, dropping them into the shallow bowl by her foot and tossing a particularly juicy specimen to the cawing hooded crow behind her. The bird stabbed at the strawberry with its beak, flinging red bits into the air and then flew off, leaving the bulk of the berry on the ground for the ants.

Having picked all the ripened strawberries she could see—there weren't more than twenty—Rhea pushed herself to her feet, eating them from the bowl as she walked through the necropolis, following the winding stone path back to her tomb-home. The fruit sat too lightly in her stomach, making her crave something more substantial. She was looking forward to some bread and olives.

So too was the red squirrel that chattered noisily behind her on the path. He knew where they were going, and he knew the routine—it had been the same routine for years, ever since the princess had nursed him back to health as a kitten. She had found him lying, eyes still unopened, near the base of the statue of King

Latinus Silvius, most likely dropped by a hawk after being nabbed from his nest. The squirrel was as tame as any pet. He even came when called by his name, Tumulto, so named for the relentless commotion he caused.

It was a commotion that had many times pulled Rhea back from the brink of madness. Tumulto's incessant chattering, knocking over of water jugs, pulling of wet linen from the clothesline, and the way he would make off with her food, chew what was left of her sandals, and clamber up her leg when she least expected it, all gave her focus. It gave her a foundation of reality and reminded her that she was still alive, still interacting with other living creatures in a living world.

Yet as she arrived back at her tomb and withdrew a loaf of bread from a round clay pot, ripping off a piece and placing it in the greedy paws of the tiny beast, she couldn't ignore the changes in Tumulto—his eyes were more sunken every day. He was slowing down, too. He didn't hop from tree to tree like he did in years past. Now, he took the easy path and followed her on the ground. She supposed it was easier on his tiny, old bones. She sat down on a bench and gave him an olive. He took it from her fingers and nibbled it, his pointed ears and thick tail twitching with happiness.

"How old are you now, Tumulto? Nine years? Maybe ten?"

She was pondering this as, very gradually, some part of her consciousness became aware of a sound in the distance. A different kind of sound. Not a bird call or a chattering rodent, not the bark of a wild dog beyond the high walls…no, it was something else. She heard it again, this time more clearly.

A voice. A *human* voice.

"Princess Rhea! Are you here?"

The shock of it brought her to her feet quickly, startling Tumulto into dropping his olive. Unimpressed, he chattered out a scolding and scurried away.

Rhea held her breath and stood unmoving, tilting her head and listening keenly, waiting to see whether she could hear it again. A few moments of silence passed. *It is just your imagination,* she told herself. *If the hallucinations come again, do not be afraid…they are not real. Tumulto is real.*

Rhea hated the hallucinations. It was bad enough when they came in the day, like this, but when they came at night it was even worse. It was always the same hallucination, too—the god Mars, in armor, wielding a bloody sword and searching for her among the tombs. More than once she had been fooled into abandoning her bed in the middle of the night and running from him, like a frantic mouse from a stalking cat, until sheer exhaustion forced her to curl up and hide behind a sarcophagus until the light of day dissolved the illusion.

Unless it was not an illusion. Who knew how the gods appeared to mortals? If Jupiter could take the form of a cloud and Vesta could take the form of fire, could Mars not take the form of a hallucination?

"Princess! Are you here? Can you hear me?"

Rhea gasped, her hand instinctively flying to her chest, her fingers gripping the fabric of her tunica in shock. That voice…it was no hallucination, no illusion. It was real.

She stepped slowly, cautiously, away from her tomb until she had a clear line of sight down the paved stone pathway that wound through the necropolis. She swayed on her feet from a current of dizziness—three men were approaching from the direction of the necropolis's entrance. One was walking in front and two, their heads covered by the hoods of their cloaks, were walking behind.

They all stopped in their tracks when they saw her. She stopped, too.

The man in front began walking again, more slowly now, toward her. He was older than she was, and his face was familiar. She searched her mind, trying to remember, when he spoke.

"Princess Rhea," he said softly. "It is me, Albus Julius. Do you remember me?"

"Yes." She took a small step backward, toward the safety of her tomb.

"We are not here to hurt you," he said, holding up a hand in reassurance. "We are friends." When she nodded—she remembered him now—Albus continued. "Years ago, you gave birth to twins. Do you remember?"

"I sent them away. With Lela...but she died."

As she gawked at the trio, one of the hooded men reached up and removed his hood to reveal his face. Rhea felt her breath leave her lungs, exiting her mouth as a single, soft word.

"Egestus?"

The man did not respond to the name, but only looked at her in bewilderment. His eyes were black and wide, confused. Rhea was confused, too. It could not be Egestus. Egestus was dead. She spoke to his spirit daily, she sat by his ashes. And even if he were alive, he would not be a young man like the one before her. He would be like her, almost forty years old.

Slowly, so as not to frighten her, the three men moved to within arm's reach. Braving it, Albus reached out and took Rhea's hands in his. He studied her face, suddenly keenly aware of the passage of time. The carefree young princess he had known was gone. She was still attractive, with a clear, healthy complexion, but her bright eyes had fine lines at the corners and her dark brown hair, while still long and full, was interspersed by silver streaks at her temples.

He swallowed the emotion that rose in him: the grief of how she had passed so many years in isolation, and his own self-loathing from not having rescued her sooner. He had failed in his duty as a Julii. Not only had he failed to protect King Numitor, he had abandoned the king's daughter. He kissed the back of her hands.

"Lela did not die in vain," he said. "She saved your children. They live, Rhea." He let go of her hands and stepped to the side, gesturing to Cinus and Caelus. "These are your sons."

Rhea's eyes narrowed as the remaining man removed the hood of his cloak. She scrutinized his young face, comparing it with the face of the other young man. *They are the same...they are twins.*

A memory returned—the image of her two sleeping infants, their faces still wrinkled from birth, as she frantically placed them in the laundry basket. She remembered the panic and desperation, and the despair of having her newborns torn from her breast. She recalled the years—so many of them now—spent in agonizing speculation after abandoning them to their fate. Had they lived? What had befallen them? Were they suffering? She felt it all anew, and her heart began to race. The current of dizziness grew disabling and expanded into nausea, and she put her hands to her stomach.

Albus took her by the elbow and guided her back to the bench. "Sit down, Princess," he said. As she did, he sat beside her. The two younger men knelt on the ground before her, their questioning eyes wild with amazement. Albus spoke again. "Your sons survived, Rhea," he said. "They were found by a shepherd. He and his wife raised them as their own." He cupped Caelus's chin and lifted his face toward his mother. "You see? They are grown now. They have come for you."

Rhea turned quickly, clutching Albus's tunica. "Nemeois! Does he—"

"He doesn't know we're alive," said one of the twins.

Rhea studied the young man who had spoken. Her *son*. He was beautiful. It was no wonder that in her confusion she had mistaken him for Egestus—the black hair and eyes, and the fine lines of worry in his brow. He and his brother were their father in every way.

Slowly, the shock began to dissipate. From some deep part of her, something else stirred—joy. It swelled and spread throughout her body, rushing through her veins, and warming her face and limbs. Her eyes welled with tears.

She slid forward off the bench, falling into her sons, clutching their hair and faces, pushing her own face into their chests and pulling them closer to her body. She could hear someone weeping loudly and realized it was her. Their arms tightened around her—not the pink little arms she remembered, but the strong, muscled arms of grown men—and their deep voices whispered in her ear.

"It is all right, Mother."

※ ※ ※

Albus had hoped to be in and out of the necropolis quickly, with no more conflict or commotion than was absolutely necessary. The small army that he had amassed for the royal twins—capable soldiers who had that morning sworn a blood oath to the Silvian brothers—had quickly and efficiently ambushed the men who guarded the city of the dead, thankfully without killing any of them.

Still, the longer they remained in the necropolis, the more likely it was that something would go wrong. A fresh shift of guards might arrive from the city at any time, or even some unexpected scout of Nemeois's. Yet as he watched the reunion between mother and sons, he could not bring himself to rush the process. The twins needed answers, and by right of birth they were owed those answers. Albus knew which answer they desired most. It was the same answer that he, Proculus, and the fifty-some soldiers whose curiosity had compelled them to enter the necropolis, all wanted to hear.

Which of the two princes was the rightful king?

Rhea had recovered somewhat from the initial shock of the reunion and was again sitting on the stone bench, admiring the twins and growing accustomed to their faces, to the way they spoke and moved. She licked her lips, realizing how dry her mouth had become.

Cinus turned to his brother. "Get her some water, Caelus."

Rhea pulled her head back, surprised. "Caelus? That is not your name." She smiled tenderly. "Of course. You don't know your names." She stroked his hair. "Caelus," she mused. "The sky. Did the shepherd name you for your eyes?"

"Yes," replied Caelus. "He told me it was the only way he could tell us apart at first. My eyes were blue"—he pointed his chin at his brother—"his were gray, so he was named Cinus. For ash."

"I remember," said Rhea. "It was how I distinguished you as well." She spoke seriously to Caelus. "Your true name is Romulus." Turning to Cinus, she said, "and you are Remus." Speaking to both, she added, "You are princes of Alba Longa. From this moment on, you will be addressed, and address each other, by your true names."

Hearing the dryness in her throat, Caelus—now Romulus— noticed Albus standing at his side, holding a cup of water. He took it from him and passed it to Rhea. As she drank, Cinus— now Remus—opened the leather sack he had been carrying since they arrived, reaching inside to withdraw the gold oak-leaf crown.

"Yes," said Rhea. "I remember that, too. I placed it in the basket. It was to serve as proof of your lineage to the Etruscan king."

"Which of us is to wear it?" asked Remus.

Rhea took it from him, exploring it in her hand. "The man who presently sits on the throne of Alba Longa, who wears a crown just like this one, is a seditious imposter and a murderer." She looked at the twins. "Since the time of Ascanius and his son Silvius, the law of primogeniture has determined the right of succession of Silvian kings. Such kingship is the greatest of responsibilities and demands the greatest of character." Her gaze shifted to Romulus. "Romulus Silvius, you were the firstborn. You are the rightful king of Alba Longa."

She placed the crown on Romulus's head. Blinking in disbelief, Romulus reached up to feel the sharp edges of the gold oak leaves. Not knowing what to do, he looked up at Rhea, waiting for direction.

"Rise," she said.

As he did, those around him knelt. The noble father and son of the Julii, Albus and Proculus, took the knee before him. So too did every one of the armed soldiers gathered expectantly before him. *His* army. It was inconceivable that such greatness, such power and potential, were suddenly his to command. As he surveyed the formidable soldiers who had sworn allegiance to him, he paused at a face that struck him as familiar. It took a moment, but then he placed it. It was the same Alban soldier who had arrested Cinus—Remus—at their farm. Only days ago, Romulus had trembled at the authority invested in this man. Now, that authority was his. The man nodded his head in respect, and Romulus nodded back.

His eyes moved to his brother. Remus was standing, crestfallen, beside him.

"Prince Remus," he said. "My brother, together we will take what belongs to us, as sons of the Silvii."

The lofty words sounded fraudulent to his ear, and Romulus knew they would sound farcical to his brother as well—someone who knew him so well, who had seen him at his weakest, at his most banal and unremarkable. Yet he could not squander the moment. He could not let the first words he spoke as the rightful king be faltering or feeble. If he wished to claim what was his—and he did—he would have to master his self-doubt and act the part until he truly became it. That would begin by asserting his dominance over Remus.

Remus regarded his brother. Romulus could see the disappointment in his posture, the conflation of pain and pride in his expression. Finally, his brother nodded in acceptance. Exploiting the moment, Proculus shouldered Remus aside and gripped Romulus's hand, thrusting it high into the air.

"*Ave, Romulus Rex!*" he shouted. Hail, King Romulus!

Albus and the company of soldiers rose with clamorous shouts of acclaim, the soldiers banging the handles of their daggers against their shields and calling out their new master's name. "King Romulus! King Romulus!"

Albus let them indulge for several long moments, then raised his arms for calm and took two officers aside. It was time for strategy now. Before they could put Romulus on the throne, they had to get Nemeois off of it…in pieces, if that's what it took.

"Mother, it is time to leave," said Remus. He glanced around, noticing the evidence of her simple, solitary life. The washbasins and clothesline, the bowls of fresh-picked fruit and the jugs of spring water. It was a small island of domesticity surrounded by an ocean of elaborate statuary and ornate royal tombs. "Is there anything you need to bring with you?"

"I must take embers from the sacred fire," she said, "and Tumulto. He is too old to find food for himself." Before the twins could ask who or what Tumulto was, she pointed to the tomb next to hers. "Come, I'll show you the tomb of your father, first."

The twins met eyes in anticipation. Finally, they would know everything—the identity of their father, the great man who had been deemed noble enough to beget them with their Silvian mother. That was the last piece of the whole: once they knew that, they could truly know themselves. They followed Rhea to the entrance of the tomb, the bronze-inlaid wooden door of which was already partly open. They stayed on her heels, and the three of them entered together. The brothers' skin prickled from the cooler air harbored within the stone walls, and their mouths fell agape at the unexpected size of the multi-room structure, the sumptuous decor.

"This is Egestus's tomb," said Rhea. "Your father's ashes are here."

Puzzlement, a silence, followed.

Romulus inquired gently: "Our father's ashes are in Prince Egestus's tomb?"

"You carry the pure blood of the Silvii," said Rhea. "Egestus Silvius sired you." She held out her hand to the statue of Mars. "You were born here, at the feet of the war god. Look at his face—you will see your father. You are sons of Mars."

Another silence.

Remus gawked at his brother. The thought of their mother and her own brother laying together... the idea that they had been conceived like *that*...no, such a dignified princess would never have done that. He leaned closer to Romulus and whispered in his ear. "She is mad."

"She is not mad," replied Romulus. "She is confused. Let's leave you here alone for years and see how you fare."

"Princess," said Remus, and then correcting himself, "Mother, please think. Who is our father? What is his name?"

Rhea turned abruptly to face him. She placed her hand on the prince's sarcophagus. "The crown prince Egestus Silvius was your father." Seeing the expression of disgust that flashed across his face, her tone grew chastening. "And you will be thankful for it," she said.

Romulus adopted a soothing smile. "Mother, may we have a moment alone in our father's tomb?" he asked. "We would like to honor him."

Rhea softened, returning his smile. She stepped past the twins, kissing each on the cheek as she did, and left them alone in the sepulcher.

When she was gone, Remus rested his palms on Egestus's stone coffer and hung his head. He chuckled, deflated. "It all makes sense now."

"What does?" Romulus asked.

"The fact that no one mentioned our father until now." He scoffed. "No wonder they avoided it." He stared at the sarcophagus. "Did Father—did *Faustulus*—tell you who he was?"

"No. Maybe he didn't know."

"Maybe not," said Remus, gesturing toward the half-open door, "but you can bet Albus and your friend Proculus knew. Did they say anything? They could have warned us."

"We never asked. And it was not their place to tell us."

Remus curled his fingers into fists and pressed his knuckles against the sarcophagus that held his father's—his uncle's—ashes. "Sons of Mars," he muttered. "We are sons of incest."

"We are sons of the Silvii," replied Romulus, "and pure blood ones, at that." He laid his own hands on Egestus's coffer, feeling the cool hardness of the *lapis albanus* against his palms. His voice was emphatic. Excited. "Don't you see what that means? There is no one closer to Ascanius, or to Aeneas himself, in all of Latium. There can be no challenge to our claim."

"To *your* claim, you mean."

"Yesterday at this hour, you were an eel-fishing peasant from the country," said Romulus. "Your eye was still swollen from being beaten half to death in a prison quarry. Today, you are a prince of the greatest city in Latium."

"And you are its king," mumbled Remus.

Romulus could hear the lingering note of spite in his brother's voice. A shout from beyond the tomb—Albus and Proculus were marshalling his army—drew his focus. "I am not king yet." He squeezed one of Remus's shoulders. "I can't do this without you. We are brothers. We are the same brothers who floated down the Tiber together in a laundry basket, who grew up together, who played with Cerva and honored the gods together. We are inseparable. The Fates cannot sink us, wolves cannot devour us, and that murderer who sits on the throne cannot keep us from our birthright."

"Perhaps you are meant to be a king," Remus said, his voice finally lightening. "You are good at giving speeches."

Romulus patted his brother's shoulder. He placed his hands back on the sarcophagus as his curious gaze moved over the colorful frescos on the tomb's walls, lively scenes that depicted their black-haired, bearded father feasting and hunting.

"What do you think he was like?" he asked.

"I think it's safe to say he was fairly serious about protecting his bloodline," Remus grinned. "*Our* bloodline. So yes, brother, I'm with you." They embraced. As they did, Remus looked over Romulus's shoulder at Egestus's sarcophagus, willing himself to feel something. But father or not, his feelings for the man were as indifferent as the stone that encased his ashes. *Ashes*. He pulled away. "I have not yet paid my respects to Mother," he said.

"Mother waits for us outside this tomb," replied Romulus, "but there will be time to honor Larentia. I promise."

Remus reddened. "Larentia? Are you serious? That is how you will refer to the woman who raised us?"

"Yes," said Romulus. "As should you."

"She was our mother."

"Rhea Silvia is our mother."

"Tell me you still have feelings for her."

"Of course, brother. But Larentia kept our identity from us. So did Faustulus. Had Vibio not stoked your anger, we might never have learned who we really are. When you think about it, Vibio did us a favor. Without him, we'd still be lambing in the barn, miserable, without the hope of anything greater."

Remus took a last look at the frescos. "Maybe," he said.

Strained but united in purpose, the brothers left their father's tomb together, stepping into the full sunlight to find Proculus already leading a group of soldiers out of the necropolis. Albus was still strategizing with two officers. When he saw the twins, he pointed in the direction of the shrine to Vesta. Rhea was there, saying a prayer over the sacred fire. Her sons approached her.

"Can we help you with anything?" asked Remus.

"I've made a sarcina," she said, holding what looked to be a bundle wrapped in tree bark. "Vesta's flame sleeps inside, waiting to be woken. You will learn to make one as well. It is a skill that all of the Silvii must learn. It is how your ancestors, Aeneas and Ascanius, carried the fire of Troy to the Lavinian shores, and then to Alba Longa."

The fire of Troy. The crown on Romulus's head at once felt heavier. And misplaced. The city of Troy. Aeneas and Ascanius. Those names were things of history and legend. Hearing the princess say them with such familiarity, such authority, made him feel even more like a royal pretender.

"We will learn, Mother," he assured her, "but right now, we need to go."

Rhea turned to him. "I cannot find Tumulto," she said. "He was probably frightened away by all the people and took to the trees."

"We will come back for him," replied Romulus. "In a day or two, at most, I promise. But we cannot stay here any longer. It is too dangerous."

She clutched the sarcina, her fingers trembling. "I leave breadcrumbs every morning for the swallows. What if they come tomorrow and there is none to be had? Tumulto has food squirreled away, but who knows about the swallows?"

Remus suppressed a sigh of impatience, but Romulus understood. She was afraid. Like him, she had grown accustomed to living in a small, quiet world—but now, without warning, the boundaries had been pushed back, and that world was about to get very big and very loud.

"Where do you leave the food?" he asked her. Rhea pointed to the spot, and Romulus called out to a passing soldier. "You," he said. "Find some breadcrumbs and leave them over there."

"Yes, Your Highness."

Your Highness. Romulus tried not to react to the title as the soldier quickly ran off to complete his task.

But Remus couldn't help it. A soft snigger sounded from his nose. "Your first command as king," he said. "To feed the birds."

Rhea put her hand on Remus's arm. She didn't know either of her sons, but she did know that both of them would need to make peace with the abrupt changes in their lives. "It is a good start, Prince Remus," she said. "A wise king provides for even the smallest souls under his command."

CHAPTER XVIII

Cloelia despised the smell of horses. It was why, whenever she was obligated to travel anywhere by carriage, she insisted the beasts be bathed shortly before they left. It didn't make much difference in the end since their unbearable odor returned within a stadion anyway, but at least it made for a tolerable departure. Still, her preference was to avoid travel whenever possible. Nemeois knew as much, so had left for the annual conference at the Ferentine Spring without her. He had also left their son, Amatus, at home after the crown prince had complained of stomach pains. It was an affliction he had recovered from almost immediately after his father's royal procession had cleared the palace gates.

His act had not fooled either of his parents. They could not be angry with him, though. Amatus had attended the conference every year since he was five years old, so missing one—especially this one, where nothing important was on the agenda—was forgivable. And anyway, who could deny the crown prince anything? There was not a soul in Latium who disliked the boy. His parents, especially, fawned over him. They hated each other, but they cherished their children. In fact, that shared affection was the only thing that had kept them from murdering each other.

It was also the only thing that could draw Queen Cloelia into the stables that she so reviled. Even though the slaves were drenched in sweat from mucking out the stalls and scrubbing everything in sight in anticipation of her arrival, she nonetheless turned up her nose and stepped disapprovingly past unavoidably fresh piles of manure as Amatus called her deeper into the large, oblong structure. She sneezed with every third step.

"Look, Mother," he said, pointing into a stall where a spotted newborn foal was trying to stand on gangly legs, its mother attentively licking its face. "Sterope just foaled! It's a colt. Isn't he remarkable?"

Despite the stench around her, Cloelia smiled. *Now I understand why you played sick*, she thought. "As you say," she agreed. "He is remarkable. Have you named him yet?" she asked, pinching her nose and forcing herself to feign interest in her son's passion.

"Not yet," he said. "I will consult with the priests of Neptune, first. The name must be auspicious."

"That is wise," said an approaching voice. "A name is a powerful thing."

Amatus greeted his friend Proculus Julius with a friendly slap on the shoulder. "The foal no sooner saw the light than he was trying to stand," he boasted, his attention still riveted on the baby animal. "And now look—he is already nursing."

"He is an exceptional specimen," flattered Proculus. He turned to Cloelia. "Your Highness, I hope you are well this morning."

"I am, Proculus," she replied. *I am even better now that you're here…now I can go back inside.* "I will leave you to admire the newcomer with my son," she said, already halfway out of the stable.

As she exited the building, she noted that Proculus had brought a number of men with him: they stood around expectantly outside the stable, waiting for their master. No doubt, Albus was sending his son on some mission or another.

Inside the stable, Amatus leaned against the stall door and clucked his tongue. "Look at that, Proculus! Have you ever seen a newborn foal so stable on its feet? It is his breeding, of course."

Proculus glanced around, speaking casually. "Tell me, where is Princess Amata this morning? Does she not care to see the foal?"

"She went to Marino with Father. She is to tend the sacred fire during the conference."

"Very good," said Proculus. "I am surprised you didn't go to the conference as well."

"I could say the same of you," replied Amatus. "It seems like we are both shirking our duties." He shrugged. "But I don't feel too guilty. I have a whole lifetime of duty ahead of me. What difference can one day make?"

Proculus smiled at his friend, but kept his thoughts to himself.

❋ ❋ ❋

The open-air meeting space located adjacent to the Temple of Concord in Marino was an ideal setting for Latium's annual political assembly, with two imposing features that fronted each other with near equal weight. The first was the huge theater-like block of thirty semicircular rows of stone seats upon which sat the leaders of Latium's most important cities. The second was the low dais that faced the assembly, upon which stood only a single seat, but that the throne.

King Nemeois reclined impatiently on that throne, watching the other leaders of Latium chatter amongst themselves while they all waited for the priests to enter and call out the rites that would bless the annual conference. Then, finally, they could get to business.

Nemeois glanced at the water clock that sat on a nearby pedestal, feeling his impatience morph to irritation at the vessel's level—in typical fashion, the priests were late. It irked him, but the influential men who filled the seats—leaders of Lavinium, Laurentum, Satricum, Ardea, and Bovillae, among others—didn't mind the delay. Although their cities were relatively close to one another, they typically only met once a year, and so had much gossiping, bragging and self-congratulating to catch up on.

The king leaned back as his young daughter, Amata, approached the bronze firebowl that sat upon the altar to Concordia before him. She placed four thick branches of oak into the sacred flames in a criss-cross pattern, and glanced toward the open double-doors that led into the temple's cella. Like everyone else, she was waiting for the priests to emerge. Until they arrived with the sacrificial offering, it was her duty to keep the fire burning.

As Nemeois watched her, her gaze still fixed on the double-doors behind him, he noticed a change—her expression seemed to transition from impatient to confused, from confused to startled. He sat forward and twisted around to look behind his throne, just as a chorus of loud voices sounded from within the temple's cella. He stood quickly, irritated by the commotion.

"Jove's patience," he said, arms out in exasperation. "Where in Hades are the bloody priests? We've been waiting since—"

A figure emerged from the temple's cella, crossing the threshold of the double-doors to enter the theater-like conference space. Nemeois dropped his arms to his sides. His breath left his body. He mouthed a single, almost inaudible, word.

"*Impossible.*"

As he stood, mouth hanging open, the hum of casual chatter around him dissipated into a stunned, disbelieving silence. One by one, every man present rose to his feet, as if standing would somehow help him trust his eyes.

She was older, but there was no mistaking her. It was Princess Rhea Silvia, dressed in a fine white *stola* and head veil, draped in shimmering gold jewelry, and carrying a sarcina.

Behind her were two young men. Twins. One of them wore the gold crown of oak leaves and a rich white tunica with an embroidered gold hem and belt: the gilded hilt of a sheathed dagger sat at his hip. The other was dressed in armor, his dagger drawn. Their similarity to Prince Egestus—who had died in this very spot over eighteen years earlier—struck each man present with the force of a physical blow.

It struck none of them harder than Nemeois himself. His lips quivering with unspoken thoughts, he rose from his throne and stared, amazed and aghast, at the trio, who now stood boldly in the center of the chamber. He stared at them as though they were apparitions, his mind assessing it all—the impossibility of it, how she had escaped, the inevitable identity of the two young men with her, what it all meant.

Finally, he recovered his wits enough to respond. "Guards!" he shouted.

"Your guards cannot hear you," said Albus Julius. Dressed in armor and accompanied by a dozen armed soldiers, the patriarch of the powerful Julii emerged from the double-doors to stand beside Rhea. His face curled into a snarl as he regarded Nemeois. "In fact, your guards can no longer hear anyone." Raising his chin, he turned to address the stricken gathering. "My friends," he said, "like many of you, I have spent too many years carrying the burden of my many shames. The shame of not bringing Prince Egestus's assassins to justice. The shame of King Numitor's death in exile. The shame of tolerating this man's false claim to the throne"—here, he pointed at Nemeois before again speaking to the gathering—"and especially the shame of my own inaction as Princess Rhea Silvia languished unseen in the city of the dead. Tell me, who among you has not looked into the innocent face of his daughter or granddaughter all these years, and not thought of the young princess we left for dead?"

Incredibly, the silence seemed to intensify, broken only by the whispered prayers of two old men from Lavinium.

Rhea moved closer to the altar, her eyes shifting to Amata. The young girl lowered her head in dread and withdrew into the shadows as Rhea replaced her before the sacred fire, the sun shining high overhead as if the gods were watching from the heavens. She placed the sarcina on the flames within the bronze bowl and faced the assembly.

"Revered fathers of Latium," she said, her voice confident and clear, "for over eighteen years, I have tended the *Iliacus ignis* in the necropolis. Today, with the blessing of Vesta, I deliver it to this assembly." Stepping back from the altar, she leveled a portentous gaze on Romulus as she spoke. "Revered fathers, by the authority of the laws of Latium, and by the will of the gods, I bring before you King Romulus Silvius, firstborn son of Prince Egestus Silvius, born in captivity, delivered to safety by the Silvian god of the great Tiber River, now here to claim his birthright—the throne of Alba Longa, and the command of all Latium." She moved her gaze to Remus. "I also bring before you Prince Remus Silvius, second in line, but no less to be feared and honored." Finally, Rhea's piercing eyes met Nemeois's. "The usurper will remove the crown from his head."

When Nemeois only blinked—Rhea could see his mind working—Albus stormed toward him. His nostrils flaring in anger, the Julian ripped the crown from Nemeois's head. "You're lucky I don't take your head off with it," he snarled. He voice rose for all to hear. "Now, traitor, kneel before your king."

Nemeois felt a line of perspiration form on his forehead, on the spot where the crown had sat only a moment earlier. His eyes darted from Albus to Rhea, before settling on Romulus. He looked at the young man in astonishment.

Romulus withdrew the blade at his side. "Kneel," he said. "Or I'll cut off your legs."

The order made something change within Nemeois. The stupor caused by the revelation—Rhea was *here*...her sons were *alive*—lifted, as contempt and self-preservation set in. After all his strategizing and efforts, he would not let this boy, this product of incest, order him to his knees.

Enraged, Nemeois called out to the gathering. "Will no one speak for your king?"

The silence remained unbroken. His heart racing, Nemeois looked into the faces of the revered fathers, desperate to see some sign of solidarity, some sign of disgust at the coup. All he saw, however, were expressions of awe, of wonder, as the gathered men gazed at Romulus as though he had descended from the clouds, god-like, to rule them all.

"Father?"

Nemeois heard Amata's voice behind him, soft and afraid. Instinctively, he turned to Rhea. The look in her eyes confirmed his worst thoughts—*Yes, I will have her killed where she stands if you do not kneel.* Trembling—his keen mind was now certain there was no other way—he knelt. The new king ascended the dais and turned to face the assembly.

"Revered fathers," Romulus called out, "I now rightfully claim the Silvian throne of Alba Longa, and dominion over all Latium, in the name of divine Aeneas, the founder Ascanius, and Father Mars."

Romulus sat on the throne, painfully aware of the palpable silence around him. Albus had told him to not react at the silence, but to remain steadfast: Nemeois had been complicit in the treason against Numitor, yes, but he had nonetheless managed Latium surprisingly well over the years—he was a better ruler than his father, Amulius, that much was certain—and his competence had earned him some respect.

Finally, the elderly ruler of Lavinium—one of the oldest and most respected cities in the Confederation—left his seat. He approached Rhea, stopping briefly to kiss her hand, before continuing to the dais. Without acknowledging Nemeois, who knelt beside the throne, he bowed deeply before the new king who sat upon it.

"My loyalty lies with the rightful Silvian king, young sir."

"And mine with you, honored father of Lavinium," replied Romulus.

The new king's chest was tight, his temples throbbed with stress, but he forced himself to speak the words just as his mother had instructed. Since her rescue, she had tutored him and Remus without rest, teaching them not only the history of the Silvii, but also the customs of Latium's institutions. That included helping Romulus to memorize the seating formality at the conference so that he could respectfully address each city ruler by name. His authoritative yet humble bearing had the desired effect. One by one, each of the revered fathers of Latium left their seats to bow before the king, swearing loyalty to him. Romulus greeted each man in turn, showing the same esteem for all, until only one remained.

The leader of Tusculum.

The years faded and the past rushed back to Rhea as she finally allowed herself to look at Mamilian. His size had always made him cut a threatening figure, and that had not changed as he neared her. She felt sickeningly self-conscious—how old must she seem to him now?—but then he looked at her, full of emotion, and she saw the age in his face, too. He walked past her without speaking to bow before Romulus.

"My loyalty lies with the rightful Silvian king."

"And mine with you, honored father of Tusculum."

With King Romulus's reign now secured, the high drama began to settle. Albus gripped Nemeois by the arm—he was still on his knees beside the throne—and pulled him to his feet. As he dragged the stupefied man off the dais, Albus felt a tug on the sleeve of his tunica and looked down to see Amata clinging to it.

"Master Albus, do not hurt my father!"

Albus's shoulders rose in anger, and he growled at one of his men. "Take her back to the palace!"

"Please, sir," pleaded Amata. "What will happen to my father?"

Standing nose to nose with Nemeois, Albus's expression again shifted into a snarl. Any pity he felt for the young girl was blighted by his hatred of Nemeois...and perhaps his hatred for himself. He should have done this eighteen years ago. "The traitor will be taken to the city of the dead and shut inside his tomb." He moved even closer to Nemeois, his snarl lifting into a smile. "I will seal the door myself."

"Albus," whispered Nemeois, "my children...they grew up with your children. Show them mercy." When Albus did not respond, he faced Rhea, his voice beseeching. "Cousin, my children are innocent—"

"Your children be damned, Nemeois." She spat on the ground at his feet. "And you with them."

❉ ❉ ❉

Of the many high-profile people and processions that left the conference near the Ferentine Spring that evening, the two processions that departed under military escort were the most interesting. The starker of the two was headed to the necropolis where the deposed king Nemeois was to be entombed alive, without food or water, in his sepulcher.

The other and far more impressive procession was headed to the royal palace of the Silvii, where the new king, along with his brother and mother, would take up residence.

Leading the procession, King Romulus and Prince Remus rode on horseback and in full regalia, surrounded by mounted Alban soldiers. Behind them, Princess Rhea Silvia traveled in a horse-drawn carriage, tossing pieces of silver and bronze outside the vehicle to the awestruck onlookers who lined the road to honor their long-lost princess and her remarkable royal sons. The astonishing news of the rightful king's return and his dramatic coronation at the conference in Marino had already spread throughout Alba Longa, and thanks to the messengers that Albus had dispatched throughout Latium, the incredible news continued to spread.

All day long, Rhea had remained strong, strong almost to the point of being emotionless. She knew it was the only way she could get through the coup at Marino without flying into a hateful rage at the sight of Nemeois, or lashing out at the revered fathers for leaving her—as Albus had said—for dead in the necropolis all those years ago.

But now, as her carriage passed through the gates of the palace and the familiar squeak of the hinges sounded in her ears—how could it sound the same after so many years?—a rush of nostalgia threatened to sap the last of her strength. She remembered each stone in the pathway, each vine that wrapped around the columns in the garden, each fountain that decorated the estate.

Even as the carriage stopped before the entrance, she fully expected to see Egestus and her father emerge from within to greet her, Egestus's brow scrunched in thought, rubbing his black beard and then finally breaking into a smile. How she longed to hear his voice again, to sit with him at supper and poke fun at their father...but both of them, now dead.

Instead, it was Proculus who greeted the procession at the well-guarded palace, six muscly soldiers on his heels. He bowed first to Romulus and then to Remus as they dismounted, then waited for Rhea to step out of her carriage before bowing to her as well.

"The palace is secure," he said, leading the three of them inside as he spoke, their way lit by rows of burning torches. "Lady Cloelia and her son Amatus are being held in their rooms. Her daughter Amata just arrived. They're bringing her through the slaves' entrance. She'll be kept under guard in her room as well."

I should have them all gutted right now, thought Rhea. But no, their punishment was not up to her. It was up to Romulus. "That is good," she said to Proculus. "The king will decide their fate tomorrow. He and the prince will rest tonight."

She turned to her sons to find them agape at the grandeur of the palace. Although they had grown somewhat accustomed to luxury at the home of the Julii, the home of the Silvii was even more expansive, more extravagant. The painted terracotta statues of the gods that lined the wide central corridor, the high ceilings, the expensive furnishings...it was all overwhelming. And it was all *theirs*.

On top of that, the spectacular history of their lineage was evident at every turn. Busts of the Silvian kings sat on marble ledges. Gold crowns of oak hung from the walls. Colorful frescos depicted historical scenes including Aeneas and Ascanius fleeing burning Troy and, later, Ascanius founding Alba Longa, pointing to the top of Mount Albanus where the first shrines to the gods would be built.

As Rhea watched her sons marvel at their surroundings, a sudden, heavy blanket of fatigue enveloped her body. She was home after all these years, and she wanted nothing more than to sleep in a real bed, her own bed, in her own bedchamber. She glanced down the corridor for a slave, but saw only troops of soldiers.

"Where are the servants?" she asked Proculus.

"Princess," he replied, "I have ordered the staff to remain in their quarters for now. There was only minor resistance as our soldiers took custody of Lady Cloelia and Prince Amatus"—he corrected himself—"I mean, the *former* prince Amatus, but nonetheless, I thought it was prudent to keep them sequestered until we can weed out any troublemakers. Meanwhile, I've brought in some essential slaves, cooks and so forth, from my father's home."

Rhea smiled tiredly at the competent young man. "You do your family proud," she said. Stepping toward Romulus and Remus, she kissed both of them on the cheek. "Proculus knows the palace," she said. "He will be your guide. I am going to bed. It's late and I'm exhausted."

"Should one of us go with you?" Remus asked.

"No, I remember the way," she said lightly, then sighed, "I am home." She touched his face. "As are you, son."

The twins watched their mother walk down the torchlit corridor, soldiers bowing deeply to her as she passed. When she was out of sight, Remus put his hands on his stomach. "I'm starving," he said.

Proculus signaled a soldier. "Show Prince Remus to his quarters," he said, "and have a slave from the kitchen bring him something to eat."

"Make sure it's a pretty slave," grinned Remus.

"As you wish, Your Highness," said the soldier.

Remus left with the soldier, leaving Romulus and Proculus alone. The king leaned against the wall and exhaled. "I am in a dream," he said. "I am asleep in my cot and any moment I'll wake up, walk through the wet grasses to the Tiber, and pull my eel trap out of the water."

Proculus leaned against the wall beside him. "There's no waking from this dream," he said. Curious at how it all unfolded in Marino, he asked, "Did Nemeois resist?"

"He snapped like a dry twig," said Romulus. "I would've expected more from him."

"What about the revered fathers? How did they react?"

"With loyal words and skeptical eyes." Romulus rubbed his chin in thought, feeling the new stubble of a thickening beard. "They are giving me time to prove myself." He rested the back of his head against the wall. "I could never have gotten this far without you and your father," he said. "I owe you everything."

"Come on," said Proculus. "I'll show you to the king's quarters."

They roamed down one wing of the palace and then another, soldiers bowing to Romulus along the way. "How do you know the palace so well?" asked Romulus.

"I've been running up and down these halls since I was a child," replied Proculus. "I grew up with Amatus."

Romulus stopped walking and faced Proculus. "He is your friend?"

"He is my closest friend," said Proculus, "but you are my king."

Finally, they arrived at the king's private wing. The mosaic on the floor transitioned to soft carpet as they strode toward the king's sitting room, flames snapping in the fireplace. Romulus slowed his step as he noticed a massive wall tapestry of the famed white sow and her litter of thirty piglets. His mother had told him the history: the animal had appeared to Aeneas in a dream, leading him to the spot where he would found the city of Lavinium and decreeing that thirty years later his son, Ascanius, would found Alba Longa, so named in the sow's honor. A large carved mahogany desk stood in front of the tapestry. Romulus hesitated—it was late, he should get some sleep—but then changed his mind and sat at the desk.

Proculus looked at him quizzically. "Can I get you anything?"

"Yes," said Romulus. "The royal treasurer. I would like an accounting of my assets."

"Right now? Would you not prefer to rest and speak with him in the morning?"

"No. Now. Also, send for your father. At the conference, I heard some of the revered fathers talking about a dispute with the Volsci and the Aequi. I need to understand this."

"I will summon them immediately," said Proculus.

"And the soldiers you have stationed in the palace…I'd like to speak with the officers."

"Of course. Is that all?"

"Yes," said Romulus. "For now."

As he watched Proculus leave, dispensing orders before he had even cleared the sitting room, Romulus remembered the day he had first ridden Xanthos into Alba Longa. He had looked up at the sprawling grounds of the royal estate and wondered how a king spent his time.

Definitely not sleeping, he thought to himself.

CHAPTER XIX

Rhea's bedchamber was surprisingly unchanged. The drapes and linens were different, but the fireplace and furniture were mostly the same. As she stood on the balcony, resting her arms on the balustrade and gazing off into the verdant hills, she could almost hear Lela and Thalia chattering in the room behind her, bickering over which dress they would adorn her in that day.

Thalia had been like a mother to her, but it was Lela who Rhea missed most keenly. Next to Egestus and her father, Lela was the person who Rhea had loved most in the world. It was heart wrenching to know that she had died in agony, without ever knowing that her actions had saved the lives of the twins. Rhea was pondering a way to honor her—a statue on the citadel perhaps—when a female servant, no doubt vetted by Proculus himself, entered the room.

"Princess," she said. "They are ready for you now."

Rhea left her bedchamber and walked down the wide corridor, smiling at the soldiers and giving silent thanks to the statues of the gods she passed, delighting in the sense that the palace was slowly coming back to life. She recognized the aged faces of the few slaves who had been permitted to once again move freely about the palace, and she had to stop more than once to console a weeping laundress or cook who was overcome with joy at seeing her again.

Reaching the royal stateroom, two young soldiers opened the doors for her and she strode inside, forcing herself to remain composed at the sight of the three figures that knelt, wrists bound behind their backs, in the center of the room—Cloelia and her two children, both siblings gagged.

Romulus and Remus, along with Albus, Proculus, and a number of soldiers, were already in the stateroom. Romulus was sitting on the raised platform at the far end of the room, on the grand high-backed throne of the king. He looked as though he hadn't slept. Remus and the rest of the men present stood around the subjugated former queen and her offspring, all brandishing daggers, their lips curled in derision.

Rhea continued to the front of the chamber, finally turning to face Cloelia. At first, Cloelia seemed perplexed at the sight of the woman standing before her, but then she began to blink rapidly, the color leaving her face. She muttered something under her breath.

"Hello, Lady Cloelia," said Rhea. Her eyes moved to Cloelia's children—the bound siblings, Amatus and Amata—and she smiled. "What beautiful children you have. How fortunate that Juno blessed them with your looks and not Nemeois's."

Finding her voice, although a trembling one, Cloelia spoke. "I had no choice," she said. "It was Nemeois's doing. All of it. He is to blame!"

"That is what I've always admired about you, Cloelia," said Rhea. "Your loyalty to your husbands."

Cloelia shifted uncomfortably, struggling against the ties around her wrists. Realizing that mercy would not come, and betting that belligerence would serve her better than begging, she glared at Rhea. "My son is the crown prince of Alba Longa," she said. "He has many followers, everyone loves him."

"What son has many followers?" asked Remus, moving to stand behind Amatus and looking down at him. "This one?"

Romulus sprang to his feet. "Remus, no!"

But it was too late. Even as Romulus called out, Remus gripped Amatus's head from above and swiped the blade of his dagger across his throat.

The young Amata released a muffled shriek of horror from behind the gag in her mouth, while Cloelia screamed, clambering on her knees toward her son and slipping on the blood that was already covering the floor and spurting out of his neck in thick gushes of red. Remus released Amatus, giving his body a spiteful shove that sent it collapsing to the floor. Cloelia let out a guttural cry of agony and fell to the floor beside her son, hands still bound, staring into his dying eyes and sobbing his name.

"Amatus! Amatus!"

The sight of Amatus's open throat and dying expression, the shock and despair of Cloelia's reaction, and her frantic, futile attempts to help him, transported Rhea back to the moment Nemeois had opened Egestus's throat before the assembly at the Temple of Concord. Even through the years of her hardened hatred of Cloelia, she felt some pity. For a mother to see such a thing...she stepped back, numb, as the spreading blood reached her sandals.

Suppressing his anger at his brother's impulsiveness, Romulus made a quick study of the room. His mother looked surprised, but Albus and the soldiers seemed unmoved. Only Proculus had turned away. Romulus felt another rise of ire. He had not yet decided on the fate of Cloelia's children, particularly Amatus. The young man was a Silvii and kin, but his line of descent made him no direct threat to Romulus's claim. Plus, his lifelong friendship with Proculus could not be ignored.

With Cloelia's screams and sobs still echoing throughout the hall, Remus moved closer to Amata. Panicking, Cloelia flopped onto her stomach, fish-like. Using her legs to push herself up, she slid on her knees over the bloody floor to reach her daughter's side.

"No, I beg you, spare her!"

Rhea moved beside Remus and put her hand on his arm. She spoke to Amata. "Are you not the girl who tended the *Iliacus ignis* at the conference?"

The young girl's eyes, streaming with tears, moved from her dead brother to Rhea. She nodded.

Rhea addressed her son on the throne. "This girl has honored the Trojan fire."

Romulus spoke levelly. "She can go to the temple," he ordered. "She can live and serve the goddess there." *It is better than the necropolis*, he thought bitterly. "Take her now."

Remus looked as though he was about to protest, but before he could, Proculus grabbed Amata's arm and pulled her to her feet. He dragged her toward two soldiers.

"You have your orders," he said to them.

Without giving the mother and daughter a moment to speak or say goodbye, the soldiers ushered the weeping girl away. When the sound of her muffled cries had receded, Rhea stood before Cloelia.

It was Cloelia who had conspired with Nemeois in every way. Her brazen lies and treason had not only engendered the seditious murder of Egestus, they had facilitated the overthrow of their father and led to his lonely death in exile. It was Cloelia whose treachery was at the heart of Rhea's own years of imprisonment, and who had ordered guards to follow Lela out of the necropolis, thus leading to her friend's agonizing death. It was Cloelia who had separated Rhea from her children, and who had tried to kill them, thus ending the royal line of the Silvian dynasty that stretched back to Ascanius himself. Rhea's hatred for the woman at her feet returned in full force, heating her blood and making her hands clench into fists.

Romulus could see it. "Kill her," he said to Remus.

Remus gripped the hair on the top of Cloelia's head and yanked it back, bringing the blade to her throat.

"Wait!" shouted Cloelia, "Rhea, your father, he would not want—"

"Do not speak to me of my father!" Rhea shouted back. "Or I'll cut out your tongue!"

"I can do better than that," said Remus. He took three incensed strides to the massive fireplace, plucked out a hot coal with a bare hand, and marched back to Cloelia, snapping her head back and stuffing the burning coal into her mouth. She screeched in protest and frantically tried to shake her head to eject it, but Remus hooked an arm around her head to hold it steady, pressing his hand firmly against her mouth and nose.

Rhea watched Cloelia writhe in an agony she could not imagine: the pain of the hot coal scorching the inside of her mouth and throat, combined with the panic of suffocation. As the deposed queen succumbed to death, her muffled groans of anguish and resistance faded, and her body twitched grotesquely. Remus let her body slump to the floor. Her lifeless arms landed in her son's blood with a soft splash. This time, Rhea felt no pity. Was this not the fate that Cloelia had wanted for her?

Romulus signaled two guards. They approached Cloelia's body and hauled it out of the room with no more ceremony than if they were lugging a peasant's corpse out of a ditch. As a traitor, she would be denied a proper interment. She would never meet the gods, never see her loved ones in the afterlife. Instead, her body would be strung up from an oak tree on the citadel and left there until the birds picked it clean. After that, her bones would be crushed into meal and fed to the sacrificial pigs. It was a well-deserved end.

Yet as far as Romulus could tell, the former prince Amatus had not deserved his death. The best Romulus could do now was ensure the young man received a dignified inurnment.

"Proculus," he said. "You may take the former's prince's body to the priests to perform the rites." Romulus chose his words. "Your loyalty to me has caused you injury. I shall not forget it."

Proculus bent at the waist. "Thank you, Your Highness," he replied.

As the soldiers carried the second corpse out of the stateroom,

Rhea stared at the liquid carpet of blood left in the center of the chamber. Almost immediately, the men behind her began to discuss the machinery of the state: the treasury, the military, the city's infrastructure and Latium's perpetual cycle of political skirmishes and power plays. She turned and exited the royal hall.

She walked along the statuary, staring absently out the windows into the courtyard. She had dreamed of this for years. She had fantasized about seeing Cloelia suffer, watching her die, and dishonoring her body in death. Yet now, despite those hateful fantasies coming to fruition, she did not feel a sense of resolution. The vengeance had been somehow unsatisfactory, oddly anticlimactic.

Something just wasn't right.

As the day wore on, the feeling of unease, of nagging nonresolution, persisted.

Rhea tried to ignore it. She ate breakfast in the dining room and then took a bath—it had been ages since she had soaked in warm water—and allowed the slaves and servants to spoil her with every luxury, every indulgence that she, or they, could think of. She received visitors, but avoided her sons and their Julian advisers, not because she didn't want to see them, but because she didn't want to intrude on the brothers' fledgling authority.

She thought about riding to the necropolis to collect Tumulto, but she wasn't ready to return there quite yet. Anyway, the soldiers who had taken Nemeois to his tomb had reported back that the princess's pet was alive and well, and as mischievous as ever. When he wasn't knocking pinecones onto their heads from above, he was stealing food from their lunch sacks. The new guards stationed at the necropolis had renamed him Chaos and had quickly adopted him as their own. She did not need to worry.

Instead, she took a short trip to the citadel to pray at the Shrine of Vesta. Upon her return home, she decided that a shrine to the goddess should be constructed in the palace courtyard, and so spent the rest of the afternoon consulting the senior Vestal sacerdotes on its design. After that, she hosted a fine supper for them and a number of other *Virgines Vestales Albanae*—important priestesses of the Vestal order in Alba Longa. During her years of captivity, they had used their influence to have extra food and comforts delivered to her, and she wanted to thank them.

It was just after nightfall when Rhea took to her bed. That was earlier than usual, but she was tired. Nonetheless, she lay restlessly, staring up at the shadows on the ceiling, moving black shapes cast by the strong flames of the oil lamps. The inner voice of misgiving that had whispered to her all day had now reached a crescendo. But why?

Nemeois was securely imprisoned—interred was more like it—and Cloelia and her imposter prince of a son were dead. The young Amata was at the temple: the girl was apparently well-liked by everyone, and Rhea was content that she had suggested mercy. Romulus's restraint with respect to the girl had reassured the important families of Alba Longa that their new young king was learning when to strike and when to spare.

Everything was going as well, even better, than Rhea and her sons could have hoped. The twins were beginning to find confidence in their birthright and identities. Via messengers, they had even convinced their shepherd-father to come to Alba Longa, which he would soon do, so that Rhea and the city could reward the humble herdsman for his role in the princes' survival.

But still, Rhea was vexed by the sense that something was wrong. She felt like she had…*missed* something. She tossed and turned in her bed, kicking off the covers in frustration, as her thoughts lightly touched on a string of memories, skipping along, like the little stones she and Nemeois used to skip across the surface of the lake when they were young.

Nemeois. She had grown up with him. They had taken their studies together, played hide and seek together in the palace, challenged each other, teased and supported each other. Her cousin had always had a natural gift for strategy, and she had learned how his mind worked. His betrayal of her and Egestus in

Marino had at the time been shocking, but in retrospect, it was utterly predictable.

Her thoughts skipped to her father's death in exile, and she realized that she did not know the location of his banishment. Nemeois's talent for strategy was accompanied, perhaps inevitably so, by a tendency for paranoia. Wherever Nemeois had sent him, it would have been a desolate place where rescue by one of her father's many allies, or even one of his enemies, would have been impossible.

Wait! Rhea, your father, he would not want—

In an instant, a half-formed thought that had been skipping along in her mind stopped, expanded into full form, and sank to the pit of her stomach. She sat upright in bed, the amorphous suspicion that had finally taken solid shape now screaming out to her, demanding to be heard, insisting to be investigated, at that very moment.

She scrambled out of bed and ran out of her bedchamber, racing barefoot down the corridor and through this wing and that, past the startled eyes of guards and palace servants, until she reached the king's private wing.

The guards opened the doors and she dashed inside to find Romulus, Remus, Albus and Proculus all sitting by the fireplace, drinking wine and still talking state business. They looked at her as if she had just confirmed their worst fear—her isolation in the necropolis had driven her mad after all.

"Help me," she said, as she walked breathlessly to the huge tapestry of the white sow that hung on the wall behind the king's desk.

The four men rose and followed her.

"Mother, are you well?" asked Remus.

Rhea ignored the question. "Hold the tapestry back," she instructed Remus and Proculus. "Romulus and Albus, come with me."

Rhea and the two men slipped behind the heavy tapestry. Once there, the princess ran her hands along a carved wood panel in the wall. Her fingers found purchase and she pulled. The panel opened outward to reveal a hidden tunnel, high enough for a man to stand upright and wide enough for two to enter side by side. Rhea turned to face Romulus and Albus.

"When I was girl," she said, "Nemeois and I ran into the king's sitting room without permission. The tapestry was down and we saw soldiers repairing this hidden door. We weren't supposed to know about it, but sometimes, when everyone was distracted by a festival or party, we'd sneak inside to play." She turned back to the hidden passage, narrowing her eyes as she peered inside. "There is a light in here," she said forebodingly.

"Let me go first," said Albus.

He gripped Rhea's shoulders and moved her backward, unsheathing the dagger at his side and motioning for Romulus to follow. They ducked through the secret door to enter the passageway, Albus doing his best to keep Romulus and Rhea safely behind him. A short distance ahead, they could make out the flame of a single oil lamp.

They moved slowly, full of fascination and dread, until they reached a wall of floor-to-ceiling metal bars. Behind the bars, the tunnel opened into an expansive and well-appointed room. Tapestries and frescos decorated the walls. A long couch with thick embroidered cushions sat on one side of the room, with a fine table in the center, dice and other playthings scattered across its large surface. On the other side of the room was a comfortable bed.

Albus gasped. Behind him, Rhea clasped her hands to her mouth and sank to her knees.

Lying on the bed was her father.

❋ ❋ ❋

"Father," Rhea whispered softly. "Wake up."

Numitor's chest rose and fell with a waking breath. Slowly, almost casually, he rubbed his eyes and sat up in the bed.

"It feels like I barely slept," he said. "What is the weather doing this morning?"

"Father…" said Rhea.

Numitor squinted into the darkness. With some effort, he swung his legs out of bed and shuffled to the oil lamp that sat on the desk, holding it out to peer beyond the bars.

"Cloelia?" he asked. "Is that you?"

Rhea withdrew her face into the shadows. She did not want to shock him. "No, Father. It is me, your daughter, Rhea," she said quietly. Calmly. Although she did not feel calm. Her entire body trembled with the joy of the discovery. Her voice trembled, too. "It is all right, Father. I am here with Albus Julius. We have come to rescue you."

He squinted harder and held the lamp out further, his voice accusatory. "Where is Cloelia?"

"She is not here," said Albus. "Your Highness, do you remember me?"

"Of course I remember you," he spat. "I'm not simple."

Rhea moved closer to the bars, the flame revealing her face. She expected her father to respond—to weep or reach for her—but he did not. A glint of recognition flashed in his eyes. Yet at the sight of her, no longer a young woman but now a middle-aged one, he appeared unmoved.

Rhea, however, balked at the changes in him. Gone were his full, healthy cheeks and fit limbs. Gone was his thick head of gray hair. Now, his face and limbs looked cadaverously thin, those features made more disturbing by an unnaturally bloated belly. He was nearly bald, with brown age spots on his smooth forehead.

"Father…"

"What have you done with Cloelia? Is she all right?"

Romulus stepped past Albus and approached the bars. Numitor's disregard for his daughter had squandered whatever sympathy he might have had for the old man.

"Cloelia is dead," he said. "And it is *you* who must answer the questions."

Numitor gaped at Romulus. He mouthed a silent *Egestus*, his mind searching for the explanation, until he shook a crooked finger at Rhea. "Your son."

"Your grandson," said Romulus. "The man who freed your daughter, deposed your traitor and wears the crown, while the rightful king squats unseen behind a wall in his own palace"—he sneered, glancing around the cell—"and plays dice."

Albus and Rhea blinked at Romulus, surprised by his uncharacteristic venom. Whatever he had envisioned his royal grandfather to be, this bent old man trapped behind metal bars—a prisoner in his own realm—was not it.

"Get him out of here," Romulus said to Albus. "Mother, come with me. You should not have to be in such a place." He turned on his heel and stormed out of the passageway, back toward the royal sitting room, Rhea nearly running to match his stride.

Mother and son passed through the door in the wall panel. Remus and Proculus were waiting, still holding back the tapestry.

"What in the name of the gods is going on in there?" asked Remus.

Romulus spoke to both of them. "Numitor is alive. Albus is bringing him out." He did not wait for their reactions. Instead, he stomped to the fireplace and slumped heavily in one of the large chairs before it.

After calling for a metal file and an axe, both of which a soldier delivered to the king's sitting room without question, Albus was finally able to enter the barred prison cell and free Numitor. He gripped the old man's skeletal arm and led him, limping, down the passageway.

Even though the king's sitting room was dim, lit only by the fireplace and some sputtering oil lamps, Numitor still shaded his eyes as he stepped out from behind the tapestry. Shaking off Albus's grip, he hobbled to a chair by the fireplace and sat.

The others stared.

"Do you need anything?" asked Albus. "Food? Water? We can have you taken to the baths and—"

"I only need to catch my breath," said Numitor. He looked around the room as if reacquainting himself with his surroundings. He coughed. "I knew something had changed when Cloelia did not visit me for two days. If she is going away, she always tells me and leaves extra supplies." He cast Romulus a reproving look. "Why did you kill her?"

The others gawked at Numitor in disbelief.

To hear her father speak affectionately of Cloelia...it was a searing insult. Rhea endeavored to speak respectfully. Patiently.

"Cloelia helped Amulius take your throne," she said. "Do you not remember, Father? She lied to the revered fathers at Marino. She said that Egestus and I planned to kill you. Nemeois—he *murdered* Egestus. You were there. You saw it happen."

"It was the last thing I saw happen," said Numitor, "before I was brought here." He glared at Romulus. "And from here, I've outlived two kings."

"Outliving is no accomplishment," said Romulus.

"Spoken with the naiveté of youth."

The old, deposed king's physical condition might have suffered from his years of imprisonment in a small, sunless space—his body seemed at once wasted and bloated—but his mind was unexpectedly sharp.

Albus suddenly realized why. "You've never stopped managing Alba Longa, or Latium, have you?" he queried. "Nemeois relied on you for advice. He kept you alive for it." He looked at Romulus, his voice incredulous. "That is how Nemeois ruled so well."

Rhea sat back in her chair, benumbed. "We should have known from the beginning," she said. "Nemeois was too smart and too religious to kill a Silvian king, but he was also too paranoid to exile one. Of course he would have kept him here." She regarded her father. "Like a secret well he could draw from when needed."

"Who knew you were here?" Remus asked Numitor.

Numitor looked at Remus, his face breaking into a smirk. "Twins," he said, as if mildly amused. Without asking for the names of his grandsons, without showing any grandfatherly interest in them, he simply answered Remus's question.

"Only Nemeois and Cloelia knew. Cloelia visited me two or three times a day. She brought me things, took out my waste. She kept me apprised of what was happening in Latium, and I'd advise her. That's why Nemeois let her visit me." His eyes moistened. "You should not have killed her."

Rhea looked away from her father. His feelings and concern for Cloelia felt like a blade of betrayal piercing her heart. She stood.

"I leave the matter to you wise gentlemen," she said, avoiding her father's eyes but nodding to Albus and Proculus, and touching her sons on their shoulders.

Remus patted her hand. "It will be all right, Mother," he said. "Rest."

The princess walked tiredly out of the sitting room. The soft carpet under her bare feet transitioned to cool mosaic, and she continued down the corridor in thought. Now that the rightful king Numitor was back—had he ever really left?—things would be different.

She thought of his coldness and the judgment she saw in his eyes. He still hated her and Egestus for what they had done. His contempt, the way he looked at his grandsons—he did not see noble young men, but only the issue of incestuous parents—was unmistakable and too hardened to chip away.

She wished that she could go backward. She would stay in her bed, drink more wine, and ignore her suspicions. She would leave her father locked away to rot in solitude, and never tell anyone about the secret room. But there was no going back. What was done was done. She kept walking, pausing now and then before a statue of a god, hoping to find some peace in their strong, divine faces.

Despite her turmoil, she found solace suddenly and unexpectedly in the face of Vulcan, god of fire, the skilled blacksmith who could forge any weapon. He had even forged Jupiter's thunderbolts and Mars's spear. She knelt before him, raising her palms up in prayer, gazing into painted eyes that seemed to flicker with life, lit as they were by the flame of a nearby torch.

The disappointment she felt toward her father burned away. In its place was the ever-expanding love she felt for her sons, her certainty that their intelligence and piety, their devotion to each other and to their bloodline, would help them claim the future they deserved. She knew it would happen, even if the gods would have to help them forge that future out of fire.

CHAPTER XX

Rhea had received a constant flow of visitors since returning to the city of the living. Noblewomen she had known since girlhood—they embraced, insisting the other had barely aged—as well as various priests, city officials, and the patriarchs of important families. They all came with gifts, words of regret over her years of imprisonment, and hopes and prayers that she, and her sons, would flourish.

She was happy to see most of her visitors, indifferent to some, and irritated, mercifully, by only a few. But she wasn't surprised to see any of them. Not until now.

Mamilian had always been handsome. He still was, perhaps even more so. He wore his hair a little shorter and his beard a little fuller. The lines around his eyes had deepened along with his complexion, as so often happened to men who spent a great deal of time outdoors riding or hunting, but he still had the same strong bearing, one that only amplified his height.

Despite his imposing frame, he entered the room uncertainly, unsure how he should greet Rhea or how she would receive his greeting. She relieved him by standing and allowing him to take her hand. They looked at each other, smilingly, until she invited him to sit. He wasted no time with small talk, but aimed directly for the only matter he knew would be on her mind.

"The news of your father's return has spread like wildfire throughout Latium," he said, accepting a cup of wine from a slave.

"Return?" asked Rhea. "The man never left."

Mamilian shook his head, still dumbfounded by the news that Numitor had spent over eighteen years incarcerated in his own palace. It was a revelation that every city in Latium, most of all Alba Longa, was still grappling with.

"It's surreal," he said. "All of it."

"My father is so changed. The blood between us has turned to ice."

"Cloelia fed him nothing but lies for years. It was inevitable they would become a part of his constitution."

"But to believe that Egestus and I were going to kill him? You know that is untrue."

"Yes," Mamilian said sincerely, "but your sons, and the way they came into being…it was hard for him to accept."

"No harder for him than for you," Rhea replied. He looked away, but she continued. "I was so young and stubborn, Mamilian. And you remember how Egestus was. He was so single-minded. I don't blame him or regret it. I chose to do it, and my sons are a blessing to me, but I do regret what I did to you. After we married, you were kind to me. Perhaps if I had only…well, it doesn't matter now, does it? It was a lifetime ago."

Mamilian tightened his hands around his wine cup. "When they first took you to the necropolis, I thought about trying to rescue you. I thought about it every day for months. I even came up with a strategy. But the months wore on, and the idea became more distant. I found excuses not to come. There were rumors Nemeois had you killed and the necropolis had been sealed off to hide the fact. It was easier to believe that than to imagine you living there, sleeping there, all alone." He set his wine cup down, sat back, and pressed his fingers against his eyes. "Many men in Latium are ashamed of their inaction, but none more than me. You were my wife, no matter how briefly. No matter what happened between us, I should not have abandoned you."

"It is the past," said Rhea. "We will start again. That is what you once told me."

"I remember," he replied, reaching out to again take her hand. It was a bold gesture, but even as Rhea gently pulled back, he held on. "Then why don't we?" he asked.

"Why don't we what?"

"Start again." He squeezed her hand encouragingly. "Come to Tusculum with me."

Rhea laughed. "I am glad we did not stay married," she said. "Your poor wife!"

"I have no wife," he said. "We divorced years ago, after our youngest daughter was born." He leaned closer to her. "Numitor will be restored to the throne, will he not?"

"Yes. It is the way of the Silvii."

"Romulus could keep it if he wanted to," Mamilian said cautiously. "The great families would support him, as would the strongest cities. That includes Tusculum. I have fine daughters, Rhea. They are sharp and beautiful, not so different than you were as a girl. You would like them. They would make excellent wives for your sons." He brushed his thumb over her fingers. "And you and I, we could marry. We could truly start again."

Rhea's skin flushed with warmth, and she found herself nodding. Mamilian's proposal was, on all counts, a wise and not unwelcome one.

Lowering her eyes, she said, "The decision must be Romulus's."

"I know, but I wanted to ask you first. Do I have your permission to present it to him?"

Why not? Rhea thought to herself. The marriages he proposed were politic and would be widely supported. And did she not deserve to be happy, after all this time? Would Vesta not approve, after so many years of caring for her flame in the solitude of the necropolis? For the first time in as long as she could remember, Rhea felt a flutter of excitement in her stomach. Excitement for her *own* future.

"Yes," she said.

They stood, still hand in hand. Rhea allowed Mamilian to draw her closer until she found his strong arms around her. It felt good, but also, for some inexplicable reason, brought her to the edge of tears. Pulling away, he brushed her hair off her face.

"The seashell," she said. "The one you gave me as an engagement present. Did you really ride to the shore yourself to get it?"

Mamilian smiled sadly at the insolence of his youth. "No," he said, "but I should have. And I promise you, if we marry again, we will ride to the shore together, and I will you pick you a hundred seashells."

❈ ❈ ❈

"Can we trust him?" asked Remus.

"Ten years ago I would've said no," replied Albus, "but now? Yes, you can trust him."

"And his daughters?"

"Penelope is the elder and Phaidra is the younger. They are as he says. Attractive and intelligent."

Remus rubbed Xanthos on his nose and leaned against the stall door to gauge Romulus's reaction to the proposal. Since Numitor was again free to roam the palace, the royal twins and their Julian advisers preferred to convene in the outdoor privacy of the stables. For Romulus and Remus, the familiar sounds and smells of work animals had a calming effect, one that helped them think clearly.

"Why would you not agree to this?" Remus asked his brother. "Mamilian is a revered father of Latium and Tusculum is a powerful city. His support would be invaluable. You can keep the crown. We can marry pretty girls and live here, in our rightful home. Even our mother can finally be happy."

Proculus leaned on the stall door beside Remus. "I have the same question," he said to Romulus. "Why not fight for what is yours?"

"It would not be a fight," said Romulus. "It would be a civil war."

"A short one," countered Proculus. "Is that not true, Father?"

"Yes," said Albus. "Numitor has his allies, but they're the old guard. There is no doubt you could defeat them."

"From what you've told me," Proculus said to his father, "many of Numitor's policies were criticized even before he was deposed. Wouldn't the revered fathers prefer Romulus?"

"It isn't about preference," Albus explained, "it's about tradition. Duty. There are cities in Latium, men in Latium, who will remain loyal to the rightful line of succession no matter what. After Numitor was deposed, Amulius suppressed a number of revolts, and quite brutally." The older man turned to Romulus. "You would have to do the same."

"Kill my countrymen?" asked Romulus. "Murder revered fathers for the sin of respecting my lineage more than I do? My rule would be forever tainted."

Remus kicked at the dirt floor. "So what will we do? I don't want to live here with this miserable old man looking down his nose at us. I don't trust him, even if he is our grandfather."

Albus turned to Romulus. "Numitor won't live forever," he said. "We have guest houses on our estate and fine villas in the country. You, your brother, and your mother are welcome to any of them, for as long as you'd like."

"Thank you," replied Romulus. "Your family has done so much for us, but I cannot accept any more of your charity." He slipped past Remus and Proculus and opened the stall door, stepping inside and patting Xanthos's neck. "I'm going for a ride. I need to think."

Romulus walked Xanthos out of the stable, donned a stablehand's riding cloak he spotted hanging over a fence, and left his brother and advisers to their frustrated devising. He knew it would come to nothing. He mounted and pulled the hood over his head, riding through the estate grounds. Declining an armed escort, he headed out the palace gates to enter the city. It was late in the day and it had started to drizzle, leaving the streets mostly empty. Those few who were on the streets were too focused on getting home for supper—the rain was getting worse every moment—to give whoever was riding an old, worn-out horse like Xanthos a second look.

Romulus rode aimlessly, his mind working through it all. In as much time as it had taken for his beard to grow in, he had burned Larentia's body, discovered his royal bloodline, rescued his condemned brother from a prison quarry, freed his true mother from the necropolis and been crowned king of Alba Longa. Now, he faced the dilemma of either abdicating the throne or waging war against Numitor, the man who, by the rules of succession, was still the legitimate king. Romulus knew that stepping down was the right thing to do.

Still, it was tempting. The contempt in Numitor's eyes, the way he looked so judgingly at his own daughter and so spitefully at his own grandsons—he openly called Romulus the "crown prince of incest"—made Romulus want to rise up and destroy the aged fool just to prove that he could. But what precedent would that set? What kind of king would that make him? He was in an impossible situation. If he killed Numitor, he would appear a tyrant. If he just waited for him to die, especially after Numitor's slanders, he would appear a coward.

He gripped the reins and rode further from the palace, sensing an incline as Xanthos clip-clopped along the smooth paving stones of the winding mountain path, the sacred road that led to the one place he thought he might find some clarity, even on a cloudy day like this—the Temple of Jupiter on the top of Mount Albanus. A little shower of stones tumbled down from the hillside, bouncing off the peperino curb and rolling before Xanthos. He snorted and shook his head, complaining about the weather and the effort the slope demanded of him. The old workhorse had quickly adjusted to life in the palace stables, eating like the king's best mount, leisurely grazing in the pastures and having stablehands groom him every morning in the warmth of the sun.

"I understand how you feel," Romulus said to him.

As they neared the summit of Mount Albanus, Xanthos's complaints grew more insistent. Conceding, Romulus dismounted and walked him past the giant rock sculptures of sacrificial animals that lined the road—a bull, a pig, a sheep, their surfaces darkened from the rain—until they reached the top. The soldiers who guarded the area had taken shelter from the storm and, quickly assessing the lone rider was no threat to the temples, statues, shrines and altars, let him enter the sacred mountaintop complex without question. He was not worth getting wet over.

For his part, Romulus did not mind the rain. It suited his mood. It suited the surroundings as well, for just as the full splendor of the colossal statue of Jupiter came into view, a thunderclap sounded loudly enough to startle him and Xanthos. Romulus tethered Xanthos to a post and left him to stand dejectedly in the rain as he proceeded to the great altar before the temple, drenched and gazing up at the king of the gods. Jupiter's mighty features, the thunderbolt he gripped in one muscular hand, seemed to float in the moving clouds. Romulus had never been on such a great height before.

He wandered along the mountaintop, looking out over the chains of mountain ridges, hills and valleys spread out below, and the temples and towns that dotted the lush landscape, getting his bearings, until he found himself staring in the direction of the Palatine Hill. A sudden clearing in the sky seemed to illuminate the area just for him.

He felt a pang of homesickness for the trees of the Palatine, the marshy grasses and flowers of the valley, and the noises and smells of the Tiber's waters. He missed the taste of salted eel, the sound of Cerva's bark, the bleating of newborn lambs and especially the snap of the fire as he and his family warmed themselves around it, telling stories and tossing bread into the sacred fire of their household hearth.

Suddenly, a bolt of white lightning pierced the sky in the distance, as if thrown down from the heavens, spear-like, by Mars himself. It struck precisely where Romulus was looking—the Palatine—with an earth-shaking force, causing a fiery explosion that he could see even from his lofty platform far away. He blinked, trying to clear the blinding light from his eyes. A deafening crack and roar of thunder followed, unlike anything he had ever heard before, muting his hearing and causing him to sink to his knees in momentary disorientation. Romulus shook his head, compelling his senses to return.

They did, and with them came a sense of certainty, of conviction, that Romulus knew could only have come from the gods. It filled his nostrils with the smell of ozone, made his hair stand on end, and pumped blood through his heart faster and with more force than ever before, perhaps faster and more forcibly than was humanly possible. For the first time in his life, he had total clarity and confidence. He could see it all from above. Like he was a god himself.

You are sons of Mars, his mother had told him in the necropolis.

In that instant, he knew what he was destined to do.

CHAPTER XXI

"You cannot marry Mamilian," said Romulus. "You must come with me. We leave today."

Rhea exchanged baffled looks with Remus and Albus, the three of them trying to make sense of the change in Romulus. He was like a man possessed, feverishly loading everything from gold and weapons to chairs and hand tools into a large cart near the entrance to the palace. Nearby, a number of men loyal to him loaded five more carts.

The palace staff and slaves eased by him, confused, while most of the guards awkwardly avoided him, similarly uncertain of how to proceed. Was their duty now to Numitor or still to Romulus? No one seemed to know for sure.

As for Numitor, once he had been informed that his grandson was leaving Alba Longa, he had chosen to simply lie low and wait for him to go, even if it meant parting with some valuables and a number of soldiers and servants—no doubt swindled by his rags-to-royalty story—who wished to follow him. It was a small price to pay to be rid of him. The old king was not keen to be challenged by the younger man, crown prince of incest or not.

"Son, where do you mean to go?" Rhea asked him.

"To the Palatine Hill," Romulus replied.

"The Palatine Hill," she echoed. "Why? There is nothing there. The shepherd is to come here, is he not? If we go anywhere, it should be to Lavinium. Romulus, you are still the rightful—"

"Alba Longa is a dying flame," he said. "I have seen it. Mars threw a spear of lightning to the earth, and I must build a city on the spot where it landed. By the Palatine."

A bewildered silence hung in the air, interrupted only by the sound of Romulus and the other men hastily packing the carts.

"You would forfeit the city that your ancestor founded?" she asked him. "That is yours by birth? That your father gave his life for?"

"Yes," said Romulus. "And not soon enough."

Rhea watched two men lift yet another trunk—this one packed with her dresses and jewelry—into a cart. She blew out her breath, her emotions vacillating between confusion and defiance, and planted her hands on her hips. "And what if I do not wish to go to the Palatine? What if I wish to marry and live in Tusculum?"

"We are family, and we still stay together," said Romulus. He stopped loading the cart and turned to his mother, his face resolved. "You have taken a lifelong vow to the goddess. If I am to succeed, you must honor it. Go to the Temple of Vesta and prepare a sarcina." He paused, then nodded to himself and added, "Go also into the vault under the temple and collect the Palladium. I will take it with me."

Rhea gaped. "It is not yours for the taking, son."

"But it is, Mother. I have the purest Trojan blood of any man alive. The sacred fire and the Palladium will reside in my city, just as they did in the cities of Ilus, Aeneas, and Ascanius before me."

Albus spat out a cough of disbelief. "I don't know what you think you're doing," he said, "but the Palladium belongs in Alba Longa. They will not let you take it."

Proculus emerged from the palace and, overhearing his father's words, spoke. "They cannot stop us," he said. "Not if they want to keep their heads. We have enough men now."

Rhea stared incredulously at Romulus's friend. Whatever fever—or madness—had stricken her son had also stricken Albus's son.

Remus stepped forward and grabbed Romulus's arm, preventing him from piling more supplies into the cart. "Brother," he said. "You must stop this."

"It came unexpectedly," Romulus said seriously, as if revealing a great secret. "The clarity of it. We have to go, Remus. Don't you see? Mars and the god of the Tiber, they brought our basket to that shore for a reason. That is where we are meant to rule. We will found a city that will make Alba Longa, and all the cities of Latium, but paving stones in a great road."

Remus laughed aloud. He gestured in the direction of the citadel, the sprawling urban homes below them and finally the temple-laden Mount Albanus. "There can be no greater city than Alba Longa."

"There already is," said Romulus. "We just have to build it." He pulled his arm away from Remus and continued packing as he spoke. "Proculus, take the men you need and go with Mother to the temple. We will leave as soon as you return."

"Wait," said Remus, now exasperated. "Why leave? Who cares about Numitor? If you don't want to fight him, then just wait for him to die. The crown will pass to you. Gods, by the looks of him, he won't make it until the festival of Juno! You'll be king of Alba Longa again by summer."

"And you'll be a mere prince again," said Romulus. "My subordinate, instead of my equal. Come with me, and we will rule together."

Albus looked at Remus—the arrow had struck a weak spot and was firmly lodged. In that instant, the patriarch of the Julii knew there was no stopping it. "How many men are with you?" he asked Romulus.

"About two hundred," Romulus replied.

Two hundred? Albus had expected no more than fifty men to follow Romulus. However, the young man's story had taken on a mythic quality. He was the abandoned prince, saved by the gods, who had returned to his city to free his princess mother, avenge his murdered father, and claim his kingdom, only to forsake that kingdom to found his own city. His identity—part royalty, part outcast—was irresistible, especially to those who, like him, sought a new life. Unfortunately for Albus, his son was among them.

And now, Remus was, too. Suddenly imbued with the same determination and single-minded purpose as the other men, he nodded in accord. "I will go with Proculus and Mother to the temple," he said. "We will take half the men with us and leave the others here at the palace to keep an eye on Numitor."

"Very good," said Romulus.

Remus and Proculus began to walk away, but halted as they realized Rhea was not following. She stood stubbornly beside Romulus.

"You cannot command me, son," she said to him.

Romulus lifted a truck into the cart, brushed his hands off on his tunica, and regarded his mother. "Go with them, Mother," he said. "Or they will take you by force."

❋ ❋ ❋

Romulus had departed Faustulus's farm near the base of the Palatine Hill alone and afraid, reeling from the loss of Larentia. He had traveled to Alba Longa on the back of an old horse, clueless as to how he would free his brother. He had worn a mended tunica and carried a gold crown sewn inside a ratty waterskin. He had still called himself Caelus, and the crown that had hung around his neck had made him feel inadequate, like an imposter.

Other than riding on the back of same old horse, Romulus's journey back to the Palatine could not have been more different. He had a new name and a new purpose. He had total clarity and confidence. He wore a fine tunica. He still had the gold crown, but now it was packed inside one of several large carts along with gold, jewels, weapons and other valuables, including the Palladium.

And he was not alone. His brother was with him, as was his true mother, who carried the sleeping flame of Troy in a sarcina. The devoted Proculus rode at his side, and behind them, followed two hundred or so men who had chosen to leave Alba Longa with him.

As the sundry convoy moved along the cobblestone road, those two hundred men had unexpectedly grown to nearly three hundred. The inspiring story of the royal twins had spread throughout Latium, moving faster than the men, horses and carts possibly could, moving with the speed at which thrilling news travels through monotonous places.

They are the descendants of Aeneas!

Their mother is the princess Rhea Silvia—she carries the fire of Trojan Vesta!

They abandoned the grand palace, rejected their birthright, to found a new city!

The cavalcade grew in numbers with every farm, country house and village it passed. Men waited on the side of the road, sometimes alone but more often in small groups, either empty handed or with their few meager belongings stuffed into a sack. They ran alongside the procession, pleading with the sons of the Silvii—"Let us join you! We will work hard and obey!"

But it wasn't just these eager men who filled the roads, and it wasn't just talk of Romulus and Remus that filled the air. During the trip, Romulus had become increasingly inspired by several reports concerning the lightning strike he had seen from the top of Mount Albanus the previous night. According to those who had witnessed it, it had struck near the base of the Palatine Hill with such force that the ground had exploded around it, and a small fire had burst to life. Amazingly, that fire was still burning—amazingly, because if the reports were to be believed, it was burning in thin air.

The road grew winding for a while, curving like a river between the stone pines, until it opened into a relatively straight stretch. Remus looked over his shoulder, noticing just how many men now followed them.

"Won't Father be amazed to see us return like this?" asked Remus. "I can't wait to see him."

"I want to see the fire first," replied Romulus.

The pace of the procession slowed, encumbered now by the packed road, everyone talking about the *ignis mirabilis*—the miracle fire—that burned in the valley on the north side of the Palatine Hill, the presence of which was now made even more propitious by the advent of the royal twins and the *Iliaci ignes Vestae* in their care.

Word spread throughout the countryside that a divine convergence of Vesta's fire—the old flame of Troy and the new flame that burned in the valley—was about to happen. A current of religious fervor ran through everyone who heard the news. They abandoned their fields, flocks and duties to rush to the blessed site.

Finally, the cavalcade from Alba Longa reached the marshy valley where the miracle flame burned. Proculus, who rode at the front, halted there: the road did not run through the valley, so they would have to go the rest of the way on foot.

Romulus dismounted Xanthos and weaved through the people, animals, and carts of the caravan to reach his mother's carriage. Pulling back the curtain, he lifted himself up to slip inside, sitting across from her. She was holding the sarcina in her lap, peering out the other side of the carriage.

"Can you see it?" she asked him.

"Not from here. We will have to walk."

Rhea looked down at the sarcina in her hands. When Romulus had first spoken of his vision— *Mars threw a spear of lightning to the earth, and I must build a city on the spot where it landed*— she had thought he was mad. She had thought the stress and disappointment of his rapid rise and fall as king of Alba Longa had driven him to delusions of grandeur.

But she had been wrong. The war god had appeared to him. She should not have been surprised. Was she not the one who had called upon him in the first place?

She remembered that night long ago...the night she had stood naked in front of the statue of Mars in Egestus's tomb and stared into the god's black eyes in desperation. Vividly, she recalled the terrifying sensation of the god in the tomb with her, circling her, wanting her.

Savage Mars, I offer my body so that you will take my sons as your own.

Her hand moved instinctively to her chest, to the place where her left breast used to be, feeling the soft mound of cloth she placed under her *strophium* every morning to disguise her disfigurement.

"Come," Romulus said to her. "Let us honor the goddess together."

They exited the carriage amidst a clamor of excitement—the chatter of voices, the snorts of horses and the clip-clops of their hooves on the cobblestone, the push of bodies all moving in the same direction. Proculus saw the two of them on the road and shouted a command to the soldiers who quickly cleared a path for them.

Everyone fell silent at the sight of the distinguished Princess Rhea Silvia making her way to the divine fire that burned, independently and incredibly, in the middle of a nondescript and swampy valley at the foot of the Palatine Hill. She strode proudly beside one of her sons, the one the crowd gleaned from his comportment to be the firstborn. A moment later, her other son—more muscular, but unmistakably a twin—took his position at her other side.

Romulus's focus was riveted on the fire ahead, but Remus's attention was drawn to a face in the awestruck crowd. It was Faustulus. Like everyone else, the shepherd had come to see the divine flame for himself. He knelt on the wet grass, clutching an urn to his chest. Tears streamed down his cheeks as he gazed upon his sons, his expression an emotional blend of surprise, relief, and pride. Remus smiled at him, sending a silent message with his eyes. *We are well, Father. We will all be together again soon.*

The crowd parted to let the trio pass. Those who were not already on their knees lowered themselves before Rhea. They had never seen such an important person: a royal woman, dressed in a fine white dress with gold bracelets winding up her bare arms, her head veiled, and a smoldering sarcina in her hands. Rhea walked past them, feeling the ground below her feet grow softer and wetter. How could a fire burn in such conditions? For a moment, she wondered whether it was all a ruse, a trick of some kind, but then she saw it—a thick orange flame burning on the ground, no higher than the level of her knees.

The earth around the flame was scorched black and cratered from the lightning strike. There was no visible source of fuel for the fire, no wood or combustible matter of any sort. It was as though the fire was burning an invisible material: it moved and swayed over the ground like any natural flame, although sustained by the supernatural.

Romulus and Remus knelt on either side of her, humbling themselves before her and the miracle fire. Rhea glanced around. Of the hundreds of devout present, she was the only one standing. All knelt and were silent, even the children. It seemed the birds themselves were perched quietly in the trees, keenly watching it all from high branches.

As Rhea looked down into the flame, as she watched it move and burn soundlessly, she was overcome by sudden amazement for the goddess. By gratitude. It was Vesta, as much as Mars, who had protected her sons. Despite the massive gathering, it felt intimate to be here with them, the three of them together as a family in the presence of the goddess.

"*O Vesta Mater*," she called out. "Accept this offering from your faithful priestess. Behold, a Trojan ember of your sacred fire." She knelt and placed her sarcina on the ground, in the middle of the fire. Its thick red tongues licked the dry bark, quickly consuming the vegetation that insulated the glowing oak coal within and emitting a series of loud snaps—the voice of the goddess. Rhea raised her palms to the sky. "*Vesta Sancta*, consecrate this holy spot."

The priestess looked down at the bowed heads of her sons, and then out at the hundreds of people encircling the flame in the marshy valley. She raised her head to look up: more people had gathered on top of the Palatine to watch, like the birds, from above.

She had to wonder. Why had Mars led Romulus here? Why had Vesta chosen this ordinary place to appear in such extraordinary form? Rhea was certain of it now—she would never understand the gods. It was probably better that way.

She held her palms over the divine flames, feeling the heat of the everlasting fire radiate into her body. She raised her voice, this time speaking as much to the devoted souls around her as to the goddess. "*Vesta Aeterna*, for as long as we honor you on this sacred ground, we ask that you protect us on this sacred ground."

CHAPTER XXII

No one called her Princess Rhea Silvia here. Here, in the valley at the foot of the Palatine, they called her Priestess Rhea Silvia. After all, the goddess had come to earth and Rhea was the only person of standing in the pastoral, sparsely populated area who could be trusted to properly honor her. The new honorific had led Rhea to an epiphany: Alba Longa was in her past. Her future was here, with the goddess. With her sons.

The *ignis mirabilis* had burned steadily for several days now. Despite its modest size, its undeniable divinity imbued the air with an aura of venerableness, as if Vesta's holy body was diffused in the atmosphere itself. People continued to arrive from places near and far to breathe it in and to pray for a glimpse of the impossible flame, or rather, the flame only made possible by the will of the gods. Many of these visitors stayed—it seemed to Rhea that her sons turned no one away—and joined the ranks of those helping to build a settlement from nothing more than the trees, rocks and clay of the environment, and the tools they had taken from the palace. It was astonishing how much they had accomplished in only days.

While both of her sons resided in huts atop the Palatine, Romulus had arranged for Rhea's temporary but nonetheless large and well-appointed tent to be erected just east of the sacred fire. Twelve times a day, she left the tent to walk the short distance to the partly constructed *Aedes Vestae*—the circular sanctum being built around the miracle flame to house it. As she neared it, people called out to her for blessings from behind the well-guarded wooden fence that Proculus had quickly ordered built.

This was Rhea's sixth visit to the fire on this day. She knelt before it, inspecting the circle of smooth stones that she had piled on the scorched ground around the flame to serve as a natural altar. Two days before, she had dispatched a messenger to the Vestal sacerdotes in Alba Longa, asking the order to send the finest marble it could. Until it arrived, the river stones would have to suffice. That seemed pious enough: they were from the river that had saved the lives of her sons.

As she was reflecting upon this, the sound of friendly chatter behind her caught her attention. She dipped a small silver *simpulum* into a terracotta bowl of oil, drizzled the libation over one of the altar stones, then rose and exited the unfinished sanctuary, proceeding to the group of men who stood waiting for her at a respectful distance.

That must be him, she thought, as her eyes settled on an unfamiliar visage.

The shepherd Faustulus was nothing like Rhea had expected him to be. He was a few years her senior, bulky and weathered in the same way that all stockmen were. His black beard had streaks of gray. She wondered how much of that was due to raising her sons. Regardless, he was far from the shrinking, fatherly type she had imagined.

Romulus and Remus were with him, all three of them escorted by her sons' men. Like her, and like the sacred fire itself, the twin princes were now constantly guarded by vigilant armed soldiers. She smiled in greeting. Faustulus knelt before her.

"Priestess Rhea, it is an honor to meet you."

"The honor is mine," she replied. "We should have met long ago." She reached down to touch his shoulders, prompting him to stand. And then she embraced him.

She had not planned to, but the irrepressible swell of gratitude she felt at meeting the man who had single-handedly saved her sons from certain death swept all decorum aside. Taken aback, the grizzled shepherd tensed. Rhea let him go and laughed.

Remus raised his chin to survey the work underway in the valley. Altars, huts, vendor stalls and other structures were in construction all around. He turned to look up to where even more work was in progress on the slopes and on the summit of the Palatine Hill. Men and animals busily and noisily carted wood, stone, vegetation for thatched roofs, and other building materials in every direction.

"The Palatine is not a good spot for building," he said, again voicing his opposition to the new city's location. "The Aventine Hill is a better choice. It has a more defensive position, and it is right along the river—"

"The Palatine has the blessing of the gods," said Romulus, "what better defense could there be? It overlooks Vesta's fire." He looked to Rhea. "The sacred flame is the city's hearth, so we must build outward from there. Is that not right, Mother?" When she nodded in assent, he continued speaking to his brother. "We will take horses and decide where the city's boundaries will be. We will have to do it soon, though. New encampments are going up every day as people arrive from other regions. We have to organize them."

Remus shook his head. "We have a more pressing matter. This valley is nearly a wetland. The ducks will be laying eggs on the altars before long." He looked sideways at Romulus. "We'll see what the gods think of that."

"Proculus found a man from Etruria who says he can drain the valley," said Romulus. "It will be dry enough."

"Drain the valley," scoffed Remus. "You might as well drain the Tiber."

"One thing at a time," said Romulus. Peering over his mother's shoulder, he inspected the progress his builders were making on her permanent home. Located behind her temporary tent, it was nonetheless near enough to the sacred flame that she could walk back and forth with ease to perform her duties. "It will not be the palace you are accustomed to, Mother," he said, "but it will be comfortable."

"It will be the finest home between here and Alba Longa," she replied. "You and Remus should have the same. I don't know why you insist on living like paupers."

"Neither do I," said Remus. "We live in huts no better than the men we command."

A leathery workman leading a donkey-drawn cart approached, pausing to scrape a clump of dirt off the bottom of his sandal. Rhea recognized him as the man in charge of building the Aedes. He bowed his head as he spoke to her.

"Priestess," he said, "we hope to finish today."

"Good," she replied. "I would like to have the exterior painted as soon as possible."

"We will invoke Mercury," he said emphatically, "we will not eat, not sleep, until we have—"

She smiled and raised a hand. "You are doing good work, my friend."

The man blushed—he did not look like the type who was accustomed to receiving compliments from women—and continued on, leading his donkey and loaded cart toward the Aedes.

Romulus watched the workman begin to unpack supplies from his cart. "The sanctum will be modest," he said, "but from what you have told me, Mother, Vesta never lives finer than her people."

"That is true enough," Rhea replied, thinking of the fine temple in Alba Longa. "I will be relieved when the building is complete. We need a proper religious space, however humble."

She thought of the delegates who were constantly arriving from nearby cities and tribes to see the miracle flame for themselves. As the nameless city's *de facto* chief priestess, it fell to her to bring them before the divine fire where they could pour wine from their own vineyards over the altar stones as offerings to the goddess. It was a religious act that required the dignity of a sanctified enclosure.

Although the ritual had originated as a strictly pious one, Romulus had quickly seen it as a politic one, too. Each day, he sent out messengers to invite even more ambassadors to the valley in an effort to establish alliances and even trading partners to support the fledgling settlement. Seeing the power of Vesta's immaculate flame dancing above the ground tended to make men more amenable.

Rhea took advantage of this, ensuring that none of these ambassadors went home empty handed. She was constantly lighting fires from the *ignis mirabilis* and sending the embers home with awestruck envoys in carefully wrapped sarcinae, urging them to light their own city hearths with Vesta's pure flame and reminding them of the Trojan fire that bound them together in history and custom. It had been a mostly successful strategy, with a number of nearby cities, including Tellenae, Gabii and Antemnae, sending gifts back in a spirit of cautious reciprocity. Even the volatile Volsci had reciprocated, hinting that the new city's reach might even extend beyond its natural Latin allies.

But perhaps the biggest surprise had come from the powerful Sabines whose reach included a modest settlement on the nearby hill they called the Quirinal, located to the north of the new settlement on the Palatine. Their envoy had been wonderstruck by the sacred flame and flattered by Rhea's diplomacy. As a result, their king had offered to send a young noblewoman from the Sabine capital city of Cures to serve as a sacerdos Vestalis, someone who could help Rhea tend the miracle flame and perform her many duties. Romulus knew the tolerant goodwill might not last. It was a good start, though, and it gave him time to gain a foothold in the region.

Yet as he noted the sober expression on the face of an approaching soldier—his name was Hostus Hostilius, and he was one of two delegates the brothers had sent to the city of Veii—Romulus suspected his mother had been correct about the aggressive nature of the people who lived on the other side of the Tiber River. The Etruscan king would not be receptive to an alliance, especially with a pair of displaced royals he would regard as self-aggrandizing upstarts with nothing of value to trade.

"Sirs," Hostus bowed to Romulus and Remus. "I have a message from King Velsos of Etruria."

"Where is Fabius?" asked Remus.

Fabius—Remus's friend since childhood—had been the other delegate. A natural diplomat, and the son of one of the better-born men in the region, he had quickly reconnected with the twins upon their return and been tasked with traveling to the Etruscan city of Veii.

"Forgive me, sir," said Hostus. He glanced uneasily at the priestess, and then down at the sack he held in one hand. "It is not fit for a lady."

"Because Fabius's head is in that sack," Rhea stated flatly.

When the man said nothing, Remus threw his arms up. "Bloody gods!" he exclaimed.

Hostus shifted on his feet. "There's more."

"We will speak inside," said Rhea. "Come with me."

She led the four men into her large high-roofed tent, which was actually three wide tents joined together end to end. Thick carpets had been laid throughout. Like everything else of comfort or value, they had come from the palace at Alba Longa. A number of dining couches, statues, and a private shrine to the gods furnished the space, while rich curtains blocked off Rhea's sleeping and washing areas. Fire from a pair of low, well-placed iron braziers radiated warmth throughout.

Rhea sat on a cushioned chair before one of the braziers as the men gathered around a rectangular table. Faustulus poured them all cups of wine, while discreetly glancing at the tent's fine items.

"We were granted an audience almost immediately with the king," began Hostus. "He's been watching us since we arrived, that's for sure. And he's not impressed that so many of his men, especially skilled men and even some priests, are leaving Etruria to join us." He looked at Romulus. "Fabius and I offered your greetings and well wishes, just as you instructed, and we gave him the gift—the terracotta statue of Mars…"

"And then?" prompted Romulus.

"He laughed," said Hostus. "He said that his grandsons could make better statues of the gods from river silt, and that we were a bunch of peasants still playing with clay. And then"—he sniffed angrily, remembering—"and then he stood, picked up the sword leaning against his throne, and cut off Fabius's head in one swipe. I moved just in time, or he would've taken mine off with it." Hostus drained his cup of wine. "After that, he ordered some of his men to take me to the citadel. I thought for sure I was marked for public execution."

"What then?" asked Remus.

Hostus shrugged his shoulders. "Then they showed me around. They wanted me to see their city, to see how much more advanced they are than us. It pains me to say it, but their temples are grander than anything I've seen in Latium, including Alba Longa. They have a sanctuary to Minerva that you wouldn't believe unless you'd seen it. It has a life-sized statue of Apollo and another of Hercules fighting the Ceryneian hind. The statues they have of their great gods, Tinia and Uni, and the skill of their metalworkers, is incredible. I saw a bronze of Mars that would stop the blood in your veins. You'd think he was standing before you. But it's their temples…they stand on high podiums, with massive columned porticos and—"

"What about their army?" interrupted Romulus.

"Terrifying," said Hostus. "As the priestess told us"—he bowed his head to Rhea and continued—"the Etrusci already have extensive trading networks with Greece and Phoenicia, even with Egypt, and it shows. Their war horses, their armor, their weapons and shields, their whole organization, it's all remarkable. They apparently have a fleet of ships at Pyrgi that stretches as far as the eye can see. Their soldiers aren't just country boys like us, either. They're elite, well-trained. Not that they have to work too hard. I think it would be near impossible to break through the city walls in the first place."

Faustulus refilled Hostus's wine cup. "So after they showed you all of this, they just let you leave?"

"They took me to the gates of Veii and an escort rode me to the Tiber. Just before I crossed, one of the king's men gave me…" he looked at the sack on the table.

Seeing Hostus's hesitation, Faustulus opened the sack and looked inside. He grimaced and pulled out the contents. A man's head.

A head that had been flawlessly gilded. Fabius's eyes, mouth and hair were coated in a second skin of pure gold, the precious metal conforming to every line and crease in the young man's lifeless face. It was a masterful, albeit grotesque, working of the splendid element.

It was also a message. *You are beyond your depth.*

"Anything else?" asked Romulus, his voice hoarse.

"The best part," Hostus said humorlessly. "The king is coming here. He wants to see the divine flame for himself. He said he expects us to comply, in the interests of diplomacy."

"Diplomacy?" said Remus. "What does he know of diplomacy?"

Rhea stood and approached the table. "Velsos has plenty of sacks," she said, looking at the one that lay crumpled next to the gilded head. "But he only used one. To him, that is diplomacy." She spoke to Hostus. "That is all."

He bowed and exited the tent.

Rhea turned to her sons and Faustulus. To their surprise, she laughed. "Your faces are more rigid than poor Fabius's," she said. She gestured to the chairs by the fire, and they all moved to sit down. "Do not mistake what is happening here, my sons," she continued. "King Velsos knows the power of the sacred flame. He knows that people are coming here from all around, even from his own cities. He may have great temples, but the gods are here."

"The gods will not fight our battles for us," said Remus.

"There will be no battle," Rhea replied. "When the king arrives, when he sees the flame and this expanding settlement with his own eyes, he will make you an offer. He will offer riches, or women, or some other desirable thing. You must reject it, for it will only weaken your position, no matter how it seems at the time. He will then become aggressive or try to undermine you in some way. Regardless of what tactic he uses, though, no matter how confident he seems, you must remember that he is afraid of you."

"He is afraid of *us*?" asked Romulus. "I find that hard to believe."

"You will believe it soon enough," said Rhea. "My son, there will always be people who seem greater, or who have an advantage. Do not fear them. Learn from them. Take what they do best and then do it better." She poured herself more wine and glanced back at the table, staring into Fabius's golden eyes. "And then, when you are powerful enough, cut off their heads."

✣   ✣   ✣

The young noblewoman who the Sabines had sent to help Rhea tend the sacred flame was named Tarpeia. Schooled in the priesthood of the goddess Ops, holy mother to Vesta, and halfway through her tenure as a sacerdos in her home city of Cures, the young woman was devoutly religious. Upon hearing of the miracle fire at the foot of the Palatine Hill, she had petitioned her father and the Sabine king to let her serve the sacred flame in the new city its presence had ignited, and to learn under the priestess Rhea Silvia. She had wept tears of awe at the first sight of the orange flame moving above the earth, burning only by Vesta's will.

Yet as much as Rhea admired the young woman's piety, she appreciated her pleasant demeanor and usefulness even more. Whether she was helping her dress, prepare sarcinae, or perform the sacred rites, Tarpeia's presence made everything easier and more enjoyable, and Rhea was beginning to realize just how much she had missed the company of other women.

The two stood in Rhea's tent, preparing the older priestess for the meeting with the Etruscan royal family. The king, along with his wife and daughter, would arrive at any moment. Tarpeia hummed a song as she secured Rhea's veil to her hair.

"There," she said, holding a hairpin in her teeth as she did a final inspection of the headdress, the one that had arrived that morning from the temple in Alba Longa: cloud white with a striking red border around the edges, it was more elaborate than the one Rhea normally wore, but more appropriate for formal occasions. "It is perfect."

"Good," replied Rhea. "We may live in a tent, but we can't look as though we live in a tent."

Tarpeia smirked. "It is magic all women are expected to perform," she said. "Like laughing at an old man's jokes or saying that an ugly child has the face of Cupid"—she kept talking through Rhea's laughter—"anyway, our houses will be complete soon enough, and Master Remus has purchased several female slaves for us."

"As he should," said Rhea. "We're expected to grace meetings and smile through banquets every day and night now. We need the help. I am glad you are here, even if it is only for a short while."

"It is my honor, Priestess."

A horn sounded in the distance announcing that King Velsos's royal procession had arrived in the valley. Rhea exited her tent with Tarpeia following close behind. As she saw the procession drawing nearer, she smiled to herself, noting that her sons and their advisers had accepted all of her diplomatic suggestions. After crossing the Tiber, the king and his family had been greeted by Proculus and Hostus. They had been collected in the finest carriage available—Rhea's, from the palace—and were now being escorted by the new settlement's most impressive soldiers and musicians in a welcoming parade that was part celebratory, part military.

She saw Romulus and Remus waiting anxiously by the now completed structure that enclosed the sacred flame. Although it had been built by the best workmen the emerging city had to offer, the design of the Aedes Vestae still reflected that of the hut dwellings most people in the region resided in: a solid, round encompassing wall with a high thatched roof and an opening in the center for the smoke from the hearthfire to escape. Although the sanctum would soon have a carved-wood door, a heavy curtain was all that currently shielded the interior.

Yet the goddess's house warranted more ornamentation, so the exterior surface of the hard mud wall had been handsomely sculpted with a high border of rosettes, and then painted in spectacular fire shades of red, orange and yellow, the artistry having been completed by a recent Etruscan settler, no less. It was beautiful work, but as a sunbeam struck the building, Rhea noticed that the paint was still wet in spots.

She walked closer to her sons. As the procession stopped before them, Rhea could see the nervous uncertainty in their eyes.

"Do not kneel before him," she whispered, before taking her position behind them.

Since she was a child, Rhea had known of the mighty king of the Etrusci. She had learned to dread him and to marvel at his strength and his achievements. She had witnessed the revered fathers of Latium fret over him, always strategizing how best to keep him at bay. Yet until this moment, she had never seen him in person.

Velsos stepped out of the carriage. As he made his way toward them, Rhea peered around Romulus's head. She had expected to see a large man, a man whose girth and physical presence was as intimidating as his reputation, a body that matched the king's well-known belligerence. What she saw, however, was a man whose power clearly resided on the inside. He was no taller than her sons, slender to the point of being too thin, with patchy brown hair and a sallow face that at one time had probably been quite handsome.

He wore an ink-blue tunica with a deep-purple cloak, and a crown of gold and gemstones on his head. And the moment he regarded her sons, Rhea knew this would not be easy. He tilted his head to the side in a manner that was somewhere between arrogant and amused, his condescending expression instantly making her clench her jaw.

"I see two lookalike men," he said, assuming control of the meeting by speaking first. "Which of you is king?"

"We are equals," replied Remus.

Velsos laughed. "You are too eager to say so, boy. That tells me your brother is the greater man."

Romulus spoke, praying that Remus would keep his temper in check. "We are humbled by your visit, King Velsos," he said. "I am Romulus Silvius. My brother is Remus."

"I know your names," said the king. "I know your story, too." He glanced around the populous valley, noting how the encampments had spread to the surrounding hills. They were far more organized than he had expected. "The common people love a good story, don't they? The only thing they love more is a miracle. And here you are, boasting both before you're old enough to stomach a full jug of wine."

Romulus took a step to the side. "You may honor my mother," he said. "Priestess Rhea Silvia."

Here, Velsos showed a flash of humility. "Priestess Rhea," he said. "A great name for a great woman. Rhea, the Titaness, the mother of the gods, who used trickery to save her son from certain death." He clasped her hands. "No doubt you drew upon that strength during your years in captivity. I was pleased to hear of your liberation. I have always admired the Silvii. Tell me, how often has fate brought our paths close, only to diverge them again?"

"Too often," Rhea answered graciously.

Velsos released her hands and she folded them respectfully in front of her as his wife and daughter emerged from the carriage. As Rhea noted was often the case with powerful men, his wife was more attractive than he was, and their daughter even more so. Like Velsos, they were dressed in the royal blue and purple of the Etrusci, their already beautiful features enhanced by shimmering makeup.

"We are grateful you could attend, Queen Tarquitia," said Rhea. "I see the rumors of Princess Laria's beauty are all true. You are blessed to have such a daughter."

"And your sons are blessed to have such a conciliatory mother," the queen replied. Her tone was genuine enough.

That's something, thought Rhea. Her eyes falling upon the terracotta jar in the Etruscan queen's hands, she gestured to the Aedes Vestae. "Come, Your Majesty. Make your offering to the goddess."

The queen made a quick appraisal of the modest structure and remained silent, while her husband was less discreet.

"This is your temple to Vesta?" he asked, an edge of goading in his tone.

His wife answered before Rhea could. "Vesta is a modest goddess, husband. The sanctuary is appropriate." She studied the exterior and turned to Rhea. "This was done by a Rasennan, no?"

"Of course," said Rhea. "The artistic skill of your people is unmatched."

The reply elicited a brief, if insincere, shrug of approval from the king. Tarpeia held the curtain aside as Velsos, his wife, and his daughter followed Rhea into the inner sanctum. There, his derisive deportment faded at the sight of the supernatural fire that floated over the scorched and cratered ground.

"*Vesta Sancta*," he breathed. "So it is true."

The royal family knelt before the circle of polished white luna marble stones—Rhea was thankful they had arrived before the royals—that stood in place of the original altar stones she had taken from the river. Queen Tarquitia poured a libation of wine over one of them as the king and his daughter held their palms up in supplication.

After saying a whispered prayer, the king studied the flame. "They say it is an emission of Vesta's fire from the earth, and that it was ignited by the lightning spear of Mars."

"They speak the truth," said Rhea. "My elder son, Romulus—the gods led him here."

"Indeed," muttered the king. He lifted his eyes to peruse the encircling wall. Several niches were carved into the wall, all but one of them housing a prepared sarcina. A look of surprise flashed in his eyes as he noticed the largest niche. It held an old wooden statue of Athena, helmeted and holding a shield and spear.

"Is that…"

"It is the Palladium of Troy, Your Highness," said Rhea.

She could see his mind working it over. *Did Numitor give the sacred relic to Romulus, perhaps with the agreement that he leave Alba Longa? Was he that afraid of his grandson? Or did Romulus and his men take it by force?* Either way, the fact that it was here, in the boy's possession, was a testament to his capability. And his ambition.

After several more minutes, Rhea and Tarpeia led the royal family out of the sanctum where Romulus, Remus and a number of their officers and advisers were waiting.

Together, they made their way to an expansive banquet tent that, like Rhea's, was made of several goatskin leather tents affixed together, its system of support beams and ropes facilitating a high roof. Its interior was comfortable, furnished with dining couches, elegant three-legged tables, and busts of the gods and the Silvian kings. Expensive tapestries hung from the walls: one depicted the plight of Aeneas and Ascanius escaping Troy, while another showed the divine abundance of the Tiber as children dined on fish and waterfowl. A particularly large tapestry dramatized Venus's birth from seafoam while, high above, Pegasus galloped through the clouds. From the scraps he had taken from the Alban palace, Romulus had managed to create a feast.

The initial formalities now over, everyone relaxed on their couches with food and drink, their conversation mingling with the sound of lively pipes and the crackling of fire from the braziers. A slave, one of Romulus's recent purchases, emerged from behind a red and gold curtain carrying a tray of mouthwateringly seasoned venison. She offered first to Velsos, who reluctantly accepted a plate of meat, his upturned nose speaking for him—*Well, if this is the best you have to offer, I suppose it will have to do.*

The slight, however, was lost on his host. For the moment, Romulus was too busy stealing the occasional glance at Tarpeia, who reclined on a couch alongside Rhea and Hostus. Hostus waved his arms in the air in the telling of some anecdote and Tarpeia snickered, her fingers moving to her lips to self-consciously cover the slightest hint of an overbite.

The Etruscan king discreetly motioned for his wife to abandon her couch next to Romulus, and then instructed his daughter, the alluring Laria, to take her place.

"Romulus," said the king. "How do you like my daughter?"

Laria lowered her eyelids demurely, letting the fire from the nearby brazier illuminate the shimmering cosmetics painted upon them.

"She is very beautiful," said Romulus.

"You know," began the king, settling back as if he was about to tell a long story, "there was a time when I intended to marry her to a son of your mother's."

"I am aware," said Romulus. "It was when my mother was married to Mamilian of Tusculum."

"That's right," said Velsos, picking at the meat on his plate. "But there are many paths to the same destiny. Perhaps we should revisit the arrangement—you and my daughter. Such a marriage would certainly be to your benefit."

"Your Highness, I thank you for your offer, but I am not yet ready to wed, especially not to one so noble. There is too much work to be done here."

"Don't be foolish," said the king. "With the bond of marriage between our cities, your work would be done for you. It would be done properly too, none of this shit-seasoned venison and peasant art on the walls."

Again, the insult failed to hit its mark. "Thank you, sir," said Romulus. "I mean no disrespect to you or your daughter, but the answer must be no."

Velsos, a man not accustomed to hearing the word "no," struggled to maintain his regality. "Think of how much you could accomplish with more Rasenna in this city. Not just our outcasts and discontents, either. I hear this city is full of refugees. Don't you want better?"

"My ancestor Aeneas was a refugee, Your Highness. What kind of fool would I be if I turned away such men?"

Velsos threw his plate of food to the floor. "You can't do this without my help, boy. I'm like King Midas. Everything I touch turns to gold."

At that, Romulus nodded in affirmation. He gestured toward the tent's entrance, where—hitherto unnoticed by Velsos—Fabius's gilded head sat on a sculpted wooden pedestal. "I cannot argue that point, sir," he said.

Unexpectedly, Laria laughed. "That is brilliant," she said to Romulus. "Is that not brilliant, Father?"

Taking the cue from his daughter, Velsos relaxed. A puff of laughter escaped his lips. "It is, Laria," he agreed. "Is she not a judicious girl?" he asked Romulus.

"She is indeed. She will make an excellent wife, Your Highness, but not to me."

Laria cast Romulus a simpering smile—she knew she was pretty enough to change a man's mind—but it was Remus who suddenly struck her as more interesting. As a twin, he shared his brother's features, although he was certainly the stronger of the two. He was looking at her intently, his cheeks slightly flushed. Licking her lips, she rose from the couch.

"It is so warm tonight," she said. "Excuse me for a moment while I enjoy the evening air."

She exited the tent, casting a baited glance over her shoulder as she walked to an outdoor brazier. Once there, she tilted her head back onto her shoulders, admiring the first stars to appear in the darkening sky. As she expected, Remus trailed only a moment behind, like a fox moving fast, afraid it might lose the scent of a rabbit.

"Your blood must run hotter than your brother's," she said boldly. "That is good to know." Emboldened by the young woman's brazenness, Remus joined her at the crackling brazier, standing closer to her than he imagined her father would have liked. Rather than shying away, she closed the distance even more, playfully patting his chest. "And if I'm not mistaken, it's getting hotter by the moment."

Remus couldn't stop the smile from bursting onto his face. "I have not met a woman like you before," he said.

"If that is a compliment, it is a cryptic one. Try again."

"You are mesmerizing." The floral words gushed out of him on a wave of pure emotion, uncensored and unchecked by reason. He instantly felt foolish and wished he could take them back, but then he felt the princess's soft lips touch his cheek in a quick kiss.

"And you are nothing like your brother," she said. "How can two men who look so alike be so different?"

"We are not so different."

She smiled, letting her tongue slip out to moisten her colored lips. "You are oil and water."

Remus smiled back, conceding. "We always have been."

"Your brother is too timid to ally with my father. He fears he will lose his status. But you? I suspect you are not so easily intimidated." She sighed, and again looked up at the stars. "I don't know what Juno was thinking when she made a man like you the secondborn. Everyone can see that you are the stronger brother."

Remus felt his body moving toward hers, drawn in by her beauty and her words. "Can I see you again?" he asked.

"I would like that."

Remus brought his mouth to hers, but the sound of voices emerging from the banquet tent made him stop. A moment later, Tarpeia, tasked with escorting the royal mother and daughter to their overnight quarters, appeared with Queen Tarquitia.

"Laria," said the queen, "we should turn in for the evening." Nothing the closeness between the two, she raised her eyebrows inquisitively at her daughter, and Laria flashed Remus a mischievous grin before following her mother and Tarpeia toward a row of well-lit and well-guarded guest tents.

Remus watched her go, and kept watching until she had disappeared into her tent. Struggling to remove the smile from his face, he returned to the banquet to find things exactly as he had left them. Velsos was red-faced with drink, clearly frustrated by his lack of headway with Romulus. Remus joined them just as the king leaned closer to Romulus.

"Look, I understand," said Velsos. "I was young once. You plan to build a city of your own, as Ascanius did. And why not? You have a founder's blood in you. However, that doesn't mean you must do it alone."

"I'm not doing it alone," said Romulus. He glanced at Remus. "My brother and I—"

"—will be at each other's throats before long," said Velsos. "There can be only one founder, and only one king. That is the nature of the crown." He leaned back, avoiding Remus's stare. "Tell me, Romulus, what do you call this city of yours?"

This time, it was Proculus who spoke. He stood by Velsos's couch, regarding the king amicably. "Your Highness, the city does not yet have a name. Although I've heard some of the men call it Silvia." He waved his wine cup casually in the air. "Others are calling it Asylium. You see, there is a small shrine to the Asylean god of refuge on the banks of the Tiber, near where Faustulus—that's him, over there—found the basket. I think it a good name, don't you?"

"I have not heard either of those names," said the king. "What I have heard is people saying they're 'going to Romulus.' They speak as though Romulus were a place and not just a person." His instigating gaze shifted to Remus. "The city will bear your brother's name. It is inevitable."

"Nothing is inevitable," replied Remus.

Velsos chuckled. "If you believe that," he said, "you know even less about the gods than you do about kings."

CHAPTER XXIII

He wasn't sure if it was the crash of thunder or the nagging urge to urinate that woke him, but either way, Romulus wished he could ignore it. The fire in the hearth had gone out and his hut was cool. He heard Magia sigh in her sleep next to him, her naked body warming his bed like a living ember.

Ever since he had been a boy and had started to think about such things, Romulus had fantasized about Magia. However, the one time he had secretly scraped together enough bronze to pay for a night with her, she had turned him down in favor of a visiting merchant who offered her silver. *It's just business, honey,* she had said.

She turned over in her sleep, causing the bedcovers to shift and letting a chill slip underneath to prickle Romulus's skin. Realizing it was hopeless—there was no way he would fall back asleep now—he reluctantly swung his legs out of bed. He stood shivering and pulled a woolen tunica over his head. A flash of lightning illuminated the interior of the hut for a passing moment, and he spotted his chamberpot. He thought about using it, but he didn't want Magia waking to the sound of a stream of urine. And anyway, the rain had not yet started. There was time enough for him to relieve himself outside.

He stepped into the night air to find two of his regular guards, Paeon and Rastus, sitting on stools, chatting idly in front of a snapping fire.

"…and then the bastard said his horse was a hand taller than mine. I had half a mind to—oh, Your Highness, I didn't hear you." Realizing that was probably the wrong thing to say, he stood. "Can we be of service, sir?"

"No," replied Romulus. "Carry on."

As the cool air stole the last of his sleepiness, Romulus walked a few steps away from his hut, toward the line of trees behind the encampment. He could hear his two guards continue their conversation—some petty dispute about horses—and lifted the bottom of his tunica, blinking absently into the blackness ahead as he relieved himself.

He flinched involuntarily as a deafening bolt of lightning turned night into day, momentarily illuminating the spaces between the thick trees. His heart pounded hard in his chest, so hard that could count the beats—one, two three—and he squinted. *Was there something there? In the trees?*

Another bolt of electric light crashed down from the heavens. This time, Romulus saw it—a figure, moving stealthily through the trees, running fast, a wild animal weaving through the woods, closing in on him. He thought back to the bear that had attacked Proculus and took a breathless step back. A third crash of lightning, another flare of white light, and the vision was upon him: not a bear, but a large man, charging out of the darkness toward its prey.

Before he could react, Romulus felt a painful impact on his side, followed by an even worse pain that traveled in a path of piercing agony down his back. He fell over and lay dazed on the ground, the shouts of his guards echoing around him, sounding strange and hollow in the still night air.

"Get his other arm! He has a dagger!"

"He's on top of me…I can't move! He's too bloody big!"

Romulus felt strong arms around his upper body, dragging him away from the struggle, toward a perimeter of torches. He looked up into the shaken but determined face of Hostus.

A heavy thunderclap boomed overhead, followed by shouting and the rush of footfalls as more men arrived, all carrying torches and swords. They all but threw themselves into the deadly skirmish, desperately trying to pry the dagger out of the intruder's hand and pull him off the two guards.

As Romulus sat panting on the ground, Remus and Proculus—both of them disheveled, obviously having been woken with a fright—squatted in front of him. The rain had just begun to fall, pasting their hair to their heads.

"What happened?" asked Remus. "Are you hurt?"

Romulus grimaced. "The bastard cut my back." He struggled to his knees. "Make sure they don't kill him!"

Leaving Hostus with Romulus, Remus and Proculus dashed to the nearby treeline where, at long last, the would-be assassin had been restrained. It had taken several men to do it, though, and they were all bleeding from their efforts.

Romulus's guards Paeon and Rastus—the first to have engaged the attacker—seemed to have taken the worst of it. Paeon, who had roughly shouldered Romulus aside, bore the marks of his heroics—an open gash to the side of his neck. Dark blood streamed down the side of his body to soak through his tunica as two men carried him off. Rastus sat on the ground, pressing his hand against a bulging eye as if trying to keep it in its socket, while another man fumbled to wrap a makeshift bandage around his head.

Hostus helped Romulus to his feet, and he limped to the thick tree trunk against which no fewer than four men were restraining his attacker. The other men stood around, sucking in air and inspecting their wounds in the rain.

"*Insanos deos!*" exclaimed Proculus. He held up a sputtering torch and they all got their first good look at the massive, battle-scarred intruder. "Hercules isn't on Olympus," he said. "He's on the Palatine!"

"I'll rip you apart like Hercules," spat the assailant.

Hostus looked at Romulus. "His accent is Samnite." He left Romulus's side to stand nose to nose with the attacker. "Who sent you?" he asked. "How many of you are there?"

The assassin grinned fearlessly, revealing a row of black and broken teeth.

"Tell us," said Remus, "and you may yet live."

"Go fuck yourself, boy." Noticing someone behind Remus, the attacker's grin grew wider. "On second thought, give me 'til dawn with that one and I'll tell you everything."

They all turned to see the priestess Rhea standing in the rain, drenched head to toe, her guards standing on either side of her. Suddenly realizing their female charge was somewhat exposed in her nightdress and light *palla*, one of the guards removed his heavy cloak and wrapped it around her shoulders.

"We could not stop her," the guard said to Romulus. "She heard the shouts and started running." He looked at Rhea. "We're lucky we could keep up."

"Go fetch Faustulus from his home," Rhea said to a soldier. "He should be here." As he darted off, she wiped the rain from her eyes and looked curiously at the attacker. "He doesn't need to survive," she said to Hostus, "but we need to know if there are more."

"Yes, Priestess." Blinking away the rain, Hostus searched the ground until he found what he was looking for: an axe, leaning against a tree, with a few other carpentry tools scattered around it. He picked it up. "Watch your heads," he said to the soldiers who struggled to control the powerful attacker.

When they were clear, Hostus swung the flat side of the axe blade toward the intruder, hitting his skull with a thump and stunning him into a more manageable state. His enormous body slumped downward and he muttered a slurred obscenity.

"Strip him," said Hostus. "Hang him up by his ankles." He pointed to a sturdy branch. "That one should hold him."

As the intruder dipped in and out of consciousness, belligerent one moment and senseless the next, it took the strength of several soldiers, who cursed the entire time, to cut the tunica off his body. It then took several more men—even the officers had to help—to hang him upside down from the tree: they worked together in the rain to hoist up his bulk, his sporadic viciousness making him even more formidable, until he hung from the ankles, though low enough that the top of his head scuffed the wet ground.

That done, the soldiers bent over, hands on their knees, heaving for breath. They looked at the suspended man. As the blood rushed to the assailant's head, his senses began to return.

"He's coming to," warned Hostus.

As the man's eyes opened and he realized his predicament, he began to thrash fiercely, twisting his body and desperately trying to curl upward enough to reach his bound ankles. After a few panic-stricken attempts, he realized it was hopeless. He changed his tactics, first clawing at the soggy earth to try to find enough purchase to pull himself down, but that also failing, began to strike out with club-like arms at anyone who dared to come close.

"Settle down," said one soldier. He dodged the deadly arms and tried to grip the man's head, but shrieked as the captive twisted his body and clamped the soldier's hand between his broken teeth. He held on for a screaming moment—just to prove that he could—then spat out a severed finger. The soldier clutched his bloody hand and stumbled away.

Remus let out a short, snickering laugh. "If that's how you want it, friend," he said to the hanging Samnite. He strode to the same pile of carpentry tools from which Hostus had taken the axe and returned with two long wooden stakes and a hammer. "Hold his arms," he ordered.

Immediately taking his meaning, Hostus—who had a brutal streak himself—directed one of the stronger soldiers to follow his lead. They each grabbed one of the assailant's thick arms and extended it outward, stepping on his fingers to hold the back of his hands flat against the ground. Remus positioned the tip of a stake over the man's left palm and brought the hammer down hard, bloodily and excruciatingly pinning the man's hand to the earth. Ignoring the string of profanities that spewed forth from his mouth, he did the same to his right hand. Squatting in front of the man's contorted face, he waited for the obscenities to subside.

"Right now, you're not Hercules," said Remus, "you're the Erymanthian boar. The sooner you accept that, the sooner this will be over. Now tell us, who sent you?"

The attacker clenched his teeth. "Fuck off," he muttered.

Remus stood and stepped back to stand beside Hostus. "I almost admire the prick," he said. "Look at him. Ass in the air, head in the mud, hands nailed to the ground, and still stubborn as a mule."

Hostus looked sideways at Remus. Had things gone a little differently, Romulus would be dead right now. He saw nothing to admire in that. "We don't have time for this," he said. He glanced at a soldier. "Get me a saw."

The soldier disappeared into the rain and returned moments later with a metal saw that gleamed with a long, serrated blade. Without pause, Hostus approached the assailant and positioned the blade between his spread legs—and then he began to cut.

The attacker screamed. His body jerked and writhed as the delicate flesh of his anus and genitals split apart. The red spray of blood mixed with the rain, and blood poured down the man's torso, quickly reaching and coating his throat and finally his face. The screams stopped as blood filled his nostrils. He snorted and coughed, frantically trying to clear his airway without the benefit of his hands, both of which were still pinned to the ground.

Hostus kept sawing until he felt the man's muscles and ligaments give way and detach—his legs shifting unnaturally as they did—and the blade reached the bone of his pelvis. The man let out a cacophony of gasps, gurgled breaths, and moans of agony. Hostus tossed the bloody saw aside and, as Remus had done, squatted in front of the man's face. He knew he did not have long to ask his questions.

He scooped away a handful of thick blood from the man's eyes, nose and mouth. The men, and Rhea, came closer.

"Who sent you?" Hostus asked him. "Tell me, and I'll end your suffering."

Although the man's voice was thin, although his teeth chattered and his eyelids fluttered—he would pass out at any moment—he nonetheless pushed an answer through his lips. "Velsos."

Hostus glanced up at his companions. No one seemed surprised by the revelation. He turned his attention back to the dying assailant. "Did anyone else come with you?"

"Just the…messenger," he said, falling into unconsciousness.

Romulus rushed forward, his rage made more potent by his pain. Falling to his knees beside Hostus, he gripped the assassin's hair and shook his head ferociously, bringing him back to what remained of his senses. "What messenger?" He shook the bloodied man's head even harder. "What fucking messenger?"

"The…the king's messenger."

"Where is he?" Romulus demanded.

But he received no answer. The man hung limply, gasping and babbling incoherently as another stream of blood poured out his nose and mouth.

Romulus spoke over his shoulder to his men. "Find him."

As the soldiers adjusted their armor, ready to dart for their horses, Romulus noticed his brother staring at the muddy ground. Remus's expression was tense and pensive, uncharacteristically subdued. He met Romulus's eyes.

"Wait," said Remus. The men froze in place, all attention now suddenly on him: he spoke directly to Romulus. "The messenger was here for me," he admitted, unable to stop a waver of apprehension from slipping into his voice. "Brother, can we talk inside?"

Romulus let go of the suspended man's head. He stood up slowly, turning to stare gravely at his brother. Instinctively, Rhea moved to Remus's side as if she could shield him from the accusatory stares of men, hard men already imbued with the spirit of suspicion and violence.

Romulus glared at his brother. "He was here for you?" A thunderclap rolled ominously across the black sky. "Have you been communicating with the Etruscan king behind my back?"

"Brother," he said. "It is not how it looks. Let us discuss this privately."

Romulus lurched forward and seized Remus's tunica at the neckline, twisting the fabric in his fist. "Answer me! Or I'll have you drowned like a trussed hog in the Tiber!"

Several of Romulus's men, including Proculus and Hostus, moved their hands to the hilts of their daggers and inched menacingly toward Remus.

Rhea reacted to the threat, to the animalist gleam in Romulus's normally thoughtful eyes. Like a wolf defending her pup, she moved to stand between the men and Remus. "Stop!" she said. "Romulus, let us go inside. We can talk." When he did not respond, she pulled the cloak tighter around her shoulders. "Romulus, please. I am cold."

Romulus released his grip on his brother's tunica. As Velsos's hired assassin quietly bled to death behind them, he limped angrily into a large hut used to hold strategy meetings. Remus, Rhea, Hostus and Proculus followed.

It was dry and warm inside the hut, with crackling braziers and enough oil lamps to light the interior well enough. Rhea brought an oil lamp close to Romulus's back and lifted his tunica to inspect his wound. "It is a long cut," she said, "but not deep. It needs to be dressed."

"It can wait," said Romulus.

Rhea was about to argue when Faustulus appeared in the doorway. He stepped inside the hut in that same winded stupor they all battled, the kind reserved for crises that strike in the dead of night.

"They told me what happened," he said.

"Really?" asked Romulus. "Did they tell you how my brother has betrayed me?"

"I have not betrayed you," said Remus.

"Did you exchange messages with the Etruscan king without telling me?"

"Yes, but—"

"Let me guess," Romulus jeered. "He offered his daughter to you."

Remus hesitated, but then threw his arms up in an exaggerated gesture of admission. "Yes," he confessed. "Now you tell me, why shouldn't I marry her?"

Romulus pointed in the direction of the door. "The reason is hanging from a tree just outside," he shouted. "Is that not enough?" He rubbed his temples in frustration, his shoulders rising and falling with heavy breaths. As he regained his self-control, he eyed his brother with renewed distrust.

Remus knew what he was thinking. "Brother," he said. "Velsos and I only discussed the marriage. I knew nothing about this attack."

Romulus wiped moisture off his forehead, leaving a streak of blood—the assassin's—behind. "You lie with the skill of Nessus," he said. "I'll find myself covered in blood if I believe you."

"Not so," said Remus, feeling his own anger rise. "You are the best liar between here and Alba Longa. What did you promise me at the Alban palace? You said that if I came here with you, we would rule our city together, as equals. But that has not happened. Since the moment we arrived, it has been your city."

Rhea stepped between them. "That is the king of the Etrusci speaking," she said to Remus. "He wishes to divide you, so that he can conquer this city from within."

"I know," said Remus. "I am not a total fool, Mother. But a marriage between our cities would change that. Princess Laria—"

"The princess is a beautiful woman," said Rhea, "but there are other beautiful women."

"I want *her*," replied Remus. "And why shouldn't I have her? Because my brother forbids it? How am I equal if I cannot even choose my own wife?"

Rhea forced calmness into her voice. "Remus, it is different with the Etrusci. Women are equal to their husbands, and royal women are superior. If you were to marry Princess Laria, her father would use his power to position her as queen of this city. Romulus would be dead, and you would be a mere figurehead. This city would be nothing more than a colony of Etruria, a means for them to expand into Latium."

"Princess Laria is in love with me."

"She is not, son. She will only hurt you."

"Oh, please, Mother," said Remus. "Do not pretend to care about me. Your only concern is him," he pointed to Romulus. "It has been that way since the day we freed you from the necropolis. He is the firstborn, he is the rightful heir, he is the first mortal son of Mars. Being secondborn to such regality is its own form of slavery."

"Remus, that is not true! I love you equally, I swear it."

"It would be easier without me, wouldn't it? You could gorge yourself on Romulus's greatness without having to throw me the scraps."

"Son, that is not how I—"

Remus turned his back to her and jabbed a finger at Romulus. "My men tell me that you finished mapping the boundaries of the city yesterday without consulting me. You know I prefer the Aventine, as do many of my men."

"You may prefer it, but the gods and I prefer the Palatine," said Romulus. "Only yesterday morning an Etruscan augur saw twelve vultures fly over the Palatine, and only half that over the Aventine. What better sign from Mars do you need?"

"An Etruscan augur? So you spurn their king but laud their charlatan priests? Your vultures were not sent by Mars, brother, they smelled a rotting sheep on other side of the hill."

"It is settled," said Romulus. "The city will be here, on the Palatine. And I was going to consult you about the boundaries, but you were busy in the valley with the drainage engineers. We can't wait any longer. The walls need to go up. The men and materials are ready and we should have started by now."

"Oh, so you get to define the city, while I drain it? You don't trust me to—"

"No!" Romulus exploded. "I do not trust you! I want to trust you, I *need* to trust you, but I cannot! Every time I need thoughtful counsel, you are too busy beating someone to death, or slicing their throat, or suffocating them. When I need loyalty, I get betrayal and secrecy. How can I trust you?"

Remus's head pounded. The primeval streak of envy and rage he felt toward his brother, the primitive and powerful desire he had for the princess and his longing to have her…it all congealed into a single feeling—hate. Without thinking, he lunged at Romulus, his fist landing solidly on his jaw.

Ever since they were children, Remus had always been the stronger of the two, the more aggressive. And so when Romulus did not react to the blow—he merely spat out a mouthful of blood as if immune to the pain—Remus could not help but stagger back, dumbfounded.

In an instant, Romulus grabbed the handle of the terracotta wine jug on the table beside him and swung it hard at Remus's head. Remus's body spun and collapsed to the floor. Through the head-splitting ringing in his ears, he could hear Rhea and Faustulus shouting muted words at Romulus.

But whatever they were saying, Romulus was ignoring it. He straddled Remus's body and began to pummel his head from above with the wine jug, even as the terracotta vessel burst apart from the force of the blows. Remus felt a stream of warm blood rush down his temple. He raised his hands to defend himself, but the beating continued until Faustulus managed to pull Romulus off him.

A dreadful silence followed.

As Romulus sat on the ground, winded and glaring spitefully at Remus, Rhea knew that her firstborn son had changed. A maniacal intensity had descended upon him, and as he pushed himself to his feet, he had not a trace of concern or sympathy in his eyes for his wounded brother. He seemed older, the last softness of youth now gone from his face.

"Velsos was right about one thing," said Romulus. "There can be only one founder. One king." He stood, his lip curled in disgust as he stared down at his brother. "Take your men and go to the Aventine. This city belongs to me. This is Rome."

CHAPTER XXIV

Rhea had been arguing with Faustulus for so long that no matter how much water she drank, her throat still felt dry. After the violent estrangement between Romulus and Remus and the latter's departure to the Aventine, she and Faustulus had spent days trying to figure out how to reconcile the twins and renew their commitment to building the city together.

In the end, Rhea had determined it could not be done. If she was honest with herself, perhaps she had known it all along.

"The power always comes between them," she said to Faustulus, as they sat together by the snapping central hearthfire in her now completed home near the Aedes Vestae. "I watched it unfold with my father and his brother, and then again with my brother, Egestus, and my cousin, Nemeois. It is the perennial curse of Silvian sons."

Faustulus shook his head in disagreement, but Rhea was already off in her own thoughts. Hearing herself speak Nemeois's name aloud had revived bitter feelings of betrayal: the shock and rage, the sting of perfidy she had felt when her once loving cousin had opened Egestus's throat. Worse, the memory of that treachery had marched her to an undeniable truth. Remus too had betrayed her and Romulus. His secret communication with the Etruscan king was not just disloyal. It was dangerous.

They are nothing alike, she told herself. *Remus and Nemeois… this is different.*

She hated herself for doubting her son. Yet how could she not? While Romulus had not capitulated to the manipulations of Velsos or the temptation of his beautiful daughter, Remus had succumbed to both. Rhea absently tugged at a stray lock of hair in thought. Did Remus simply have a more pliable disposition, or did the breach of trust stem from envy? She thought back to the crisis on the Palatine—to how quickly, how naturally, most of the men had marshalled around Romulus, even to the threshold of committing violence against Remus. No matter how much Romulus had tried to assert that he and his brother would be equals in their new city, the gods simply did not make men that way.

Faustulus pushed aside a plate of bread and figs and chewed his lip instead. "I know they can be reconciled," he insisted, talking as much to himself as to Rhea.

"Perhaps they can, but for how long?" she asked. "A month? A year? Until another king offers an even prettier daughter? Perhaps it is time to accept the nature of men and the will of the gods." She stoked the fire, and a thick, orange flame crackled to life. Rhea stared into it. "When I was in the necropolis," she began, "I used to dream all the time. I don't know if the dreams kept me sane or brought me closer to madness, but they came almost every night. I remember one of them. I was sleeping by the sacred fire when the ribbon fell from my hair. I sat up to retrieve it, but it began to grow into two trees. One of them grew to a natural height, but the other kept growing. It grew until it covered the whole world." She stoked the fire again. "If we go to Remus together, he may listen to us. He may be content to be prince."

"I will not tell Remus to bow to his brother," said Faustulus. "They are meant to be equals."

"You are too naïve, Faustulus. They are not children fishing for eels in the river anymore. They are men fighting for a kingdom. And there is a natural order to kingdoms. Everyone must know their place. That is the only way to keep the peace. It is the only way for them to be brothers and not enemies."

"I cannot choose one of my sons over the other." Although he tried to hide it, Rhea heard the edge of insinuation in his voice.

"They are *my* sons," she said. "You will defer to my decisions, or I will have you banished from the city. Do you understand?"

He paused. "Yes, Priestess."

Rhea considered softening her tone, but decided against it. Faustulus may have raised the twins, but he was not their father. Their days of lambing and listening to the advice of a shepherd were over. She stood.

"You can go," she said.

He left without saying a word. Rhea watched him leave, then wrapped her cloak over her shoulders and made her way to the Aedes Vestae. Tarpeia was just emerging and greeted her with the warmth of a much-needed smile.

"I have performed the morning rites, Priestess," she said. "Just as you instructed."

"That is good, Tarpeia. I am going to speak with Romulus. I will return soon."

As her guards trailed her at a respectful but watchful distance, Rhea walked briskly up the Palatine and toward the nexus of huts where Romulus lived. She was met pleasantly by Proculus and Hostus. They looked as though they had just finished delivering the day's orders to Romulus's other top officers, who were in the process of dispersing. When Romulus heard them greet her, he emerged from his strategy hut.

"*Salve*, Mother," he said. "Did you sleep well?"

"Well enough," she lied. There was no point telling him that she and the shepherd had been bickering since sunrise. "I thought we could take a walk together."

"Would you not rather rest? You already walked here."

"It is a mild morning. Let's walk, son."

They strolled together comfortably to the *Aedicula Vestae*, the small shrine to the goddess that Romulus had ordered built near his hut. Rhea had used flames from the *ignis mirabilis* to light its altar fire. Romulus poured a libation of oil over the altar and drizzled a stream into the flames. Strolling along, they reached the north side of the Palatine, which offered an unparalleled view of the valley below, as well as the hills beyond. A wisp of smoke from the sacred fire snaked out of the opening in the roof of the Aedes Vestae and floated upward until it dissolved into the morning air.

"Priests from Delphi arrived just before sunset last night," said Rhea. "They wanted to see the sacred flame."

"Delphi," said Romulus. "Where the Oracle is?"

"Yes. They told me the eternal fire that burns in the Temple of Apollo there began the same way. It burned for months on its own, a miracle, before the flames began to fade and the sacerdotes were required to sustain it. If this fire begins to weaken, I will need more help than just one priestess if I am to keep it burning at all times."

"You will have it," said Romulus. "A number of cities have asked to send sacerdotes. That includes Maleventum, if you can believe it. They regret the assassin was a Samnite and wish to keep the peace."

Rhea nodded. "That is good news, but you must only accept women who are already betrothed," she said, "like Tarpeia. Not all orders follow that custom."

"I will try," he said, but his thoughts seemed to drift.

"After the Greek priests left," Rhea began again, "we had even more visitors—a group of *Amazónes*."

"Yes, I heard about that this morning," grinned Romulus. "Apparently they made quite an impression. As desperate as my men are for the company of women, they were unwilling to approach them."

"That was a wise decision," smiled Rhea. "Son, you are fortunate it was a Samnite and not an Amazon who wielded the blade against you. They live up to their reputation as warriors. They showed great reverence for the flame, though, and said your city's fame spreads more each day."

"That is why it must be the greatest city in the world," Romulus replied. "Have you seen how much land we're clearing along the river and south of the Palatine? Those will be camps where my soldiers and war horses can train." He looked down into the valley below them. "Faustulus told me that when he was a boy, villagers from all over these hills used to bury the urns of their loved ones here. I will develop this whole area from their ashes. There will be homes here and a market. It will serve as a forum for people who come here to live or trade." He pointed to the hill just northwest of them. Like the Palatine, it also overlooked the valley. "They call that the hill of Saturn," he said. "My citadel will be there, and great temples will cover the whole hilltop, grander than anywhere else in the world. The other day I stumbled upon the strangest flint stone there—you should go see it, Mother, it is shaped just like a thunderbolt!—and so I pledged to build a temple to Jupiter on the very spot. And do you see those men working down there by the shrine to Vulcan? They are building a *Comitium* where I can hold assembly and honor the gods."

"Like the meeting place of the revered fathers in Marino," said Rhea.

"Yes, but better."

She smiled. His enthusiasm for the future was contagious, but memories of the past always came with a touch of melancholy. She turned her head and stared off into the distance, in the direction of Alba Longa: she could almost imagine the green hills meeting the blue sky. It was not a terribly long way away, but the distance between her old life in Alba Longa and her new life in Rome seemed suddenly immeasurable.

Was she really the same person who had once skipped rocks in the lake with Nemeois, played dice with Egestus and her father, and shared girlish laughter with Thalia and Lela? How could people who had at one time seemed so fundamental to her life now seem so foreign?

"I received a messenger from the high priestess of the Vestal order in Alba Longa," said Rhea. "She again expressed her discontent that you have taken the Palladium."

"Her discontent is of no concern to me."

"It is to me, son. She is a woman to be respected."

After a pause, Romulus said, "I will not return the Palladium, but I will send her a personal message, explaining my reasons for taking it. I know she advocated for you during your captivity. I will express my gratitude and send a rich gift to the temple." He looked at Rhea. "I will be respectful, Mother."

Rhea knew it was pointless to argue, so she left it at that. "The high priestess also said that Numitor is fading. He will die soon. Romulus, if you still refuse to take the Alban throne, you will need to decide on a successor. Perhaps..." she ground the toe of a sandal into the ground.

"Speak freely, Mother."

"Perhaps you could put Remus on the throne. With him as king of Alba Longa, and you king of Rome, all of Latium would be—"

"Never," said Romulus.

"Then do not make him king. Let him rule as a prince, in your name."

"No." He frowned, his posture stiffening. "That would put him in command of the Alban army. I don't trust him enough for that. You are correct about naming a successor, though. I have already been thinking about it, and I have chosen Sextus Julius—a nephew of Albus Julius, and a cousin of Proculus. I'd appoint Proculus himself, but I need him in Rome with me. Both Albus and Proculus say that Sextus is capable enough. He is only seventeen years old, but Albus will serve as regent until he is ready."

Rhea looked away. So there it was. The end of the Silvian kings in Alba Longa. She had privately hoped that Romulus would change his mind and return to the city of his birth to wear the crown of his ancestors, but now it was clear that would never happen. "A Julian on the throne of Alba Longa," she mused. "It is a politic choice. I still wish you would at least speak to your brother, though. So does Faustulus. Perhaps you can meet at your new Comitium—"

"There will be no negotiation, Mother. Remus is building his encampment on the site of an abandoned settlement on the Aventine. That gives him an advantage. He's fortifying the existing walls and gathering an army, and his man Luperco is recruiting men from the countryside. Proculus and Hostus have confirmed it. My brother's actions are not those of a man inclined toward peace."

"Proculus and Hostus have always been loyal to you," said Rhea. "They have never supported Remus. What if they are not telling you the truth?"

"I sent additional scouts out in secret," said Romulus. "I needed to be certain. They came back with the same information."

"I cannot believe it."

"Remus spreads the lie that I am a tyrant, that I commit sacrilege by saying I am the son of Mars." He faced Rhea. "But I *am* the son of Mars. It is not a sacrilege to say so. I was born at the feet of the god. He sent a spear of lightning to bring me here, and then he lit the sky to save me from the assassin's blade. I will not feign mediocrity just to appease my brother."

He turned his back to her. When he did, she noticed a small spot of blood had soaked through his tunica from where the attacker had cut him.

"You are bleeding," she said. "Are you having the dressing changed every morning?"

"Yes."

"My new slave, Polyxene, will treat you. She makes a warm peppermint tonic that cures even the worst headache. She will know how to heal the wound."

"I will see her as soon as I can."

Rhea stepped closer to her son: her firstborn, the one born with the blue eyes and the frowning face. She and Romulus were unified in their common purpose to build a city where the gods had ordained it, but the unresolved break with Remus, and the hard change in Romulus—a change that increasingly bordered on the egomaniacal—now brought an undercurrent of tension to each conversation.

Rhea tried to soothe it. Looking again at the Aedes Vestae in the forum below, she smiled. "Your ancestors would be proud to know the fire of Troy burns here."

He followed her gaze. Wisps of smoke rose out of the circular roof. It was a sign to Romulus, to everyone, that *Vesta Aeterna* now resided in his new city. "The fire of Troy has gone out, Mother," he said. "That is the fire of Rome."

※ ※ ※

There was no doubt that life in the new city of Rome—at least for those in Romulus's inner circle—had transitioned from a life of getting by, of having only the necessities and eking out an existence, to a life of some ease and even a few luxuries. No one enjoyed more luxuries, or more admiration, than Rhea. As mother to the city's young king and priestess of the sacred flame, everyone from sweat-stained laborers to visiting kings took care to honor her.

And yet Remus still refused to see her. All of her messengers were denied entrance to his growing encampment on the Aventine, and were sent away unheard. She could not stop hearing his words, though.

It would be easier without me, wouldn't it? You could gorge yourself on Romulus's greatness without having to throw me the scraps.

The words were hurtful enough, but the real pain came from knowing there was some truth to them. She loved Remus, but his refusal to accept the law of primogeniture, as practiced by the Silvii for generations, continued to cause discord, distrust and unrest.

Yet as she waited in her sitting room for Mamilian to arrive from Tusculum, she had to wonder: had she not also defied the laws of the Silvii by refusing to be Mamilian's queen and bear his sons? Like Remus, she had rejected the expectations of her birth. Her ambitions and her actions had caused the death and suffering of those she loved. As she thought about Mamilian, and all those lonely years she had spent in the necropolis, she could not help but think that she would have been happier had she simply done what was expected of her.

If only Remus would hear me, she thought. *I could tell him how I should have fulfilled my duty as a Silvii. I could make him understand his own duty and accept it.*

Her slave Polyxene pulled back the curtain to her sitting room. "Priestess," she said. "Master Mamilian has arrived."

"Show him in."

He entered, and Rhea felt the familiar pull toward him.

"Let me guess," he said magnanimously. "You've decided to marry me after all."

Rhea tilted her head, disguising her weakness for him with wit. "How strange," she said. "It is unusual for a man to develop a sense of humor this late in life."

"I have two daughters," he replied, sitting. "It was either develop a sense of humor or lose my mind."

As Polyxene poured them both a cup of wine, Rhea grew more serious. "How are your daughters? I am told they are exceptional."

"Don't all fathers think their daughters are so?"

Rhea looked at the wine cup in her hands. "My father does not," she said. "I cannot blame him."

"Your father is a foolish old man, Rhea. If Albus Julius didn't still feel obligated to prop him up on the throne, he'd fall off of it. Not that it will matter soon. He is frail and failing. He won't last the summer."

"I have been thinking about that, Mamilian. When he dies, the Silvian line of Alban kings will die with him."

"It will be the end of great era."

"And the beginning of a new one," she replied. "I have a proposal for you."

He settled back in his chair. "I'm listening."

"I would like you to use your leverage as a revered father of Latium to have my son's city, Rome, recognized by the Confederation."

"And in exchange?"

"Romulus has decided that Sextus Julius, a nephew of Albus Julius, will succeed my father as king. I am told he is a fine boy, and Albus will serve as regent until he comes of age next year. If you agree, I will arrange for Sextus to marry one of your daughters. She will be the next queen of Alba Longa. Your other daughter may come here, to Rome. She can serve her tenure as a sacerdos here, and after that, you can decide on a suitable husband for her. Romulus has established alliances with some wealthy cities. She will do well for herself while expanding your influence in Latium, and beyond."

Mamilian nodded his head, first in thought and then in approval. "Agreed,"

he said. "With one condition."

"Name it."

"You take me to the Aedes Vestae, and we'll honor the goddess together."

※ ※ ※

As it turned out, Mamilian stayed in Rome for several days. In a turn of events that proved to Rhea that the gods were as unpredictable as they were inscrutable, he and Romulus had connected, and the more experienced man had offered the young city founder some invaluable advice.

Mamilian had been particularly interested in the large swath of field that Romulus was clearing in the valley on the south side of the Palatine Hill, between it and the Aventine. People in the region had for years called it the Valley of Murcia for the abundant myrtle trees that grew there, but those were now mostly gone to make way for a rectangular equestrian field. Mamilian, however, had the idea that it instead be constructed as a great oval so that horses could be raced around its perimeter, both for training and for sport, and Romulus had immediately thrown his engineers into disarray by insisting on the change. And so the Valley of Murcia would now be Rome's hippodrome, the Circus.

But the visit was not all business. Romulus and Mamilian had celebrated their alliance with a number of evening banquets during which Rhea had tried, although unsuccessfully, to put thoughts of Remus to rest for a few hours while she enjoyed the food, drink, and company.

Still, she could not deny that spending time with Mamilian, being close to him in such an informal way, felt good. He seemed to feel the same way, and had taken her by the hand several times during their walks along the Tiber before catching himself and letting go. They both knew that time had passed them by. Her duty to Vesta and to Rome made it impossible now.

They said their goodbyes in the early morning hours of the sixth day of Mamilian's visit. He had embraced her in parting, leaving her with a strangely hollow feeling in the pit of her stomach. She watched him go, and then headed unhurriedly to the Aedes Vestae. Tarpeia would already be there, scrubbing the previous day's libations off the marble altar stones with spring water and performing the morning rites.

Rhea neared the circular structure, noticing that three workers were busy replastering a section of the exterior wall. They were chatting easily with each other and with the guards, laughing as they worked, until one of them stood up straight and pointed in concern at a fourth man who was carting a load of plaster inside the sanctum.

The guards' relaxed demeanor disappeared, replaced with sudden alarm. Rhea watched, her heart hammering in her chest, as the pair of guards and the trio of workmen all raced inside the Aedes Vestae. Shouts followed—a cry of protest from Tarpeia and the sound of men struggling.

"Get his other arm! Bloody Jove, watch his feet!"

Lifting the bottom of her tunica, Rhea dashed toward the Aedes Vestae. She opened the door and gasped. Inside, it was chaos. Both of the guards and one of the workmen were struggling to restrain the intruder: he fought and screamed in defiance, but a swift kick to the head by one of the guards silenced him.

But that was not the worst of it.

Rhea heard herself cry out, "No!" at the sight of a spreading puddle of thick, wet plaster that had been dumped on the *ignis mirabilis*. She stumbled over the fighting men and dropped to her knees beside Tarpeia who, along with the two other workmen, was frantically clawing at the plaster, desperately trying to stop it from suffocating the divine flame.

Rhea joined their efforts, pausing only to extinguish a flare of fire that had caught the ends of Tarpeia's long hair. Yet the more they tried to sweep away the heavy plaster, the more it was evident to all of them that it was no use.

The fire was out.

As the men sat back, their heads in their hands, Tarpeia began to weep.

Yet all was not lost. Rhea crawled to the wall and reached up to a niche, within which sat an expertly bundled sarcina.

"It's still warm," she said to Tarpeia. "Run and get a bowl!"

The young woman was gone and back before Rhea had even caught her breath. Together, they set the sarcina in the bronze firebowl that Tarpeia had brought. Carefully, Rhea unwrapped the precious bundle and placed dry tinder on the red-hot coal inside as Tarpeia collected a few smoothened branches of oak from a niche in the wall. Rhea leaned over the ember and gently blew, waking the sleeping flame. A flare of orange burst forth, snapping and consuming the tinder, and soon reaching out for more. Rhea placed the oak branches on top, and within a few moments, the infant flame had grown into a strong fire.

The two women sat back and clasped hands in relief. Behind them, the shaken guards and workmen offered prayers of gratitude.

"We will take this as a sign," Rhea said, her voice trembling but resolute. "The goddess has finished doing our work for us. Now, it is our duty to keep her flame burning."

CHAPTER XXV

"I've seen him before," said Hostus. "He's Luperco's kinsman."

"Luperco?" asked Proculus. "Remus's right-hand man?"

Hostus nodded soberly. "We can assume Remus is behind the attack."

Romulus squatted down to examine the face of the dead man on the ground outside the Aedes Vestae. The guard had kicked him so hard in the head that his neck had snapped. Romulus wished it had not. He wished the man was still alive so that he could kill him. A snapped neck was too easy a death for the criminal who had violated the goddess's flame.

"Take the body to the Aventine and dump it in front of the gates to my brother's encampment," he said. "Then position newsreaders along the road and on the hills. Have them spread word that Remus's sacrilege failed. The sacred flame still burns."

"At once," said Proculus. "Thank the gods the priestess could save it."

"Yes, but she will need more hands to keep it burning," said Romulus. "I will dispatch messengers to several of our allied cities. They will send women to help her."

"More women," grinned Hostus. "That's never a bad thing."

"They will be sacerdotes of Vesta," said Romulus. "So you will still have to make do with prostitutes for now." Standing, he looked over his shoulder toward his mother's house to see Faustulus exiting. The shepherd was walking quickly, with his shoulders up and his head down, angrily mumbling to himself. "That is all for now," Romulus said, dismissing his men. He marched to Faustulus, meeting his eyes. "What is the matter?" he asked.

"Your mother is the matter," Faustulus replied. He brushed by Romulus and kept walking.

Cautiously, Romulus entered his mother's house. She was kneeling in prayer before a small shrine to Vesta, weeping softly. Without speaking, he knelt beside her. He dipped his fingers into the terracotta bowl of oil that sat on the shrine, and then dripped the oil into the flame of a lamp, making a silent offering to the goddess. He waited for her to speak.

"Mother Vesta came to me in the necropolis," she said at last. "When I was pregnant and afraid, she answered my prayers. She delivered you and your brother, alive, in the city of the dead." The flame of the oil lamp swayed as a draft from the open door reached it. "Hostus told me…" Rhea continued, her voice raspy with emotion. "…he told me that Remus is the one who did it. To think"—she wiped her eyes, her expression hardening to anger—"to think that my own son would now dishonor the goddess so."

"Remus does not just dishonor the Virgin," said Romulus. "He dishonors you and your lifetime of service to her sacred flame. He defies the will of Mars as well. There is no limit to his impiety or his hatred of me." He looked into the lamp's flame. "Mother, did you and Faustulus have words?"

"We disagree on what must be done," Rhea replied. "He is naïve."

"He thinks my brother and I can be reconciled. He is wrong."

"I know," said Rhea. "I've known all along." She sat back on her heels. "I've known since the moment…"

Romulus stared at her with sudden intensity. "Since what moment?"

Rhea put her hands on the shrine. "All those years ago, after Lela snuck you and your brother out of the necropolis, Nemeois came to see me. He told me that Lela had been captured and that she had died a terrible death. He told me..." her voice trailed off, as if swept away by the trauma of remembrance.

"Mother, please. You must tell me."

She forced composure into her voice. "Nemeois said to me, 'Your suckling is dead, too. Eaten by wolves in the forest.' When I heard him say that, I knew he had not found you. He did not know there were two of you." She began to speak faster, reliving the panic and anxiety. "But I knew his men would still be searching. I knew they would look in every home, every stable, every tavern and temple, until they found you. I was powerless to stop them. I could do nothing but turn to the gods. So I turned to the vengeful god. The god who Egestus had prayed to for a son."

"Mars," said Romulus. "My divine father."

Rhea used her veil to wipe away the fresh tears that now coated her cheeks. With shaking hands, she gripped the neckline of her tunica and pulled the fabric down. Romulus's eyes narrowed at the sight of the raised, jagged scar that filled the space where her left breast should have been.

"I offered my body to him," she confessed. "I sacrificed my breast, the one that nursed you, so that you would survive." She pulled the fabric back up, and looked at Romulus with pleading eyes, eyes that begged for understanding. For forgiveness. "But I only had the strength to sacrifice one. It was so painful, Romulus...I could not cut off the second. It was my weakness that caused Mars to favor you alone, and to turn his back on your brother." Wearied, Rhea's voice took on a tone of resignation. "Now we must do the same."

CHAPTER XXVI

As the man in charge of defending Remus's walled encampment, Luperco was very accustomed to hearing the obscenities of soldiers and the shouts of messengers at the gate. He was not at all accustomed to hearing the cries of women.

By the time he climbed the ladder to look over the wall, the women's soft sobs had attracted several of his men, their feminine voices drawing them to the gate like hungry animals drawn to the cries of wounded prey. When he laid eyes on them, he felt his own hunger grow.

He counted thirteen, all of them looking up at him in fear, desperation, and fatigue. They all wore dirty, torn tunicas. Their hair was pinned up, although matted from exposure and neglect. A few had ragged bandages wrapped around their arms or legs, the fabric stained with spots of blood and pus. One particularly dazed girl had dried streaks of blood down the inside of both legs and shivered miserably in the cool morning drizzle. Whatever they had undergone to arrive at the fortified gate of his encampment, it had been traumatic.

One of the women—she looked to be oldest, perhaps in her

early thirties—looked up at Luperco. "Is this Rome?" she called up to him. Although she did her best to hide it, her voice quivered as much as her body. Her accent was thick and pastoral, and although unfamiliar to Luperco, he could understand her well enough.

"Why?" he asked.

"We have heard that you honor the gods of refuge," she said. "We seek sanctuary. We were trying to get here when we were attacked...they came out of nowhere, in the middle of the night."

"Where are your men?"

The woman's expression stiffened, but she held back the tears. She put her arm around the young woman beside her, the one with the bloodstained legs, as the girl began to weep. "All our men were killed. Even the little boys. They took the women captive, but some of us managed to escape."

Still perched on the top of the ladder, Luperco cranked his head to look down at his next in command, a square-jawed man by the name of Florus. "Have there been any reports of marauders in the region?" he called down.

Florus looked up at him. "Our scouts found an overrun caravan on the road yesterday, quite a ways to the south. The dead were all males, maybe fifteen or twenty altogether. They hadn't been dead long, by the look of them."

Luperco turned back to the women. *Their loss is our gain*, he thought. Doing a quick survey of the area and receiving the all clear from the sentinels, he shouted for the gate to be opened and descended the ladder.

The women passed through the gate together, moving as one, like a skittish herd of animals finding safety in numbers. Their arms were crossed over their chests, as if that would somehow shield them from scrutiny or attack. The same woman who had spoken previously faced Luperco.

"These are respectable women," she said. "Most are still innocents. I hope your men will honor that." She shifted her eyes to Remus, who had been watching several steps away, but who now stood beside Luperco. His better armor, and his authoritative demeanor, suggested he was the man in charge.

"This is not Rome," Remus said to her. "This is Asylium. And we are all respectable men here." He laughed, though not maliciously, and grinned at Luperco. When the anxious woman failed to see the humor, he adopted a more reassuring tone. "I am Remus. None of you will be harmed. We are building a city, not a slave camp."

"You will find use for us, Master Remus," said the woman. "We will earn our keep."

Florus let out an involuntarily snort—it was clear where his mind had gone—but Remus cast stern eyes at him. Of course, his mind had gone to the same place, but being obvious about it would not help to put their newest and fairest citizens at ease.

"What is your name?" he asked the woman.

"Kyme," she answered. Noting how his eyes gravitated to the young woman beside her, the one with the bloody legs, Kyme put a protective arm around her. "This is my niece, Athea."

As he regarded Athea, Remus felt a strange mixture of sympathy and attraction. It was clear she had been violated—the thought made his anger rise—and yet her eyes, pretty and pleading, drew him in. He understood her aunt's instinct to protect the younger woman. He felt it himself.

"We are not equipped with finery for women," he said to Athea, "but we have a decent bathhouse and plenty of food, and I promise that you will not be harassed."

The young woman pulled away from her aunt and knelt at Remus' feet, bowing to him. "You are merciful," she said. "I am yours to command."

Remus bade her to rise. He put his hand on her back to direct her toward the cook's tent—she flinched at his touch, but did not protest—as his men prompted the rest of the demure women to follow. Outside the tent, several fires burned in braziers. Pots of gruel warmed over some, and stakes of cooked meat stood by others.

"That is fresh boar's meat from the morning hunt," said Remus.

Although the meat smelled enticing, it was a basket of steaming bread, balanced on the edge of a wooden trunk, which drew Athea's eye. She looked to Remus for permission before taking a piece. Her hunger getting the better of her, she also grabbed a cup of wine sitting on the trunk and dipped the bread into it before pushing a large piece of the wine-soaked bread past her lips. Her posture seemed to relax as she swallowed.

"Make sure they have their fill," Remus said to Florus.

"Yes, sir."

As Remus's men eagerly yet respectfully hosted the women's feast, Remus and Luperco stood guard, making sure the increasing number of men who surrounded the cook's tent—all inspecting the women with a singular purpose they could hardly hide—knew the rules. No harassing, no taking by force.

Luperco spoke quietly to Remus. "Will we let them choose?"

"No," said Remus. "Officers get first choice. I'll have a mutiny on my hands if I do it any other way."

He squared his shoulders and looked at Athea, trying not to picture Princess Laria. It still hurt to think of the Etruscan beauty. A few days after establishing the foundation of his encampment on the Aventine, Remus had sent a messenger to her, explaining his reason for breaking with his brother and asking her to join him in his settlement as his wife. The messenger had returned the next day with her cutting reply: *No, and don't ask again.*

Luperco followed Remus's eyes to Athea. "I'm assuming you want her for yourself."

"Yes," Remus replied. Athea was young and attractive enough. She would make an impressive wife once she was clean and plumped up. "You can choose next, and the others in order of their command."

"Understood," said Luperco. "Thank you, sir."

Oblivious to the deliberations occurring only several paces away from them—or perhaps simply resigned to the knowledge that it was inevitable—the women sated their hunger before being ushered through the encampment's central plaza to the baths. Although still in the early stages of construction, the area was sufficiently stocked with clean water, oil, laundry facilities and latrines.

Remus ordered that the women be left in privacy. He and his officers had chosen their wives, and their first night would be more pleasurable for everyone if the women were free of the blood and grime of their trauma.

It wasn't until nightfall that the women had finished washing themselves and their clothes. With hair and tunicas still damp, and with bellies full, they seemed only slightly less anxious than when they had arrived. The sight of the thirteen men standing in a row in the otherwise empty plaza could only mean one thing. They were about to be distributed to their new husbands.

Remus faced Athea who stood shivering in the early evening air, her shoulders hunched and arms folded over her chest. Around her, one by one, her friends and kinswomen were selected by officers and led off to the barracks. That included her aunt Kyme, chosen by one of Remus's older officers. Unlike the younger men, he showed no signs of bravado, but greeted her humbly and spoke at length before leading her off.

Alone now with Athea in the plaza, Remus felt a twinge of awkwardness. The girl might be a refugee, but she was no slave, no prostitute. She was not like the girls he sometimes took to the back rooms of the tavern or behind the stables. She was to be his wife, and in time, she would also be the queen of his city.

The young woman sensed his uncertainty. Interpreting it as waning interest—where would she be then?—she forced herself to let her crossed arms drop to her sides in an act of capitulation. Remus could just make out the tiny point of a nipple under the fabric of her tunica. His awkwardness gave way to his desire for her and he took her hand, leading her toward the barracks.

His private tent was large and well stocked, and as Athea entered, he felt a surge of pride that he could offer her such comfort after the harshness of her journey. He led her directly to the bed at the rear of the tent. She sat on the edge, watching him add wood to the brazier.

Moving to stand before her, Remus removed his tunica and the loincloth underneath. Athea's cheeks flushed with color. Her chest began to rise and fall, although he was not sure whether it was from fear or excitement. Either way, the sight excited him and he pushed her back onto the bed. His fingers found the bottom of her tunica.

One of Athea's hands flew to her mouth to stifle a sob, while the other gripped Remus's hand, holding it still.

"You can leave it on," he said. "I will just lift it enough."

Closing her eyes but opening her legs, she surrendered, allowing him to use her body as she knew he would. Thankfully, he did not take long. He finished quickly, then exhaled in pleasurable exhaustion and rolled off her. A moment later, he was asleep beside her, leaving her to stare at the ceiling of his tent as the light from the crackling fire cast strange, moving shadows across its surface.

❋ ❋ ❋

Remus woke to the pleasure of Athea's warm body against his. He could feel her chest pressed against his back and her hands moving down, cautiously exploring his body. He kept his eyes closed, feigning sleep, letting her satisfy her curiosity. But soon, he could not resist. He turned over lazily, relishing the anticipation as she climbed on top of him.

He had been too excited to think about sating her last night— he felt foolish about that now—but she was young and healthy, driven by the same urge for release that he was. He pressed the back of his head into the mattress as her warmth enveloped him. The morning sun that filtered into his tent was just enough to see her by, and he looked up to watch her sigh in satisfaction. He stroked her legs before lifting her tunica and peering underneath at her bare body.

What he saw made him wither inside her.

Her right breast was missing.

Frantically, he twisted his body to reach for the dagger he kept at his bedside, but it was not there—or rather, it was suddenly too much there, its blade pressed threateningly against the delicate flesh of his throat.

He looked up to see Athea's face change before him. Gone were the pleading eyes of the innocent refugee, replaced now by the self-satisfied grin of an Amazon.

The Amazons, the race of warrior women who famously cut off their right breast in order to better draw their bows. Remus felt his body break into a cold sweat as he realized the gravity of his naiveté and negligence. He cursed himself.

It was clear to him now. The bodies his scouts had found…they were not the husbands and sons of the women who had appeared at his gate the day before. They were their victims. Victims, no doubt, of the same Amazonian strategy: infiltrate and then slay from within.

Athea, his own Trojan horse.

A teeth-clenching self-hatred overcame him. He despised himself for his carelessness. For his stupidity and his gullibility. Yet despite how much that hatred overwhelmed his thoughts and his senses, he managed to save a little hate for the one person who could have devised and delivered such a masterfully fatal gift. The one person who was more imbued with the strategic blood of the Silvii, more alive with their legacy, than any other.

Romulus.

Still straddling his body and pressing the blade against his throat, Athea shouted loudly. "*Ela edó!*"

There was a flourish of voices and a clamor of movement around him. More fierce faces stared down at him from above. One of them was Kyme, her face transformed, hardened and assured. She cast Athea an expression of approval. The younger woman carefully dismounted Remus and directed him to stand.

He rose and stood naked beside the bed. Six Amazon women

were now in his tent, all of them holding weapons he recognized, including Luperco's sword and Florus's dagger. The blades of both were bloody.

The women led him out of his tent to where the rest of the Amazons were gathered and waiting. If there was any doubt left in Remus's mind, any last hope in his heart, that his men were still alive, he abandoned it the moment he stepped outdoors. There were bodies everywhere.

Some were dressed, lying in thick pools of blood that drained out of their throats or stomachs. A few were naked, like him— Luperco was one of them. The soldier lay unmoving just a few steps from his tent, as if he had fled but soon collapsed. Two long stick-like objects protruded from his neck. Remus recognized them as the hairpins the Amazons had worn the day before.

As the Amazons led him naked along the barracks, Athea grabbed a laundered tunica off a clothesline and thrust it into his chest. Dejectedly, he pulled it over his head, although it did nothing to hide his shame from them or from himself. Two other Amazons approached him, each grabbing one of his arms and wresting it roughly behind his back, binding his wrists together.

And then they prodded him along through the dead-quiet plaza and toward the wide open gate of his failed city, talking and laughing amongst themselves, as if he were nothing more than a lame sheep they were taking to slaughter, content to fetch whatever price they could for his flesh.

CHAPTER XXVII

Rhea's arguments with Faustulus had become an hourly occurrence. He would agree to nothing less than a total reconciliation between his sons—her sons—and no matter how many times she and Romulus tried to convince him that it was impossible, he did not believe it.

The last argument had ended badly, with Romulus banishing Faustulus from Rhea's home and the Palatine Hill, and Faustulus accusing Romulus's adviser, Proculus, of stoking discord between the brothers, perhaps even being the mastermind behind the attack on the sacred fire. Romulus had only relented on the banishment after Rhea's pleading.

For her part, Rhea was doing her best to stay busy. Distracted. She did not want to think about what was happening on the Aventine. If she started to think about the thousand things that could go wrong, she would go insane. Only the gods could see what was happening on that hilltop, so she left it to them. They had already guided every step of her and her sons' lives, so she saw no reason they would stop now.

She emerged from her house, blinking into the bright afternoon sun. Thin lines of smoke from the Aedes Vestae were rising through the opening in the roof. There was no urgent need for her to visit the flame. Now that she and Tarpeia had more help—several young noblewomen from Gabii and Antemnae had arrived to serve as sacerdotes—she could relax a little. Yet after the attack on the Aedes Vestae, she knew things would never be the same. Romulus had posted additional guards around it, and although the religiousness of the area remained, there was an unmistakable military presence to it now. Perhaps that was inevitable.

She saw Tarpeia standing in a grove of nearby trees and walked over to join her. The younger sacerdos was staring up at the branches of a tree, from which hung long locks of her hair. After it had been singed during her attempt to save the miracle fire, Rhea had had no other choice but to crop it short. Together, they had hung the long strands high on a tree to ensure the goddess saw Tarpeia's sacrifice. It was now affectionately known as the *Capillata* tree—the hairy tree.

Tarpeia saw Rhea coming and greeted her with a sympathetic embrace. "Any word?"

"Not yet."

Tarpeia smoothed the sides of Rhea's veil in a soothing gesture. "It will be over soon."

"I hope so. Not knowing…that's the worst part."

Hoping a change of topic might divert the priestess's worries for a moment, Tarpeia tucked her short hair behind her veil and spoke lightly. "If it is not insensitive of me to say so," she began, "I have news that has made me happy. My father is coming here from Cures. He will serve as commander of the citadel. That means I will stay in Rome as well."

Rhea smiled. It was welcome news. She was about to say so when a noisy commotion and a flurry of activity on the hill of Saturn caught her and Tarpeia's attention. She squinted in the sunlight—even from where she stood, there was no mistaking what it was.

It was the Amazons, marching Remus onto the citadel hill.

Rhea could make out the group of them walking together, driving a lone figure in front, at the tip of a long spear. Despite Remus's sacrilege, seeing him this way—defeated, captive—made her heart sink.

"Go to the Aedes," Rhea said to Tarpeia, her voice breathy with haste and sudden anxiety. "Offer into the sacred fire, just as I showed you."

"I will, Priestess. I will pray for you."

Within moments, the drama on the hilltop had spawned a convergence of bodies rushing toward it, and Rhea found herself having to weave through people who were gathering in the Forum below to watch, all pointing up and speculating, all loud and on fire with the expectation of some awful event.

As she neared the base of the hill, she noticed that, strangely, the area of the Comitium had been cordoned off by Romulus's soldiers. They stood shoulder to shoulder, blocking her view of what was happening behind them. She rushed over.

Seeing an officer she knew by name—a nobleman who had recently come to Rome from Sabinum—Rhea called out. "Appius," she said. "What is happening?"

"Priestess," he bowed. "Master Faustulus was causing a disturbance. I regret that General Proculus has had to detain him."

"Merciful Concord," breathed Rhea. "Let me through."

Appius made a space for her to slip through into the Comitium. As soon as Faustulus saw her, he jabbed an angry finger at Proculus. "Tell this man to let me pass," he said. "I will speak to my sons!"

"You cannot interfere, Faustulus," Rhea replied.

"I am not *interfering*," he nearly spat back. He pointed up at the hilltop. "Why such a public spectacle? They should be here, in the Comitium. It is a place for peaceful negotiation, is it not? They can speak here, privately, as brothers. I am their father, they will listen to me!"

"You are *not* their father!" shouted Rhea. "You are a shepherd who pulled a basket out of a river! Their father is Prince Egestus Silvius of Alba Longa!"

"I'm curious," said Faustulus, his voice hard and cynical, "what would the noble Prince Egestus Silvius think of all this? Was he as cold hearted as his sister is? Would he have so quickly forsaken one son and favored the other?" He shook his head, trying to govern his contempt, but it was impossible. "I should never have shown Caelus that crown." He looked hatefully at Rhea. "You have destroyed the relationship between my sons."

"They are not your sons, shepherd. They are sons of the—"

"The Silvii be damned!" roared Faustulus. "They were brothers until they knew that name! If their mother was alive, she would—"

At that moment, Proculus knew the shepherd had gone too far. He saw the order flash across the priestess's face and, ready for it, he lunged forward to plunge the thick blade of his dagger into Faustulus's chest. The blade pierced his heart and Proculus stepped back as Faustulus's body slumped to the ground.

Yet even before he fell, Rhea regretted it.

Faustulus's lifeless body rolled onto its back. The dead man's mouth was open, not in a cry of pain, but in a cry of protest. He had died believing that the twins' sense of brotherhood was stronger than the chaos, the violence, infused in their blood.

Rhea gaped down at his weathered, work-worn hands—hands that had pulled her sons' basket from the river. That had lifted two helpless infants out of the crumpled linen and placed them in a mother's arms. Hands that had shielded them from Nemeois's relentless search parties and ruthless spies, and yet preserved their legacy, despite the risk to himself.

In that shameful moment of regret, of excruciating guilt, she knew that Faustulus's love for them was at great as her own. Perhaps, in some ways, it was even greater. He had known and loved them as children, as part of the family that he and Larentia had created. He had watched them grow. She had barely come to know them, and only as men.

She turned and ran, pushing through the soldiers and the crowd, racing toward the hilltop.

She had to stop it.

✲ ✲ ✲

Romulus felt the hate course through his veins. It flowed faster than blood, faster than impulse, faster even than thought. When he breathed, he drew it in, and it soaked into his tissues.

Clutching the spear in his hand, he stood his ground atop the hill of Saturn while the Amazon warriors marched Remus toward him at the tip of an ivory spear. His brother looked ragged, beaten. His mouth was gagged and his hands were bound behind his back. He was too hopeless to even lift his head.

The chief Amazon, the one named Kyme, jabbed her captive with the point of her spear, prompting him to walk faster. When Remus turned around to scowl at her, Romulus could see the point had pierced his skin, leaving a bloodstain on the back of his tunica. A stream of blood ran down one leg.

Romulus cast his eyes around. His officers and soldiers had gathered on the hilltop, some smiling in satisfaction at Remus's capture, others frowning warily at the arrival of the well-armed Amazonian warriors. The soldiers' hands rested on their weapons, ready for anything, ready to defend their city and its king to the death.

Romulus turned his head to survey the Forum below. His people—his citizens and subjects—looked up at him in amazement and reverence. They looked up at him the way that he looked up at the gods.

And why not? He was the son of a god.

Kyme brought Remus before him, and Romulus studied the powerful woman. Her face was feminine, but her expression merciless. Like the Amazons with her, she wore her hair wound in a headband. Her sleeveless, short tunica exposed muscular arms and legs, and the bracelets around her wrists fit snugly, there for defense rather than mere ornamentation.

She nodded respectfully to Romulus and struck the back of Remus's legs with her spear, causing him to cry out in pain. He collapsed onto his knees at Romulus's feet, landing hard on rock.

Remus winced as the jagged stone edges dug into his kneecaps. He bit his lip, determined to not cry out again. The Amazon saw his weakness, though, and sniffed in disgust. She lifted her chin, waiting for Romulus to speak.

Romulus looked past his brother to address her. "You have fulfilled your end of the bargain." He signaled to a soldier. "This man will take you to collect your payment."

The Amazon grinned. "Twenty horses," she confirmed, "of my choosing. And a gold spear, as promised." Her eyes fell on the spear in his hand. "Solid, not gilded."

"Yes," said Romulus. He held the spear out to her. "This spear belonged to King Romulus Silvius of Alba Longa. My namesake. It is yours."

She took it. "My ancestor, Penthesilia, fought for the Trojans in Troy," she said, studying the fine weapon. "She fought for your kinsman King Priam, but she was slain by Achilles. I am obligated by history to ally with kings of Trojan blood." Her hands tightened on the gold spear. "But not for free." She smiled at the Roman king and bade her warriors to follow her.

Remus lifted his head enough to watch Kyme lead her army, including Athea, off the hilltop. He glanced at the faces around him. They were mostly strangers, Romulus's men, and they stared back with hard expressions, unfriendly and unmoved by his plight. He searched the faces for one more sympathetic—Faustulus, or his mother. Even Magia or an old friend from the tavern.

But there were none to be seen. There would be no reprieve, no sudden act of mercy by Romulus. A soldier passed Romulus a sword and Remus could tell by the way his brother stood, the way he gripped the hilt and regarded the people around him—he was gone. He was a madman, possessed by the need to fulfill his own destiny. Or perhaps he was not mad at all. Perhaps he really was a god.

As Remus awaited his own destiny, he spotted a cricket in the tall grass. This hilltop. He and his brother used to explore this area as children. Here, they had caught crickets and chased Cerva, and thrown rocks at each other in jest until they hurt each other, made amends, and ran home, their wounds already healed. He looked up at Romulus and felt the breath catch in his throat at the sight of his brother's metamorphosis. The deep lines around his eyes, the lip curled in derision, the black hair that had grown just a little too long, giving a look of wildness to a man who had always been the essence of restraint. But mostly, it was the hate.

For some inexplicable reason, seeing the hatred in Romulus's face dissolved what remained of his own. As he looked into his brother's eyes, he felt only the love he had felt for him in simpler times. He struggled to push the gag out of his mouth, but could not manage it.

Romulus saw his efforts. He reached down to rip away the gag.

Remus sat back on his heels. "Caelus," he said, just loud enough for his brother to hear. "Do you remember when we brought Cerva here as a puppy? She started to run away from us. We both called her, but she came to you. She always came to you first. I hated you for that." As he spoke, he saw no acknowledgement on his brother's face, no sign that his words meant anything to this man named Romulus. "I don't hate you, Caelus. You are still my brother. You are still the boy who fished with me for eels in the river. You are still the boy who stopped on the way home to pick flowers for Mother. I love you, brother."

Romulus raised the sword, and Remus lowered his head.

The blade came down squarely on the back of his neck, separating his head from his body. Remus's head rolled twice through the dirt before stopping, face down. His body fell to the side in a heap.

Romulus stepped over the headless corpse and reached down, gripping his brother's head by the hair and lifting it high in the air. He shook the head as he shouted to the mesmerized crowd, his people, his soldiers, his officers.

"I am Romulus!" he proclaimed. "King of Rome!" His soldiers on the hilltop, and his followers in the Forum below, looked at him in silent awe. "I will defend this city from every traitor, every rival, who challenges it, be they from Etruria or from my own mother's womb! All who threaten this city will feel a Roman sword against their neck! From this hilltop to every land, to the ocean and beyond, all will kneel to Rome!" His maniacal intensity seemed to set his followers ablaze. They chanted his name and cheered for the glory of Rome. Romulus glared at Remus's headless body and held the head higher. "Rome, the city of the gods! The eternal city!"

※ ※ ※

It took only moments for Rhea to reach the top of the hill. The blood drained from her face at the sight that awaited her: Romulus standing tall, his sword raised, looming above Remus who was on his knees, his hands bound behind his back.

Rhea tried to call out, to stop it…she tried to run faster, hoping to reach them in time…but the horror of it sapped her voice and stole the strength from her muscles. She moved as if underwater, her body and senses muted and slow, as the blade came down.

She stumbled, and suddenly Hostus was at her side, holding her up. He said something—her hearing too muffled to understand it—and tried to pull her away, but she resisted.

Her son's head was rolling on the ground in front of her. Her vision grew blurry as she kept stumbling toward it, driven by the instinct to take it in her arms. But then a hand appeared from nowhere and grabbed the head, thrusting it high into the air.

Rhea stood unsteadily, Hostus all but supporting her, as Romulus held his brother's head high in the air, shaking it madly as he spoke. She blinked, disoriented.

A ringing sounded in her ears and slowly her hearing returned.

"…the city of the gods! The eternal city!"

A flourish of triumphant cheers rose up around her. She could feel Romulus's unbridled pride and the aggression that emanated out of him. It radiated out of his body like heat from a flame, penetrating every one of his soldiers and citizens, filling them with the same pride and aggression. They looked at him with veneration. He was their founder. Their king. Their god.

But then the god looked at her, and she saw only her son. One son, holding the head of the other. She pushed Hostus away and stood straight to meet Romulus's eyes. There was no doubt in them, no regret. The blood and the history of the Silvii flowed through him, and he had shown his people what it meant to be a king.

She pushed her grief down into some deeper part of her, and forced a proud smile onto her face. She could not let him see her regret or her grief. She would not give him that burden. As king of Rome, he would soon carry enough without it.

"*Ave,* King Romulus," she said.

CHAPTER XXVIII

She could not guess how many banquets she had been to in her life. When she was Princess Rhea, she must have attended hundreds. Most were in the palace in Alba Longa, but many had been in other cities throughout Latium.

If she closed her eyes, she could almost imagine she was at any one of them. The music and the revelry, the calls for more wine, the foreign accents of envoys, and the din of men eating and drinking, telling stories, blending the art of negotiation with the art of socializing. It was always the same.

In fact, if she listened very carefully, if she used a little imagination, she could hear voices from the past, barely audible through the ribald laughter and clatter of wine jugs: Numitor flattering an ally; Nemeois strategizing with a diplomat; Egestus forging a new alliance; Lela speculating on the sexual stamina of the revered fathers...and their sons.

She decided that she had made enough of an appearance, so she rose from her couch, said her goodnights, and walked out of the banquet tent. Just outside, enjoying the cool night air, Romulus was speaking with Proculus and Hostus. When Romulus saw her, he took her hand and kissed it.

He is Egestus reborn, she thought. No matter how much she studied his face, the amazement never wore off. Surely no son in history had ever resembled his father so absolutely. He looked at her the same way Egestus used to look at her, too. With affection, but also a glint of possessiveness, as if he were keenly aware that she was a vital component of his own power and legacy. She could not fault him for it, and she did not resent it. She understood.

Despite her insistence that it was safe enough for her to walk alone, Romulus signaled for two guards to accompany her. They bowed obediently first to him and then to her.

They called her the Mother of Rome. Rhea did not dislike the honorific, she was simply indifferent toward it. She preferred to be called Priestess or even Princess. Then again, what difference did it make? The gods knew who she was.

She tolerated the guards as they walked behind her along the top of the Palatine Hill, until she reached the spot where she could imagine seeing the mountain ridges of Alba Longa in the distance. Tolerating the guards slightly less, she made her way down the Palatine, into the Forum, to the Aedes Vestae.

Inside, two young women from Gabii were tending Vesta's sacred fire: it now burned in a firebowl atop a round stone altar, positioned immediately over the spot where the *ignis mirabilis* had once burned. Rhea asked the sacerdotes to wait outside for a few moments so she could make a private offering. It was not an unexpected request. They knew the priestess's father, King Numitor, had died that morning. They embraced her and left her alone.

The fire crackled, and Rhea heard the voice of the goddess echo within the circular space. That was a good sign. Vesta only spoke when she was pleased. Reaching under her wool palla, she retrieved the small dagger from her belt, the one that Romulus now insisted she carry at all times for her own protection. Moving her veil aside, she clutched a long lock of hair and brought the blade to it, cutting it off. She placed her hair in the fire.

"Holy Vesta," she said. "As my ancestors honored your spirit in the fire of Troy, my son now honors it in the fire of Rome. Protect his city, goddess. Let it spread to consume the world, as your flames spread to consume this offering."

That done, she left the Aedes Vestae and wandered through the Forum, trying unsuccessfully to increase the distance between her and the two guards. They were dutiful, she had to give them that, and they did not question her as she kept walking all the way to the banks of the Tiber. Had they known she would lead them on such a meandering moonlight trek, however, they might not have been so eager to accompany her. She smiled to think of the whispered complaints they were no doubt exchanging.

She reached the area of shore where Faustulus had found the twins' basket. A large rectangular stone altar had been erected on the spot to honor Father Tiber, the river god who had brought the basket safely to shore. Offerings—cups of milk and wine, round loaves of bread, dried fish, a seashell—had been left on and around the altar. Someone had even left a rough terracotta statuette of a wolf. Its snarling face and bared teeth looked ominous by the light of the moon and the flicking torches.

But Father Tiber had not always been a god, and the river had not always been called the Tiber. In days gone by, it had been known as the River Albula. It had been renamed the Tiber in honor of her ancestor, the Alban king Tiberinus Silvius. He had drowned himself in its waters as a sacrifice, to protect Alba Longa from its enemies. His piety had moved the gods, and so they made him one of them. A god.

Rhea had no such aspirations. She sat on the ground on the far side of the altar, thus blocking the guards' view of her. They would assume she was praying and would leave her alone. Then, for the second time that evening, she reached for her dagger.

It was not the first time Rhea had cut her own flesh with a blade. Yet as she opened one wrist, and then the other, she was surprised to find it did not hurt much at all, certainly nothing like she remembered. That was a relief. She was not afraid of death, but dying…that was the part that gave her pause. Regardless, it was done now. There was nothing left but the waiting.

So she lay down on the river's edge and extended her wrists over the water, feeling the blood leave her body to join its timeless flow. And then she closed her eyes, letting the river and the nightingales sing her to sleep.

EPILOGUE

Tarpeia stood on the south end of the hill of Saturn and looked out over the Tiber. She could almost see the spot where Rhea's body had been found along its shore. The discovery had sent the king into a rage. His officers and friends had tried to console him, but they could not get close enough to him for that. The only person he would permit inside his hut was Tarpeia.

She had walked in apprehensively to the sound of his manic prayers, prayers that vacillated between grief-stricken petitions to Juno and embittered words to Jupiter. His mother had been his greatest adviser, and her death had left a void not just in his heart and city, but in his kingship as well.

He had turned to Tarpeia, Rome's next most senior priestess of Vesta, to fill that void. It was an appointment she had not asked for and had quickly learned to fear. The king was not an easy man to manage.

She had told him what she knew Rhea would have wanted her to say. Fortunately, it was the same thing that Romulus wanted to hear.

Your Mother did not kill herself out of grief…she sacrificed herself to the Tiber for you, for Rome. That is her legacy and her gift to you. That is how much she loved you and your city.

As she walked along the hilltop, she looked down at the Aedes Vestae in the Forum below. Since Rhea's death, Tarpeia had been tasked with so many duties that she hadn't performed a full watch over the flame in days, hadn't even stepped inside the sanctum in days. Fortunately, she didn't need to. A number of young women from surrounding cities had come to finish their six-month tenures as maiden Vestal sacerdotes in Rome, the city that the powerful goddess had blessed with the *ignis mirabilis*. After their tenure, they would be married off to a merchant or nobleman of their father's choosing. Tarpeia's own father would arrive any day to take command of the citadel. She could not wait.

Wisps of white smoke, Vesta's sacred breath, rose out of the Aedes and vanished into the ether of the morning sky, just as the smoke from Rhea's burning body had risen from her funeral pyre to join the clouds the day before. It had been Rome's first state funeral, and Romulus, despite his sorrow, had seemed pleased by the reverence that citizens, soldiers and dignitaries had paid to his mother and his city.

Afterward, Tarpeia and Romulus had gathered Rhea's ashes and put them in a simple urn. A visiting dignitary—Mamilian of Tusculum—had asked to join them. To Tarpeia's surprise, Romulus had allowed it. The man had wept openly as he scooped the wet ash into his hands and put them into the urn. When they had finished, he insisted on taking the ashes to Alba Longa.

She would want to be next to Egestus, he had told Romulus.

This time, the king protested. But Mamilian did not relent, even when Romulus threatened to relight the pyre and throw him on top. In the end, Romulus had allowed the urn to leave. It had left him bitter, though, and less open to granting further favors, even for Tarpeia. It had taken much cautious pleading before he had agreed to grant her one request.

I only do it out of friendship for you, he had told her. And then he had stared at her for just a moment too long, making her skin prickle with trepidation. She could never tell what he was thinking.

Tarpeia slowed her step as she reached the edge of the hilltop. She swished away a black cloud of flies that swarmed around her head, took a deep breath, and forced herself to look up.

For over a week now, Remus's head had been sitting on a spike on the hilltop overlooking the Forum. It had become something of a notorious sight. In fact, people had now started calling the hill of Saturn the Capitoline Hill—the hill of the head.

Tarpeia hated it. She knew Rhea would have hated it too, but there was nothing she could do about it now. The most she could do for the priestess was to remove her son's head from the hilltop and spare it further humiliation.

The Capitoline was swarming with nearly as many soldiers as flies. Tarpeia spotted the two men who had been charged with protecting Rhea the night she had died. They had very wisely kept their distance from the king. She beckoned them to approach and they ran to her.

"Pull the stake out of the ground," she ordered. "I am taking it down."

"Yes, Priestess."

One of the men wrapped his hands around the stake and pulled it up, out of the earth. He carefully lowered the stake—Remus's head still impaled on the tip—until it was at Tarpeia's level. The head had spent days decaying in the sun and had been incessantly picked at by the birds. It threatened to fall off the stake at any moment.

Tarpeia lifted her palla off her shoulders. Swallowing her revolt, she placed the fabric around the rotting head and pulled it off the stake, like meat off a skewer. She wrapped the cloth around it several times until it was completely covered. Now, she could take it somewhere private and perform the rites. Perhaps, then, Rhea's secondborn son could finally know peace.

The soldier who had pulled the stake out of the ground glanced uneasily at his companion and shuffled nervously on his feet. "Lady Tarpeia," he said. "We regret Mother Rhea's death as much as anyone in Rome. We can assure you, we did not—"

"You could not have prevented it," she said. "Her fate was ordained long ago." She gave the guards a reassuring smile and they both exhaled, relieved to have been spared punishment.

The priestess began to make her way off the Capitoline. Doing her best to ignore the stench of the rotting head in her arms, she approached another group of soldiers. Their eyes settled on the head as one of them spoke.

"Sacerdos Tarpeia, can I perhaps carry that somewhere for you?"

"I can manage, thank you," she replied. She glanced over her shoulder. "Those two men behind me were Mother Rhea's guards." The soldiers glared disapprovingly past her at the unsuspecting pair now trying to alleviate the boredom of their watch by stomping on the crickets in the grass around them. "Throw them both off the cliff back there."

"At once, Priestess."

Tarpeia walked along. She did not look back and was not moved by the guards' desperate pleas for mercy as they were seized. As she reflected on the new city, as she contemplated its future, she felt certain that mercy would soon be a thing of the past.

The First Vestals of Rome
Book I – Rhea Silvia
Book II – Tarpeia
Book III – Amata

Thank you for reading.

To see the author's other books on Vesta and the Vestal Virgins, please visit DebraMayMacleod.com.

You'll also find a wealth of supporting content on the author's website: articles, ancient history, videos, a gallery of images (including artifacts and coins either found in Debra's novels or which inspired certain elements in them), and much more.

Printed in Great Britain
by Amazon